Dear Readers,

Many years ago, when I was a kid, my father said to me, "Bill, it doesn't really matter what you do in life. What's important is to be the *best* William Johnstone you can be."

I've never forgotten those words. And now, many years and almost 200 books later, I like to think that I am still trying to be the best William Johnstone I can be. Whether it's Ben Raines in the Ashes series, or Frank Morgan, the last gunfighter, or Smoke Jensen, our intrepid mountain man, or John Barrone and his hard-working crew keeping America safe from terrorist low lifes in the Code Name series, I want to make each new book better than the last and deliver powerful storytelling.

Equally important, I try to create the kinds of believable characters that we can all identify with, real people who face tough challenges. When one of my creations blasts an enemy into the middle of next week, you can be damn sure he had a good reason.

As a storyteller, my job is to entertain you, my readers, and to make sure that you get plenty of enjoyment from my books for your hard-earned money. This is not a job I take lightly. And I greatly appreciate your feedback—you are my gold, and your opinions *do* count. So please keep the letters and e-mails coming.

Respectfully yours,

William Johnstone

WILLIAM W. JOHNSTONE

THE FIRST MOUNTAIN MAN: PREACHER AND THE MOUNTAIN CAESAR

BLOOD OF THE MOUNTAIN MAN

PINNACLE BOOKS
Kensington Publishing Corp.
http://www.kensingtonbooks.com

PINNACLE BOOKS are published by

Kensington Publishing Corp.
850 Third Avenue
New York, NY 10022

All Kensington Titles, Imprints, and Distributed Lines are
available at special quantity discounts for bulk purchases for
sales promotions, premiums, fund-raising, and educational or
institutional use. Special book excerpts or customized print-
ings can also be created to fit specific needs. For details, write
or phone the office of the Kensington special sales manager:
Kensington Publishing Corp., 850 Third Avenue, New York,
NY 10022, attn: Special Sales Department, Phone: 1-800-221-
2647.

Pinnacle and the P logo Reg. U.S. Pat. & TM Off.

ISBN-13: 978-0-7860-1901-4
ISBN-10: 0-7860-1901-8

First Pinnacle Books Printing: July 2007

10 9 8 7 6 5 4 3 2 1

Printed in the United States of America

THE FIRST MOUNTAIN MAN:
PREACHER AND THE MOUNTAIN CAESAR
7

BLOOD OF THE
MOUNTAIN MAN
301

THE FIRST MOUNTAIN MAN:
PREACHER AND THE MOUNTAIN CAESAR

1

There's a limit to everything, by dang it, the mountain man known as Preacher fumed to himself. At least that's how he saw it. Birds twittered musically overhead; a fat, white-tailed deer bounded across the meadow in this lush, deep basin. Water burbled, clear and pure, in the narrow stream that cut diagonally through the upper end of the valley and left by way of the entrance gorge to the south. Only marginally on the east side of the continental divide, water courses often did not follow the rule of the land. Tangy pine scented the clear, crisp air, while small puff-ball clouds floated by overhead.

So, why in tarnation would a body come along and spoil a perfectly relaxful fall? Yet, here they were, five of the most vile, stomach-churning, unwashed, buzzard pukes Preacher had ever laid eyes upon. Worse, they looked to be fixin' to ruin his peaceful layin' up for winter by settling down in the selfsame valley he had staked out for its high mountain walls to the north, east, and west. Preacher found himself jealous of sharing the sure, swift stream that ran through the middle, and the ample tall, slender fir trees which abounded on the slopes, from which he could make a stout little cabin and enjoy a source of plentiful wood for heat and cooking. No, it wouldn't do, not at all. But despite that, Preacher decided to drop down and invite these hog-dirty, walking, talking slop jars to depart.

Preacher meandered down to where the scruffy frontier trash had put up a disreputable lean-to, and hashed together a pine bough lodge which would not shed water or keep out the cold. Stupid flatlanders, no doubt, he reasoned as he neared. Preacher halted a goodly distance from the men, who had to be bone-stupid to have not noted his approach, and hollered up at the camp.

"Hello, the camp!"

"Howdie, mister. C'mon in an' fetch up a cup of coffee."

"Thank'e. I'll come in right enough." Preacher came to within three long paces of the rude camp, then screwed a ground anchor and tied his horse to it.

Preacher entered the camp, his posture one of complete dominance. This was his valley, by damn. One of the unshaven quintet studied their visitor with open curiosity. Only a bit over what passed for average height in these days, the man had an air of power about him. From his broad shoulders and thick chest to his narrow waist, he radiated strength. The man Preacher viewed as an intruder raised a hand in a greeting. "Rest yourself, stranger. There's coffee over yon."

"I'll not be stayin' for coffee, thank you all the same. M'name's Preacher." He noted how their eyes widened at this news. "I come to offer you an invitation."

"That's mighty nice. What's the invite for?"

"I'm askin' you fellers to pack up your gear and be outta my valley before sundown." His gray eyes, they noted, were cold and hard.

Surprised looks came from the five men. Lomax and Phelps grew angry at once. Windy Creek produced a snarl that came off more like a sneer, while Rush and Thumper separated from the others slightly, to get an advantage. Preacher noted all of that and accepted the fact that his invitation could be a bit more difficult to deliver than he had anticipated. They showed other obvious signs of how unkindly they took his words.

"Lomax, Windy," barked the only one who had spoken so far. "Looks to me we have to learn this boy some manners."

"You got that right, Phelps," Rusk growled from nearly behind Preacher.

From a similar position at Preacher's left rear, Thumper uttered the wheezing gasp that served him for laughter. "This is gonna be easy, Rusk. All we gotta do is jump on him and hol' him down while Phelps and Lomax work him over a bit."

A low chuckle came from the one Preacher identified as Windy. "Then we take him off with us like we was told. He—he—heee." The sound of his laughter came out even worse than that of Thumper. Preacher raised his big hands, palms up and open. He took a deep breath and sighed aloud as he spoke.

"Well, hell, fellers, if you're set on joinin' the dance, I suppose I have to accommodate."

While they took time to digest the meaning of Preacher's fancy words, he exploded into instant, furious action. He whipped out with one big hand and popped Lomax along the jaw. The contact sounded like a rifle shot. Preacher kept his momentum and spun to snap a hard right fist into the bony chest of Windy Creek. The skinny border rat grunted, and his eyes crossed momentarily.

Preacher followed up with a left to Windy's unguarded cheek. Blood sprayed at the contact. A right cross produced a screeching sound from Windy's mouth that set Preacher's teeth on edge. The spry, if momentarily befuddled, Windy began to spit out teeth as he danced backward. Rusk and Thumper grabbed Preacher from behind the next instant. Preacher raised a heel into Thumper's crotch and got a satisfying squeal of pain in return. Then the punches began to smack into Preacher's middle and face.

Phelps and Lomax closed in, working with the efficiency of steam engines. Lomax, an ugly brute of short stature, pistoned his arms forward and back, pounding Preacher in the belly with hard-knuckled regularity. Phelps, tall and skinny, worked over his crime partner's head, driving cutting, jarring lefts and rights to the planes of Preacher's face. Blood began to flow from a cut high on one cheekbone. A ringing filled Preacher's head as Phelps lopped him one in an ear. Pain exploded in his left eye, and the tissue began to swell immediately. He'd have a good mouse out of that one, Preacher reckoned.

He chose to ignore the efforts of Lomax. The short, pudgy hard case furiously drove his fists into slabs of work-hardened muscle to no effect, save to sap his own energy. Lomax tagged Preacher on the point of his chin, and stars blazed behind the mountain man's eyes. Preacher sucked in a deep breath and shifted position.

"Well, hell," he drawled, "that's about enough of this."

Preacher stomped a high instep on a foot that belonged to Rusk, yanked himself free, and boxed the ears off Lomax. Howling, the squat piece of human debris clapped hands to both ears and spun away from Preacher, to receive a solid kick in the rear as further reward. Eyes widening, Phelps took a step backward and tripped over a snub piece of granite protruding from the grassy turf. He caught a solid punch under the heart that knocked the air from his lungs and momentarily froze his diaphragm. He hit the ground seeing stars and listening to the birdies sing.

Ignoring that pair, Preacher turned his attention toward

the remaining three. Rusk, Thumper and Windy Creek stared in confused disbelief. No one man had ever stood up to them like this. Not even just two alone. They had not been told something about this Preacher, the trio immediately suspected. Most of all, how goddamned mean he could be. Rusk, Thumper and Windy Creek exchanged worried glances. Windy was known as a champion free-for-all wrestler. It seemed his responsibility to take care of Preacher. The expressions of the other two said as much.

Windy shrugged his shoulders until they hunched to protect his neck, snuffled, and shifted his feet on the ground. When his partners in crime feinted to distract Preacher, he jumped forward, spread his arms and sought to clasp the wiry mountain man in a ferocious bear hug. Only Preacher was not there.

"Huh?" Windy grunted, then let out a howl as pain exploded in the side of his head.

How had Preacher gotten over there without him seeing it? Windy turned to face the threat, feeling ready now. No time for finesse, he reckoned. He'd just plow right in and throw his man with one massive twist of his shoulders. Or would he get clobbered in the head again?

Much to his surprise, Windy got a good hold on Preacher. He put the point of his shoulder in deep against Preacher's ribs and set his powerful, tree-stump legs. Arms locked at the wrist, he heaved and felt the sudden give as Preacher left the ground. Elation filled Windy as he slammed his opponent down hard on the ground.

Preacher grunted, shook his head and let his mind absorb the pain that radiated from his ribs. It took him only a moment to realize that his assailant lacked the polish and skill of a true grappler. The ancient Greek art of wrestling was better understood by the Cheyenne and the Sioux than by most white men. That gave Preacher a decided advantage as he saw it. He had learned his wrestling from the Cheyenne.

While Windy scrabbled to find new purchase, Preacher drew his legs up in front of him.

When his knees reached the middle of his chest, he had Windy humped up like a bison bull mounting a heifer. The illusion lasted only a second, as Preacher put all his effort into violently thrusting his legs outward. A moment's resistance, and then Windy went flying.

Preacher bounded to his feet in time to meet Rusk and Thumper. Rusk caught the brunt of Preacher's fury. Hard fists pounded his chest and gut until Rusk dropped his guard; then Preacher went to work on the youthful, if dirty, face of the junior thug. Rusk's grunts and groans changed to yips of pain. Preacher spread the nose all over Rusk's face a second before Thumper grabbed him.

Thumper had only begun to pull Preacher around when he got hit low and painfully, an inch above his wide trouser belt. The power in Preacher's punch lifted Thumper off the ground. Before he even had time to wonder where the blow had come from, Preacher sent him into a hazy twilight land. The big, thick-legged mountain man spun around to see what opposition remained.

In that instant, he discovered that the fight had turned serious. Off to one side, Windy Creek held a .70 caliber horse pistol. To Preacher's front, Lomax stood hunched over, breathing hard, and he had a knife out, held low, the edge up in a ripping position. From behind Preacher, Rusk, coughing and retching, pulled a short, ground-down sword. That made the day look a little darker, Preacher reasoned.

"We . . . gonna . . . fix ya . . . for this, ya . . . bastid. You boys," a panting Phelps grunted, "throw down on him. We'll . . . hold him . . . while Lomax . . . carves out his liver." Then he, too, drew a big .70 caliber horse pistol.

Faced with this opposition, Preacher did a quick reappraisal. Confronting the .70 caliber muzzles, and wickedly sharp edges, he found their attitude decidedly hostile. Cranky enough, he reckoned, that he'd best do something about it. He twisted his face into a semblance of amiability and raised a distracting left hand.

"Well, heck, fellers, why'in't you tell me this was supposed to be a gunfight?" With that he dropped his other hand to the smooth walnut butt-grips of one of his marvelous .44 Walker Colt six-shooters and whipped it out with a suddenness that left the others still thinking about what they should do next.

With cold precision, he blasted two of the woolly-eared men into the arms of their Maker. His first two slugs punched into Phelps's chest. He rocked back and sat abruptly on his skinny butt. Preacher ducked and spun, to send two more rounds into the surprised face of Windy Creek. Belatedly, Windy's .70 caliber horse pistol discharged into the ground with a solid thud. Preacher ignored it to turn and menace the remaining simpleton trash.

Rusk and Thumper fired as one. A fat ball moaned past Preacher's ear, low enough to the shoulder that he could feel its wind. He gave the shooter, Thumper, a .44 slug in the hollow of his throat. It landed the thug backward in a heap beside the dying Phelps. Rusk's eyes went wide. He had fired his only barrel and had no time to reload. He gained precious seconds, in which to go for a second pistol in his belt, when Lomax charged with a bellow, his knife at the ready.

"Some of us just never get the word," Preacher said with tired sadness as he shot Lomax squarely in the chest. "A feller never takes only a knife to a gunfight," he explained to the dying man at his feet. Then Rusk fired again.

His bullet cut a thin line along the outside of Preacher's left shoulder. With an empty six-gun in his hand, Preacher dived and rolled for cover behind a fallen tree trunk while he drew a second magnificent .44 Walker Colt, which he had taken off the outlaw named Hashknife a couple of years earlier, and answered Rusk with fatal authority.

Rusk dropped his suddenly heavy pistol and staggered backward. Preacher took the precaution of cocking the Colt again. Then he looked around himself. None of the enemy moved, except the gut-shot Rusk, who moaned and curled up on himself, his legs trembling feebly. Preacher crossed to him. He knelt beside the dirty-faced low-life and spoke with urgency in his voice.

"What brought all that on?"

"Come to get . . . you, Preacher," Rusk panted.

"Why? What got into your heads to do a fool thing like that?"

"We . . ." The dying man's voice took on a cold, haunting note as he gasped out his last words. *"We was sent."* For a short while convulsions wracked the body; then Rusk went stiff, his death rattle sounded and he relaxed into the hands of the Grim Reaper.

Preacher rose slowly, his mind awhirl with puzzlement. " *'We was sent,'* " he repeated. "Now who in tarnation would have a mad-on at me big enough to send five worthless trash bags like that to even a score?" He let the question hang in the warm, late-August air while he went about rounding up the tools needed for grave digging.

No stranger to the process of burial for his fellow man, Preacher much preferred that the task be left to others. For his own part, when he ever gave it thought, Preacher much preferred a Cheyenne or Sioux burial platform when it came time to give up the ghost. Let them deck him out in his finest, lay him on a bed of sweet pine boughs, on a platform made of lodgepole pine saplings and rawhide strips, exposing him before God and man, to let the elements do their best with him. Preacher had neither wife nor, as far as he knew, living child to mourn him, or to quarrel over any possessions he might leave behind—although he wasn't real certain about the children bit. That's what Preacher hated most about the white man's way of caring for the dead. If a feller had anything to amount to a hill of beans, and had so-called loved ones left behind, getting possession of that hill of beans always made enemies of those who professed to most love the departed. Instead of supporting each other in their mutual loss, they quarreled like greedy children to divide even the clothes the poor feller left behind.

Preacher stopped in his task of digging holes for the hard cases he had fought. Why couldn't they do like the Injuns, and gather to lend support to one another? And in the process, leave a feller in peace? Let him take his most prized belongings with him to *Nah'ah Tishna*—the Happy Hunting Ground? Preacher sighed, wiped a trickle of sweat from his brow and returned to the chore he had given himself.

They came upon him shortly before twilight. An old man, his gray hair hanging to his shoulders, unkempt and stiff from being a long time unwashed. He was brewing coffee at his small camp in a mountain valley when the skinny pair of urchins drifted silently out of the woods and stood staring gauntly at the cooking fire. It took a moment for the old man to notice their presence. When he did, he gave a start and grasped at the left side of his chest.

"Land o' Goshen, youngins. You gave me a real start. Don't you know better than to slip up on a camp like that?" His eyes narrowed with suspicion and unacknowledged alarm. There could be others out there, lurking, to attack when he became distracted.

"We—we got lost," stammered the skinny, yellow-haired boy with the biggest, cornflower blue eyes old Hatch had ever seen.

"Where you from?"

"We—uh—we don't know, 'cause we don't know where we are now," the boy answered evasively.

"Now that ain't any sort of answer. Whereabouts is your home?"

Together they looked at the ground. "Other side of the high mountains. We got took off by some bad folks."

Hatch doubted that. Even so, he pressed for something by which to identify them. "You got names put on you?"

"Yes—yes, we do. I'm Terry, an' this is my sister, Vickie."

Hatch canted his head to one side and made a smile. "Vickie—Victoria, eh? Like the English Queen, huh?"

"I—I suppose so, sir," her sweet, young voice responded.

"What's your end handle?" Hatch demanded.

"We—uh—do you mean our last name?" Terry asked.

Hatch studied them closer then. Both were barefoot and in threadbare clothes that were hardly more than rags. They had missed a good many meals; bones stuck out everywhere. Their eyes were a bit too bright, feverish mayhap. The boy had a ferret quality to him, his face narrow, hollow-cheeked, eyes close together; and he was somewhat buck-toothed. He wouldn't look a person directly in the eye, either.

The girl, Victoria, if that was her name, had a precious quality about her. For all her grime and stringy yellow hair, she could smile enough to charm the demons outta perdition. Her figure, although still undeveloped and boyish, held a certain promise. She stood before him now, toes turned in and touching, the hem of her skirt swaying around her knees as she twisted and turned, hands behind her back. Her attitude convinced Hatch.

"There's some extra grub. Welcome to it. But first, you gotta go to the crick and clean up a mite."

"Oh, thank you, sir," Vickie chirped. They started off to the creek hand-in-hand.

"Hold on there," Hatch called after them. "You can't go in there nekid together. One at a time."

"At home we never have . . . ," Terry blurted, then paused, an expression of nervous wariness flickering across his face. "I mean—er—we never had to do it that way when we had a home."

"Well, you're gettin' too old to jump in bare together. Just do as I say."

They took their turns, looking unhappy about it, then returned to the warmth beside the fire. Hatch handed them plates piled high with stew and fresh, flakey biscuits.

"Go on. Eat hearty. You could use a little meat on those bones."

Eloy Hatch glowed with an unusual contentment when he rolled up in his blankets that night. It made him feel good to do something kind for others. Especially youngsters cut off from hearth and home. Tomorrow he'd see about trimming the lad's hair. Maybe scare up a button or two so's to cover more of their bodies. He might even take them along with him to the trading post, where Ol' Rube would know, if anyone did, where to find them a home.

He drifted off to sleep with these good thoughts. They held him in such deep slumber, until near midnight, that Eloy Hatch never felt a thing when Terry slid the slender knife blade between Eloy's ribs and pierced his heart. When Hatch's death throes ceased, Terry and Vickie quickly stripped the corpse and campsite of all valuables, took the prospector's horses and stole off into the night. Half a mile from the scene of their latest murder and robbery, they paused to embrace. Vickie shivered with the excitement of their bloody handiwork, and her skin was cold to the touch.

Terry quickly warmed her in the shelter of his strong

arms. Their eyes got lost in one another's, and they sighed heavily. "But he was *nice,* Terry."

"If we hadn't done it, we'd get a powerful beatin' when we got home, Vic, you know that."

A sigh. "Yes, you're right, Terry." She raised on tiptoe and kissed him on one cheek. It would be all right now, she knew; it would be like always.

2

Face hidden entirely behind the slouch brim of a disreputable, soft, old felt hat, the man moved with exaggerated caution between the lodgepole pines on the northern slope. To his left, another buckskin-clad figure paused, brown eyes searching the terrain from under a skunk-skin cap, a long-barreled Hawkin rifle at the ready, until his partner halted behind a large fir tree. Then he went into motion, downhill, for a short distance. He pulled up sharply behind the protruding bulb of a gigantic granite boulder.

The first man advanced again. The loose coat he wore opened in the slight breeze to reveal a barrel chest and a narrow waist, which put a lie to the salt-and-pepper hair that protruded from under the dirty old hat. With practiced ease, they continued to leapfrog to the valley floor. They glanced back up the steep slope. Each tried to figure out how to get the other to offer to make the long climb back to get their horses and pack animals. A voice spoke to them from the cover of the treeline.

"One-Eye, Bart, you boys coulda saved yourselves a pas-sel of extra walking if you'd just rid straight in."

One-Eye Avery Tookes cocked his head to one side. "Preacher? B'God's bones, it is you, ain't it?"

"Alive an' in one piece," Preacher allowed. "An' I saved you the trouble of bringin' those mangy critters down here."

That set well with both visitors. They let out satisfied bel-lows when Preacher came into the open, leading their live-stock. Then the one Preacher called Bart pursed his thick lips and appraised his old friend with soft, brown eyes.

"We been lookin' for you," Bart Weller advised. He cut his eyes to the fresh mounds of earth and stones close by. The turning of his head caused the tail of his disreputable cap to sway as though alive. "Looks sorta like trouble found you first."

Preacher sighed heavily and rubbed his hands together. "That it did, an' puzzlesome at that. But the tellin' will go better over a pot of coffee an' a bit o' rye." He led the way to his partially constructed cabin and added fuel to the fire in an Indian-style beehive oven-stove combination. He told his old friends about the five men and their actions in the valley. While he talked, the water in the pot came to a boil. Preacher added coffee and an egg shell. One-Eye noted that the shell had considerable size to it and was of a bluish tint. Preacher spotted his curiosity.

"Duck eggs. When I first come into this hole, I found some ducks that liked it rightly enough that they made it a year-round home. Every couple of days, I'd nick an egg from each of the six nests. Et the eggs, saved the shells for coffee. Nothin' settles grounds quite so good. Now, as I was tellin' ya," Preacher said launching back into his account of the scruffy intruders.

While he talked, he paid close attention to his visitors. He had known Bart Weller longer. Why, from way back at the Rendezvous in '27, he thought. Didn't seem that his hair had a strand more of gray in it than the day they'd met. A quiet fellow, he had already partnered up with One-Eye Avery Tookes before the Rendezvous. Been together ever since. One-Eye Avery was a legend all to himself.

Of an age with Preacher and, like that venerable mountain man, one of the last of the breed, he had not sacrificed an eye to obtain his High Lonesome moniker. Indeed, he still had the clear, light blue orbs with which he had been born. The first white man who, in a drunken rage, had attacked a then much younger Avery Tookes had been bent on snuffing out the life of the adventurous, youthful trapper. Avery had defended himself admirably, until the huge brute got him in a bear hug. Not eager to kill the man, Avery had resorted to his only other line of offense. He had gouged out the man's eye with a long, thick thumbnail. Howling, the lout had given up, and Avery answered the questions as to why he had not finished the job with the remark that he reckoned one eye was enough. His newfound friend, Preacher, had promptly dubbed him Ol' One-Eye.

That had been years ago, yet both men had maintained their health and strength. If you saw them from behind, it would be difficult to distinguish one man from the other. From the front, One-Eye's big, bulbous red nose was a sure giveaway. Tookes had invited Preacher to spend the season trapping with him and his partner. Preacher knew Bart Weller to be a man with plenty of sand, and more knowledge about beaver than any human should possess. He had readily agreed, and they had spent the next three seasons together. Like it so often happened, they'd drifted apart at one Rendezvous, only to make infrequent contact over the years. Now, here they were in his valley. He decided to ask them why.

Bart studied that for a while, then made a reply. "Well, we come across several collections of similar trash. Most been headin' northwest, into Wyoming country."

"Wonder what this batch meant by being sent?" One-Eye asked.

"That sort of has me in a hassle, too," Preacher admitted. "Just who an' why would someone send such unclean riffraff into the High Lonesome?"

Bart swept the skunk-skin cap off his head and ran fingers through his thick mane of hair. "Lord knows the place is too crowded as it is." He paused, thought a moment. "You did say these unsavory lads had been sent to get you, right?"

"Right as rain, Bart. I'm flattered someone thought it necessary to send five fellers, but I'm damned if I can put a name to who it might be. Why don't you two light a spell, get rested. Maybe in a day or two we can figger out what this is all about."

One-Eye patted his belly. "Suits. You bein' such a good cook an' all. An' we got some other tall tales to tell. Just for an instance, Bart an' me done heard of some place in the far off; supposed to have a bunch of shiny white buildings. A right colorful sight, I'd say."

Preacher shot him a frown. "You got it all wrong, One-Eye. White is the *absence* of all color." That set them all to guffawing, and Preacher set out the Monongahela.

Three mangy, woolly-eared drifters crested a rise in the Ferris Mountains of Wyoming. They had barely raised their heads to the horizon when they halted abruptly, thunderstruck by what they saw. The one in the center mopped his thick, gaping lips and smacked his mouth closed noisily. He shook his head in an attempt to clear his vision. He saw the seven hills, with their buildings in various stages of construction.

"All them purty buildin's," the sallow-faced lout on his left said in an awed tone.

"What you reckon they's here for, Hank?"

Henry Claypool, the one in the middle, wiped his mouth again and stared across the wide, deep basin. "Don't rightly know, Jase. There's one thing I do know. They don't rightly belong here."

"But we was *told* . . . ," the shallow-faced Jason Grantling bleated.

"I know what we was told, idjit. I didn't expect nothin' like this, though. But, yep, this is the place all right, the one we was told to find."

"Who ever saw a place like this?" the flatland trash on Hank's right asked.

"Ain't got a clue, have you, Turnip Head? I'd say we done took a step back in time."

Turnip Head, whose real name was Alvin Wooks, and Jason Grantling stared at Hank Claypool as though he had lost his mind.

"H-how you come to mean that?" the slightly dumber Alvin Wooks asked.

Impatient, Hank gigged his horse forward. "I say we ride down and find out for ourselves."

Negotiating the inner slope of the basin proved easier than had the ascent. The smell of rich, fresh grass made their mounts frisky, their tails up and flying in the stout breeze that blew from the far-off structures. It brought with it the tangy scent of raw pine boards. At the foot of the incline, Hank and his companions were forced to rein in abruptly once more.

This time, a group of burly, hard-faced men confronted them. They all carried long poles that looked like spears and had funny round, knobby leather hats fastened on their heads by thick straps with cheek pieces that had been shaped like large leaves.

"Oh-oh, what kind of clothes is them?" Jason asked in a worried whisper.

* * *

Silas Tucker peered nearsightedly at the trembling pair before him. Tobacco juice stained his full, pouting lips and discolored the scraggly beard that surrounded the ugly hole of his mouth. He cut his shoe-button black eyes from one child to the other, despising their pale complexions, fair hair and cornflower blue eyes. Didn't look like any kids of his at all—at all. His gaze went over their shoulders to where Faith stood in the doorway of the tumble-down cabin he and his women had labored to erect three summers past.

He'd managed sure enough to stamp every one of the brats he'd given her. How had that peaked Purity managed to override his dark, hill people's blood? Course what with Faith bein' his younger sister, the blood held true, didn't it? Then there were these two. Cotton tops, with their mother's coloring and eyes. But, she sure was a good romp in bed. Li'l Faith hadn't had that much energy since she had given birth to their oldest at thirteen. That was when Pop had run him and Faith off, clean out of the Appalchian country.

"Cousins is fine and good, but yer sisters are jist for practicin' yer plowin', not plantin' a crop," the old man had bellowed when he shooed the shame-faced pair off the rocky hillside that constituted their farm. Well, hell, this place wasn't any better. Biggest crop each year was rocks. Now he had to make sure these ghost-pale kids of his an' Purity didn' leave anything behind at the old man's campsite that could be traced to him. His expression grew stony, and he pinned the boy with those obsidian orbs.

"Tell it again, Terry. You sure this pilgrim ain't gonna go to Trout Crick Pass an' yap to the law?"

"Ye—yes, sir. I done slid that pig-sticker in betwixt his ribs like you showed me."

"D'ya thrash it around like I said?" Silas asked from the depths of his shrewdness.

Silas knew himself to be a dimwit, due to the inbreeding

in his family, or at least that was what that circuit-ridin' doctor had said about the whole passel of Tuckers in the hills back home. But he also knew he was as shrewd as the next feller. More so than a lot. Now he watched with a growing dread as the boy blanched even whiter with guilty knowledge.

"I—ah—I—er . . . forgot."

Rough and horny from hard work, the right hand of Silas Tucker popped loudly off the downy cheek of the frightened cherub in front of him. Tears sprang to Terry's eyes.

"Dangit, boy! How's we's supposed to stay safe if you keep forgetting the most important part?"

Long hours, days, even weeks alone in the wilderness had given Terry a new sense of self-worth, of independence. It prompted him to an unwise decision at this point. "Maybe . . . maybe if you'd come along and do some of the dirty work for a change, we'd be a whole lot safer."

Silas Tucker had the boy's trousers down and the child bent over his knee in one swift move. His belt hissed out of its loops, and he used it expertly to flail at Terry's exposed bottom. Bravely, the lad resisted the impulse to scream out his pain and humiliation. Not so, his sister. Vickie shrieked, stamped her small feet on the hard ground, and pounded ineffectual little fists on the back of Silas Tucker.

"Stop it! Stop it! You're hurting him," she wailed.

"That's what I damn well intend to do, Missy. An' if you don't shut up, you'll git yours next." He did stop, after seven strokes that left angry red welts on the pale flesh of Terry's posterior. "All right. Here's how it's gonna be. You'll both go to bed without any supper for the next week. Bread and water twicest a day is all you see otherwise. The next time you go out, you make sure you stick those fellers good an' proper. Wouldn't do for word to go around that Silas Tucker's brood is doin' sloppy robberies. Now, go. Get out of my sight.

An' you best yank up them britches before you give your sister bad ideas," Silas added with a lewd wink.

Hurt and shamed, Terry did as he had been bade. He and Vickie knew all about what Silas had so nastily hinted at. They knew it went on among their half brothers and sisters. For them it had never held an appeal. Each loved the other and had had to look out for one another for as long as they remembered. They didn't have time for that sort of foolishness. Besides, the Good Book said it was evil. Oh, they had read the Bible all right, only in secret.

None of the rest of the Tuckers could string three letters together to make a word, let alone read. And Silas—Poppa— hotly cursed the Bible and preachers in general all the time. He claimed that man had been put on the earth to take his pleasures where he wished, and that book-learnin' an' religion got in the way of that something fierce. Only went to show, Silas didn't know everything about anything. Terry had wiped away the last of his tears by the time they got to the cabin. Their momma, Purity, stopped them and asked what had happened and what Silas had decided.

"We got punished for not makin' sure of that last pilgrim we robbed. Sila—Poppa says we get no supper for a week, an' we have bread and water only for our other meals," Terry reluctantly revealed.

Inwardly, he was thinking: *If only there were some way we could leave here and not come back. If we could just he free forever.* Terry had no way to know that his sister shared her version of the same desire, or that the opportunity to escape lay just beyond the next couple of ranges.

One-Eye Tookes and Bart Weller bent over the large cast- iron skillet, biscuit halves in hand, to mop up the last of the pan drippings left from the fresh venison steaks Preacher had fried for their breakfast. The tender meat had gone well with cornmeal mush and fried potatoes and onions. Avery Tookes glanced up from his efforts and eyed the surroundings.

"Mighty larrupin', Preacher. Course it woulda been better iffin we had some aiggs. Why don't you get you some chickens and keep a store of aiggs?"

For a brief moment, Preacher eyed One-Eye, uncertain if he was funnin' or not. "I ain't no farmer, One-Eye. Ain't made to chase after some old Dominickers or Rhode Island Reds. Let nature provide, I alus say."

Orneriness twinkled in the pale blue orbs of One-Eye Tookes. "Couldn't be that you're too lazy to tend to some measly chickens, could it?"

Preacher popped upright, spluttered, cussed and slammed his hat on the ground. "Lazy, is it? Who cooked that breakfast to feed your worthless hide and bottomless belly?"

One-Eye patted the slight mound at his middle and produced a fond smile. "And right good it was, Preacher. I'm obliged I didn't have to wrassel you for it, like I hear some visitors got to do."

Steam escaped from Preacher. "That ain't true. Not a word of it. I've never begrudged a man a bite to eat, iffin he be friendly." He drew up suddenly. "Say, who was it told you I made a body fight for his meal?"

Tookes looked him straight in the eyes. "Bloody Hand Kreuger, that's who."

"That Kraut is a liar, plain and simple. An' I'd say it to his face if he was present to hear it. There's a bit of—ah—bad blood betwixt us. Has been for a few years now. I ride my trails, an' he rides his. We both like it that way."

One-Eye wouldn't let it go. "Might be he knows something about these strange doin's in the High Lonesome. Story is he's been up north the last couple of years. That bein' where all this riffraff is headed, he could be the key to what's goin' on."

Preacher made a face. "I'd as soon kiss a wolverine as be beholdin' to Karl Kreuger by askin' him about it."

Both guests came to their boots and ankled it over to their already loaded packhorses. They adjusted the cinch straps while speculating further on the meaning behind the recent intrusions. Tookes summed it up for the three of them.

"You ask me, it's gonna mean trouble. Too many of those light-in-the-saddle types driftin' up outta Texas ain't good for man nor beast. They all think they're good with a gun and proddy as Billy-be-damned. If we run across Bloody Hand, you don't mind if we ask him what he knows, do ya, Preacher?"

"Nope. Go right ahead. You ask me, though, I say we'll learn what is going on soon enough anyhow."

Bart Weller, the worrier of the partners, agreed, then added, "We should hope we don't learn of it to our regret."

Arms tightly around each other, Terry and Vickie clung close together. Each could feel the warmth of the other through their thin nightshirts. There was nothing arousing about it, only comforting. They were too bony; Terry knew that for certain. Far too little to eat. He and Vickie were always treated like outcasts. As though they did not belong to the family. When he had been littler, they had both cried about that. Now he was too old for things like that.

He had to find a way for them to get something more out of life than stealing and lying and sneaking around. He refused to think about the killing. He hugged his sister tightly and whispered in her ear. "Are you awake?"

"Yep. So are you," Vickie observed with the logic of a ten-year-old.

"I hate it here," Terry muttered softly.

"So do I," Vickie agreed.

Terry gathered courage. "Sometimes I think the thing we best do is to run away for real."

Vickie stiffened, her eyes suddenly bright in the starlight that seeped through the tiny window in their loft room. "Do you mean it, Terry? Really mean it?"

"Y-yes, I do. D-do you want to?"

"We . . . could try. When? Oh, when, Terry?"

Terry gave that considerable thought. "Why not the next time Poppa sends us out? We could go and just keep going."

"To where?"

"Somewhere. Anywhere. We could find something."

Vickie had become quite agitated. Her slender form trembled against that of her brother. "Let's do it. *Please,* let's do it."

After a long moment, Terry answered in a hollow whisper. "All right, we will."

Chance decided it in the end. Philadelphia Braddock had been of several minds as to where to go for the approaching winter. He had a standing invite from two old friends who had a tidy cabin on the Snake River. They put out a good table, what with smoked salmon, plenty of elk and venison, a root cellar full of camus bulbs, wild onions, yucca root, some grown turnips and other eatables. Yet, they also kept a pouch of juniper berries to flavor the raw, white liquor they distilled each summer for the following cold time.

When they drank that awful stuff, they got snake-pissin' mean. Philadelphia could not count the number of times he had been caught up in one of their brawls. The two of them spent most of each winter covered with lumps and bruises. And Lord help the outsider who strayed within range of their fists. Naw, he concluded. He'd best avoid that situation.

He also had a standing welcome from the Crow to visit them in Montana Territory. They had always been friendly to the whites exploring in their land. He even knew he would have a nice, tractable bed warmer to occupy his lodge. Only Philadelphia reckoned as how he had more than his share of half-Crow youngsters runnin' around the High Plains already. No need to build another.

That left him with the long journey to Bent's Fort. In this late year of eighteen and forty-eight, the place was but a pale shadow of its past glory. Only two factors remained, neither of them related to the Bent brothers. There'd be whiskey. Good, clean whiskey, aged in barrels and filtered through charcoal. But a winter there would cost him an arm and a leg. The soft, deerskin pouch around his neck still hung with respectable weight, but the gold would be soon gone at Bent's. Better pass that up for another day.

Which brought him to his final choice. He could head southeast and check out the Ferris Mountains in Wyoming. If that didn't suit, and the weather held, he could go on south to Trout Creek Pass. There, he had heard, some of the good old boys had taken to hanging out over the cold months. He could jaw a little, play cards and checkers, and have a warm bunk to roll up in at night. No pliable Crow girl, nor any hard floosie, for that matter, but a comfort to a man getting on in his years.

By jing! That's just what he would do. Check out the rumors about a man willing to pay out real gold for fighting men in the Ferris Range; then, if it didn't pan out, he'd go on to Colorado country and the High Lonesome. He might even run into his old sometime partner, Preacher. What with the fur trade all but moribund, Preacher and some of the old boys had taken to hanging a mite closer to civilized living. Might be he could benefit by that, too.

Philadelphia Braddock clucked to his packhorse and yanked on the rope around its neck. Long ride to Trout Creek, but only a day or two now to this outfit in the Ferris Mountains. He'd give them a look-see—that's what he'd do.

3

Three days later, in a wide valley, set off by seven low hills, Philadelphia Braddock stumbled upon a sight he could not believe. Alabaster buildings shined from the crests of several of the seven hills that clustered in the upland vale. It became obvious to Philadelphia that some serious construction work was going on along the slopes of the three still vacant hills. Flat, layered plain trees had replaced the usual aspen, and tall, slender pines, of a blue-gray color Philadelphia had never seen before, lined a wide, white, cobblestone roadway that led from the south end of the basin to tall gates in what looked like a plastered stone wall that surrounded a portion of the four occupied hills. From his angle, Philadelphia could not tell if the rampart ran all the way around. This was one whing-ding of a puzzler.

He had never heard of any settlement sprouting up in the Ferris Mountains. Certainly nothing like this. Why, it was a regular city. "I'll be blessed," he said aloud to his horse.

The animal replied with a snort and shake of its massive head. A spray of slobber put diamonds in the air. A peremptory stomp of a hoof drew Philadelphia's attention to a knot of men who broke off from the workers, one of them pointing in his direction. Too far off to see details, the former trapper decided to wait them out. When they drew nearer, he noted that the men wore bright red capotes—no, he corrected himself, longer than the ubiquitous mountain man garb, more like cloaks. A horseman joined them.

"Odd-looking fellers," Braddock advised his mount, while he patted the visibly nervous beast with one hand to calm it.

When they came even closer, he saw that they wore overskirts of leather strips studded with brass knobs. Below that, they wore short skirts. For a giddy moment, Philadelphia wondered if they might be sissies. On their heads they had brown, leather-covered pots of some sort. Odder still, he noted, they carried lances and shields, like Injuns. He changed his examination of the approaching men to the one on horseback.

Wasn't he a sight! He had an even longer capote, scarlet in color, with shiny brass coverings on his legs, chest and helmet—for that's what it was, bright red roach of horsehair and all. The polished cheek pieces were shaped something like oak leaves. Then Philadelphia made out another feller, who jogged along behind the horse. He held some sort of long pole with a big metal banner on top. On closer examination, Braddock saw that it was an eagle, with spread wings, head turned in profile, and something written under it.

Now, old Philadelphia wasn't too strong on reading, but he could make out his letters as good as any man. These read: *S.P.Q.R.*

Within seconds, the rider reined up right close to Philadelphia, rudely crowding his space. He pulled a short, leaf-bladed sword and pointed it somewhere above Braddock's head. "Hold, there, barbarian!" the man bellowed with all the officiousness of a government man in a swallow-tail coat. "What business have you in Nova Roma?"

From habit, Philadelphia made the plains sign for coming in peace as he spoke. "I was only lookin' for a place to hole up for winter. An' I ain't no barbarian."

Glowering, the challenger proved arrogant enough to not need to consult anyone about his opinion. *"This* is not the place. Unless you bear a scroll of safe passage, you are trespassing on the territory of Nova Roma."

Philadelphia's forehead furrowed. "I ain't got no paper on me."

His interrogator motioned two men forward with his sword as he spoke. "Then you are under arrest. You will be put to work with the rest of the slaves, to build our magnificent city."

Philadelphia Braddock did not like that one bit. His eyes narrowed. "Is that so? How long do you reckon I'll be doin' that?"

"Until you prove your worth to be a citizen of Nova Roma."

"That long, huh?" Philadelphia followed his first instinct.

His reins given a turn around the saddle horn, Braddock moved swiftly, hands closing around the handstocks of a brace of .64 caliber Chambers horse pistols. He yanked them free before any of the startled soldiers could react. The muzzles centered on the two closest to him, and he blazed away.

Loud, flat reports shattered the bird-twittering silence, and twin smoke clouds obscured everything for a moment. His actions served his purpose, Philadelphia observed as the greasy gray mass whipped away on a light breeze. The two who were to arrest him lay on the ground, writhing, shot X-wise through their right shoulders. The footmen had scattered, and the snarling leader had been put to flight.

"Appears to me you need a lesson in manners, fellers," Braddock told them.

Satisfied with the results, Philadelphia reholstered the discharged pistols and slid his Hawken rifle free of its scabbard. With a final, careful appraisal of his would-be foe, he turned the head of his mount to the south and started off, away from this inhospitable place. By then, one of the footmen had recovered himself enough to spring up on his sandals and cock his arm, the hand holding his pilum behind his right ear. He let the spear fly with deadly accuracy.

Sharp pain radiated through Braddock's right shoulder as the smooth point penetrated flesh and bone and pinned his shoulder blade to his ribs. Stunned by the sudden, enormous pain, Philadelphia nevertheless managed to swivel at the hips and bring up his Hawken. Leveled on his assailant's chest, Braddock cocked and triggered the weapon. The big, fat .56 caliber conical bullet smashed through the soldier's sternum and ripped a big hole in his aorta.

His sandals left the ground, and he crashed backward, head over heels, to sprawl in the dirt. His valiant heart rapidly pumped the life from his body. Philadelphia Braddock did not wait to check his results, though. He put boot heels to the heaving flanks of his mount and sprinted for the distant pass that opened on the white cobblestone roadway.

With each thud of a hoof, new agony shot through Philadelphia's body. The lance flopped wildly up and down, caught in his muscular back. He did not stop, though, until safely beyond the crest of the ridge. Then he scabbarded his Hawken and painfully wrenched the pilum from the wound it had made. His last thought was, *What the hell did I stumble into?* Only then did he allow himself to pass out.

Preacher began his morning with the usual grumping about, slurping coffee too hot and strong to bear for normal persons, and a lot of scratching. He interspersed these activities with a lick of a brown wooden lead pencil and careful application of it to a scrap of precious paper.

He preferred the newfangled gypsum plaster for chinking

logs in his cabin walls. Clay mud did all right, he allowed, but often came with an unwelcome harvest of bugs. He also needed some nails to hold door and window frames together and to build furniture for his digs. When he saw the size of his list, he decided to call it a day for the work in progress and head off for Trout Creek Pass and the trading post.

He could also pick up flour, cornmeal, beans, sugar and more coffee beans. With the meat he had already killed, dressed out and smoked, he figured to be set for the long, cold months just around the corner. But he would also have to get a bag of salt. He had not as yet built a corral, so he had to chase down his hobbled mount, the big roan, Cougar, and the sorrel gelding packhorse. That accomplished, he carefully stored all his supplies safely out of the way of raccoons, bears, and wolves alike, and departed. He didn't even cast a casual glance over the graves of those who had so recently come to kill him.

Slowly, the late-summer, pale blue sky frosted over with a thin skein of high cirrus clouds. At first, Preacher paid it no mind. The weather often did this in late August. An hour later, the leaden overcast had blotted out the sun and brought a single worry that furrowed to Preacher's brow. What the heck. It was too early to snow, he felt certain of that.

Fat, black bellies slid low over the highest peaks an hour and a half later, the temperature had dropped twenty degrees, and Preacher began to worry about how close winter really was with this harbinger of a late-August snowstorm. Odd, he considered. Even a tenderfoot counted on snow not beginning in the High Lonesome before September.

Had his mental calendar slipped a cog? No, not likely. Shoot, the big, gray Canadian honkers had not yet put in their annual appearance far below and beyond the eastern slopes of the Shining Mountains. What a joy they were to observe from on high, their heavily populated vee formations winging their way south for the winter. With the same regularity they used to hail the approach of the cold, each spring they were also the first heralds of warm weather returning. Yet, it seemed that this time nature had even outsmarted them.

Tiny flakes, invisible to the eye, began to land on Preacher's face and the backs of his hands. Cold and wet, they did not remain for long. Their bigger brothers and sisters would be along soon enough for that, Preacher reasoned. He began to take closer note of his surroundings. One of these northers could blow up in a matter of minutes, and a man caught in the open would soon be buzzard meat. Temperatures could, and often did, drop forty degrees in less than ten minutes.

Given that this late in August, the high for the day hovered around forty-eight to fifty, that could have fatal results. Memory played its map pages in his mind. A ways farther south, he knew, there was an old cabin, part of a failed mining attempt. Beyond that, in a rocky gorge, another small cabin fronted a natural cave. Preacher had often wanted to poke around in there, only to have circumstances get in the way. He would put his trust in his own instincts and see how far he got.

For, no matter what he hoped for, he knew dang well it was going to snow. "Best eat some ground, Cougar," he advised his trustworthy mount.

The invisible flakes changed to freezing rain half a mile along the trail toward Trout Creek Pass. Preacher broke out a sheepskin jacket and bundled up, the collar pulled high. His breath came in frosty plumes. Cougar snorted regular clouds of white. No question, this one would be a heller.

* * *

Fat, wet flakes drifted downward, twirled by the flukey breeze that sent them skyward again, or into spirals that danced vertically across the ground. Little cold pinpricks where they lighted on the exposed skin of Preacher, they grew steadily in number. Before he could account the time, Preacher observed that the horizon ahead of him had been curtained off by a swirling wall of gray-white.

In a place where visibility usually stretched on forever, unless impeded by a mountain peak, Preacher could not see even half a mile off. And, dang it, he'd been caught out away from any of the shelters he knew of. Better than two miles to the cave, about three-quarters of a mile to the mine. He took time to wrap a bandana around his head, tied it under the chin, to protect his ears, plopped his hat on his head again and turned up his collar.

"Cougar," he advised his roan horse, "we're deep in the buffalo chips if we don't find shelter. Just keep a-movin', boy."

Over the next half hour, the snowstorm turned into a regular, full-blown blizzard. Preacher remained silent through the ordeal, batting his eyelashes rapidly to blink away the clinging flakes that settled after icily caressing his face. Only the largest tree trunks stood out as black slashes in the thick, wild gyration of white. So dense was the downfall that he almost missed the cabin over the mineshaft when he at last came to it.

Preacher saw the reason for that soon enough. Over the years, the abandoned place had sagged to a ruin that more resembled a raw outcrop of rock than a man-made structure. No relief from the storm here, right enough, Preacher regretfully realized. He must push on for the cave, and hope that last year's thunderstorms and resulting fires had not destroyed the cabin there.

Numbness had crept into Preacher's fingers and toes a quarter hour later when he stopped to pull a thick pair of wool socks over his feet and return them to the suddenly chilled boots. *Fool,* he chided himself. He should have thought to bring along gloves. Or those rabbit-fur mittens, a leftover from the previous winter.

His world had become a wall of white now. To rely on dead reckoning to navigate from one place to another was to lead oneself astray, Preacher reminded himself. And to stay where he was invited a slow death by freezing. He had heard most of his life that it was peaceful, going that way. Then he snorted with derision. Who in hell had ever come back to tell about how easy it was?

Just keep Mount Elbert on my right shoulder, Preacher repeated over and over in a sort of chant. For all its size, the mountain loomed a dark gray, rather than the usual green-shrouded black. In fits and starts it disappeared entirely in the whirl of dancing snow. Preacher rode on, the comforting tug of the lead rope of his packhorse against his left thigh. In that blind world, all sense of time abandoned him.

Whenever he opened his heavy coat to check his timepiece, the resultant small movement of his hands jolted him. The numbness began again in his feet. *Frostbite!* The terribly real possibility of it ate at his vitals. His ears alternately burned and tingled with awful cold. They would be affected first. Preacher ground his teeth and urged Cougar onward. At last his fat old Hambleton registered the passage of an hour. His goal had to be near. Each breath of man and beast brought forth clouds of white. The wind increased steadily.

Preacher found himself leaning into it and realized with a start that he must have somehow circled, for the wind had been at his back from the beginning of the storm. How long had he ridden away from the safety of the cave? Accustomed, over long years in the High Lonesome, to suppressing desperation, he fought back the welling of panic from deep in his gut. Turn around, find Mount Elbert, and carry on.

It sounded so easy. Something a man could do in a fraction of a minute. But not in this raging blizzard. Preacher reversed himself easily enough. Then, try as he might, he could not find the nearby peak. Lowering clouds scudded through the snow now and blanked out everything. All he could think of was to keep going.

Another half hour crawled by, and Preacher began to note a lessening in the density of the snowfall. To his right the dark gray mass of Elbert swam out of the maelstrom. Reoriented once more, Preacher struck off a couple of points to the west of due south. At least by his reckoning, that's what he did. Within a hundred heartbeats, a darker, regular shape showed itself intermittently through the gyrating clots of flakes. Preacher's eyes stung and burned, and he blinked away more snow that assailed his face. Was that it?

Had he made it to his objective? A dark smear resolved into a straight, black line. A few labored paces farther, another smooth slash joined the other at a steep angle. A roofline, by God! Reserves of strength sent a warm flush through the cold body of Preacher. He could not contain the anxiety of his tormented flesh. He leaned forward in the saddle and peered intently.

Yes! There she stood, the tiny cabin perched on a shelf above the floor of the gorge. He had found his refuge. Straining his eyes, Preacher picked out the start of the ledge that led to the eroded cutback and the so welcome sight of the tiny cabin. He kneed Cougar toward it, hardly feeling the touch of his legs against the ribs of the horse. They made five small paces forward; then Cougar floundered in a snowbank.

With a frightened whinny, the animal sank to its neck in a hidden wash that paralleled the hillside. Preacher nearly pitched out of the saddle. He held on though and bent forward to scoop away enough of the powder to free Cougar's shoulders. Next he worked a space that would allow him to apply a touch of spur. Cougar responded with a burst of nervous energy that sent a plume of snow above his rider's head.

The roan's rear haunches bunched, and he plowed forward in a succession of sheets of white.

Gradually Cougar gained a purchase and surged onto the narrow ledge. Squealing in confused fright, the packhorse followed. In what seemed no time at all to Preacher, he reined up in front of the low, crudely made hut. Painfully, he dismounted. First, he eased an icy .44 Colt Walker from the holster and tried the small people's door. He found it unlatched and it opened easily.

The whole front of the cabin swung outward, Preacher recalled, to give access to horses. He pulled the wooden pegs that held the structure together and eased the facing wall out enough to allow his animals to enter. Out of the direct wind, it felt a lot warmer. He used a lucifer to light a torch, and took note of signs of recent occupancy.

Dry wood had been stacked by a stone stove, which showed a residue of burned-out coals. The cobwebs had been cleared above a double bunk on one wall, and over the single one opposite. He led his animals farther back, where he found evidence of more ancient residents. Petroglyphs carved and painted into the walls of the cave spoke of visits by early man, hunt stories, and some sort of ritual. They made the hairs rise at the nape of Preacher's neck.

After he had secured Cougar and the packhorse, unsaddled them and rubbed them down, he returned to the cabin portion. He quickly kindled a fire, retrieved his cooking gear from one of the parfleches on the pack frame and set to boiling coffee, made from snow scooped up outside. Real warmth flooded the secure little shelter.

When the first cup of strong, black brew had become a thing of the past, Preacher shredded thin strips from a dry-cured venison ham into a skillet and brought out a scrupulously clean bandana, into which he had tied half a dozen biscuits. He chose two and set them to warm on the rock beside the gridiron over the stove. A little grease from a crock, some dried hominy from a bag he soaked in a small clutch oven, and Preacher considered himself to be in hog heaven.

He poured another cup of coffee and settled back to enjoy it. Exhausted from his fight to resist the cold and battle the storm, Preacher's head began to droop. His chin all but touched his chest when he jerked upright suddenly. What was that he had heard?

He thought chirping birds had disturbed his sleep. Yet, the storm still raged outside, and night was fast coming on. Birds did not twitter in such conditions. There. He heard it again. Preacher came to his boots and edged closer to the front of the cabin.

A more careful listen and the chirpings resolved into human voices. *Small* human voices. Little kidlet voices. Preacher reached up to wipe the astonishment off his face. What in Billy-be-damned would brat-kids be doing wandering around in such a blizzard?

Taking a covered, kerosene lantern from his pack rig, Preacher lighted it and bundled up before stepping out into the storm. He found it greatly reduced, the wind down and the snow light streaks in the twilight gloom. The voices came from below him. He could make out the words now.

"Help! Someone help us!"

"We're gonna freeze out here, I just know it."

"Oh, please, help. Hello! Someone, anyone, help us!"

Preacher investigated the ledge and found it still passable. He raised his lantern on high and called to the youngsters below. "Hello. Stay where you are. I'll come to you."

"Oh, thank you. Thank you, thank you, thank you," a squeaky voice babbled.

Within five minutes, Preacher had descended and located

the children. They shivered and shook, and hugged him, fighting back tears. They stiffened, though, when Preacher asked their identity.

"I-I'm Terrance," the slightly built boy replied in a gulp.

"I'm Victoria."

Preacher forced a scolding frown. "What are a couple of babies like you doing out here in this storm?"

Terrance shoved out a thin lip in a pink pout. "I'm not a baby. I'm twelve."

"Well, loo-di-doo. What about you, girlie?"

"I'm ten. Terrance is my brother. We're cold, mister."

"You can call me Preacher. C'mon, I've a warm place up yonder, and some victuals if you're hungry."

Terrance's eyes widened, and he put a hand to his stomach. "Are we? We're starved."

Preacher led them back, moving as swiftly as he could in the drifted snow. He had taken note, in the lantern light, of their pale skin and blue-tinged lips. Both children shivered so violently, they appeared to be caught in some sort of seizure. Once secure inside the cabin, he poured them cups of coffee and urged them to drink. Their coats were threadbare, hardly more than rags. Terrance had strips of cloth wrapped around his feet instead of boots or shoes.

Recalling a pair of moccasins in his kit, Preacher rose and turned to both shaking youngsters. "Now, you strip outta them clothes, down to your long johns, and get close to the fire."

Victoria flushed a deep red. "We ain't got no long johns, not any kind of underclothes."

"Well, then, wrap up in blankets and skin outta your clothes. They need to be warmed and dried. For you, boy, I got a pair of moccasins. They's a tad mite too small for me, an' I figger you'll be able to swim in 'em. But, they're rabbit-fur-lined and a lot warmer than those rags."

Terrance lowered long, blond lashes over wide, pale blue eyes. "I'd be obliged, mister."

"Call me Preacher. Ev'ryone else does."

Terrance snapped his head upward at that. For all his furtive, rodentlike manner, he stared wide-eyed now at Preacher. "Gosh. You're famous."

It became Preacher's turn to blush. "Some fool folks try to make it that way. But, I was alus just tryin' to do my job as I saw fit. Let me git them moccasins, an' then I'll rustle you up some grub."

He turned away to do as he had promised. The fire's warmth, the food, and hot coffee did their job. The children became more animated. When Preacher considered them past the point of desperation, and relaxed enough to answer sensibly, he opened a little inquiry into their background.

"I know you said you were Terrance and Victoria. Only, what's your last name?"

Terrance gave him that now-familiar ferret stare. "Are you a real preacher? A Bible-thumper?"

"Nope. I reckon I'm about as far away from that sort as a man can get. Though I do consider myself on good speakin' terms with the Almighty."

"What's your name, then?" Terrance challenged.

Preacher hesitated a moment. "Arthur's m'given name."

"What's your family name?" the boy persisted.

The mountain man puzzled over that a while. "Well, by dang, if I don't think I've plumb forgot it. Folks have called me Preacher for so long, it's sort of stuck."

Terrance brightened. "Then, I reckon that's the case with us. We don't know what our family name is . . . or even if we've got one." He gave Preacher a "so there" look.

"I'll buy that. Now, tell me, how come you were out in that tempest?"

"That what?" Victoria asked, puzzlement on her wide, clear face.

"How'd you come to be out in that blizzard?'

Terrance took up the answers. "We've been wandering

around for days—weeks now. Those we were travelin' with
got lost in the woods. They stumbled around, and the food
got real short," the boy continued, his expression one of far-
off construction. "When they runned clean out, they abandoned us. Just dropped us off in a canyon one day."

Preacher scowled. That didn't ring true. "Who were these
folks?"

Terrance scrunched his high, smooth brow. "Some real
mean fellers. They—they stole us from our home far, far away."

This had begun to sound to Preacher like one of those
melodramas in one of the Penny Dreadfuls. "An' I suppose
they made you do all sorts of awful things?"

"Ye—yes, sir," Terrance acknowledged.

Preacher's flinty eyes bore into the boy. "Like what?"

Terrance flinched. "No—nothin' below the belt. Me an'
Vickie wouldn't allow that."

"If they were that mean, what choice would you have?"
Preacher taunted, having not the least interest in pursuing
the salacious topic he had introduced. He merely wanted a
means of verifying the boy's truthfulness.

"They—they really weren't that mean until they got lost
and ran short on food. One time they made us rob a cabin
that the folks were away from. Another, they offered to sell
us to some Injuns." Preacher noted that Terrance would not
look him directly in the eye. The boy's own pale blue orbs
shifted nervously as he related his tales of horror.

After half an hour of what Preacher considered the largest
collection of fibs he had heard in a long time, during which
Terrance continued to stuff himself with venison ham, the
lad's eyelids began to droop. Preacher took advantage of that
to hustle them off to bed.

"Time to turn in, I'd say. Snow'll be down enough by
midday, so we can head out. You'd best roll up an' get some
sleep."

Yawning, they agreed. Preacher saw them settle in, then

curled up in his blankets, a thick buffalo robe over the top. After the day's ordeal, sleep came quickly and went deep. Well into the night, when everyone should have been sound asleep, Preacher heard some creaking from the twin bunks across the room. He breathed deeply and turned his head that way in time to see two small, naked forms rushing swiftly toward him. It quickly became obvious they intended to subdue and rob him. The larger of the pair competently held a long, thin-bladed knife.

4

Although loath to harm children, Preacher had to fight for his life. For all her frail build and small size, Vickie turned out to be a wildcat. Scratching and biting were her game. She raked Preacher's left cheek with bitten nails, hardly long enough to break the skin. She bit him in the shoulder when he attempted to throw her off him. Screaming a blue string of obscenities Preacher doubted she knew the meaning of, she kicked him in the ribs with a bare toe.

For all of Vickie's ferocity, Terry proved the greater danger. The knife he wielded flicked through the air an inch from Preacher's eyes, then whipped downward, a hairbreadth from the skin over his ribs.

"Dammit!" Preacher roared. "What's got into you? Leave be. I ain't gonna hurt you."

"We want it all, everything you've got," Terry shrieked.

Preacher grabbed his wrist behind the hilt of the knife and bent the arm away with ease. Vickie kicked Preacher in the groin. Hot pain exploded through Preacher's body. He gave a shake to Terry and flung the boy across the cabin. The kid cried out when he struck the rickety table and sent it crashing to the floor. He quickly followed while Preacher came to his feet.

Small pebbles bit into the bare soles, and Preacher was thankful that he wore moccasins most of the summer and spent time barefoot. Vickie came at him again. She bit him on the belly, just above the drawstring top of his long john bottoms.

"Ouch! Don't do that, dammit," he barked.

Preacher's thumb and forefinger found the nerves at the hinge of Vickie's jaw and pressed firmly. Her mouth flew open, and he yanked her off her feet. She instantly began to kick. Sighing away the last fragment of any regret, Preacher began to administer to her a solid, tooth-rattling shaking.

It reduced the slender girl to hysterical tears in a matter of seconds. He gave her a single, hard swat on her bare bottom and hurled her onto the upper bunk across the room. "Now, you stay there, hear?" he growled.

Preacher turned in time to see Terry lunge at him. He sidestepped and smacked the youngster alongside the head. Stunned, Terry lost his grip on the knife. Preacher yanked Terry high in the air and shook him until sobs nearly choked the boy. With them both relatively calmed, Preacher lighted his lantern and sat them, draped in blankets, at the table.

"Someone goin' to tell me what that was all about?"

Terry and Vickie exchanged silent glances. Preacher leaned close to their faces.

"You'd best one of you open up. I don't abide sneak-thieves. Nor those who abuse a body's hospitality. Turns out you're guilty of both. I promise it will go easier if you do. You"—he nodded to Terry—"you said I was famous. Then you must know that if I am who I said I was, an' you crossed me, I would squeeze the life out of both of you and never blink an eye. I could skin you alive, an' not feel a pang." He loomed over Vickie. "I could eat your liver."

Vickie turned deathly pale, and her lips trembled. "Oh, no—no. *Please!*"

"Then you'd best be tellin' me what's true and what's not."

Terry mopped at the single tear that ran down his soft cheek. "We—we were abandoned by our parents more'n a year ago. They hated us, said we were even more violence prone and bloodthirsty than they themselves. There weren't no other mean fellers. We been out here ever since. We've lived since by takin' things from unsuspecting travelers we come upon who were dumb enough to take us in."

"Like me." Preacher prodded, his anger not entirely quenched.

"No, not like you," Terry hastened to correct. "You're different altogether. Not like them at all. I—I kinda like you, an' I'm sorry we tried to rob you."

"If I hadn't whupped you, would you be sayin' that?"

Terry looked at Preacher in naked horror, and his face dissolved. "You—you're right. We're both awful, ugly kids." He buried his face in his hands and sobbed wretchedly, no longer a would-be killer, only a small boy alone and frightened.

Uncertain as to what to do, Preacher decided to hog-tie them for the rest of the night and take them along with him to Trout Creek Pass. Surely someone at the trading post would be able and willing to take charge of them.

Pacing the polished granite floor caused the purple stripe on the hem of the tall man's toga to ripple like a following sea. Through the window, beyond his broad shoulders, the western peaks of the Ferris Range gave off a rose glow from the rising sun opposite them. The newborn orb struck highlights from the rings that adorned six of his eight fingers and the gold and silver ornaments on his bare forearms. Anger gave his long, narrow face a scarlet hue that clashed with his sandy blond hair. He reached the limit of the large, airy room and turned back. Before he spoke he drove a fist into an open palm.

"Five men have failed to return and no one says anything about it? Why was I not told of this at once?" he demanded of the other man in the atrium.

"The centurion of the guard did not consider it an important event, First Citizen."

The sandy-haired man shook his head sadly as he examined the other. He saw a burly man, with wide-set legs, thick and muscular, protected by shiny brass greaves. A barrel chest, encased in the brass cuirass of a Roman officer, rode above a trim waist and was topped by a full neck and large, broad-faced head. The horsehair-crested helmet tucked under one huge arm seemed a part of him. His white and red kilt was skirted by brass-studded leather strips. On his feet, the plain, brown leather marching sandals. Taken together these factors made him every inch the mighty general of the Legions of Nova Roma that he was. Yet, he allowed laxness and mistakes to weaken those powerful forces.

Any newly made corporal would have known to see that such vital information be relayed upward. The First Citizen sighed before he spoke. "Gaius Septimus, I chose you as my constant companion and commander of my legions because you are awfully good at what you do. The years you spent with the barbarian army before leaving their ranks for—ah—a freer life are invaluable to Nova Roma. You must maintain the proper attitude among your subordinates. Is that not possible?"

Gaius Septimus Glaubiae, whose real name was Yancy Taggart, responded with such vehemence that it shook the pleats of his kilt and rippled his long, scarlet cloak. "Not when all I have to work with is border trash and frontier riffraff, Marcus Quintus." They had been speaking in the classical Latin as taught at Harvard and other schools in the East. Gaius/Yancy now changed to English for the benefit of the three men standing behind him as he went on. "Speaking of which, I have brought the new men along this morning to introduce them to you. Then there is some rather bad news to relate."

Marcus Quintus raised a hand imperiously. "Spare me that for now. Bring these newcomers forward."

Gaius gestured to the trio standing a respectful three paces behind the general. They came forward and made a halfhearted effort at the proper salute: clinched right fist brought upward to strike the left breast. Gaius winced. Then he took on the formalities.

"First Citizen, let me introduce our newest recruits for the legions. This is Claypool, Grantling, and Wooks. Men, the First Citizen of Nova Roma, Marcus Quintus Americus."

They saluted again, and Marcus Quintus smiled at them, rather like a shark contemplating an unguarded baby dolphin. "You could not have come at a better time. You will be given proper Roman names once you have proven yourselves in the ranks and learn Latin. Until then, your barbarian names will have to do. Gauls, aren't you? The names sound like it. Never mind," he hurried on. "I am entrusting to you an important mission, outside the realm of Nova Roma. Recently, five of your fellows were sent out to capture a notorious individual who might be a threat to Nova Roma. I have learned only this morning that they have failed to return, with or without their captive, the legendary mountain man, Preacher. It is his destiny to fight gloriously in the coliseum," Marcus Quintus continued.

While he rambled on, Gaius Septimus let his thoughts roam over what he knew of the man who called himself Marcus Quintus Americus and had the audacity to take the title First Citizen. Glaubiae/Taggart considered Quintus to be more than a few flapjacks shy of a stack. Born Alexander Reardon, into the fantastically wealthy Reardon family of Burnt Tree Plantation, Duke of York County, Virginia. He'd had the best education affordable. Only, somewhere around the end of his primary school, Yancy Taggart recalled, Alexander had begun to fixate on Ancient Rome. As little Alexander grew, so did his mental disorder.

By the time he had graduated from Harvard, he was, as the rough-and-tumble mountain men would put it, "nutty as Hector's pet coon." When his father died in a riding accident, Alexander inherited. Alex quickly converted everything into gold and set out to establish his dream, *Nova Roma,* the New Rome. Yancy saw Alexander as some sort of combination of Caesar Augustus and Caligula. For, oh, yes, Alexander had a vicious, sadistic streak. And his sexual appetite would have shocked even the emperor Tiberius.

In addition to a number of slaves he had brought from the old plantation, Marcus Quintus had enslaved many Indians, and the hapless victims of raids on cabins or wagon trains. These he had put in the charge of Able Wade, now named Justinius Bulbus, master of games and owner of the new Rome's gladiator school. Over the years, Quintus had constructed a replica of the Circus Maximus and the Coliseum of Trajen. And he had revived the practice of throwing Christians to the lions. In this case, cougars, Septimus corrected himself.

The physical appearance of Quintus lent to his persona as a Roman emperor. Although tall and broad shouldered, Quintus was built close-coupled, with a bit of a pot belly, and a balding pate, fringed with yellow-brown hair. In a toga, with his gold-strapped sandals and golden circlet of laurel leaves, he looked every inch the emperor. Gaius Glaubiae reflected bitterly that he had deserted from the United States Army for something far better than this madman. Yet, he never sought to put it all aside. He yielded far greater power, and enjoyed far more comfort and luxury now, than even the product of his wildest dreams. He jerked slightly to free his mind as he realized that Marcus Quintus had been addressing him.

"Yes?" he asked coolly.

"I want you to see that these men have everything they will need for a long journey in the wilderness and send them on their way."

"Right away, of course." Septimus gestured for the three scruffy drifters to leave the room. "Now, I have something else. I regret to say it is also the doing of Centurion Lepidus."

"Go on," came Quintus' icy invitation.

Quickly, Septimus outlined the situation in which two legionnaires had been wounded and a third killed, and how the mountain man who had done it had managed to escape. He concluded lamely with the familiar remark: "The centurion saw nothing in that threatening enough to report it until this morning. It happened two days ago."

Rage boiled in the face of Quintus. "He is *Legionnaire* Lepidus as of now. I'd have him in the arena if he weren't a citizen. By Jupiter, this is outrageous. I want you to put out cavalry patrols at once to find the trespasser. He must not be allowed to carry his story to the outside world.

"It is far too early, as you must know, for New Rome to begin a war of conquest among the Celts and Germanic tribes. They, and the barbarian Gauls, must remain in ignorance for a while longer. There are still more of them than there are of us," he cautioned. Then a twinkle came to his eyes. "Although I have a way to make each of our legionnaires the match of any ten of the savages. It will be revealed at the auspicious time."

"And when will that be, Quintus?"

A crafty look stole over the face of the First Citizen. "Mars will make it known to me."

Mars! My God, he has gone totally mad. Septimus shook

such thoughts from himself and made to answer. "It shall be as you will, First Citizen. I will not fail you. And Lepidus shall be dealt with. *Ave Caesar!*"

Once Septimus departed, Quintus left his audience chamber and passed down a narrow, dimly lighted corridor into the bowels of the palace. Two turns and down an incline, he came to what appeared to be a solid, wooden plank wall. Behind a hanging tapestry, his hand found a lever and pulled it away from its recessed niche.

A hidden panel swung outward, and Quintus swept the tapestry aside and entered. Flint and steel provided the spark to ignite a pine-resin torch. The flames danced through the room, banished shadows and revealed a soft, metallic glow from the long racks of carefully maintained weapons.

Several makes of the finest, most modern rifles lined the walls. It always calmed Quintus, gave him renewed confidence, to view his magnificent arsenal. Now he crossed to a rack of Winchester .45-70-500 Express Rifles and caressed the butt-stock of one while he purred aloud his sense of impending triumph.

"Soon now, my beauties. Very soon now, I will call in all of this border trash my good Septimus has recruited and enlisted in the ranks of our legions. Their testing will be done before long. When my legions are welded into ranks, they will be trained and honed into a fine-edged fighting machine. Then we will march to the north against the red savages, acquiring new colonies for Nova Roma." He paused to stroll over to where a rank of six twelve-pound Napoleons rested on their high-wheeled carriages. He patted the muzzle of one affectionately.

"That will test the mettle of my men for the time when they will conquer the true, Gallic enemy to the east. We shall claim every scrap of land from Canada to Mexico and east to the Mississippi. Oh, how mighty shall be the name of Rome!"

* * *

Preacher spent an uneasy night. It just weren't natural, but them two brat-kids insisted on sleepin' all huddled together like peas in a pod. Swore they didn't do anything naughty, only that they couldn't sleep any other way. Weren't right at their age. Though from his observations, they seemed a good mite younger actin' than their ages would account for. Boys of twelve were usually on the edge of being *serious*.

This Terrance, or Terry as his sister called him, seemed no more grown up than an eight-year-old. It worried Preacher. Was they both touched in the head a little? Could be, what with all their talk of violence, robbin' an' killin'. Huh! What was he doin' wastin' his time frettin' over the lives of a couple of woods waifs? It didn't sit right. He had set out for Trout Creek Pass to jaw with others about strangers comin' into the High Lonesome. Couldn't take time to stew over a couple of candidates for an institution for wayward children. Take what they had done just this afternoon.

It wasn't warm enough for a man to take a decent bath, what with this late snowfall and the coming of fall. Yet, when they had stopped for their nooning, those two scamps had flung off their clothes and jumped into the creek buck naked. For a swim! Not a hurried bath, mind, just to play. Enough to drive a man to the crazy house. Preacher had yanked them out, one by one, and wiped them dry with an old flannel shirt. Gave them a good talking to, he thought. At least until he heard their giggles behind his back. *What was a body to do?*

Hunkered down in the brush, Philadelphia Braddock hid on the edge of a stand of golden aspen and watched the strange men from the valley search for him. He was good, one of the best, and he knew it. Braddock had left a confusing trail that should keep these amateurs meandering through the Big Empty country for a good long time. And they would never catch a glimpse of him.

A good thing, too. His shoulder hurt like the fires of hell. In a fight he would have to rely on pistols. He remembered the spear cast that had wounded him. It had been from a distance that made a pistol shot an iffy matter. It made him shiver to think about it. Ah! There they went. Hounding off on another false scent. Must be light-headed from all this blood loss. And maybe infection, though he didn't want to think of that. Thing was, those fellers all seemed to be in some sort of uniform.

And they acted like soldiers. But whose? He'd never seen the likes in all his born days. Not live ones, anyhow. He had to get back to Bent's Fort and tell someone what he had stumbled onto.

Through the haze of fatigue and weakness, Philadelphia Braddock recalled that Trout Creek Pass lay a lot closer. That would have to do, he decided. He couldn't hold out much longer than that. Quietly he eased back into the aspens, their brittle yellow leaves giving off a dry bone rattle as they quaked in the slight breeze.

With a maze of zigzags over the next hour, Philadelphia Braddock left the last of the thoroughly confused soldiers far behind. When he lined out on the trail south out of Wyoming Territory, headed for Trout Creek Pass, he had time to reflect on the men he had seen. *Funny,* he mused, *they looked like them fellers I seen in paintings of the Crucifixion of Christ.*

He held that thought until he made night camp and refreshed himself on broiled rabbit. He could sure use some bison. Man feeds himself regular on bison heals right fast.

5

Thin ribbons of white smoke rose above the saddle that separated Preacher and his young charges from the trading post in Trout Creek Pass. Preacher had never been so weary of a self-imposed duty as this one. Had this pair been grown up, their bones would be picked clean by buzzards and coyotes by now. Being as how they were children, he felt obliged to spare them and bring them to folks who would see to their proper upbringing.

Although, he had to admit, it might be too late. It was written in the Bible that a child must be made straight in his ways by the age of seven or he was lost to righteousness. It was a hard thing to think of little nippers of eight, nine, ten or eleven roasting forever in hell because they had not been brought up right the first seven years of their lives. That was deeper theology than Preacher had delved into for a long while. He shook the images from his mind and plodded on. Terry and Vickie sat astride the pack saddle frame on a not-too-willing horse.

"When we gonna get there?" Terry asked.

"Yeah. We've never beened there before," Vickie chirped.

"You've never *been* there," Preacher corrected the girl.

She made a face. "That's what I said."

Preacher calculated the angle of the sun. "We'll be there by mid-afternoon. Those are the noonin' cook fires, an' ol' Kevin Murphy's smokehouse you see beyond the rise. He makes the bestest smoked hams. An' his bacon will melt in your mouth."

"Ugh!" Terry blurted. "I wouldn't like that. I like to *chew* mine. Is it spoilt or something?"

"Just a figger of speech. Means that his bacon is delicious. Now, you two quit pullin' my leg. I've got a sudden, bodacious thirst a-buildin', an' I figger to tend to it soon as I get you all settled in."

"Where are we gonna stay?" Vickie demanded.

"I been over all that before. You'll go to whoever will take you in."

Fear showed in both their faces. "You won't split us up, will you?" Terry asked nervously.

It was the first time Preacher had seen such emotions displayed by either, except for when he'd broken up their attack on his person. "I'll try not. No tellin'."

"We won't go to different folks." Terry grew stubborn.

"If you send us, we'll run away." Vickie cut her eyes to her brother for confirmation. He nodded solemnly.

Preacher lost hold of it for a moment. "Dang, can't you blessit tadpoles ever make things easy for a feller? I can't guarantee anythin' because I don't know what situation we're gonna come into. Put a rein on them jaws until we get there."

Terry and Vickie resumed a sullen, sulking silence. Terry's pink underlip protruded in a pout. Preacher snorted in disgust.

*   *   *

Preacher reached the trading post at a quarter past two that afternoon. "Tall" Johnson, as opposed to his cousin and partner, "Shorty" Johnson, greeted Preacher from the roofed-over porch of the saloon half of the frontier general store.

"Preacher, you old dog. I heard that you were holed up for the winter." His eyes widened when he took in the children. "You a fambly man now, Preach?"

"Not for any longer than I can help it, Tall," Preacher grumbled. "You wouldn't happen to be in the mood to play father, would you?"

Tall Johnson wheezed out his laughter. "Shorty would never hear of it. He sees kids as somethin' like warts. A feller needs to cut them off his hide as soon as possible. Besides, brats needs wimmin. An' we ain't got no wimmin. Decent ones, that is. Just a couple of Utes."

Preacher faked a disapproving glower. "Utes is ugly, Tall."

"Not this pair. Now, you just take that back, Preacher, or you buy the first drink."

Preacher's eyes sparkled with mischief. "I'll not take it back, an' I'll be proud to buy you the first drink. Soon's I get shut of these youngins."

Tall Johnson made his point markedly clear. "A feller could die of thirst before that happened."

Preacher chuckled. "Chew a pebble, Tall."

He dismounted and helped the children down. He took them with him into the trading post side of the large, stout log building, which had been built like the corner tower of a fort, the windows narrow, with thick shutters into which firing loops had been cut.

Ruben Duffey, the bartender, greeted him warmly. "Hograw, if it ain't Preacher. What you got there?" he asked. "Sure, it's a couple of partners you left out in the rain to shrink?"

"Nope. They's kid-chillins right enough."

"Seems I might know them, don't I? Lemme get a closer look?" Duffey studied Terry and Vickie a moment, and his full lips turned down in distaste. "I was right, Preacher. Ye've got yourself a pair of genuine juvenile criminals on your hands, don't ye know? Sure an' it's a better thing if ye bring them with me. I've got the right place for them. Come along then, won't ye?"

Preacher led the youngsters in Ruben's path, out through the back hallway, past a storeroom. Outside, the smiling Irishman directed them to a small storage building with a low door and no windows. He opened up and made a grand gesture with a sweeping arm to usher them inside.

"Faith now, an' we'll just lock those heathen devils' spawn in here for a while. Could be we might get enough men together later on to decide their fate, don't ye know?"

"They are that bad, Ruben?"

"Aye, every bit of it an' more, I'm sayin'."

They walked back inside, and were joined by Tall Johnson. Ruben poured whiskey for the three of them; then he told Preacher the real story behind Terrance and Victoria. His tale, in his lilting Irish brogue, took the listening men back three years.

"There was this family, there was. Name of Tucker. Sure an' they was dressed like rag-a-muffins. Don't ye know, I, like most folks, saw somethin' strange about them right off, we did. A whole passel of kids they had, an' nerry a whole brain among 'em, there wasn't. There was something even more strange about them, wouldn't ye know? This Tucker and his mizus looked enough alike to be brother and sister. Sure an' they could be, for all I know. They squatted around the post for a few days; then they hauled out to a canyon some thirty miles northeast of here.

"That's when things started happenin'." Ruben leaned close and spoke in a confidential manner. "Sure an' things started disappearin'. A man would lose his shovel, or a pig, or maybe a couple pair of long johns a-dryin' on a bush. Then a prospector turned up dead. One day, ol' Looney Ashton come in for a nip of the dew. He swore an' be damned that two nights before, out around his digs, he saw that two-headed pair sneakin' off with a brace of mules that belonged to Hiram Bittner. It was the full moon an' he saw them right clear."

"Stranger things have happened," Preacher said dryly.

"No stranger than this tale gets. Ya see, the two little nippers were stark naked."

Silence held for a moment. Then a cherry-cheeked Preacher added verification to Ruben's story. "They do like to get out of their clothes a lot. I found that out on the way here."

Ruben raised both hands. "So there it is, isn't it?" He took note of the empty pewter mugs and poured more whiskey. "Whose payin' for these?"

Preacher and Tall turned to each other. "Preacher." "Tall."

"Ah, saints preserve us, I'll buy, 'cause it's good to see you again, Preacher, it is."

Ruben dropped coins into the wooden till under the bar and went on to tell how the little depredations, and an occasional killing, went on right up to the present. He concluded with a suggestion. "So, if ye'll tell me what dastardly act you caught this pair performing, maybe it is we can drag the whole family in and dispatch them."

Silence lengthened while Preacher thought over all he had heard. Try as he might, he could not visualize these two as so profoundly evil as Ruben painted them. He had brought the children here to find them a good home, with stepparents who would raise them properlike. He could not turn his back on that promise in good conscience.

"I dunno, Ruben. I'm thinkin' they can be shown the error of their ways and, given a good home, turn out all right."

"Don'cha tell me ye've turned soft-hearted, Preacher, don't ye?"

"Ruben, if you weren't such a little-bitty feller, an' all frail-like, I'd break you in half for sayin' that. I'm the same man I've always been. It's only that I've got to know them over the past two, nearly three days. They can be sweet-tempered enough and obey right smartly, if a firm hand is applied."

"To their bottoms, I presume, I do." Ruben poured another drink. For all of Preacher's disparagement, Ruben stood six-two in his stocking feet and had the body of a double beer barrel.

"I have yet to do that. Though when they come at me to rob me, I shook 'em until their teeth rattled. That seemed to get their attention."

"I wonder why?" Tall Johnson spoke for the first time. "You were serious, then, when you asked me about bein' a poppa?"

"Not really. I know how you and Shorty live. Not a place for kids. No offense intended."

"None taken. There's a feller over a couple of valleys, runs horses. I hear he's been wantin' to take in a couple of yonkers to help work on the place. If that's any help."

"He have a woman to wife?"

"Sure does. And three kids of his own."

"Sounds fine. I might look into it, failing I find any closer."

A sudden shout and curse in French from the cook at the hostelry brought the old drinking friends out of their cups and onto their boots. Preacher, wise in the ways of his captives, reached the back door first. He got there in time to see the cook on his rump, legs splayed and upraised, a pot of as-yet unheated potato soup soaking him from floppy stocking cap to the toes of his moccasins. Beyond him was the open door to the store shed—and the rapidly disappearing backs of Terry and Vickie.

"You had the right of it, Ruben. They's nothin' but trouble," he shouted as he set off afoot in swift pursuit.

Being no stranger to running—Preacher had engaged in many a foot race against Arapaho and Shoshoni braves—the rugged mountain man soon managed to close ground on his quarry. Terry lost more precious space with frequent, worried glances over his shoulder. With longer, stronger legs and more endurance, Preacher far out-classed the youngsters. Then providence gave the children a much-needed break in the form of several habitués of the trading post.

"Hoo-haa! Lookie there. Ain't that ol' Preacher playin' the nursemaid?"

"Shore be. Don't he look cute a-high-steppin' it like that?"

"Shut them yaps, Ty Beecham, an' you, Hoss Furgison. Them kids is my responsibility."

"Strike me dead. Preacher's done become plumb domesticated." Tyrone Beecham rubbed salt in Preacher's wounded pride. "Nextest thing we know, he'll take to wearin' an apron and skirts."

That did it. Preacher slammed to a stop and whirled to confront his detractors. No man, unless he was a tad light in the upstairs, ever suggested that a denizen of the High Lonesome might have sissy inclinations. To question a fellow's manhood most often called for a shooting. Preacher did not want to kill these old friends, and sometime partners, but Beecham had stepped over the bounds. The least that would satisfy now was a good knuckle drubbing.

And Preacher was just the man to deliver it. He stepped in without a word and popped Beecham flush in the mouth. Surprise registered in the dark, nearly black eyes of Tyrone Beecham as he rocked back on his boot heels. He swung a wild, looping left at Preacher's head, which, much to Beecham's regret, missed.

Because Preacher did not. He followed his lip-mashing punch with a right-left-right combination to Beecham's exposed rib cage. Each blow brought an accompanying grunt, expelled by the rapidly depleting air in Beecham's lungs. Droplets of red foam flew from Beecham's mangled mouth. His head wobbled with each blow. Right about then, his friend, Hoss Furgison, decided to join in.

He came at Preacher from the mountain man's blind side. Raw knuckles rapped against Preacher's skull, behind his left ear. Sound and sparkles erupted inside, and Preacher stumbled before he delivered a final right directly over Beecham's heart. Then he spun, his left arm already in motion, and drove his back fist into Hoss Furgison's nose.

Blood spurted, although nothing had been broken. Preacher continued his punishment with a right uppercut that cropped Furgison's surprised jaw closed. Furgison stomped on Preacher's right instep. Preacher gritted his teeth and ignored the pain. He still didn't want to hurt these two badly, only drive home the lesson that there was still a lot of spit and vinegar in this old coon. Everyone witnessing their battle had seen two-on-one plenty of times, sometimes even four or five. Most had seen Preacher handle those odds with ease. It didn't take long for the betting to begin.

"I got a cartwheel says Preacher pounds them both onto their boots," Tall Johnson declared.

An old-timer next to him elbowed Tall in the ribs. "I got me a nugget that assays as one and a quarter ounce pure says those younger fellers will plain bust his bum for him."

Thirty-five dollars, Tall thought. A reg'lar fortune. Temptation, and his confidence in Preacher, overcame his usual prudence and his near-empty purse. "You're on, old man."

Preacher made to dodge between his opponents, then

stopped abruptly and reached out to snag the fronts of their shirts. He thrust himself backward on powerful legs and slammed his arms together at the same time. A coonskin cap went flying from the top of Ty Beecham's head as the two noggins clocked together. It was time for them to see stars and hear birds sing.

Preacher did not let up. He shook both combatants like small children and then threw them away. Ty Beecham bounced off the ground and started to get back on his boots. Preacher reached him in two swift strides and towered over the fallen man.

"Don't."

All at once, Beecham saw the wisdom in this and remained down. Not so Hoss Furgison. He came at Preacher with a yodeling growl. Preacher mimicked it and danced around like an Injun, flapping a hand over his mouth in time with the sound that came out. Somehow that further enraged Furgison, who, blinded by the taunts, abandoned all semblance of a plan.

He walked into a short, hard right to the chest, which he had left unprotected in order to grapple for a bear hug. Unkindness followed unkindness for Hoss. Preacher stepped in and pistoned his arms into a soft belly, until Hoss hung over the arms that punished him. Preacher disengaged his arms and stepped away. Hoss fell to his knees.

"You'd do yourself a favor if you stayed there, Hoss. I wasn't fixin' to do any real harm. Push it, an' by dang, I surely will."

"You win, Preacher. You win," Hoss panted.

Tall Johnson looked to the old man. Grudgingly, the graybeard dug under his grimy buckskin shirt and pulled out a small pouch. From it he took a large gold nugget, crusted in quartz. Tall reckoned it to be worth what the old feller said.

"You got enough in yer pocketbook to have paid, had yer man lost?" the ancient demanded with ill grace.

Tall puckered his lips and threw the sore loser a wry look. "Well, now, we'll never know, will we?"

"Don't get another hidey-ho goin', Tall," Preacher admonished. "I still have to go after those brats."

"So you do," Tall answered cheerily. "And I wish you the joy of it."

"Dang it, Tall, if my knuckles weren't so sore, I'd knock some of the dust off 'em on that ugly puss of yours." So saying, Preacher stomped off for the front of the trading post and his trusty Cougar.

Preacher reined in and dismounted. The troublesome pair had found a stretch of slab rock that made it impossible to track them. Instead of crossing directly over, Preacher skirted around the edge counterclockwise, leading Cougar. He had gone only a quarter of the way when he found traces. Something about them bothered him.

Then he saw it clearly. These prints had been made by moccasins, right enough, and Terry had been wearing the pair Preacher had given him. But these were of a different pattern than those the boy had. These marks had been put down by an Arapaho. Preacher continued his search, and found no sign of where the children had left the wide stretch of exposed granite. Had the Indians taken the boy and girl?

One way to find out. He set out to follow the trace left by the Arapahos. An hour later, he encountered their evening camp. Among them he soon found old friends. Bold Pony was an age with Preacher, and in fact they had spent several summers together as boys in their late teens. Now the Arapaho settled Preacher down to a ritual sharing of meat and salt.

Bold Pony had held his age well, Preacher noted. He still made a strapping figure, his limbs smooth and corded with muscle. He wore the hair pipe chest plate of a war chief and proudly reintroduced Preacher to his wife and three children. His boy was eleven, with a shy, shoe-button-eyed little girl of eight next, followed by a small boy, a toddler of three.

"Makes a feller know how many summers have gone by," Preacher confided. "Last I saw of you, that biggest of yours was still peekin' at me from behind his momma's skirts."

"You have weathered the seasons well, old friend," Bold Pony complimented.

"Yep. Well . . . beauty is as beauty does." Preacher's observation didn't mean a damned thing, but Bold Pony nodded sagely, arms crossed over his chest.

"What brings you into the hunting place of the Arapaho?" Bold Pony got right to the point as he pushed aside his empty stew bowl.

Preacher described in detail his encounter with Terry and Victoria, described them and recounted how they had managed to bowl over Frenchie Pirot and make an escape from the trading post. Bold Pony nodded several times during the explanation, then sat in silence as he lighted his pipe.

After the required puffs sent to the four corners of the world, and the two to the Sky Father and Earth Mother, Bold Pony drew one more for pleasure and passed it to Preacher. "We know of these children," he said with a scowl.

Preacher repeated the ritual gesture and sucked in a powerful lungful of pungent smoke. "Do you now? Any idea where they might be right now?"

Bold Pony accepted the pipe back, puffed and spoke. "I may know that. My son and his friends"—he nodded to the other lodges in the small encampment—"range far on their boyish hunts. It is possible they saw these young white people not long ago. It is possible that they are with their no-account family in a canyon not far off. One that is hidden from the unskilled eye."

"Is it also possible," Preacher asked after another drag on

the pipe, "that you can give me directions on how to find that canyon?"

A hint of a smile lighted the face of Bold Pony. "It is possible, old friend. I could tell you simply to follow your nose. They are dirty, an unwashed lot. You can smell them from far off. Or I could tell you to follow your ears. There are many children there, and they seem to squabble all the while— very noisy. Or I could tell you to journey half a day to the east until you come to a big tree blasted by the Thunder Bird. There you would find a small stream that comes from a narrow opening to the north. Follow that and you will find them."

"I am grateful, old friend."

"It is good. Now we must eat more or my woman will be unhappy."

"I'd rather to be off right away. But—" he looked up at the stout, round-faced, beaming woman and waggled one hand in acceptance—"I reckon another bowl of that stew wouldn't do no harm. Half a day will put me there a mite after the middle of the night. I can hardly wait," he said to himself with sarcasm.

6

Eight men, who were dressed in traditional diaperlike loincloths and spike-studded sandals, marched out of a stone archway after the clarion had sounded and the portcullis had been raised. Four of them looked entirely unwilling. They had every reason to be, considering that they were captives from an ill-fated wagon train, not professionals, as were their opponents. When the eight reached the lavish, curtained box, they halted and raised their weapons to salute the *imperator* in the sanctioned words.

"Ave Caesar! Morituri te salutamus!"

And, right here on the sands of the Coliseum of Nova Roma, they really were about to die. At least the four pilgrims were, who possessed a woeful unfamiliarity with the odd weapons they had been given. One had a small, round, Thracian shield and a short sword. The second had the spike-knuckled *caestus* of a pugilist—a fistfighter. The third had the net and trident of a *retiarius*. The fourth bore a pair of long daggers, with small shields strapped just below each elbow, in the style of the Midianite horsemen. The professionals bore the appropriate opposing arms. They looked expectantly beyond their soon-to-be victims of the *imperator*.

Marcus Quintus Americus rose eagerly and gave the signal to begin with his gold-capped, ivory wand. At once, the gladiators ended their salute, each squared off against his primary opponent, and the fight commenced. Shouts of encouragement and derision rose from the stone benches filled with spectators. Many of these people, the "citizens" of New Rome, had been here for years. Not a few had formerly been the inmates of prisons and asylums for the insane. Whatever their origins, they had acquired a taste for this bloodiest of sports. That pleased Quintus, who resumed his seat on the low-back, X-shaped chair beside his wife, Titiana Pulcra, the former Flossie Horton of Perth Amboy, New Jersey.

"Rather a good lot, this time, eh?" Quintus asked the striking blonde beside him.

Pulcra/Flossie tossed her diadem of golden curls and answered in a lazy drawl. "Come, Quintus, you know the games bore me. They are so gruesome."

From her far side, the small voice of Quintus Faustus Americus, her son, piped up. "But that's what makes them so exciting, Mother."

Pulcra gazed on him coolly. "I was addressing your father, Faustus. Really, Quintus, for a boy of ten years, he has truly atrocious manners."

"Eleven, my dear," Quintus responded. "He'll be eleven on the nones of September."

"Which makes it all the worse. He needs a proper teacher. There's geography, history, so many things, including manners, he should be taught."

"Eleven is a good enough time to begin formal education," Quintus countered. "A boy needs to be free to indulge his adventurous spirit until then, doesn't he, son?" he added fondly as he reached across his wife to tousle the youngster's yellow curls.

Quintus Faustus Americus had his mother's coloring, her gray eyes and pug nose as well. A thin, wiry boy, he had inherited his father's sadistic traits. He enjoyed tormenting small animals and treated all other children as inferiors. Gen. Gaius Septimus Glaubiae summed up the lad best, as being mean-spirited, filled with a deep-seated evil.

"Yes, Father. Oh, look!" Faustus blurted, pointing to a small, nail-bitten finger on a fallen man on the sand. "He's gone down already. I *told* you he was too old and frail. You owe me ten dinarii."

"Done, my boy. Right after the games end," Quintus responded laughing.

Out in the arena, the oldest immigrant lay in a pool of blood, his life slowly ebbing, while the professional gladiator who had downed him with a simple, straight sword thrust with his *gladius* stood over him. He looked up at the box. Quintus gave him the sign to dispatch the unfortunate.

A short, sharp scream came from the old fellow when the *gladius* pierced his heart. To the left of the unfeeling gladiator, a sturdy young farmer, who had been bound for Oregon, smashed a surprising blow to the face of his opponent with the *caestus*. Blood flew in profusion. A chorus of boos came from the audience.

"I say, rather good!" Quintus cheered on the amateur. "Smack him another one."

Before the brave farmer could respond, his opponent's length of his chain with the spiked ball at the end lashed out and struck him solidly in the chest. Yanked off his feet by the effort to extract the spike point from the deep wound, the farmer fell face-first to the sand. His opponent closed in and stood above his victim while he swung the wicked instru-ment around over his head. The farmer rolled over, eyes wide with fright, and lashed out with his blade-encrusted fist. The tines dug into the partly protected calf muscle of the professional gladiator, who leaped back with a howl.

"He's going to die anyway, isn't he, Father?" The small hand of Faustus tugged at the edge of his father's toga.

"Yes, of course, they all are."

Gray eyes alight and dancing, Faustus clapped his hands. "Oh, good."

Two attendants rushed from the gladiator entrance portal to help the wounded professional off the sand. Another, armed like a Nubian, complete with zebra-print shield and long spear, took his place. He quickly finished off the second of the four pilgrims. With the farmer dead, that left only two. Faustus grew more excited with each feint and thrust of the four men before him. He stuffed his mouth with popped corn, a feat made difficult by the broad, wet smile that exposed small, white, even teeth, like those of a wolverine. A great shout came from the crowd as one surviving immigrant stumbled over the body of the first man slain and went to one knee.

"Oh, splendid!" Faustus squeaked as the gladiator in Thracian armor swiftly closed in on the off-balance amateur.

With cold deliberation, the Thracian swung his curved sword and cleanly decapitated the downed outsider. Faustus bounced up and down on his cushioned chair, his breathing roughened, as little gasps escaped his lips. His eyes grew glassy. He moaned softly as the headless corpse toppled sideways to flop on the sand. To his right, his mother gave him alarmed glances.

"Hasn't it been quite a good day at the games, my dear?" Quintus remarked idly to Pulcra.

"Yes, I suppose it has. Apparently Faustus thinks so."

Faustus licked his lips repeatedly now and groped for

more popped corn while he fixed his lead-colored eyes on
the death throes of the last captive. A low, soft moan escaped
as the hapless man breathed his last.

Quintus spoke in low, confidential tones to his wife. "I
only hope the men I sent will be successful. And, that they
get back in time for the birthday games for Faustus. We will
have the spectacle of spectacles when that living legend,
Preacher, is on the sand. What a crowning event that would
be for the boy's birthday!"

Preacher had other things on his mind at the time. Slipping unseen through the woods in late afternoon, he spied
out the Tucker compound shortly before sundown. To grace
it with the name of "compound," Preacher reasoned, had to
be a gross exaggeration. It consisted of a low, slovenly cabin,
the second story of which seemed to have been added as an
afterthought. A rickety corral stood to one side, partly shaded
by a huge old juniper. The mound and the recessed doorway
of a root cellar occupied space on the opposite side. Right
off, Preacher spotted a dozen brats.

They stair-stepped from a toddler of maybe two to a gan-
gly youth of perhaps fifteen. The younger ones went about
blissfully naked. The older ones were every bit as ill-clothed
as had been Terry and Vickie. While Preacher observed, he
began to note that all of them appeared to have some physical or mental defect. All except Terry and Vickie, who showed
up in the last glimmer of twilight.

Perhaps they had a different poppa, Preacher speculated.
Or another momma? A moment later, the situation became
clearer when three adults showed themselves in the tree-
shaded, bare, pounded ground in front of the cabin. The man
and one woman looked enough alike to be twins, both with
black hair and eyes, like most of the children. Preacher recalled the speculation on the part of Ruben Duffey.

That seemed to make more sense when he studied the other woman, whom he saw to be fair, with long, blond hair and pale blue eyes. To Preacher's consternation and as an assault on his sense of propriety, the man was openly affectionate to both women. He hugged them and bussed them heartily on their cheeks, held hands with the dark one while she gathered in the children.

Like most youngsters, the black-haired tribe frisked about some, holding out for only a few minutes more before surrendering to the indoors. The dusky woman cupped hands around her mouth and let out a raucous bellow.

"All right, that's enough. Inside this minute or no supper for anyone."

They scampered for the house with alacrity. All except Terry and Vickie, who coddled along as though reluctant to face a meal in that house. Terry continuously scuffed a big toe against the firm ground. Preacher continued to watch until the adult trio disappeared inside. Disgusted by this *ménage à trois,* and apparently an incestuous one at that, he settled back to lay plans for how he would deal with them. Some of the alternatives he came up with seemed distinctly grim.

Deacon Phineas Abercrombie and Sister Amelia Witherspoon stood stock still, thoroughly astounded. The men who surrounded their three-wagon train, which comprised their "Mobile Church in the Wildwood," looked exactly like soldiers of Ancient Rome. Yet, how could that be? Here, in Wyoming Territory, in the year of our Lord 1848? One of them came forward into the flickering bonfire-lighted clearing from the surrounding woods.

He bore a large Imperial Eagle on a long, wooden rod; the laurel leaf wreath, which, like the eagle, appeared to be of pure gold, encircling below it the famous emblem of Rome—

S.P.Q.R., *Senatus, Populusque, Romanus*—Deacon Abercrombie recalled this from his Latin studies. "The Senate and the Roman People." What madness could this be?

One, obviously their leader, stepped forward, haughty, fierce-eyed, every inch the domineering Roman centurion in his crested helmet, cuirass, kilt and greaves. "What are you barbarians doing in the realm of Nova Roma?"

New Rome? the stunned deacon echoed in thought. That accounted for it, then, his dizzied mind supplied. Still unsettled by this apparition, he spoke in a near babble.

"Why, we are not barbarians. We are Christian missionaries. We have come to spread the word of God to the heathen lands, to do the work of the Lord."

Cutting his eyes to a subordinate, the centurion commented, "Good Christians, eh? We'll get to see the lions again, eh, Sergeant?" His smile was decidedly unpleasant, Abercrombie thought.

His *contubernalis* (skipper) produced a wicked smirk. "That'll be just jolly. I hope they save this fat windbag for last," he went on, with a nod to Abercrombie.

Astonished that he had no difficulty in understanding their Latin, Deacon Abercrombie flushed with crimson outrage at the depiction of himself. He was about to launch into an indignant protest when the centurion's next words stoppered his mouth.

"All right, round them up and get them in chains. First I want to ask a couple of questions." He turned to Abercrombie and spoke in perfect English, albeit heavily laden with a Southern accent. "We're looking for a man. He's been wounded, and probably traveling slow. Have any of y'all seen such a person?"

While Deacon Abercrombie struggled to frame a reply that included a protest, a startled yelp from his right silenced him. "Take your hands off me," Sister Amelia snapped. "I'll not abide any man to touch me, let alone a rude stranger."

A hard-faced legionnaire barked back at her. "Shut up,

lady. The *contubernalis* says we put you in chains, that's what we're going to do."

"Why, the very idea! The nerve. How dare you treat us like this?"

"Sister, please," Abercrombie interrupted in an attempt to defuse the situation.

The soldier acted as though he had not heard a word. "Because we've got the weapons, Sister. Now, cooperate or suffer for it."

Quickly the twenty men and sixteen women were rounded up and thrust into chains. Few voiced protest. Several women began to pray aloud or to sing hymns. The crude legionnaires laughed among themselves and made nasty comments. Soon, the job had been completed. The centurion had as yet to get an answer to his first question. He bore in on Deacon Abercrombie.

"You seem to be in charge of all this. I want an answer, or it will go hard on y'all."

Abercrombie tried to compose himself. "What was the question?"

"Have you seen a wounded mountain man?"

"No."

"That's all? Just no?"

Deacon Abercrombie sighed in frustration. "No, none of us has seen such a person."

With eyes narrowed, the centurion put his face right in that of Abercrombie. "You sure y'all ain't hidin' somethin'? Not bein' entirely truthful?"

"Sir, I am a churchman. I do not lie."

The centurion pointed contemptuously at the Bible tucked under the deacon's left arm. "You ask me, that's all you do, is lie. Pack of nonsense between those leather covers. I'll ask one more question; then all of you back in your wagons or on horses. Have you, by chance, encountered a scruffy man goes by the name of Preacher?"

Several of the cowed missionaries shook their heads in the negative. Abercrombie drew himself up and glared defiantly at his interrogator. "Of that, I am absolutely certain. Had we encountered anyone with so outlandish a pretension in this wilderness, we would have remembered."

"Am I to take that to mean no?" the centurion asked with a sneer.

"Precisely. It is possible that this wounded man you are looking for saw us first and hid himself. So it may be that we have passed by him on his way, without knowing so. As to this Preacher you are speaking of, there's been no such person."

"So, if you are going to stick to that, you might as well load up. Maybe the curia's torturers can loosen some tongues."

"Where are you taking us? I demand to know," Abercrombie unwisely blustered.

"To New Rome, of course. Y'all are in our country without permission. The First Citizen will likely call you all Gallic spies. Whatever he decides, it's the coliseum for the lot of you."

At the news of this, wailings and lamentations rose among the faithful.

By ten o'clock that night, Preacher had it figured out. He waited until midnight, then glided out of his place of concealment. Bent low, walking in moccasins for quiet, he crossed the clearing to the tumble-down cabin. A stench of neglected, spilled food and unwashed bodies leaped out to assault him. His nose wrinkled. The shambles of an outhouse behind the log structure gave evidence of being a total stranger to quick lime.

He had been upwind of the wretched hovel, Preacher recalled as he closed on the rickety front porch. He made not a sound as he crossed the warped, weathered gray boards to the front door. There Preacher paused while he reached for the latch string. Strangely, considering where the cabin was located, it hung outside as a welcoming.

Preacher eased it upward and winced at the slight scraping sound the bar made as it raised. When it came free, Preacher waited tensely, one hand on the butt of a Walker Colt. After half a hundred heartbeats, with no alarm shouted from inside, he eased the door inward. Another mistake in wild country. The hinges should provide added resistance against anyone trying to break in. Sucking in a breath, Preacher edged around the open portal.

He made not the slightest sound as he entered the smelly structure. He eased the door shut behind himself. A long wait to allow his eyes to adjust to the dimness within. Slowly, objects began to define themselves: a counter along one wall, with crude cupboards above; a cast-iron stove, tilted rakishly because of a broken leg; a hearth and fireplace mantle; a large, leather-strung bed beyond a gauzy curtain. Satisfied, Preacher ghosted past the slumbering adults lying together in a tangle of naked arms and legs.

Carefully, he tested the rungs of a ladder that gave access to the loft where, he surmised, the children slept. He gingerly put weight on the first and thrust upward. No squeal betrayed him. Preacher took a second and a third step. Surprising for the slipshod construction in general, the ladder still did not give off a single betraying squeak. In due time, Preacher brought his head above the level of the elevated flooring.

Here and there in the starlit darkness he made out the huddled forms of sleeping children. Beyond their relaxed bodies, he found Terry and Vickie, asleep together as usual, fully clothed, their arms around each other. With that accomplished, he went back down to take care of the adults.

What a ruckus that caused! Perhaps Preacher had not chosen the wisest way of extracting brother and sister from the family bosom. What he picked to do was stand in the middle of the cabin floor, by a large table, and bellow his intentions to the parents.

"All right, folks. I want you to stay tight in that bed. Don't even twitch an eyeball. I've come to take those towheaded youngins outta here to someplace decent."

In the next instant, the women erupted in a hissing, spitting, nail-clawing cat-fight mode. Bare as the day her mother birthed her, the blond one hurled herself at Preacher with fingers arched into wicked talons. He deflected her with his raised left forearm, but not before she raked his cheek with sharp nails.

"You bastid, keep yer filthy paws off my babies!" she howled.

"They as much mine as yorn, Purity. T'same man fathered them as mine," the other wailed, closing in on Preacher's right.

Preacher backpedaled and shoved the black-haired vixen away, toward the bed. Silas Tucker had not moved a hair. He sat in the middle of his harem bed with a bemused expression on his ugly face. He laughed at the startled look on Preacher's face.

"You done kicked a hornet's nest, mister," he declared through his mirth.

Preacher shook his head, determined not to be bested by a pair of fillies. "More'n likely *they* did."

They rushed him again and Preacher had to duck. A sizzling kick hurtled toward his groin. A hot rod of pain thrust into the outside of one thigh. This could prove more than he bargained for, the mountain man reckoned. Shouts from the loft joined in the pandemonium. Blond curls flying, the mother of Terry and Vickie charged in while Preacher held off the other woman.

Her fists pounded ineffectually off the broad, firm back of Preacher while she cursed and spat at him. He felt the wetness of her saliva on his neck, and it rankled some.

"Enough of that," he bellowed as he backhanded her in the upper chest.

She went tail over tea kettle across the table. Preacher had time to gather only a short breath before the dark one bounced in the air and came at him with fists flying. He ducked, blocked what he could and took a stinger on the already black eye. It smarted more than he would admit. All of a sudden, the other woman had him around the ankles.

She held on for dear life. It deprived Preacher of any means of avoiding the wrath of the one throwing fists and feet at him. It began to look worse with every passing second. Then Silas Tucker roused himself enough to get into the fray. He came at Preacher low and mean, a long, wicked-bladed knife held in one hand.

7

Preacher swatted the blonde aside and cleared a space for a swift kick. His moccasin toe bit into the meaty portion of Silas Tucker's right forearm. The knife went flying. Preacher quickly hurled the furious black-haired gal full into Tucker's chest.

Tucker went flying with a yowl, which quickly turned into a bellow of pain when his bare rump made contact with the still-hot stove. He came off it mouthing a string of curses, and his hand groped blindly for a weapon. He found the short, hooked, cast-iron stove poker and launched himself at Preacher. Evidently the blonde woman had learned her lesson. She hung back and satisfied her outrage by hurling metal cups, plates and other cookery items at the dodging figure of Preacher.

A white-speckled, blue granite cup clipped him as it zinged past Preacher's ear. He jumped to the opposite side, having his moccasin caught up in the tangle of legs and arms of the dark hoyden. Abruptly, he went down in a heap. Black curls swirled over his face as his wily opponent scrambled on top of him. She immediately began to pummel him with her fists.

"Git back, woman," Silas Tucker bellowed. He came at Preacher with the poker.

Faith Tucker rolled off Preacher in the wrong direction and at the wrong time. The descending poker caught her on the exposed point of her left shoulder. Her shriek of pain ended with a curse; then she added for emphasis, "Idjit, you done broke it."

Stunned, Silas looked upon his injured sister and dropped the metal rod as though it had been heated in the fire. Preacher used the brief interlude to spring to his feet. A large stew pot filled the entire range of his vision. He ducked and received only a slight graze across the top of his head. That bought valuable seconds for Silas Tucker.

He bolted to the corner of the cabin, by the fireplace. There his hands closed around the smooth, polished hickory handle of a double-bit axe. He hefted it once, grinned stupidly and advanced on Preacher's back, the deadly tool held high, ready to split the mountain man's skull. He learned how stupid he had been a moment later.

A shout—he thought it could have come from Terry—warned Preacher. He spun, took in the menace, now only four feet from him, and drew in one swift, sure motion. The hammer came back on his .44 Walker Colt and then dropped on the primer of a brass cartridge. Fire flashed in the cabin in time with the comforting buck of the six-gun in Preacher's hand. Smoke billowed, but not before Preacher saw the axe fly from Tucker's hands, and a spray of blood from the back of the man's shoulder showered both of his women.

They went berserk. Howling and screaming, they rushed to their wounded male, like females in a pride of lions. They completely ignored Preacher, who turned and headed for the loft. Pandemonium reigned above. Suddenly awakened, the children shrieked, screamed and wailed in confusion and fear. When he loomed up through the opening in the loft floor, Preacher rightly read a warning of fight in some of the older youngsters. Two of them came at him before he gained purchase on the flooring.

Preacher cuffed one of them aside and climbed off the ladder. He lightly felt a stinging blow to his side and yanked a naked, spluttering boy of ten or so off his feet. Preacher gave a disapproving cluck of tongue against teeth as he tossed the lad into three more who advanced on him.

"Enough!" he roared. The command had its effect.

Some of the smaller children clapped hands over their mouths and went round-eyed. Yet another brat challenged him. Growing amused, Preacher batted at the ineffectual blows in the manner of a man swatting mosquitos. His diversion lasted only a moment, until the sturdy boy of about thirteen snapped a kick at Preacher's groin. It connected before he could block, though without striking any vital targets. Preacher popped the youngster high on the cheek in reply and sat him down on his bare butt. The rest drew back in fear.

Preacher advanced toward the dormer alcove where Terry and Vickie had withdrawn. "C'mon, I'm takin' you outta this hell-hole," he commanded.

Accustomed to mistrusting all adults, Terry responded with defiance. "What if we don't want to go?"

Preacher cocked his head to one side. His expression clearly declared that he would not take a lot of that. "Do I have to hog-tie you, like before, an' drag you outta here? It can be easy or hard, your choice; either way, we gotta move fast. 'Cause them she-cats down there are like to recover from their weepin' an' wailin' over their head he-coon and come after me with a vengeance."

"One of them is our momma," Terry said as he continued his challenge.

A flint edge turned Preacher's eyes; and sarcasm, his words. "You got any idee which one?"

Terry had not expected that tack. "Why-why, the yeller-haired one, of course."

"If you expect to see her go unharmed, then you'd best move fast. There's knives and forks and things down there that can do a feller real harm. I don't intend to stand around an' let her poke any of them into me."

His head of steam deserted Terry, and his frail chest deflated under the raggedy shirt. "We'll go."

"Yes, Preacher, we'll go with you anytime," Vickie added, her cobalt eyes dancing in starlight.

"Now, that's more like it. 'Sides, you'll be better off where I'll be takin' you, better by far than livin' with this sordid riffraff."

Terry produced a pout. "She's still our maw."

Enough had come and gone for Preacher long ago. His face clouded, and his words rang in a hollow command. "Git down them stairs. Grab what belongin's is yours, especially any coats."

"Coats? You flang the only ones we had in the fire," Terry protested.

Nonplused, Preacher could only shrug. "Rags. They was mostly rags," he defended his action. "Now, scoot!"

Oblivious to the deep chill, the youngsters scampered barefoot down the ladder. Preacher followed. The thirteen-year-old, still smarting from the punch Preacher had laid on him, shouted after. "Paw's gonna wrang your necks oncest he catches up to y'all."

Preacher turned his iron gaze over one shoulder. "You tell him to come on, as I reckon it'll be me does the wringin'."

On the ground floor of the cabin, the women still whooped and hollered over the wounded Silas Tucker. Silently, Preacher wished them the joy of it, then led the way to his horses.

* * *

"I don't *want* to sit still!" Terry Tucker sassed Preacher from atop the packsaddle at midmorning the next day. "It hurts my behind, ridin' like this."

"You spook that pack-critter an' I'll show you a hurt behind," Preacher warned.

Terry tried his repertoire of the cutest. "Why can't I ride with you?" he asked coyly.

"Cougar ain't used to carryin' double," Preacher grumbled.

"He can *learn.*"

"Not now, he cain't, Terry. Not no-how," Preacher insisted.

Right then, Cougar's ears twitched. The packhorse whuffled. Preacher reined in sharply and listened. His ears, then his nose caught the message. Injuns! Friendly, without a doubt. Else they would not have let the three whites ride in so close. Preacher nodded, raised his right arm and signed the symbol for peace. Then he waited.

Always perceptive, Terry spoke in a mere whisper. "What's wrong?"

Preacher's lips barely moved. "Cain't you smell it? They's Injuns out there."

Terry's eyes went wide and round. "They gonna scalp us?"

"I don't think so."

Fear and insecurity shivered through the boy's skinny frame. "You don't *think* so?"

"Take it easy, boy. No sense in gettin' them riled . . . if they ain't already."

Preacher signed again. This time a familiar figure walked his spotted pony out onto the trail. Preacher raised in the saddle and signed "friend."

"Ho! Ghost Walker, we meet again."

"Ho! Bold Pony, it is a good meeting."

"The hunting is plenty. We stay to fill our travois." He

looked pointedly at the two towheads on the packhorse. "You found them, I see."

Preacher thought over the ordeal of last night, and the trials of this morning. The kids had taken to being bratty, as usual, right after breakfast. "Yep. More's the pity."

"You would tell me about it?" Amusement twinkled in the eyes of the Arapaho war chief as he rode in closer. He examined Preacher's face. "The parents were not so pleased with parting with their dear ones?"

Preacher grunted. "Sometimes your eyes are too keen, Bold Pony."

He went on to relate the visit to the Tucker house. The more colorful his description grew of the brief fight in the cabin, the more Bold Pony laughed and held his sides. Although unaware of why, the amusement of Bold Pony had an effect on the children. Before long, Terry and Vickie broke into fits of giggles with each revelation Preacher made. It put him in a scowling mood.

Preacher rounded on them to growl. "That's enough of that." He turned back in appeal to Bold Pony. "You see what I mean? These two have been a pain in the behind from the git-go." Then he told of their morning's fractiousness.

Bold Pony studied the predicament in which Preacher found himself. At last he answered cautiously, albeit with a hint of laughter in his words. "If my people did not believe that spanking a child is wrong, I'd suggest that you do just that."

Preacher soberly considered his friend's words. "Well," he announced at last, a gleam in his eyes, "these warts ain't exactly Arapaho. So, mayhap a willow switch would be just the thing."

Bold Pony nodded sagely. "I will leave you to your important work. May the sun always rise for you, Preacher."

"May the wind always be at your back, Bold Pony."

Without a backward glance, Bold Pony turned his mount

and rode off silently. Preacher turned his attention to the youngsters, who had grown deathly pale. He dusted his hands together and kneed Cougar in the direction of a creek bed, where a long, narrow stand of weeping willows beckoned.

Terry read Preacher's intent in a flickering and blurted his appeal, thick with tears. "Oh, no, you ain't gonna do that. Please. You ain't gonna whup us?"

"You broke my only fire trestle, burnt the cornbread, dang near ran off the packhorse, an' shamed me by jibberin' like a pack o' monkeys in front of Bold Pony. Suppose you tell me just why I shouldn't?"

" 'C-'cause Paw always whups up on us somethin' fierce."

Determined now, Preacher ignored the boy. At the creek bank, he dismounted and tied off both horses. Then he selected and cut a suitable willow switch. Stripped of its leaves, it made a satisfactory whirr as he flexed it through the air. Face somber, Preacher walked over to the children.

"You first, Missy," he directed to Vickie.

Reluctantly, she came down from the packsaddle. Her eyes flooded as Preacher knelt and bent her over his knee. He upended the hem of her skirt and exposed a bare bottom. Swiftly, without any show of anger, he delivered four sound whacks. Vickie bit her lip to keep from crying out, but her whimpers tore at Preacher's heart.

Dimly, from memories best left buried, he dredged up images of the few times he'd been thrashed as a boy. Once begun, though, he could not stop in midstream, so's to speak. He set her on her feet and went for Terry.

"Don't touch me," Terry wailed. "I'll git'cha. I'll git'cha in your sleep," he threatened to no avail.

Preacher had him in the strong grip of one hand and hauled the slight lad off the packsaddle. The willow switch between the third and little fingers of the other hand, he quickly had the boy's britches down and his wriggling torso over an upraised knee. For only a moment did Preacher hesitate; then six fast, expertly delivered smacks left red spots, but raised not a welt. Returned to his upright position, instead of pulling up his trousers, the silently sobbing boy yanked on his shirt to expose his chest and back.

Angry, fresh red lines, knotted here and there with spots of infection, showed over the welter of earlier scars Preacher had seen in the cave. "See? You're no better than he is, Preacher." Then Terry broke into a gushing flow of tears. Vickie joined him.

Seeing the terrible punishment meted out by the animal who called himself the boy's father and hearing their pitiful sobs tugged at Preacher's heart. Impulsively, he reached out and hugged them to him. He held them tightly while their blubbering subsided.

"Nah—nah, that's all right, yonkers. You ain't hurt that bad this time. An' a feller's got to learn that he does wrong, he's gonna git punishment, swift and sure. It's what distinguishes us from the animals." Preacher stopped and jerked his head back, a surprised expression on his face. "Listen to me, speakin' words with more syllables than my tongue can tickle over. Next thing you know, I'll be takin' to Bible-thumpin'."

Out of their anguish came laughter. Preacher continued to press his case. "Understand, I want things to go right for you. I promised I'd find a home for the both of you, with someone who will love and care for the both of you. An' I'm gonna do it."

Sniffling, Terry and Vickie dried their eyes and padded barefoot back toward the packhorse. Vickie spoke first. "I promise not to give you a hard time anymore, Preacher. Really I won't."

"Me—me, too, Preacher," Terry croaked hoarsely. "It's hard. After so many years of bein' bad, it's—it's a *habit*."

Preacher answered gruffly, his own throat constricted by a

lump of memory. "See that you tend to your p's and q's an' we'll git along just fine."

He restored them to their perch atop the pack animal and mounted up. Preacher led the way out, much relieved, the children considerably subdued.

Preacher crouched by the hat-sized fire he had built in a protecting ring of stones. He looked up from the skillet of fatback and beans, savoring the aroma that rose. He had found some wild onions, added dried chili peppers, salt and a dab of sugar from his supplies, and water from the creek that flowed soundlessly a hundred yards away.

Only a fool, or a greenhorn flatlander, camped right up beside a noisy mountain creek that burbled and gurgled over rocks and made musical swirls as it rounded sandbars and bends. A whole party of scalp-hungry Blackfeet could sneak up on such a foolish person. Preacher had learned that before his voice changed. It had saved his hair on numerous occasions. He paused in his cooking duties.

"Terry, go fetch that foldin' bucket full of water for the horses."

"Why didn't we just camp by the crick?" Terry offered in a revival of his earlier attitude.

There you go, Preacher thought to himself. Flatlanders an' fools. He drew a breath, ready to deliver a blistering rejoinder, then mellowed. "Because it's foolish, even dangerous, to camp where the sound of water fills your ears and you can't hear anyone sneak up on you. Didn't I explain all that to you before?"

To Preacher's surprise, Terry flushed a rich scarlet. One big toe massaged the top of the other. He cut his eyes to the ground right in front of them. "I—reckon you did. I—I . . . forgot."

"Well an' good. You owned up to it, an' that's what counts."

Unaccustomed to praise for any reason, Terry glowed, his eyes alight and dancing, his cheeks pink for a far different reason. Preacher gave him scant time to rest on his laurels.

"Git on, now. Gonna be dark before long."

After her brother scurried off on his errand, Vickie came to Preacher. With all the natural wiles of a woman, she draped one forearm on his shoulder and bent toward him with an expression of earnest absorption. "When will we be at the trading post, Preacher?"

"Some time in the mornin', provided you two carry your end. We git up, eat, clean up, an' git. All before the horizon turns gray."

Vickie made a little girl face. "Why do we have to wake up so early? I like to sleep until the sun is up far enough to shine in the loft an' I can smell breakfast a-cookin'."

"There's no loft here, an' we be in a hurry," Preacher answered shortly.

"What's the hurry for?" Vickie asked in sincere ignorance.

Preacher studied her a moment. "You don't think your poppa an' them herri-dans of his'n is gonna kick back and say, 'Ol' Preacher done stole our prize pupils. Ho-hum.'"

Vickie's eyes went wide. "You mean . . . they's a-comin' after us?"

"Count on it. Sure's there's stink on a skunk."

Twenty minutes passed, with Terry not yet back from the creek, when Preacher's prediction proved true.

His teeth gritted against the constant pain in his shoulder, Silas Tucker had held steadfast to his determination to exact revenge upon the crazy man who had broken into their cabin and stolen his best earners. Why, then two could steal the gold from a man's teeth without him knowin' it. And the boy, even though Silas had no intention of letting him know it, was turning into a right capable killer.

With those two bringin' in the goods, Silas would soon have his women dressed in silks and himself in a woolen suit. Reg'lar nabobs they'd be. Then, along comes this mountain wild man and spoils it all. Silas' brow furrowed, and he flushed with mounting anger as he looked down into the small valley where Preacher and the children had made camp. They'd soon see, Silas decided. He turned to Faith and spoke in a whisper.

"Be sure not to hit them brats. I know you're a good shot, m'love. Allus was. That's why I want you to stay back up here and give cover fire, y'hear?"

"I know, Silas, I know. It's that Purity cain't shoot for beans."

Silas gave her a broad wink. "That's why she's comin' with me. I c'n sorta keep an eye on her." He paused and gave consideration to something that had been gnawing on him since Terry and Vickie had been stolen. "You know, I been thinkin' maybe I should git a couple more brats offen her. They's whip-smart, her git."

Faith hid the jealousy that nearly gagged her. "What's wrong with me?"

"We gotta face facts, woman. Those youngins of ourn ain't travelin' with full packs. Somethin's sommat wrong with them."

"They're kin an' kin to our kin," Faith defended stubbornly.

Silas ground his teeth. "So be it, woman. Now you just get ready."

Preacher had poured himself a final cup of coffee when a bullet cracked sharply over his head. He lunged to the side and rolled to where he had rested his Hawken against the trunk of a grizzled old pine. The finely made weapon came into his hands with fluid ease. He turned back to the direction from which the shot had come.

His eyes took in a flash, bright enough in the twilight to be readily seen, and a puff of gray-white powder smoke. He sighted in the Hawken. The hammer had not struck the percussion cap when a fat lead ball smacked into the tree, two inches above his head, and Preacher flinched in a natural reaction. Bits of wood and bark stung as they cut the back of his neck. That caused his round to go wild. A hell of a shot, whoever it might be, Preacher considered.

"You youngins stay low. Hug the ground."

"It's Silas, come to git us," Terry announced, his voice quavering with his fear of the man.

Preacher mulled that over. "May be, but if so, he's gonna leave his bones here for the varmits."

"No," Vickie wailed. "No, he's gonna kill us all."

More shots came from closer in. Preacher dived for another position. But not before one ball cut a hot path across the top of his left shoulder. He came up in a kneeling position and took aim at a hint of movement among the aspens along the trail. The reloaded Hawkin bucked and spat a .56 caliber ball into the tree line.

A grunt and muffled curse rewarded Preacher's effort. He put the rifle aside and drew one of the pair of new-minted .44 Walker Colts. Another shot came from uphill and forced Preacher into a nest of rocks at the edge of the camp. Vickie yelped, and Terry uttered words that should never be in the mouth of a twelve-year-old. Preacher fired into the aspens and moved again.

Emboldened by Preacher's apparent retreat, Silas Tucker came into view. A red, wet stain glistened in the waning light of the sunset. He had taken Preacher's ball in the meaty flesh of his right side. Enough fat there, Preacher reckoned, to make certain nothing vital had been hit. Still, even a cornered rat had a lot of fight left in him. Silas peered shortsightedly around the clearing and located Terry, hunkered down on the grassy turf. Sudden rage at the boy's defiance blotted out his earlier evaluation of the youngster's worth. He raised a single-barrel pistol and took aim at the boy's slim back.

A hot slug from the .44 Colt in Preacher's hand shattered the radius of Tucker's right forearm a split second later. Impact caused his .60 caliber pistol to discharge skyward. Instinctively, he dove for a hiding place. Preacher started after him when another shot cracked from the aspens.

This could be a little harder than he had expected, the mountain man admitted to himself. He sure hated to kill a woman, but who else could Tucker have with him?

8

In rapid succession, three bullets sought a chunk of meat from Preacher's hide. He banged off two fast slugs at the hidden shooter and again moved to better cover. A fallen log seemed to offer the best advantage.

He had barely settled into position and begun to lament the lack of his rifle when a scurry of movement in the open caught his attention. On hands and knees, Terry scampered toward Preacher, with a Hawken, powder horn, ball pouch, and cap stick slung over his slender back.

"Git back, you little varmint!" Preacher shouted at him.

Terry kept coming. "You need these," he countered.

Well, damned if I don't, Preacher acknowledged to himself.

Terry reached the fallen tree in under five seconds. He paused as a ball smacked into the bark inches above his towhead. Then he adroitly flew over the rough surface of the trunk. At once, Preacher snatched the rifle from the boy, taking time only to pat the lad on his head in gratitude. A moment later Silas Tucker made his move.

"Git out there, woman," he bellowed as he charged, a pistol in each hand.

First one barked, then the other; lead cracked overhead and Terry scrunched lower behind the tree. The ramrod still in the barrel of the Hawken, Preacher set it aside and answered the two-person charge with his .44 Walker Colt. A freak change of direction on the part of Silas Tucker caused Preacher to blow the heel off the degenerate's right boot.

Preacher exchanged six-guns as Tucker and the woman bore down on him. Biting his lip, Preacher sighted in on the center of the woman's chest. She fired at him, missed by a long ways, and Preacher saw her golden hair streaming from under a bonnet. The mother of Terry and Vickie! Imperceptibly, Preacher changed the aiming point of his Walker Colt and triggered a round.

Hot lead tore a shallow crease along Purity Tucker's rib cage. She stumbled and sprawled headlong in the dirt. "Momma!" Vickie screamed.

Silas Tucker did not even miss a stride. Hobbling, he came on, determined to end it right there and then. Preacher was glad to oblige him. His .44 Colt bucked once, then again. Silas Tucker jolted to a stop, turned partly away from Preacher and looked down in amazement at the twin holes, which formed a figure eight in the center of his chest. He made a feeble attempt to raise his weapon again, then crumpled bonelessly into a heap on the ground, while his lifeblood pumped into his chest through a shattered aorta.

Made haunting by distance and the echo effect of the basin, a curse descended upon the living in the clearing. "You baaastarrrd!" A shot followed.

Calmly, Preacher completed the loading drill for his Hawken and hefted it to his shoulder. "You up above. You can give it up now. No harm be done to you if you do."

He waited for a reply. It gave Faith Tucker time to reload. A shower of bark slashed down on Preacher and Terry. Preacher grunted his reluctance away and took aim. He fired with cool precision. A weak wail that wound down to breathless silence answered his shot.

"D'ya git her?" Terry asked hopefully.

Preacher sighed heavily. "I reckon so, though I sure am sorry to have had to do that. Killin' a woman's not somethin' a man lives with easily."

"She treated us as mean as Silas did." To Preacher, Terry's justification lacked conviction enough to vindicate what had been done. "What about our momma?" the boy asked.

Recalling the grazing wound he had given the woman, Preacher came to his boots. He swung a leg over the downed tree and cleared it with ease. Terry quickly followed. Rapid steps brought them to the side of the fallen woman. Preacher knelt and felt her wrist for a pulse. He found one, strong enough, if a bit rapid. She moaned, turned her head, and opened one eye.

"My babies?" she asked first off, surprising Preacher. "Are they all right?"

"Sure are, ma'am," Preacher assured her. "Terry's right here beside me."

"Silas would have killed them. Sure enough that black-haired bitch sister of his would have."

Preacher broke the news with the usual mountain man's lack of delicacy. "She won't be doin' no killin' anymore."

"She's dead?"

A straight face hid Preacher's feelings. "Yep. She was tryin' to take my head off with that rifle."

"She is—er—was a good shot."

"Shootin' downhill throws a body off some. Now, there's somethin' I need ask of you. In fact, I damn well insist you do it. Once I get you patched up, I want you to go back for the rest of the children and lead them to the trading post at Trout Creek Pass. If you have any love for your own two, you had best do as I say, and mend your ways. You're gonna have to do that, and give them the care and love they deserve."

"They have done some terrible things," Purity offered in the faint hope of sloughing off her responsibilities.

"I know that. But they's youngins an' were forced into the life they led. You're not and nuther am I. We got rules to live by, and for you to teach this pair. Let me get on about fixin' you up."

"What if I just leave here an' keep on goin'?" Purity sought yet for a way out.

Preacher cut his hard, gray gaze to her eyes. He remained silent long enough to cause Purity to flinch. "Well, consider this. If you have any idea of duckin' out, with or without those other youngsters, keep in mind that I will hunt you down and drag you in to the tradin' post, where they'll be obliged to put a rope around your neck."

Purity Tucker swallowed hard and nodded her understanding. With her children gathered around, Purity sat still while Preacher cleaned up the shallow gouge in her side, packed it with a poultice of sulphur, moss and lichens, and bandaged it. Then he lighted the fire and set out the makings for coffee.

"Come morning, you set out north; we're headed south." Purity started to raise her voice in protest. Preacher showed her the palm of one hand to silence her. "Nuf said. Now, do I have to tie you to a tree?"

Purity shook her head and settled down to sip coffee in silence. An hour later everyone lay down for a restless sleep.

Dawn seemed to come extra early. After one of Preacher's substantial breakfasts, Purity sent Terry to recover the horses used by her and the dead pair. Preacher admonished the boy to gather all of the weapons. When Terry returned, Preacher tightened the cinch on one animal and helped Purity to mount. Without even a good-bye to her children, she rode away to the north.

Terry turned imploring blue eyes on Preacher. "Think she will really come back?"

Preacher shrugged and snorted. "I wouldn't bet more'n a nickel on it."

With that he assisted the boy and his sister into the saddles of the newly acquired mounts, and the three rode off toward Trout Creek Pass.

Philadelphia Braddock looked up from the moccasin he was repairing on the front porch of the trading post at Trout Creek Pass. He worked with a bison bone awl and a curved, fish rib bone needle. He sewed the sinew thread in precise, neat stitches. He was putting on thick, smoke-cured, bull hide "traveling" soles. The soft, distant sound of approaching horses had attracted his attention. Philadelphia squinted his bright green eyes. The brown flecks in them danced in the tears this produced. He peered over the top of the hexagonal half-glasses perched on the bulb of his nose.

From the cut of him, that big feller in the lead could be Preacher, he reckoned. Philadelphia ignored a small twinge in his shoulder wound, which was mending nicely under the care of an unlicensed doctor, who had journeyed west, turned to trapping and later to hard drink. To his credit, the pill-roller abstained religiously whenever he had a patient who needed the best of his professional skills. Yep, he saw more clearly now. Couldn't be anyone else.

Philadelphia shook his long, auburn hair in eagerness, which made his over-large ears, with their long, floppy lobes, flutter like wings. He snorted his impatience as it seemed to take forever for Preacher and the smaller folk with him to descend the high grade to the northern saddle out of the pass. Did his eyes play tricks, or did those folk ride some ways behind Preacher?

No, he realized a minute later as Preacher drew near

enough to make out his face. They were kidfolk. Preacher with a pair of brats? And whose, at that? Be they his? Philadelphia literally danced with urgency, yet he knew he would learn the answers soon enough. Preacher swung clear of the main trail and entered through the gateway of the palisade that surrounded the trading post compound. Already, his keen vision had identified Philadelphia, and he waved enthusiastically to his old friend.

"Whoo-weee! Preacher, as I live an' breathe," Philadelphia exploded, unable to contain himself.

When Preacher reined in and dismounted to tie off his big-chested roan stallion, Philadelphia rushed forward with a wild war whoop. Preacher spun and met him midway. Both had their arms extended and charged into a chest-banging embrace that raised a cloud of brown around them. At once they started a toe-stomping fandango that raised more dust. The longer they went on, the more violent their greeting became. Concern began to crease the high, smooth forehead of Terry Tucker. At last he could contain himself no longer.

"Hey! Hey, mister, go easy," he shouted at Philadelphia. "He's been wounded."

"Hell, that's never slowed Preacher none, boy. Mind yer business an' we'll mind ourn."

All of the improved deportment he had learned in Preacher's company deserted Terry. He looped the reins around the saddle horn and jumped off the back of the horse acquired from the Tuckers. "That done it!" his squeaky voice declared. "Damn you, old man, I'm gonna kick you right in the balls!"

Terry charged forward, only to be plucked off his feet by Preacher, who grabbed the boy by the tail of his shirt and the waist of his trousers. Terry squirmed and made ineffectual thrashing with his legs and arms. "Lemme go! Lemme go. I'll fix 'em, Preacher."

Their hugging welcome ended by Terry's intervention,

Philadelphia Braddock stepped back and turned those star-
tling green eyes on the lad. He cocked his head to one side.
"Whose your bodyguard, Preacher?"

"He's not a bodyguard," Preacher growled. "He's a bother."

Philadelphia gave Preacher a fish eye. "Since when you
be travelin' with children?"

"Ain't the first, won't be the last time, nuther," Preacher
rumbled.

For some reason, Preacher felt loath to go into all the
lurid details behind Terry and Vickie. Philadelphia would
find out soon enough, and no call to embarrass the youngsters. He clapped Philadelphia on the shoulder and changed
the subject.

"I got a powerful thirst, Philadelphia. Be you buyin'?"

"I be. Best get these babies some milk." He made a face
at the prospect. "An' a sugar stick to suck on; then we can
settle down to some serious depletin' o' Duffey's supply of
Monongahela whiskey."

Preacher lowered Terry to the ground and looked hard
into the boy's eyes. "You gonna behave yourselves? Not
gonna pull a stunt like last time?"

Terry shrugged skinny shoulders. "We ain't got nowheres
to go."

"That mean you'll stay?" Philadelphia cocked an eyebrow at Preacher's manner of speech.

"Yes."

"Yes, what?"

"Yes, sir."

"Fine. Now, go help Vickie down an' scoot inside. Ask
Duffey for something to eat. C'mon, Philadelphia. Let's go
wet our throats. By the by, I see you look a mite peaked.
Been off your feed a little?"

"Not perzactly. It's a long story. One best told over a
flagon of rye."

Once settled at a crude table in one corner of the saloon

side of the trading post, Philadelphia related his tale of the strange city and the stranger men, how they dressed and acted and that they spoke in a funny, foreign tongue. When he had finished, they drank in silence for several long minutes while Preacher wondered at it. At last he made up his mind.

Slapping a big palm on the damp wooden tabletop, Preacher spoke plain and clear while he looked Philadelphia straight in the eye, his own orbs hot with invitation. "I reckon I needs to see these people. I want to learn all I can about them."

"Suits. I got my curiosities aroused, too."

"There's more. That city you told me about. Seems I've heard of it somewhere before. Something is nigglin' in the back of my brain pan, says I've seen such a place, or read about it. Buildings is all white, right?"

"Seen 'em with my own eyes," Philadelphia assured him.

"Hummm." Preacher drained his pewter flagon and hoisted it to signal for another round. Ruben Duffey complied with a will. When he departed, Preacher went on. "Thing that really rubs me where I cain't itch is all these folks, an' all those buildin's bein' out here in the first place, an' me not knowin' a thing about it."

Philadelphia tried to hide his own eagerness. "Well, I cain't say I blame you a bit for that."

"Tell you what, Philadelphia. When that shoulder wound you got from them downright unfriendly fellers heals, I'd be mightly beholden if you were to lead me to this strange city growin' in the wilderness."

For an instant, relief flashed in those brown-flecked, green eyes. "You got yourself a deal, Preacher, that you surely do."

Chariot wheels rattled noisily over the smooth, nicely set cobbles of the wide Via Iulius, which led to the foot of the

Pontis Martius—the Hill of Mars—and the gladiator school of Justinius Bulbus that nestled in its shadow. Swelled with pride, young Quintus Faustus Americus held the reins as he stood beside his father. Although usually the task for slaves, driving the chariot had made the day into a golden one for the patrician boy. His bony chest swelled even more when he slowed the horses at the proper time and received a fond pat on the head from his father.

He halted the animals in good order and stopped the vehicle without incident, due to the hand brake, an improvement over the original design. Bulbus stood in the gateway to welcome them. Born Able Wade, Justinius Bulbus looked the ideal director of a school for gladiators. His thick, burly body, low brow, jutting jaw and hairy ears made a clear statement of his past as a brawler and a thug.

Cunning and ruthlessness lighted his pale blue eyes, rather than intelligence. When recruited out of the dockside slums of Boston by Marcus Quintus, Able Wade had been more than enthused by the proposition made to him. He had babbled on and on about various weapons and fighting styles of the ancient gladiators. It became clear to Quintus that Wade had likewise shared the benefits of a classical education. Only the lack of a keen intelligence, and his father's sudden loss of a vast fortune, such as that of the Reardon's of Virginia, had ended that schooling abruptly and left Able in the lowest strata of society. Quintus could not have cared less. So long as the newly named Justinius Bulbus could run a school to teach men exotic ways to slay their fellows, he would be amply rewarded. Quintus now returned the greeting salute of the master of games and dismounted from the chariot.

"You are just in time, First Citizen." Bulbus had had little difficulty becoming fluent in Latin, recalling snippets of it from his years in the finest schools. "We are about to begin the morning session. Come, join me in my box."

"With pleasure, good Justinius. You know my son, Quintus Faustus?"

"Of course—of course. A bright lad." Bulbus peered closely at his guest. "He certainly takes avid interest in the games."

"That he does. The games to honor his birthday are coming soon. I am sure you have prepared a magnificent program?"

"Oh, yes. You see, we have this new contingent of Christians. I'm sure the boy will fair pop a—ah—button at the spectacle I have planned."

Faustus brightened even more; his face writhed in expectation. "Christians, Father? How wonderful." He clapped his hands in emphasis.

Bulbus directed his important guests to the small, private box that overlooked the practice arena. Exactly one-third the size of the coliseum, it afforded space for only two pairs to fight at once, or for rehearsal of half of one of the "historicals" or farces at one time. The rest of the participants in the latter two presentations looked on from behind bars set into one wall of the arena. They studied the movements of their counterparts, then changed places and did the routine themselves. Final rehearsals would naturally be held in the coliseum. Bulbus made sweeping gestures to cushioned chairs in the front row, and father and son seated themselves.

Bulbus raised an arm. "All right, let it begin."

"Will Sparticus fight first?" Faustus asked the master of games.

Offended by this slighting of his star gladiator, Bulbus answered sharply. "Certainly not. Sparticus is my grand finale. Lesser-knowns are for opening the show. Today, and this will be a preview of your birthday games, young man," he confided, "Baccus Circus will open. He has taken to training well and shows real aptitude."

"He's a magnificent specimen." Quintus brought the subject back to Sparticus, who had appeared while Bulbus spoke to the boy, and was working out in a side cage that could be seen beyond the wall of the arena. He nodded to the huge black man.

"Our legionnaires found him wandering on the high plain east of here. No one in Nova Roma knows his real name. He's a runaway slave, of course. And, frankly, I don't care to know his identity. He is the best gladiator in Nova Roma, as I am sure you know. But, a slave is a slave, so Bulbus owns him. Sparticus likes his work.

"He's never been intractable or rebellious. That must also be true from before he came here." Quintus paused. "If you examine him closely, you'll find there's not a whip mark on him."

Bulbus was not to be put off a lecture on his favorite subject. "Timing is everything with the games. It is like the theater." He would have said more, but the shriek of wrought-iron hinges interrupted as the Porta Quadrila opened and two gladiators stalked out.

Big and burly, the first blinked at the sudden, bright sunlight. Thick muscles rippled in his shoulders and arms. He bore a spiked club and a small shield. His opponent, Baccus Circus, carried a round "target" shield and a twin-bladed dagger. Of nearly sword length, it made a formidable weapon. They paced across the sand and saluted Bulbus and his distinguished guests.

"Begin," Bulbus commanded in a bored tone.

That this would not be a fight to the death soon became obvious. The middle-range fighter squared off with Baccus Circus, and they began a series of set-piece drills. They consisted of four or five varied attacks, at the end of which they engaged shields and weapons and rotated a quarter way around the arena. Both men soon glistened with sweat. Their smoothly shaven bodies sparkled in the sunlight. The speed of their drill increased with each engagement. Quintus, bored by so routine a performance, looked to his son.

Faustus stared intently at the battling men, jaw slack, lip parted, eyes glazed with excitement. His breath came harshly from a dry throat. Slowly, the pink tip of his tongue slid out and licked his lips. It was not, Quintus noted, a quenching gesture, rather one of unhealthy arousal for a boy so young. He quickly cut his eyes back to the contestants.

Their contest ended in the third quarter, when Baccus caught one of the spikes in the head of his opponent's club between the two blades of his weapon and disarmed the man. Quickly, Baccus stepped in and laid the flat of his dual knives against the throat of the other.

"Well done!" Bulbus shouted over his applause. "You are doing magnificently for a beginner, Baccus Circus." He turned to Faustus. "Now it is time to see some real blood flow, eh, lad?"

Faustus brightened. "Yes! Oh, yes . . . please.

Bulbus made a full arm gesture and called to his staff. "Bring in Sparticus. And . . . one of those teamsters from the freight wagons, I think."

Baccus Circus winced when he heard that. He hated the name given him. To himself, he would always remain Buck Sears. He hated what he had been forced to do. Most of all, he hated it when a fellow teamster captured in the high plains or the mountains was slaughtered needlessly to slake the appetites of some crazy fool who believed he lived in ancient Rome.

Buck had been brought here six months ago, after his train of freight wagons had been ambushed by men in the weirdest outfits Buck had ever seen. When he heard them speaking a foreign language, Buck at first thought the country had been invaded by the Mexicans. Only two years past the big war with Mexico, it seemed likely to him. Put into chains and forced to walk with the other survivors and captives, his first sight of New Rome stunned Buck.

This could not be. He didn't have a lot of book-learning, only six years of grammar school. Yet, he had a haunting suspicion that he should recognize the sprawl of shining white buildings and the seven hills they occupied. Rage almost earned him the lash when the captives had been led to the market, stripped, and sold like those unfortunate slaves in the South. He and half a dozen others had been purchased by a man whose function he did not then know.

Then he had been taken to the gladiator school. No stranger to fighting, the idea did not bother Buck, until he discovered that the contests were to the death. For all his moral objections, eventually he became resigned to it. At first, their training had been in English, with some Latin words worked in as they grew familiar. Now he spoke Latin with all the ease of those born in Nova Roma. Buck glanced up as they neared the portal and passed through with the first sensation of regret he had known in a long time. Against his better judgment, he quelled his reflections and remained at the iron lattice to watch the slaughter of his brother teamster.

Sparticus gazed coolly at the sorry specimen standing beside him. This wouldn't take long. The best Sparticus could recall, this one had not been at the school more than a month. What could he have learned in that time? Oh, well, the white boss says, "You do dis," you sho'nuf do it. He says, "Do dat." You do that. He shrugged it off and raised his arm.

"Ave Maestro! Morituri te salutamus."

"Give us a good show, Sparticus," Bulbus told the big black gladiator.

Now, that would be a hard one. Sparticus lowered his arm

and prepared to step into position. Frightened to desperation, the shivering teamster did not stand on formalities. He struck swiftly and without warning. Only by the barest of margins did Sparticus elude death.

"Bis dat qui cito dat!" the spoiled little boy jeered down at Sparticus.

He gives twice who gives quickly, Sparticus thought angrily. That was supposed to apply to charity—snotty little brat. He made a quick lunge. His opponent dodged clumsily. Sparticus pressed in on him.

With wild slashes, the hapless teamster defended himself. Metal shrieked off metal, a spark flew. Then another. The clash of blades became a constant toll of chimes. In a surprisingly short time, the teamster's wrists began to weaken. Sparticus played with him like a cat with a mouse. Small cuts began to appear and stream blood from the chest, arms, and belly of the amateur. Eventually the big black man grew bored with his sport. Swiftly, with a confusingly intricate movement, Sparticus struck again.

The short, Etruscan sword went flying. For all his furious action, the teamster went pale. Sparticus loomed over him. Tasting defeat, his opponent lowered his shield and let his chin droop to his chest. Sparticus looked up at the box.

Before Bulbus could signify the fate of the teamster, Quintus interposed a request. "Since it is close to his eleventh birthday, and he will be *imperator* at the games in his honor, I'd like to make a present to Faustus at this time."

"Go ahead, Your Illustriousness."

"Faustus, you may have the honor of deciding the fate of this wretch."

Faustus gaped. "Thank you, Father." Then young Faustus leaned even farther over the arena and thrust out his arm, the fist closed, thumb extended. With an exalted expression of ecstasy, he made a quick, jerking movement and turned the thumb down.

9

By the third day after their return to Trout Creek Pass, Preacher had to admit he had all he could handle to keep up with Terry and Vickie. Much of it centered around behavior *they* considered entirely ordinary, yet that which most of society frowned upon, or saw as outright immoral. If ever he was to find a family to take in the youngsters—he had long since given up on the return of their mother—Preacher felt obligated to instruct them in manners and other socially acceptable conduct. To that end, he established an open-air classroom in a stand of fragrant pines.

Squirrels chittered and birds sang from above while the children sat on the low stumps of trees harvested to build the trading post. It was going the same way it had during the past morning and afternoon sessions. Terry and Vickie sat politely, still and attentive, their cherubic faces upturned to Preacher. One by one, Preacher dealt with their moral shortcomings, as he and his culture saw them. They listened, he felt sure of that. Then, in the most innocent of words, they dismissed entirely every manner of conduct that differed with the way they wanted to do things. This afternoon's session had finally gotten around to their sleeping habits.

"Now, over the past days, I've been tellin' you a lot about how decent people do things. Also about the sorta stuff the good folk would never do. Some of it, I'm sure you understood. What sticks in my craw is how you manage to make it sound out of the ordinary and your way to be better. To tell you straight out, that cain't be with what I want to talk about this afternoon. There comes a time—ah—when youngins reach a certain age—that decent folk just don't countenance them sleepin' together, if they be of opposite sorts."

"What do you mean?" Vickie asked, all sweetness and light.

"Take the two of you. Terry is twelve, you ten, Vickie. Decent boys and girls of those ages don't sleep together nekid, especially if they's brother and sister. They don't even sleep together in nightshirts. Or even like you sometimes on the trail, in all your clothes."

"Why not?" Terry prodded.

Preacher's face clouded. "We been over this before. You both told me you knew about animals an' stuff. How they get their young. An' that sort of thing went on a lot among that brood of kids with your folks. Well, if you an' Vickie continue to sleep like you do, other folks are gonna think it goes on betwixt you."

"But we *don't!*" they protested in chorus.

"I know that. But decent folks are gonna *think you* do.

Terry took on an expression of sullen defiance and challenge. "If they think those kinda thoughts, seems to me they cain't be too decent themselves."

Preacher's cheeks turned pink. "Now, there you go, boy. Deep in my heart I know I'm right, especial for brother an' sister. Yet, danged if I don't have to agree with you. Only dirty minds could dwell on those sort of notions."

Terry and Vickie gave him a "so there you are" expression. Preacher cut his eyes from one to the other, stomped the ground and turned away. Images of Indian children, all curled up together in furry buffalo robes, marched through his head. Over his shoulder he announced to them, "All right. Dang-blast it, all right. School's out for today. At this rate, I'll never make you fit to live among proper folk." He grumbled to himself as he walked off.

Preacher did not get off the hook that easily. Early the next morning, over a plate of fried fatback, beans and cornbread, he found his good mood spoiled by Anse Yoder, the factor of the trading post. A strapping, amiable Dane under most circumstances, Yoder had his visage screwed up into the best expression of disapproval and anger that his broad, pink face under a tousled mop of straight, blond hair could produce.

"Preacher, those little hellions of yours have gone too far. Hoot Soames got howlin' drunk last night. When he passed out, I put him to bed in the common room. Those devil's spawn snuck in there, and they dribbled molasses all over Hoot's face. Then they cut his pillow. He woke up this mornin' thinking he had been tarred and feathered."

Preacher's first response was to let go an uproarious belly laugh. He restrained himself and considered the situation over another cup of coffee. From what he had dragged out of Terry and Vickie, the children saw their former criminal activity as high adventure. It had taken some powerful talking for him to convince them to find another outlet for their charged spirits. He hadn't expected them to turn to stinging jokes on the customers at the trading post. He would definitely have to do something about it. That decided, Preacher prepared to relax, when Anse dropped the other boot.

"Just the other day it was Olin Kincade, near to killing himself trying to get out of the chick sale. Ya see, what those *schnorrers* of yours did was to rig some rattlesnake rattles under the bench in there, right by the opening. They had dem so that they made a purty real sound when a string got pulled. So, what happens? Olin went in to answer a call of nature. Those brats waited until he got settled all well an' good, then let go. Olin came up off that seat with a roar and nearly tore himself apart tryin' to get out. He forgot he had slid the latch bolt closed when he went in."

"Now, that's nothin' that ain't been done before," Preacher defended, all the while making a powerful attempt to hold in his laughter.

"That's grown men playing a gag on one of their fellows. No, sir, I tell you, Preacher, I tell you true. You have to find a home for them and damned fast at that."

Grumbling to himself, Preacher finished his breakfast and looked up from his place. "All right, Anse, I'll do just that." With that he left to find Terry and Vickie.

"Nope. Sorry, but I heard about them two already. What I want is for them to be as far away from me and mine as anyone can get."

Preacher found the story the same wherever he went. Not a single household wanted anything to do with Terry and Vickie Tucker. After one silver-tongued effort to beguile a thickly set timber cutter, and father of four, the man rounded on him, double-bit axe in hands made hard by work.

"No, sir. I'd as leave have the devil hisself move in. Why that pair would pollute my youngins faster than a man can say 'Go.' Those Tuckers was nothin' but trash. Plain ol' hill trash from the west part o' Virginny. They just natural have the morals of an alley cat and the urges of a three-peckered billy goat. It's those mountains they growed up in, I think. Even the Injuns called them big medicine. The Cherokees, before they was removed from Carolina and Georgia, wouldn't set up a camp there. Only went for religion things. Whatever it is, it's done twisted those white folk that live there. Say what you might, Preacher. I just ain't gonna have them here."

After they rode off, Preacher's keen hearing hadn't any difficulty picking out the faint sound of sniffling. The children had dropped back slightly, so he turned to see what caused it. Tears filled the eyes of Terry and Vickie. Caught in an embarrassing moment, Terry took a quick swipe at his nose with the back of one hand.

"There ain't anyone wants us, is there, Preacher?" Vickie asked, her voice shaky with weeping.

Preacher roughly cleared his throat. "We ain't seen *everyone* yet."

"Don't matter," Terry fretted. "No one's gonna take us in."

Eyes squinted, Preacher challenged the boy's conviction. "I wouldn't be takin' any wagers on that, Terry." He sighed and looked back at the roof peak of the cabin they had just left. "Maybe we ain't gone far enough."

"But, you already said we'd come ten miles from the tradin' post."

Exasperated, Preacher snapped. "Right enough. Only maybe that ain't far enough, considerin' the reputation you Tuckers has hangin' on you." Then he softened his harsh words. "We'll look some other places."

After four more refusals over the next three days, Preacher had about talked himself into accepting Terry's cynical version of their predicament. He had even agreed with his doubting side that given another turndown, he would return to Trout Creek Pass and keep the kidlets with him, at least until he had time to journey to Bent's Fort and hopefully hand them off to some unsuspecting pilgrims.

What an awful thing to do to both sides, he thought charitably a few minutes later. He had crested a low saddle and saw beyond a tidily built, inviting-looking cabin of two stories, complete with isinglass windows that sparkled in the afternoon sun. Thin streams of smoke rose from two well-constructed chimneys at opposite wings of the building, one of them of real brick. A lodgepole rail fence surrounded it, and defined a generous kitchen garden to one side of the front. A corral of the same material featured high sides, and a sided lean-to for sheltering stock from summer's heat and spring's rain.

A half barn abutted it, no doubt the remaining portion dug into the hillside. Then, on another small knoll, with a huge, gnarled old oak shading the plot, he noted three small, fresh mounds of dirt behind a split-rail fence that guarded the final resting place of those who had departed. Preacher confounded the youngsters by removing his battered, floppy old hat and holding it over his heart as he rode past. At a hundred yards, he halted and hailed the house.

"Hello, the cabin!"

"Howdy, yourself," came the answer from the doorway to the barn, where a man appeared, a pitchfork in one hand.

"We be just the three of us. These youngins an' me are friendly, oncest you get to know us."

Their host squinted, then nodded. "I know you, right enough. Know *of* you anyway. You're Preacher, right?"

Terry groaned. "We might as well ride on," he said under his breath.

It didn't escape Preacher. "Now, hold on there, boy. Let him tell us that." To the stranger, he answered, "That I am."

"Ride on in, then. My wife's bound to have coffee on the stove. An' there's buttermilk or tea for these two," he added.

"My goodness, *tea*, as I live and breathe," Preacher said from the corner of his mouth. It brought a giggle from the children. "Mighty obliged, mister."

Down at the cozy, large cabin, Preacher learned that they

were Cecil and Dorothy Hawkins. Two rug-crawlers clung to Dorothy's skirts and peeked shyly at the mountain man, their eyes widening when they saw Terry and Vickie. Tears sprang into Dorothy's eyes as she studied the towheaded youngsters.

"Are they . . . yours?" she asked in a low, grief-roughened voice.

"No, ma'am. They're not. You might say they is orphans. At least for sure on their pappy's side."

Cecil interrupted in an effort to spare his wife more sorrow. "You can tell us about it over some plum duff and coffee, Preacher."

"Obliged, Mr. Hawkins."

"Call me Cecil."

They entered the house, the children showing the nervous excitement common to the good smells they picked up. This Mrs. Hawkins must be the best cook in the whole world. Seated at a large, round oak table in the center of the main room of the cabin, Preacher felt himself relaxing—this was a house full of love. This was also a house that had experienced a recent tragedy. He longed to ask about it directly. Good manners prevented him from doing so.

"What brings you this way, Preacher?" Cecil asked as though their earlier conversation had not occurred.

Preacher took a big bite of the plum duff that had been set before him. "Well, like I said, Cecil, I'm lookin' for a home for these tadpoles." His hosts lowered their eyes. Preacher made a note of that. *Strike,* he thought in a cliche that had originated long ago in some army's surgical tent, *while the iron is hot.* "Did I say anything wrong?"

A long silence followed. At last, his eyes brimming with unshed tears, Cecil Hawkins answered him. "No, Preacher. Likely you said something right for the first time in a long time."

Always sensitive to the emotions of others, Preacher spoke softly. "How's that, Cecil?"

"We—we just lost our three oldest youngsters, Preacher. It was—was a fever that sort of sprang up all of a sudden. There ain't any doctors anywhere around here, not for a thousand miles. We didn't know what to do. We doped them with goose grease and sulphur, put cold cloths on their heads and chests. Nothin' did any good. It . . . took a long time. We buried the last only three days ago."

Sadness drew down the corners of Preacher's mouth. "I'm powerful sorry to hear that. The Almighty gives and He taketh away. It don't matter no-how what we wish things to be; the final outcome is in the hands of our Maker. I don't imagine, in your grief, you'd be willing to take on responsibility for two wild colts?"

Cecil and Dorothy cut their eyes, one to the other. A long, silent message seemed to pass between them. Cecil drew a long breath. "You say they are orphans?"

"Same as. I kilt their pappy, an' their momma has gone and deserted them."

"Are they well-behaved?" Dorothy asked.

Preacher took a deep breath, then let the words out in a rush. "They could be, if you've a strong hand and a powerful will of your own."

Another silent conference occupied the Hawkinses. Cecil scooted back his chair and came to his boots. "You'll excuse us for a moment?"

"Certainly. Take your time."

Preacher drummed his fingers on the table while the pair left the cabin. Their muted voices came from outside. He could make nothing of what they said. At last, they returned. Expectation lighted Dorothy's face. Cecil cleared his throat, his hands doing nervous things with one another.

"We—ah—we talked it over, Preacher. Losin' those babies almost destroyed Dorothy. Our oldest was about an age with this boy. You're Terry, right?" Terry nodded, his face blank.

"We know that—that you could never completely fill the place in our hearts that Tommy held, but would you . . . will you try?" He turned to Preacher again. "We want them to come live with us. We need their help and we believe they can help us. Our other two are so young, and Dorothy says she is—in a family way again. With a new baby, she'll need someone to help with the chores. So, if it's all right with you, Preacher, and you children? We'd like to make you a part of our family."

Beaming, Preacher came to his boots. "Them is splendid words, Mr. Cecil Hawkins. I'm mighty happy for all of you. What do you say, Terry, Vickie?"

"Yes," Terry blurted. "I—I guess."

"Your two children are so cute, Mrs. Hawkins," Vickie made her thoughts known. "I'd love to help you with them, if I may."

"Of course, my dear." She opened her arms, and Vickie rushed into her embrace.

Preacher cleared his throat, finding it quite restricted. "Well, then, that's all settled. You two might as well stay here. Philadelphia an' I are headin' to the northwest to look into what is going on in the Ferris Range. I'll drop off your things on the way by."

"Oh, thank you, Preacher," Vickie squealed, rushing to hug him and turn up her face for a kiss.

"Thank you, thank you, thank you, Preacher," Terry squeaked. Then he pushed out his lower lip in a pout. "But I really would like to go along and see those strange men."

"Another time, boy. Not now. Well, I'd best be gettin' on my way. Thank you folks for bein' such good Christian souls." He cut his eyes to the ceiling. "I'm sure the Almighty will give you a fittin' reward." If he was aware of the irony, he didn't show it.

Filled with deep-rooted satisfaction, Preacher rode away

some ten minutes later. Terry ran down the lane to catch up and leap up on Preacher's leg. The mountain man caught the boy, which freed Terry's arms to give Preacher a big hug.

"I'll never forget you, Preacher. Goodbye." The boy turned his head away to hide the rush of tears.

Preacher released the lad and brushed a knuckle at the corner of one eye. "Goodbye to you, Terry. Remember what I taught you about the things decent people expect of children."

And then he rode away.

Preacher counted the days on his fingers. He had been off on his quest for a week and a half by the time he saw the chimneys and rooftops of the trading post. He gigged Cougar into a fast trot. When he drew near, he recognized the stout figure of Philadelphia Braddock on the front porch. Philadelphia spotted him at the same time and bounded down the steps, his body visibly charged with energy. They met fifty yards from the double cabin that formed the trading post.

It instantly became obvious to Preacher that Philadelphia had made great strides in his healing. His face held its usual ruddy color, and he bounced around like a young puppy. His eyes twinkled with mischief as he questioned Preacher.

"I see you're alone. What happened, Preacher? Them two runned off again?"

"No. I found them a home. Let's go get the trail dust out of my throat and I'll tell one and all at the same time."

Inside the saloon, Preacher downed one pewter flagon of rye, signaled for another and waited for it to arrive. All the usual hangers-on crowded into the room. Their faces revealed how anxious they were for a good tale. Preacher soon obliged them.

"Yep, my quest ended in success," he declared the obvious. He went on to detail the search for a home, told of the

Hawkins family and the evident pleasure Terry and Vickie had shown at being taken in by them. He concluded with an observation.

"Strange enough, they did not appear too happy about partin' with me. For all I drubbed their heads and switched their bottoms."

Ruben Duffey answered with sober sincerity. "Not so strange, Preacher, I'm thinkin'."

Preacher blushed. "What's done is done. Tomorrow Philadelphia an' me are off to the Ferris Range. I aim to get me a good look at these strange soldiers, or whatever they are."

"Need some company, Preacher?" a couple of the regulars shouted.

Preacher pursed his lips and gave it a moment's thought. "That's mighty nice of you, Clem. You, too, John. This first time, though, I reckon the less of us they see, the better. But stick around. Might be we'll want some help later on," he added prophetically.

Buck Sears sat on a stone bench in the dressing room of the public baths of New Rome. Gathered around were five of the new "gladiators." One man wore a hard, belligerent expression. He ground a fist into one palm when Buck told them that the penalty for refusing to fight or attempted escape was death in the arena. No matter how many a fellow fought and bested, he would die there on the sand.

"I don't wanna go back to those cells they keep us in. Filthy, smelly, with rats and other critters runnin' around at night. I'm willin' to risk death to get out of here."

"Good. That's one of you."

"What are you getting at, Buck?" the pugnacious one demanded.

Buck studied him a long moment, while all five leaned

toward him in anticipation. "I've found a way out of here. I need me some good men, ones with enough fire and fight in them to make an escape."

"But you just said yourself that the penalty for attempted escape is death," one pilgrim with a receding chin and pop-eyes protested.

Buck stared him down. "That's only *if you get caught.* I don't intend to. From what I hear, the trouble is in those big ol' black dogs this so-called Bulbus keeps. We try to break out of the school, they give the alarm, and any who doesn't get eat up are condemned to the arena."

"How'er you gonna get around that?"

Buck studied the mousey little fellow. "I'm tellin' that only to those willin' to go with me."

Pop-eyes averted, the captive gladiator turned away. "Well, I—I don't know. At least, we're still alive."

Anger flared in Buck's chest. "For how long? Sooner or later, we're all gonna be pitted against Sparticus. When that time comes, you'd better be ready to meet your Maker."

The angry one looked at his timid companion with contempt. "Count me in. I don't aim to be dog meat, an' I sure know I'm no match for Sparticus."

Buck cut his eyes to the others, hope shining in his face. "How about the rest of you?"

Slowly they turned away, shame-faced, and muttered feeble excuses. Disappointed, Buck stomped out through an archway to wait for the guards to escort them back to the gladiator school on the Field of Mars. A moment later, his only recruit joined him. He extended a hand.

"M'name's Fletcher. Jim Fletcher. When do you reckon on doing this?"

Buck gave him a relieved look. "Soon, friend Jim. Soon's we have enough to make it work."

* * *

Later that night, when the inmates of the school slumbered in deep exhaustion, the skinny pilgrim with the receding chin quietly left the small cell he occupied, being released by a discreet guard. Blinking in the bright light of oil lamps, he was brought into the presence of Justinius Bulbus. Bulbus studied him over fat, greasy fingers.

"You have some information for me?" he asked, licking meat juices off the tips.

Voice shaking, the informant replied softly, "Yes, I have."

Bulbus gestured to a tray piled high with steaming meat. "Have some roasted boar. It's really quite delicious. Besides, you need the meat to build you up."

In spite of the obvious intent behind the invitation, the betrayer indulged himself greedily while he informed Bulbus of what he had overheard at the baths. Bulbus listened carefully and considered the problem a while before making answer.

"You have been most helpful. Circus is a splendid gladiator. It would be a shame to lose him. Perhaps . . ." Bulbus paused, thinking. "Yes, perhaps a flogging, administered by Sparticus, would serve as an object lesson to all concerned." He turned to his chief trainer, who lounged on a couch at right angles to Bulbus.

"See to it, will you? Say, ten lashes. No lead tips on the flail, either. I don't want him marked up." Bulbus sighed heavily. "Ah, such a magnificent specimen. When his time comes, I want him to shine. See that it is done tomorrow morning, right after breakfast."

10

Philadelphia Braddock halted and turned in the saddle to look directly at Preacher. He gestured to a notch in the ridge ahead. "By jing, if it ain't been a week's time since we left Trout Crick. Over yonder is that strange city I told you about."

Preacher thought on it, as he had been doing over the past seven days. "I reckon if they have people out scoutin', we'd best hole up somewhere until dark, then move in close."

"Good idee, Preacher. But, first, don't you want to size it up in daylight?"

"Of course. If we stay inside the tree line, we can reach the back slope of the ridge unseen. We can pick a spot from there."

It went as Preacher expected. Near the pass that led through to the basin, his keen ears picked out the brassy notes of several bugles, yet they saw no sign of soldiers beyond the gap. On the opposite side, he found an entirely different, and amazing, situation.

Philadelphia had been right. Large, shiny white buildings

now covered the slopes and tops of four of the seven hills. Construction, even at this distance, could be seen to go on at a feverish pace. Horsemen in scarlet cloaks and shiny helmets cantered around through the organized confusion. On the Campus Martius, formations of soldiers raised clouds of dust as they drilled with precision. Preacher studied the scene for a long while, then grunted his satisfaction.

"Over there." He pointed to a thick stand of slender pines, as yet not fallen to the hunger of the axemen. "We can ease our way over there and be within range to look over that place by spyglass."

Philadelphia licked his lips. "Now, that shines. If I'd 'a had my smarts about me, I coulda done the same thing." For a moment he looked crestfallen. "Only m'spyglass is broke."

Preacher gave him a smile. "No time like the here an' now, I allus say."

Silently, and with the great skill of the mountain men, they worked their way to Preacher's suggested vantage point. They left their horses muzzled with feedbags to silence them, and crept through the undergrowth which crowded the stand of lodgepole pines. Preacher settled in, his Hawken rifle across his lap, and extracted a long, thick, bullhide tube from his possibles bag. From that, he slid a brass telescope.

He fitted the eyepiece in place and peered at the scene below. Men dressed in only sandals and diaperlike loincloths sweated in the warm afternoon sun. Many, Preacher noted, had scars from a heavily applied lash on their backs. Overseeing them were men in tunics and rough leather aprons. Here and there stood uniformed soldiers. Preacher blinked, and pursed his lips.

"Danged if they don't look just like them old-timey Romans. But, that cain't be. T'weren't any Romans got to the New World."

"That's what I thought," Philadelphia whispered back.

"Then I reckoned my wound had got infected and I was seein' things. But, by gol, if you see 'em too, then they must be real."

"Only too real. We can't learn too much about them from here. We'll wait until night, then go down among them buildings and see what they're up to."

That suited Philadelphia fine. He settled back for a comfortable afternoon snooze. Preacher continued to study the oddly dressed men. He saw what he believed to be a chariot, pulled by a pair of sparkling white horses. Some big shot no doubt. Twenty men in uniform marched down a wide avenue toward the largest hill. They all carried long, slender spears. An hour shy of sundown, a shrill note sounded, as though from a reed flute, and the men quit working. They lined up and had chains fastened on their arms and legs. Then the men in tradesmen's aprons marched them away, out of Preacher's sight. Slaves, Preacher thought with disgust.

Preacher did not hold with slavery. Far from a frothing-mouthed abolitionist, he still did not think it right for one man to own another, like a horse, or pig, or cow. Quite a few Indians had slaves, mainly captive women or children from other tribes. Most times, once they had learned the ways of those who captured them, the children were adopted to fill the place of a child that had died, or the women married men affluent enough to afford two or more wives. Somehow, that didn't seem to Preacher to be so harsh a system. What was going on here, though, rankled.

"May an' have to do something about that," he whispered to himself.

Time edged toward sunset. Preacher stretched out the kinks in arms and legs and munched a strip of jerky. An hour after dark, he awakened Philadelphia. He bent close and spoke lower than the serenade of cicadas.

"Eat yourself a bit o' somethin' an' we'll move out in another half hour."

"I'll admit I ain't looking forward to this too much, though it does have my curiosity aroused."

"Not a big problem. Certain sure they ain't got senses half as sharp as an Injun. We've sure snuck into enough Cheyenne and Blackfoot camps to know how it's done."

"Even so," Philadelphia warned, "we could die here."

Silent as ghosts, Preacher and Philadelphia crept through the streets of New Rome. Every block brought new marvels. In moccasins, with rifles at the ready, pistols loaded, primed and waiting in their wide belts, they accosted marble statues; tall, alabaster columns of the same material supported high porticoes over stately porches. Philadelphia pointed a finger in amazement when they came upon a large, bronze brazier flaming with the eternal fire before the Temple of Vesta.

"Lookie there," Philadelphia whispered in awe. "I'll betcha someone is paid to keep that goin' all the time."

"More likely a slave," Preacher amended in a sour note, his mind on the shackling of the workmen at quitting time. "Cost less that way."

"Any way you look at it, somebody has to tend it. That must be some sort of church."

"More likely a pagan temple, if this is what we think it is."

"Better an' better." Philadelphia rubbed his hands in anticipation. "That's where they hold them orgies, huh?" He pronounced it or-*ghees*.

Preacher and his friend had no time to contemplate that vision. They rounded a corner in the forum and came face-to-face with the night watch. Armed with cudgels, flaming torches held above their heads, the city guards reacted instantly. With a shout of alarm, they dashed at the two surprised mountain men.

"Looks like folks know we're here," Philadelphia declared flatly as he flung away one of the watchmen.

Preacher saved the talking for later. Two burly sentries closed on him, their cudgels swinging with competence. When they raised them to strike, Preacher ducked low and stepped in under the weapons. Quickly he popped one with a right, the other with a left, under the chin. They rocked back on their heels. The chubbier of the two sat down abruptly, eyes wide with wonder. Preacher turned to finish the other one, when a cudgel caught him in the side.

He grunted out the pain and shock, then delivered a butt-stroke from the half-moon brass butt plate of his Hawken that broke teeth and cracked the jawbone of his attacker. The clatter of fast-approaching sandals on the cobbles sounded like hail on a broad-leafed plant. A swift check of the immediate area told Preacher that between them they had accounted for four of the six. With a little luck, they still might make it.

Good fortune deserted the mountain men. A dozen more of the night watch rounded into the *Via Sacra* and pounded down on the Temple of Vesta. Preacher caught a blow from a closed fist in the side of his head that made lights flash and bells ring. A short sword flashed in the hand of one watchman, and Preacher forgot all about his determination not to use firearms.

The Hawken barked. Burning powder sparked in the wake of flame that erupted from the muzzle. Smoke rose in front of Preacher while his opponent twisted his mouth into an ugly gash, stumbled backward and clutched at his ravaged shoulder. Then the other guards arrived, and the great square of the forum became a welter of struggling human shapes. Many of the blows delivered by the sentries fell upon their fellows. Enough found their intended target to bring an end to the battle.

A ringing, thudding pain exploded in Preacher's head, and the Hawken slipped from numbed fingers. Shooting stars cut through the darkness that gathered in his head. He tried to turn, to put his back to that of Philadelphia, though he knew it to be already too late. Philadelphia had sunk to his knees, hands around his head to protect it, while the heavy blows of cudgels rained on his bent back. The next smash with the thick-ended nightstick made the darkness complete for Preacher.

Early the next morning, Preacher and Philadelphia awakened in a small, damp, slimy cell. The odor of human vomit hung heavily in the dank, still air. Preacher's head throbbed, and he located four separate goose-egg-sized lumps on it. The sour taste in his mouth told him who had vomited. Beside him, Philadelphia groaned.

"Where are we?"

Preacher answered glumly. "In the lockup. Damn, my head hurts."

"So's mine. Ah! Aaaah—aaah, my back, too. They tried to turn my kidneys into mush. I'll be piddlin' blood for a month."

"Be glad it ain't runnin' out your ears."

Philadelphia quickly forgot his own misery. "You hurt that bad, Preacher?"

"No. But no thanks to those fellers."

Footsteps tramped loudly in the corridor outside. A jingle of keys came to Preacher's ears. They sounded sharp and tinny through the buzzing in his head. A key turned noisily in the lock, and a low, narrow door banged open.

"Come out, you two," a voice commanded in clear English.

"Where are we going?" Philadelphia wanted to know.

"You've got a hearing before the First Citizen."

Preacher scowled. "I don't like the sound of that. If I recollect, I've heard that before. It escapes me what it means."

Outside the cell, each man was given a bowl of water and

a crudely woven towel with which to freshen up. Then the in-different turnkey passed over a lump of coarse bread and a clay flagon of sour wine. "Eat up, eat up," he snapped. "We don't have all day."

Preacher shot him a flinty gaze. "Maybe you don't."

Three uniformed soldiers joined the procession at ground level. In short minutes they found themselves once more in the open area of the forum. At this early hour few citizens filled the walkways and steps of the temples. They were directed to a building next to the Senate. Above the columns, inscribed on the portico of the Capitol, was the single word *"Curia."*

Preacher saw it and shrugged. "Looks like we get our day in court."

Inside, they were rudely shoved through a curtained archway into a brightly lighted room, a hole in the domed roof to allow smoke out and sunlight in. Before them, three men sat on a marble dais. The one in the middle had a wide purple band around the hem of a toga. The ones flanking him had two thin lines on theirs.

"Who brings charges against these men?" the burly man in the center demanded.

"The tribune of the watch, Your Excellency."

"What are those charges?"

A tall young man, his head swathed in bandages, stepped forward from a stool to one side. Preacher recognized him as one of those he had smacked with his rifle butt. "I, Didius Octavius Publianus, tribune of the *vigilii,* charge these criminals with trespassing in the domain of Nova Roma, of being enemies of the State, and spies for the Gauls."

Gauls? Preacher thought. How silly could someone get? He could not let that one lay. "Why, Your Worship, this whole thing is crazy. Downright redic'lous in fact. What Gauls? There ain't any Gauls anymore, an' this sure as hell ain't ancient Rome."

Quintus raised a restraining hand. "Ah, but it is, my talk-ative spy. It is Nova Roma, New Rome. Let me introduce myself. I am Marcus Quintus Americus, First Citizen of Rome. These are my fellow judges, Publius Gra—"

Before he could complete the introductions, Preacher exploded. "By damn, I remember now. First Citizen means dictator."

Quintus displayed a surprised, impressed expression. "Why, that's quite correct, my good fellow. Duly elected to that honored position by the Senate. You seem quite learned for such a rough and rude specimen of the frontier."

"Just because I've spent most of my days out here, don't mean I didn't get any learnin'. I studied history, includin' ancient Rome, at the University of the Shinin' Mountains."

"How odd. I've never heard of it."

Preacher eyed Quintus suspiciously. "Small wonder. From that accent, I'd say you got your book-learnin' way back east somewhere. Maybe Princeton? Or Harvard?"

Quintus widened his eyes at this astuteness. An amused twinkle lighted the gray orbs. "You amaze me. That's quite remarkable. Harvard it was. Class of Thirty-six. I would really like to take some time to talk with you about this university of yours." He sighed. "But, the duties of office, and your crimes, make that impossible. Tribune, are you ready to put on your case?"

"Yes, Your Excellency." Quickly the tribune outlined the encounter in the forum the previous night. His version markedly differed from Preacher's recollection. He made note to dispute them when his turn came. The opportunity came too quickly for him to marshal his arguments.

"Is there anything possible you can say in your defense?" Quintus leaned forward to ask condescendingly.

"Only that it ain't so. Not the way he tells it. We was just takin' a little stroll through your fine city, seein' the sights, so's to speak. We come around this corner and these fellers jumped us right off. We had no idea who they might be, so we had to fight back. I will admit he was right about how many we downed before it was over. Musta been a baker's dozen or more." He gingerly touched his head. "An' I must say they got in their licks, too. Well, no real harm done, an' no hard feelin's I say. Now, to that bein' an enemy of the state," Preacher went on.

"We ain't enemies of no state. Not at all. An' we come here on our own. We don't spy for anyone. At least not anymore, nohow. There was a couple of times we done some scoutin' for the Dragoons. I suppose some as would call that spyin'." Preacher put his hands behind his back and began to pace. "Like I said, there ain't any Gauls anymore, so that charge is out the window, too. Taken all in all, we'll just say we're sorry about bustin' up your watchmen here, and bid you a peaceable farewell."

"I think not!" The voice of Marcus Quintus cracked like a rifle shot. "My fellow judges and I will confer and render our verdict. Jailer, take them away."

Preacher and Philadelphia found themselves in a small, windowless room with a sobbing young girl. Curiosity prompted Preacher to ask her what had brought her here and caused her distress.

"I—I'm to be branded as a runaway," she wailed, her English rusty. "But I didn't really run off. I was caught by a terrible thunderstorm and had to stay over the night at the farm of Decius Trantor. It wasn't my fault. But the watch caught me before I could reach home and explain to my master."

"Why, that's hardly fair," Preacher commiserated. "What brought you here in the first place?"

"We—my family—were on our way with some others to the Northwest. Our wagons were attacked. I was—I was—they had their way with me, and then I was sold into slavery."

"Why, them black-hearted devils. How long you been here?"

"It seems forever. At least two years. I remember my last free birthday was my fourteenth. We had a party right on the trail. There was music from a violin and a squeeze box." She put her head in her hands and began to sob wretchedly.

Preacher cut his eyes to Philadelphia. "When we get out of this fuss, we're gonna have to do somethin' about that."

"Yep," Philadelphia agreed readily. *"If* we get out."

Shortly before the noon meal, the guards came for Preacher and Philadelphia. Hustled into the trial room of the curia, they again faced Marcus Quintus and his fellow judges. Quintus looked at them sternly.

"It is the considered decision of this court that you are guilty as charged. You are to be scourged, then sold into slavery for life. Give your names to the clerk."

Preacher gave Philadelphia a quick wink first. "M'name's Arthur. I don't rightly know what my last handle happened to be. I been out here since a boy not yet in my teens."

Eyes suddenly aglow with interest, Quintus leaned down toward Preacher. "That's most interesting. Come now, do you also happen to answer to the name Preacher?"

Preacher hated deliberate lies. He swallowed his objection to untruthfulness and answered with a straight face. "I heard of him, of course. Why is it you ask?"

"I'm . . . most interested in this wildman Preacher. I've sent men after him, to have him fight in our arena, but none have returned."

"With good reason, too," Philadelphia answered sharply. "Preacher's the wildest, wooliest, ringtail he-coon in the High Lonesome. 'Less you send about a dozen or more, you'll never see hide nor hair of Preacher, other than he wants you to."

Anger tightened the skin around the eyes of Quintus so that they became flinty points. "You'll learn manners as a slave, or you'll be dead at a young age. Tribune, have the guards take these men off to be scourged." Quintus paused and sighed. "It is too bad you are not Preacher. What a glorious fight we would witness on the sand. See they are whipped quite soundly, but do not mark them. And notify Justinius Bulbus of these splendid fighting men we will have on the sale block."

11

"Everything is turned topsy-turvy in this dang city," Preacher lamented as their escort conducted them to the small square off the forum, where a raised platform filled the center.

A crowd of men pressed close to the edges, faces turned up, eyes fixed on the shapely young woman standing there beside a burly fellow with a coiled whip over one shoulder. He held a long reed pointer in one hand, and gestured grandly as he called off what he clearly saw as selling points.

"She's broad-hipped and will deliver with ease. Notice those smooth, straight shoulders, gentlemen. She can carry heavy burdens. All in all, a treasure for a bargain price. Now what am I bid?"

"Six," a voice called from the throng.

"What? Only six *sestercii?*"

"No. Six *denarii,*" came the answer, followed by laughter.

"Surely you jest? Why, I would gladly pay ten talents for her myself."

"Then you buy her," the heckler taunted.

A more serious buyer bid himself in. "I bid four talents."

Brightening, the auctioneer located his bidder. "Now, that's more like it. I have four, who'll give me five? Five-gimme-five—five-five—yes! Now six." His chant rolled on until he had worked the sale price to eleven talents. A lot of gold for a young woman.

Her new owner claimed his prize and took her to the cashier's table to pay his fee. The auctioneer motioned for the next sale lot. A muscular, bullet-headed assistant shoved forward two small boys. Their red hair, freckled faces, and dark brown eyes marked them as brothers.

"Lot number seven. Two house servants. They are brothers, aged nine and eleven. They were taken from a wagon train one month ago, and have mastered enough Latin to show they are quick learners. They will make ideal body servants for sons of gentlemen. Now, I'm going to open the bidding at ten sestercii, take your choice."

"They been cut?" a suspicious buyer demanded.

"No, sir. I'll guarantee that."

Not satisfied, the skeptical one pressed on. "A good look's the best guarantee I know of."

Sighing, the auctioneer tucked his pointer under one arm and reached for the white loincloths the boys wore as their only item of clothing. He gave hard yanks, which exposed them to all eyes, and humiliated the lads to their cores. Blushing all over, they stood with heads hung, tears running down their cheeks. "As I said, they have not been gelded."

"Why, that egg-suckin' dog," Preacher growled. "I'll fix him good when I get up there."

Philadelphia nodded to the javelin-wielding guards at the side of the platform. "More likely those bully boys would pin you with their pig stickers while that feller used his whip on you, Preacher."

Not one to waste breath on "if only," Preacher sighed heavily and accepted the inevitable. "It sure ain't the High

Lonesome anymore. This sort of thing is downright shameful."

"Then maybe we oughta be thinkin' about takin' our leave," Philadelphia muttered silently.

"Now your talkin', Philadelphia. We'll both work on that, keep our eyes open. First chance, we be gone."

"Count on it."

Their turn came sooner than either mountain man had expected. Not surprisingly, a burly man with a face mean enough to stop the charge of a bull bison purchased them. "You'll make fine additions to my gladiator school," he told them as armed and armored men hustled Preacher and Philadelphia away.

Hoisting a gold-rimmed cup, Marcus Quintus called across the expanse of table to his principal guest, Gaius Septimus. "The two barbarians who were captured night before last will make excellent additions to the birthday games for Quintus Faustus, will they not?"

Septimus curled his lower lip in a deprecating sneer. "That sort of man is entirely too independent to make a good slave, let alone a gladiator. Do you not agree, Justinius?"

Bulbus, the third guest, glanced up from his intense study of a lovely young dancing woman. "Quite to the contrary, Septimus. They are quick and strong, and used to fighting for their lives. Once their spirit is—ah—molded to my liking, they become marvelous in the arena. Some are absolutely fearless."

"Yes, like Preacher, who I fear is still on the loose," Quintus snapped.

"Will I get to watch your new slaves die?" Faustus, at the fourth table, asked.

The two senators who had been invited hid their reaction to the boy's rudeness behind pudgy hands. Bulbus glanced idly at the youngster, who had been included at this all-male dinner party by his doting father. There was something . . . not at all right about the child, Bulbus thought, not for the first time. His reaction to the games was—odd. Were he a couple of years older, Bulbus considered, it might be ascribed to the erotic fires of puberty. For all his suspicions, he answered cordially enough. After all, the youth was the son and heir of the First Citizen.

"No, young Faustus. They show much too much promise to be dispatched so soon. Unless, of course, someone lands an unfortunate blow."

"Why is that?" Faustus asked, genuinely interested.

"Keeping a crippled gladiator is like having a pet elephant. The cost of feeding him is ruinous." Bulbus laughed at his own joke. "But, you are quite right, Marcus Quintus, these last two specimens are in superb condition. I will intensify their training so that they can appear at your son's birthday games."

Flattered by this, Quintus ignored the admonition of Bulbus about sparing them for future games. "Wonderful. It will surely be marvelous. They will die magnificently," he burbled on, his eyes fixed on some unseen distance.

In a numbing cadence, the bored voice of the drill master barked out the commands. "Strike left . . . strike right . . . strike left . . . strike right."

Another chanted to his victim of the moment, "Shield up! Parry! Strike target! Parry, dammit!

"Duck! Duck, you idiot!" quickly followed as the heavy wooden ball on the opposite arm of the practice frame swung around and clobbered the hapless former immigrant. His dreams of the Northwest had long been abandoned in the rigors of the gladiator school. He looked up pitifully as Preacher and another gladiator stomped by, trading sword blows with weighted wooden weapons. The metronomic throb of the drumbeat used to mark movements accelerated to a rapid roll and ceased.

At once, the student gladiators ceased and headed for the large fountain in the center of the training yard. Dripping with sweat, they plunged bare torsos in to the waist. Preacher found himself a place beside Philadelphia.

"To carry off that escape we talked about," he observed to Braddock, "we must first get out of this dang-blasted gladiator school. An' I don't allow as how I've figgered out a way to do that as yet, what with them big dogs."

"We'd best find it soon. We've been here the better part of a week now. I've got bruises where I didn't know a man could get them."

Standing to Philadelphia's right, Buck Sears listened with interest. Here was a pair who sounded like they still had some grit left. A quick check over his shoulder showed Buck that the trainers were occupied elsewhere. He decided to take a chance.

"Don't worry about that. I have it all figured out. And, believe me, it's the only way you can get out of the school." He paused to check on their overseers. "If you promise to take me along, I'll show you how."

Philadelphia gave him a gimlet eye. "Got it all figured out, huh?"

"Yep." A smug smile brightened by sudden relief bloomed on the face of the teamster. "I'll tell you all about it at the baths after tomorrow's training session."

"Mighty decent of you, Buck," Preacher said agreeably. "We'll be obliged for the help. An', sure, you can go along."

"That's a relief. I can't stand it in here much longer."

Preacher nodded and smiled back. "None of us can, son. Not a one."

* * *

Due to his lifestyle, Arthur proved to be a magnificent standout at gladiator training. In early afternoon the next day, a bemused Justinius Bulbus stood in his private box watching the ripple of muscles in the arms and shoulders of the big mountain man. He could not believe his good fortune. Bulbus had his doubts that the legendary barbarian, Preacher, who so preoccupied the thoughts of Marcus Quintus, could be much better.

Whatever the case, the master of games intended to match this one against Preacher when, or if, the famous denizen of the mountains was captured. Bulbus' shaggy eyebrows rose as he watched the big one batter down another of his trained gladiators. He raised an arm to halt the man scheduled to next face the powerful barbarian.

"Crassis, you take him," he instructed one of the trainers.

With a big grin born of overconfidence, the heavily muscled Crassis came forward; his small shield, strapped to his forearm, was held up to protect his chest; his blunt sword was poised. Bounding like a panther, Preacher surged out to meet him. He struck the wooden shield with such force, it split down the middle and broke the forearm behind it.

An expression of surprise flashed on the face of Crassis, but was quickly replaced by a grimace of pain. Preacher swung again and caught Crassis against the side of his head with the flat of the blade. Rubber-legged, Crassis stumbled away to drape himself over the lattice of iron strips that formed the training ring. A ragged cheer went up from among the captive would-be gladiators. Preacher looked around for another opponent.

Bulbus quickly provided one. A bigger trainer, one who taught the net and trident, came forward. "Julian, bag him with your net and teach this upstart a lesson," Marcus Quintus called from the cushioned chair upon which he sat, beside his wife, Titiana Pulcra.

They had arrived unannounced and put the school into a

tizzy, not the least Bulbus, who wanted always to put on the best of shows for his benefactor and patron. He had hastily devised this test of strength for the enormously powerful mountain man. It now seemed to have turned out ill-advised. Even his trainers could not best the agile, resilient man. Bulbus cut his eyes anxiously from husband to wife.

At least Pulcra appeared to be enjoying the exhibition. She squirmed in her seat with each excellent blow by the mountain man. Now, while Bulbus covertly studied her, she crossed her legs and began to swing one nicely turned ankle. A sure sign a woman had a naughty itch to soothe, Bulbus thought lasciviously.

"I'll have you down to size in no time," Julian taunted. "Then I'll prick your hide to give you a good lesson."

Julian feinted to the right, dodged back to the left, spun a full circle on his heel to gain momentum, then whipped out his weighted net. Preacher ducked, picked up the edge of the fan-shaped snare and did a wrist roll that collapsed it into a long, folded filament. This he quickly climbed, mock sword in his teeth. When he reached the forearm of Julian, he let go with one hand and dosed his fist around the hilt.

A swift swat to the temple and Julian went down, a stone dropped into a fathomless pool. And with hardly more than a ripple. Preacher came to his moccasined feet and turned toward the box. A steady flow of sweat blurred his vision and stung his eyes. It kept him from clearly seeing the occupants, though he rightly guessed one to be Bulbus and another Quintus.

Exasperated, Bulbus clapped his palms together. "I'll have an end to this at once! Two of you, have a go at him at the same time."

A pair from the training staff came forth. One wore a *caestus,* its usually sharp bronze talons blunted with India gum. The other bore a curved Persian sword. Preacher greeted them with a nasty grin.

Above him, Pulcra veritably writhed in her chair, her leg swinging ever faster, small beads of perspiration breaking out on her upper lip. Fascinated by this enthralling demonstration by the mountain barbarian, Marcus had eyes only for what went on in the arena.

Preacher went for the swordsman first, after a glance at the blurred figures in the box. He came in low, leading with his sword. The tactic thoroughly distracted his opponent, who raised his weapon to parry the blade with enough force to knock it from Preacher's hand and do a quick reverse that would have, had his own been sharp, disemboweled the hapless antagonist who so insulted their abilities. Only it did not work that way.

At the last second, Preacher let the tip of his sword drop, so that the edge of the other one slipped across the flat without making contact. Startled, the trainer stumbled off balance while Preacher drove straight in. He rammed the point of his weapon into the helpless man's gut. It drove the air from his lungs in a gush.

Preacher wasted no time on finishing him, and then spun to confront his second threat. The armored fist lashed out at him and forced the mountain man to duck. Even with the sticky gum on the four triangular blades, they could inflict a terrible injury. Preacher avoided the *caestus* and hacked at the trainer's belly. Far quicker than the man with the sword, the trainer dodged the blow and tried to backhand Preacher in the head.

In a flash, Preacher went down at his knees and extended one leg. With a powerful push-off from one hand, he spun on his heel and swept the feet from under his opponent. A startled yelp came from twisted lips as the burly brawler left the ground and painfully landed on his rear. Preacher jumped to his moccasin soles and towered over the dazed man. He reversed his hold on the practice sword and rapped the trainer soundly at the base of his skull.

Preacher stepped back and let him fall. Then he placed one foot on the unconscious man's chest. Slowly he raised his eyes to the box.

"Blast and damn! Enough. You are through for the day, Arthur," Bulbus bellowed angrily. "You have won more than you have lost, so you get early baths, along with the other winners. Now, get out of here."

Beside him, Titiana Pulcra reached over and touched her husband's arm. "I'm going to leave now. The sun is too hot, and glaring. It has given me a headache."

"Very well, my dear. There is snow-chilled wine awaiting us at home."

She smiled sweetly. "I know I'll enjoy it."

Someone else had watched Preacher's performance—albeit with far less cupidity than Titiana Pulcra. Sister Amelia Witherspoon saved her feelings of desire for an image of Preacher as deliverer. When they had arrived in this horrid New Rome, they had been condemned to die in the arena, thrown to the lions.

Now, Sister Amelia was quite familiar with the heroic stories of Christian martyrdom in the days of the mad Nero. Yet, deep in her heart, she knew that she was not ready to be fed upon by beasts for the sake of her faith if it could be reasonably avoided. She saw no conflict between her retreat from the martyr's role and the depth of her belief. Amelia had a healthy respect for life. And she wanted to escape from this horrid place like all get-out.

From the first time she saw this magnificent specimen of male prowess, Amelia just *knew* he was the answer to her prayers. Arthur would save them. Like her captors, Sister Amelia did not know that this brave, strong man was the legendary Preacher. She knew him only by the name those hated Romans called him. Now she felt all trembly at the sight of how swiftly and surely he had handled those men. How could she make her plight, and that of her brothers and sisters of the Mobile Church in the Wildwood, known to him? She hurried off to make her thoughts known to Sister Charity and to seek her advice.

Thick steam rose from the surface of the large pool in the *calderium* room of the *thermae publicus* of New Rome. Preacher gratefully sank his bruised hide and aching muscles into the hot depths. During his six days in the gladiator school, while he learned the ways of the strange new weapons, he had taken his share of punishment. He would ache for a while yet, he felt certain.

Taking a bath in the raw, in the presence of other men, had never bothered Preacher. He vaguely recalled weekly Saturday excursions from his early homelife in a single, large, wooden tub, and older brothers squirming around in it together with him. The first time he discovered that women, and children of both sexes, readily joined the men of New Rome in their baths, he had been quite disconcerted. Now he handled it with greater ease. He took care, though, to look the other way as best he could. He also made an effort to banish the blood-racing thoughts certain of the ladies engendered in his mind. All of which left him unprepared when a loud splash announced the presence of a shapely young woman who made a shallow dive into the hot pool.

She swam around him in circles, as graceful and as wriggly as an eel. At last, she let her legs descend and stood before him, the water up to her shoulders. Her long, blond hair hung wetly down her back. She smiled and touched a small, slender finger to his chest.

"You're that exciting new gladiator at the school of Bulbus," she stated coyly in English.

Tension added bluntness to Preacher's words. "Not by any choice of my own."

Teasingly, she moved her hand to his shoulder and draped it across the top. "You should be grateful. If you fight well, win a lot of battles, you could gain your freedom. You could even receive the *rudis*."

"What's that?"

She puckered her mouth. "You really don't know. It's the wooden sword that is the symbol of your retirement from the arena. A free man, a citizen, and one who no longer has to fight. It's something to work for."

A sudden suspicion bloomed in Preacher's mind. "Are you allowed to talk to slaves?"

"I'm allowed to speak to anyone I choose. I'm Pricilia," she responded with no small heat. "Let's scrub down. I'll scrape you and you can scrape me. Then we can move on to the *tepidium*."

Preacher found himself less reluctant than he had been when she had first appeared. After all, it had been a long time since any woman, especially one so young and attractive as this one, had shown interest in the rugged mountain man. It might be fun, he decided, shedding another inhibition, to partake. After all, she wouldn't bite. He screwed up a smile.

"If that's what you want, it's fine as frogs' hair with me."

"How quaint," she said through a titter.

After a thorough cleansing, the pair swam across the wide pool and climbed out. In the next room, the *tepidium*, they entered the luke-warm water eagerly. It made their skin tingle. Preacher had grown painfully aware of their nakedness while scraping her silken skin with a *stigilis*, the curved, bronze, knifelike implement used in the manner of a washcloth.

Now they frolicked like youngsters. Exactly like . . . Terry and Vickie, he thought suddenly. Soon the bright pinkness left their skin, and the water began to feel less refreshing. Pricilia tapped Preacher on the chest, her head canted to one side atop her long, graceful neck.

"Race you to the *frigidium*."

"You're on!" said Preacher through a shout of laughter.

Now, that would be more like it, Preacher thought. Cold water being something he was most familiar with, he expected that a dip in it would calm the odd stirrings that teased his body. He crossed the pool with powerful strokes. Out and onto the warm tile floor. Through the curtained doorway.

Preacher beat her by half a length to plunge into the icy water that flowed directly into the pool from the stream outside. They splashed and swam for several minutes, until goose bumps appeared on Pricilia's shoulders and arms. She edged to the shallow end and drew herself out of the water to her waist on the marble-tiled steps. She threw her arms wide in a gesture of invitation.

"Come warm me, Arthur. I'm frozen."

After all his efforts to resist, Preacher found himself beguiled into dumb obedience. He crossed the frigid water in five long strokes and entered her embrace. After he had twined his strong arms around her, she drew his lips to hers.

In no time, they caused the icy liquid of the *frigidium* to reach a near-boil with the energy of their amorous romp.

12

Fully sated, Preacher lay on a bench, covered by a towel, when Pricilia made her departure. Entering as she left, Buck Sears and Philadelphia Braddock got a good look at her. One glance at their companion and they knew what must have gone on.

"You loon-witted he-goat!" Buck Sears blurted in shocked surprise. "You tryin' to get yourself killed before we can escape?"

Preacher sat upright, the sappy expression wiped from his face. "No? Why? What did I do that could cause that?"

Flabbergasted by Preacher's response, Buck worked his mouth for several moments before he could get any sound to come. "Don't you know who that was?"

Preacher blinked, suddenly suspicious of his recent amour. "Not for sure. She said her name was Pricilia. She was quite . . . friendly."

"I'll just bet she was. That happens to be Titiana Pulcra, the wife of Marcus Quintus Americus." He struck his forehead with the palm of one hand. "I wondered why those guards were not letting anyone enter the baths. If the Praetorian guard learns that we got by their watch at the door and saw—anything at all, they'll kill us along with you."

Preacher could not believe what he heard. Fooling around with another man's wife was definitely not a part of his code. Anger blended with self-disgust as he questioned Buck further. "Are you sure? D'you mean she's the dictator's woman—his wife?"

"I am only too sorry to say that I am sure," Buck lamented.

"Dang-bust it, I've been tricked. She done lied to me." His face turned dark red. "Me dossin' another man's wife. I'll never live it down. Though I don't reckon I should waste time tryin' to explain it to him. Only one thing for it now. We gotta go ahead with our plan to escape. Suppose you tell us how you got in mind for us to do that, Buck?"

Buck shrugged, then produced a smug smile. "It's plain as could be. In fact, it's right under your noses."

"What'er you gettin' at?" Philadelphia growled. He, too, felt his friend's chagrin.

"We all agreed we could not escape from the school. So that leaves having to be outside the school to make a break. And the only time we are outside is to get to the coliseum to fight or here to the baths."

"They told us we go to the arena by tunnel."

"That's right, Preacher, they said that," Philadelphia agreed.

"Then it has to be here. What about the guards?"

Buck gave a slow answer, his expression one of awe and bemusement. "You . . . are . . . *the* Preacher?"

"That I am, Buck. But there's no time to talk about that. How do we get out? What about the guards?"

Buck produced a sunny smile. "They are a sufficiently lazy lot. They're convinced there is only one way in and out of this place. I found out better, before I was sold to be a gladiator for hittin' my so-called master."

Preacher exploded with curiosity. "Go on—go on, tell us."

"I worked here at the baths. Part of my job was to clean out anything that got caught in the water system. The water comes in big tunnellike things. There is a way to get to them from behind a wall of the cold room. All we have to do is get to there, then walk and swim our way to freedom. Because, all the water that comes in has to go out."

"That shines. I like it. Don't stand there, show us the way."

"You mean right now, today?" Buck seemed uneasy.

"Do you want to wait around until that Marcus feller finds out I rode his filly?"

Buck grimaced at that graphic depiction. "All right. Come with me."

Preacher stopped him with a hand on one arm. "One thing, though. I don't figger to leave without my brace of Walker Colts."

Buck dismissed him. "We'll deal with that when the time comes. First thing is to get away from here and out of the far end of the entrance tunnel."

Preacher squared his shoulders and reached for his clothes. "I'm game. Let's go."

At first progress came easily. Ledges had been cut into the tunnel walls, a good two feet above the water that flowed with regularity into the *frigidium* pool, and beyond into those of the heated tanks. After some thirty paces, Preacher estimated that they had reached a place somewhere out near the middle of the forum. Only the single long, covered opening presented itself to them.

Preacher, Philadelphia, and Buck followed it beyond what must have been the southern edge of the forum. The walls grew wet and slick. Thick hanks of roots hung down above their heads. From his spyglass reconnoiter, Preacher recalled a garden, with bushes and hedges trimmed into the shapes of animals. That had to be what they passed under now.

Their pathway became narrower and closer to the water. The latter swirled by in oily blackness, its surface alone illuminated by the torch in Buck's hand. He had taken the lead, naturally enough, since it had been he who discovered this way out of Nova Roma. Preacher came next in line, with Philadelphia bringing up the rear. Little light reached the big-eared mountain man, and he stumbled occasionally, with a muffled curse for each time.

Philadelphia had about run out of cuss words, when an even worse situation came to them. Buck halted his companions and gestured ahead with the torch. "We walk in the water from here. At about what I guesstimate to be a hunnard yards from the inlet, we have to swim for it."

"So nice, this route of yours," Preacher told him acidly.

Buck removed his slave's tunic and wrapped it atop his head, then stepped off into chest-deep water as he spoke. "Be glad there is any trail out of here, Preacher. These New Romans are damned thorough in everything they do."

One by one they followed him. Chill water swirled around them. Buck reasoned aloud that once out, so long as they moved through the city with an air of going about their usual business, their slave costumes would not be a danger to them. They could even get to within a hundred paces outside the walls.

"Then we cut and run," he added grimly.

Preacher eyed him sternly. "Now, that's why I want my Colt re-volvers an' Cougar. I can run a damn sight faster on a horse."

Buck lectured him in how to accomplish that. "There are storerooms in the house of the master of games for all that sort of captured things. Also a stable. Since it is built into the outside wall of the school, on the Via Martius, we should have no trouble getting there. It's the getting away that bothers me."

Preacher gave him a grunt and a knowing nod. "You let me an' my Walker Colts handle that."

Shaking his head in wonder, Buck spoke with awe. "You actually have a pair of those Texas guns?"

"Sure enough. An' a dang good Hawken. I left my fancy Frenchie rifle at Trout Creek Pass." He nodded to Braddock. "Philadelphia's got him four of the nicest two-shooter pistols a feller could ever want. Sixty caliber they be. Ain't no spear-chucker can stand up again' our firepower for long."

"And I'll have my pick of what's in there, too," Buck added with a note of anticipation.

He led off once again and soon discovered that this late into summer, the water level had fallen enough that they did not have to swim at any point along the tunnel. Soon, a soft, gray glow emerged in the distance, around a bend. When Buck reached the turn, he paused a moment.

"Dang, I was afraid that might be," he spat.

"What's that?" Philadelphia asked.

"I worked the tunnels. All we ever dragged out was small bits of wood, a dead rat or two, some other animals caught in the water. Stood to reason they had a way of keeping bigger things out of the water course. See up ahead? There are bars across the opening to the river itself."

"Then we're stuck here?" Philadelphia demanded.

"Not necessarily," Preacher advised. "First let's get a look at them bars."

To Preacher's delight, they found them old, rusted and neglected. The current was stronger here and threatened to sweep them off their feet. Preacher gauged the weakest-appearing ones and took hold. He dug his feet into the sandy silt on the floor of the tunnel and heaved with all his might.

A bit of rust flaked off, nothing more. "You two, get in

place to the sides. Each take a-holt of one of these and pull when I do," he instructed.

This time a faint groan could be heard above the rush of the water. The muscles in Preacher's bare shoulders bunched as he exerted even greater effort. Philadelphia braced himself and heaved again. Opposite him, Buck planted his feet against a smooth rock and strained against the resistance of the worn iron bars.

At first, nothing happened. Then a mighty shriek came from the grommets into which the rods had been fitted. Small chunks of stone and mortar rained down on the heads of the escapees, and the first bar popped free. Philadelphia flopped backward in the water.

"Consarn it," he yelped.

Preacher eased it into the hands of his friend and turned to put his full force on the iron rod in Buck's grasp. Together, they tore it loose with seeming ease. A gathering of driftwood floated through the opening in a lazy spin. Preacher studied the situation.

"Another one."

Facetiously, Philadelphia added, "Make it two more an' we can drive a wagon through there."

"All right," Preacher agreed readily. "Two it is. Your side seems weaker. We'll take those next in line."

"Awh, Preacher, one'll do," Philadelphia retracted his attempt at sarcasm.

Fate turned a jaundiced eye on the fleeing men. The next barrier held stubbornly in place, refusing to pop out of its header or footing. Buck and Philadelphia lined up on one side, Preacher on the other. He anchored himself on the neighboring bar and surged with his legs. In the back of his mind—as in those of the others—he held the thought that the alarm could be given, at any moment, of their being missing.

It added the necessary extra energy. With a grinding,

cracking sound, the upright came free. They let it fall where it would. Quickly they waded through and up on the sloping bank of the river. Panting, Philadelphia wiped himself partly dry and put on his tunic. Preacher and Buck followed suit.

"I wish I had a wax tablet," Buck announced. At the look of curiosity from Preacher, he explained. "Anyone with a tablet of some kind is accepted as being at something official, and he's ignored. At least, that's the way I've seen it around here, and before in big cities, like St. Louie."

Preacher grinned and clapped him on one shoulder. "By jing, if you ain't got the right of it, Buck. Maybe we can—ah—borrow one somewhere on the way. Now, show us the way back to the school and that storehouse you talked about."

Buck cut directly across the burgeoning city of New Rome. He walked with the stride and head-up posture of an important slave. Preacher and Philadelphia followed suit. Few cast them a glance. At a market stall, Preacher paused. While Philadelphia distracted the owner with talk about onions and turnips, Preacher filched a wax tablet from a ledge inside the display of vegetables. They quickly caught up with Buck, and Preacher handed it to him.

"There you go," Preacher told him jokingly. "Now you can be as important as you've a mind to."

Amazement glowed on Buck's face. "Where'd this . . . ?"

"No, don't ask."

"Thank you, Preacher, but stay close from now on."

On the far side of the forum, well away from the Via Iulius, the street took on a twisty course around the base of the Hill of Mars. Buck slowed and gestured the others close for a quick word.

"If the alarm has been given, we'd best try to make for the outside."

"And if it hasn't?" Preacher prompted.

"Then we get what we need and head for the high country."

Shut away in her private wing of the nearly completed palace, Titiana Pulcra lay sprawled on her downy bed. Her heart still fluttered from the intensity of her magnificent encounter with Arthur. Her body glowed. She hadn't felt *this* good in a long time. What advantage was the life of the rich and powerful if one's appetites could not be fully indulged at will? That thought brought her mind to the disturbing topic of her son's recent conduct.

She supposed all small boys took pleasure from tormenting insects and small animals. Her own brothers, in another life, another world, had often gleefully tormented cats. That violent aspect of the conduct of Quintus Faustus did not unsettle her, although being on the cusp of eleven seemed awfully old for such behavior. No, it was something else.

Since that time three weeks past, she had paid careful attention to his conduct at the games. Reflection on the hour just past made all too vivid images of how he had responded to the nearly naked bodies and violent deaths of those who lost on the sand. In her memory, his gasps and quiet moans had sounded utterly too much like her own strident ones in the strong arms of Arthur. She stifled a thrill of horror. Surely Faustus could not be so—so *twisted*. She forced a change of subject.

Would she enjoy Arthur's presence soon again? Could she possibly risk it? Her husband was entirely too dense to ever suspect her. This wasn't the first time that a handsome gladiator slave had aroused her beyond caution. Pulcra was practical-minded enough to realize it would not be the last. Silently she offered a petition to the gods that Arthur prove a really good gladiator and last a long, long time. An anxious, if servile, scratching at the doorpost diverted her.

"What is it?" she demanded.

A clearly agitated slave entered, his forehead and upper lip bedewed with oily fear sweat. He advanced awkwardly. "A message for your husband, my lady."

"He is occupied elsewhere."

"May I ask where?"

"You may not. He is not to be disturbed." At least not until she had bathed. "You may give it to me."

"It's a matter of state, my lady."

Temper, mingled with sudden guilt, flared. "Dammit, must you be so obstinate? Give me the message."

Trembling now in fear of the arena, the slave stutteringly complied. "Three of the slave gladiators are missing, my lady."

Alarm stabbed at Pulcra. "Really? Their names?"

"Philadelphias, Baccus, and the champion of the day, Arturus."

Oh, God, Pulcra thought in pain. *I am alone. Utterly alone.* Duty demanded she rally herself. She girded her frazzled nerves. "Have the games master organize a search. I assume he has already conducted a roll call?"

"Yes, m'lady."

"Good. He's not the lack-wit I suspected him of being. Tell Bulbus to have the city searched first, top to bottom. Then the surrounding fields. They are not to be allowed to get away. More lives than theirs depend upon it."

She cast a quick glance into a mirror, evaluated her posture while reclining on her bed. Her pride swelled as she saw the steel she had in her when she needed it.

13

Ahead lay the entrance to the home of Justinius Bulbus. Two professional gladiators stood outside in light armor, with a pilum at the ready. Behind them, along the Via Iulius, Preacher, Philadelphia, and Buck heard the sounds of a search being organized. That told them they had been found out. They had to move fast. Preacher came up with a rudimentary plan.

"Wait here. I'll go up and get the attention of those two."

"How do you figger to do that?" Philadelphia inquired.

"By telling them what they expect to hear." With that he set off.

Preacher approached the two sentries with a blank, slave expression plastered on his face. "I have a message for your master," he announced.

"He is out."

"Where is he?"

"In the city. You need know nothing more."

"Yes, I do. Look, I have it right here. Do either of you read?" Preacher bent low, groping in a fold of his tunic.

Automatically the two guards leaned with him. When Preacher had them where he wanted them, he balled both fists and slammed them hard at that sensitive point under the jaw. Both men went down in a clash and clatter of bronze. Philadelphia and Buck came on the run.

"Quick, put on their gear and take their places."

Preacher went in like a wraith. He slid silently past the steward's office and followed Buck's directions down a long hall to a tall, thick, double door. An iron ring served as an opener. Preacher yanked on it, and it swung on well-oiled hinges. He went through and pulled the door to behind him. He found himself in a roofless courtyard. From one side he heard stable noises, and his nose identified it at the same time. Hugging the slim concealment afforded by the balcony overhang, he skirted the wall that enclosed the yard from the house. A two-piece door yielded easily.

Inside, he located Cougar and Philadelphia's mount, and the pack animal. He picked one for Buck, saddled all, and led them from the stalls. Outside, he took the animals at an angle across a tiled area where a fountain splashed musically. He ground reined them while he opened the portal that should lead to a treasure trove of belongings and weapons.

Buck's description proved to be right on the money. Preacher quickly found his .44 Walker Colts and Hawken rifle. Philadelphia's weapons came next. Dressed in buckskins again, Preacher fastened his wide, leather belt around his trim waist. He stuffed his knife and war hawk behind it, adjusted their position and added two .60 caliber pistols, then covered it all with his slave tunic.

Padding softly along the line of firearms, he selected a serviceable rifle and four pistols for Buck. Then he set about loading all. He doubled up on powder horns, boxes of percussion caps and conical bullets. He added sacks of parched corn, a big bag of jerky, another of coffee beans, flour, and a final of cornmeal. Salt and sugar concluded his shopping list.

Outside again, he packed away all his booty and started for what had to be the gateway that led outside. Its latch gave with a mild squeak; then the hinges squealed with noticeable protest. Preacher winced. At once, a wizened little clerk appeared through the doorway to the steward's office, a scroll clutched in one hand. His eyes widened and showed a lot of white when he saw the man in slave's clothing with four horses.

"What are you doing here?" he demanded in Latin. Preacher looked blank, and the clerk gestured toward the horses, changing to English. "What are you doing here with those animals?"

"Oh, I come to get them for the—ah—master of games," Preacher bent the truth slightly.

Emboldened by his freeman status and accustomed to having slaves cringe before him, the bean counter took two steps forward. "Not with all those weapons. You're—you're trying to escape, that's what you are doing."

Preacher gave him an expression of genuine regret. "Now you had to go and say too much for your own good, didn't you?"

Lightning fast, Preacher closed the remaining distance between them. His arm shot out, and he grabbed the surprised clerk by the throat. He throttled the frail little man into unconsciousness, then turned to leave.

"Not so fast," came a more authoritative voice behind the broad back of Preacher.

Preacher turned to find a man in the by-now familiar uniform of a centurion. He had his sword half drawn and advanced with a menacing tread. Preacher reached under his tunic and drew his Green River knife, with a blade almost as large as that of the *gladius* in the hand of the centurion.

"Well, shucks," Preacher said through gritted teeth.

No doubt, the Roman soldier had been well trained. He completed his draw and held the leaf-bladed short sword competently as he brushed past the sparkling fountain in the middle of the courtyard. His only weakness came from the fact he had rarely fought against another armed man, particularly one so well versed in the various means of killing his fellow creature.

With a soft, grunted challenge, the centurion launched his attack. Preacher parried the thrust easily enough and slid the keen edge of his Green River along the muscular forearm of the soldier. It laid open the back of his hand and the meaty portion at the elbow. The young officer cursed and jumped back. Preacher just jumped back. They squared off to face one another.

"You still have time to look the other way, Sonny," Preacher suggested.

"It's my duty to protect the home of my employer," he rejected Preacher's offer.

A little job on the side, eh? Preacher thought. They circled while Preacher evaluated what he knew of this man so far. At last he worked out something. "You cain't have been borned here, your English is too good. When were you captured?"

Strange emotions surged across the broad face of the centurion. "About—about six years ago. At least I think so. What is it to you?"

Preacher favored him with a comradely smile. "Then you ain't one of them Roman lunatics. Think of your past, man. Think of getting back there?"

Loyalties warred on the face of the wanderer, who'd had his life turned upside down some six years ago. He had once had a wife and three children. Where were they now? Yet, he had won recognition and been rewarded by his captors, many of whom became his friends, or he now commanded. What was life supposed to be for him? Maybe he should ask *which* life? Past and present swirled in his mind, merged, and forged out his decision. With a shout, he launched himself at Preacher.

"Wrong choice, friend," Preacher told him sadly.

Nimbly, Preacher stepped outside the arc of the *gladius* in the centurion's hand. The tip of his own knife found the gap between the breast and the back plates of the officer's cuirass; the wide, sharp-edged metal quickly followed. Preacher wrenched sideways, twisted the blade, and freed it. Slack-legged, his opponent gasped out his final sigh and fell dead. Off to his left, Preacher heard the hurried scurry of sandaled feet. More trouble from that direction.

He turned to see a quickly retreating back. Time to hurry. He cleaned his knife and replaced it, then went to the horses. Swiftly he led them out of the compound and toward the front door to the residence of Bulbus. His two friends saw him coming and instantly abandoned their pretense of being guards. Philadelphia Braddock swung into his saddle with practiced ease. Grinning, he patted the stock of his favorite rifle.

"I see you found old Betsy. Now, we'd best take our leave of this place."

Jokingly, Preacher made himself appear in a casual mood. "What's your hurry, Philadelphia?"

Braddock frowned. "One of the servants of that Bublus feller come squawlin' out the door, didn't look left nor right, just runned off down the street like ol' Nick hisself was after him. I reckoned you had a part in that, an' also that our escape is no longer a secret."

Laughing, Preacher patted Cougar on the neck. "Right you are. We'd best go while we still have a chance."

Buck nodded and started them along the *Via Iulius*.

It was utterly reprehensible, Deacon Phineas Abercrombie thought to himself for what must have been the hundredth time. It was so degrading, so demoralizing, to be herded together like this in a single, large cell. Not a hope of a moment's privacy. Men and women, whole families thrust cheek and jowl against one another. And that foul-smelling trench at the narrow end of the holding pen as their only place to relieve themselves. With not a curtain or blanket to conceal the most private of personal acts.

Voiding themselves right out in the open, like animals! Unspeakable. He could find no other word for it. He had complained at every opportunity. Only to be laughed at and told to turn his back if he did not wish to observe. It smelled so foul in here, so fetid, and dank. It had come to the point where he could no longer eat. Even if he tried, it came back up. Would they ever see the light of day again, or the light of freedom?

Somehow he doubted they would experience either. Sighing, he turned to hear the appeal of young Mrs. Yardley. "Deacon, my boy, Johnny, he's got himself a case of the runs. Real bad. Says his belly aches somethin' fierce, and it is sore to the touch."

Deacon Abercrombie followed the woman to where a small boy of eight lay on filthy straw near the center of the herd of missionaries. The child whimpered when Abercrombie knelt beside him and lifted up his tattered shirt. At least no unusual swelling, the untrained man diagnosed. That could bode even worse if cholera got loose among them. Well, he would have to tell the Yardley woman something.

"I'm afraid you are right, Sister Yardley. See that he gets all the fluids you can find for him. Keep him covered, and all we can do beyond that is pray."

For a moment, anger flared hot and red in the eyes of Mrs. Yardley. "We've *been* praying, Deacon. All of us, day and night. As yet, it appears the Lord has not seen fit to hear us."

Abercrombie's eyes widened. He raised an admonitory, pudgy hand. "Careful, Sister, lest you stray into blasphemy. I will tell the others, and we will join in group prayer for your boy."

Chastened, Mrs. Yardley lowered her chin and spoke meekly. "Thank you, Deacon. Thank everyone for me. I'll try to find Johnny some water."

Pursuit began at the edge of the Forum of Augustus. Shouts came from the *vigilii* posted there, and they set off on foot after the mounted fugitives, leather straps slapping their scarlet kilts. People along the way, most in the grubby garb of "common citizens," pointed accusing fingers to direct the watchmen.

At least one thing served as an advantage to the fleeing men. All of those forced to accept life in New Rome had long ago learned that the clatter of horses' hooves in the city streets signaled to get out of the way. As in its historical counterpart, Marcus Quintus had found it necessary to erect vertical stone plinths across the avenues to slow the speed of young rakes in their chariots. That forced the horsemen to zig and zag, yet kept them well ahead of the policemen. Slowly, they even gained some. Then the main body of searchers joined the chase.

They came at right angles to the *vigilii*, effectively forcing Preacher and his companions to swerve onto another street that did not lead directly to a gate that gave access to the outside. Several of the newcomers rode horseback, and they pushed on ahead of the yelling men behind them. The gap began to narrow. That's when Preacher noted some of the details of the construction that went on all around.

A block ahead, a tall engineer's scaffold had been erected. It consisted of a beam that pivoted from a central point. Equipped with a counterweight, it allowed large blocks of stone to be lifted by ropes and lowered into place by means of pulleys. The mechanism was operated by a horizontal capstan, manned by sweating slaves. At present, Preacher noted, a huge, rectangular slab of marble hung suspended over the street. More slaves pulled frantically on ropes to swing the walking beam. Without hesitation, Preacher rode in among those around the capstan, their pursuers almost at the heels of his horse. Their mounts filled the center of the street.

Preacher pulled his war hawk from his belt and gave it a mighty swing. It severed the thick cable to the capstan with a single blow. The braided hemp parted with a musical twang. The pulleys responded instantly. With a loud shriek, they payed out the loose rope and allowed the three-ton marble slab to descend in a rush on top of the mounted searchers.

Preacher could not resist a backward glance. The carnage was terrible. Only one horseman had escaped the bloody pudding that had been made of his companions. He sat slumped in his saddle, numbed by shock. Once more, the gap between fugitives and hunters widened. Preacher estimated another three blocks, once back on the Via Ostia, the main route to the gate and freedom.

He led the way around one corner, then a sharp turn to the right on the Via Sacra. With only a block remaining, Preacher discovered that the word had gotten to the soldiers. The legion cavalry had joined the search. They thundered forward to cut off Preacher and his friends along the Via Ostia. Ahead, the sentries labored to shut the heavy gates.

Preacher held back in the small plaza formed directly inside the gate to empty a cylinder load from his .44 Walker Colt. It slowed the cavalry considerably. Preacher exchanged his marvelous six-guns and watched as Philadelphia, then Buck, streamed through the narrowing gap in the gate. His turn now. He spurred Cougar and bent low over the animal's neck. They hit the opening at a full gallop. Preacher further slowed its progress by blasting one guard into eternity with a .44 ball.

Outside, the trio did not slacken their pace until they had

ridden beyond the last cultivated field. Gasping in excitement, Philadelphia slapped one thigh. "We got away. By jing, we done it."

Preacher looked beyond him at the nearly closed gates. "I'd not break my arm pattin' m'self on the back just yet. Them gates is gonna slow the cavalry, but they're comin' after us. You can be certain sure of that."

At the crest of the southern pass, Preacher called another halt. He and his companions looked back. Far back among the plowed fields they observed hurried movement along the roadway. Preacher took out his telescope and extended it. Peering through it, he made out the billowing scarlet cloak and dancing plume of a centurion. Behind him, the mounted troops of New Rome were strung out in a ragged formation that more resembled men fleeing for their lives than determined hunters. He nodded, satisfied at the lead they had, created by the confusion at the gate.

"They won't be catchin' up any time soon. Well, boys, what's your pleasure now?"

Philadelphia considered that a moment. "I say we hightail it to Trout Crick and gather up as many good ol' boys as we can. Then come back here and kick us some crazy Roman butt."

"Sounds good to me," Buck agreed. "But, I ain't a mountain man. Will they accept me goin' along on this?"

Preacher considered him with keen eyes. "If you kin hit what you shoot at, they'll welcome you like a long-lost brother. If you kin do that and not make noise goin' through the woods, they'll give you their sisters."

Buck turned him a straight face. "I know better than to walk on my heels. Spent some time with the Kiowa whilst I was freightin' on the Santa Fe. They taught me to walk on the edge of my foot, and I'm at home in moccasins."

Preacher and Philadelphia nodded solemnly. "You'll do.

Only first, I think we ought to confuse them fellers a little before we leave these parts, don't you?"

Broad grins answered him. They set off, making no effort to conceal their tracks.

The stratagem worked. For only a moment the legion cavalry reined in where the escapees had halted. Then they set off at a rapid trot. Totally lacking in scouting skills, they made no effort to look ahead or to the sides. They stared only a few yards in front of their horses' heads, eyes fixed on the sign of those they sought. It didn't work.

The Roman soldiers soon found themselves in a box canyon. Confused and disoriented, they milled about at the face of the high wall that denied them further progress. Centurion Drago cut his eyes from one to another of his men. He was up for *primus pilus*—first spear, or adjutant to the legate— and dared not fail in this mission. Tradition in the *Legio XIII Varras Triumphae* said that the *primus pilus* was always elevated to command of the legion upon the retirement or death of the legate. He wasn't about to throw that away.

"Find how they slipped out of here without our seeing the trail," he commanded.

Thirty minutes later, a young cavalryman trotted up and saluted. "We have found it, sir. They crossed over the stream and used the trees to screen them."

"Brilliant. A first-week recruit could figure that out. How many are they now?"

"Only two, sir."

On the heels of his remark came a solid, meaty smack, followed by a brief scream and the rolling crack of a rifle shot. Before Drago and his troops could recover, the centurion heard the rapid drum of departing hooves. Right then, Centurion Drago made an uncannily accurate observation to his men.

"Jupiter blast that man. First Citizen Americus may not know it, but I think he had this mountain man, Preacher, in his hands all the time."

Philadelphia looked up as Preacher ghosted in to the grove of aspen where he and Buck waited for the crafty mountain man. A broad grin spread when he saw the new layer of powder grime on Preacher's right hand. Preacher slid from the back of Cougar and dropped the reins. At once, the broad-chested stallion went to munching grass.

"There's one less of them."

"How far behind us are they?" asked the always practical Philadelphia.

"I'd reckon at least half an hour. Most likely more, their horses haven't had any rest, like ourn."

"The bad news is there is only one trail out of here, unless we want to spend our lead climbing one ridge after another. Well, back to the trail."

Preacher led the way. Two miles down the wilderness road they found another meander that circled a steep pinnacle and went beyond, with a side-shoot that ended atop it. They rested up there, eyes fixed on the winding trail through the Ferris Range, while they munched strips of jerky and crunched kernels of parched corn. By the fat turnip watch in a pocket of Preacher's vest, forty minutes went by before the greatly subdued cavalry rode into view. At once they put away their eats and reached for rifles.

Preacher honed in on the third from the last man in the column. Philadelphia took the second; and Buck, the rear soldier. They fired almost as one. Swiftly, Preacher and Philadelphia began to reload. Below them, the trio of legionnaires jerked in their saddles and fell sideways off their horses. Shouts of dismay echoed upward to the ears of the shooters. Buck finished reloading last. Once more they took aim.

Three shots rippled along the canyon walls. Cries of alarm raised again, and Drago halted the column. A terrible mistake. It allowed the intrepid mountain men to reload and take three more from the backs of their mounts. Then Preacher was up and leading the way to their horses. Ten down, and they still had a quarter-hour lead.

Preacher led the cavalry of Legio XIII into four more blinds and successfully ambushed them, carving great gaps in the ranks. They had only settled down in another spot to pick off more, when the thunder of hooves alerted them to a danger they had not anticipated.

Fully fifty mounted troops, most foot soldiers unaccustomed to horseback, lumbered awkwardly toward their hiding place. Drago rallied his cavalry and charged with determination. No matter how well they fought, regardless of how many they killed, Preacher knew at once that they were doomed.

The Roman troops swarmed over them, took dreadful losses from the rifles, pistols and revolvers of the mountain men. Several received nasty knife wounds, and two had their skulls split by Preacher's tomahawk. At last, though, they prevailed. After suitable punishment for their prowess, the soldiers trussed them up and slung them over their saddles. Preacher, Philadelphia and Buck found themselves on their way back to Nova Roma.

Marcus Quintus Americus looked up sternly from the written report of Justis Claudius Drago. His brows knit, while anger ran rampant across his features. His words were formed carefully.

"Our laws are clear on this. Not only have you murdered twenty-seven members of our Thirteenth Legion, but you have escaped. The penalty for escape is death in the arena. My only regret is that you will not have long to regret your deeds and fear your ultimate death. My son's birthday is three days from today. There will be games, of course. You three will be the central attraction."

14

Excitement sent an electrical charge through the missionaries of the Mobile Church in the Wildwood. During all of their lengthy captivity they had never heard of anything so hopeful. Blue eyes shining, her long, golden curls a-bounce under the fringe of her modest, white-trimmed, gray bonnet, Sister Amelia Witherspoon hastened to take the latest news to her friend, Sister Carrie Struthers.

"It's a sign from God," Sister Amelia declared confidently. "If someone can escape from this dreadful place, then someone else can as well."

"But you said yourself that they were men," Carrie complained, her freckled face agitated below a wreath of auburn curls. "What can we possibly do, mere women?"

Amelia looked at her friend, blinked and answered sharply. "What can we do? We can put our foot down, that's what. Demand that the *men* in this company make some effort to effect our escape."

"Well, I'm not so sure . . . ," demure Carrie began, long, coppery lashes lowered over dark brown eyes.

Fists on hips, Amelia responded forcefully. *"I am sure! The least they can do is try to get away from this insane community."*

Deacon Phineas Abercrombie bustled over, his considerable girth inflated with righteous indignation. "Here now, what is this all about?" Amelia quickly told him. It did not sit well at all. He peered disapprovingly at her down his long nose. At last he spoke his mind. "I am sure you will agree. If it is God's will that we become martyrs, then so be it. Who are we to question Him?"

Stubborn, Amelia continued to press her point. "What sort of martyrdom is it to be killed by lunatics who believe this wretched place is some rebirth of Ancient Rome?"

Abercrombie dismissed that reasoning. "That is for the Lord to decide, Sister. I am afraid I must forbid you to discuss this topic with any others of our flock. Besides, I hear that the men who escaped have been recaptured. It is really all so futile," he concluded with a bored sigh.

Not one to be easily intimidated, Amelia Witherspoon flounced off to speak with others of their small congregation. In open defiance of the deacon, she urged them to join in making some sort of plan to effect an escape. Watching her from a distance, the deacon grew angry at the impertinent young woman. He made a casual, angled course to the bars at the front of their communal cell. There he made a covert signal to one of the guards.

A few minutes later, with Sister Amelia still urging at least resistance if not actual escape, a centurion arrived outside the iron gate to their prison. "Which one is Deacon Abercrombie?" he demanded.

"I am he," the deacon volunteered.

With a curt gesture, the centurion sent two burly guards into the holding pen, and they roughly dragged Deacon Abercrombie out into the stone corridor. Without another word,

the centurion started off with his prisoner in the firm grips of
the pair of thugs.

Buck Sears looked across the dining table in the gladiator
quarters at his new friends. "We're going to be taken over to
the coliseum tomorrow. There are to be rehearsals for the
spectacles."

Preacher looked up, lines of concern etched in his forehead. "How do you rehearse being fed to the lions?"

"It's them Bible-thumpers, ain't it?" Philadelphia asked.
"You're worried about them."

"There's women and children among them," Preacher explained.

"Fools for comin' out here, I say. An' to'd you just a short
while ago."

Preacher sighed. "You're right, Philadelphia. On both
counts. It's only with them bein' youngins, it's all so—so un-
civilized bein' a cougar's light lunch."

"No matter. There ain't a thing we can do about it."

"Right again. Only keep your wits about you, and if an
opportunity comes to . . . well, just be ready, hear?"

Philadelphia pulled on one large ear lobe. "Oh, yeah. For
certain sure. I don't know what sort of weapon they might
give me, but I sure would like to wet it in a little Roman
blood."

Preacher forced a laugh he did not feel. "That's the spirit.
How about you, friend Buck?"

Buck shrugged. He had been giving that question considerable thought since their recapture. "I'd rather be dead than
forced to fight every time they have some sort of holiday."

Preacher rubbed dry, calloused palms together. "That's
settled then. We'll look to give them a show like they've
never seen before."

Philadelphia's sour expression belied his enthusiastic words. "Beats daylight outta sittin' around wonderin' which one o' them profess'nals is gonna do us in."

Bejeweled fingers aglitter, Marcus Quintus Americus caressed the gold wine cup he held, then set it aside as the centurion from the gladiator school entered with a portly, pompous-looking man with graying hair and the eyes of a prophet. The first citizen had dined sumptuously on roasted bison backribs, stuffed quail and an enormous fish. Recalling it made Quintus salivate. Then a flicker of annoyance shot across his face. Why could they never get the wine just right? It always tasted more like vinegar than a vintage selection. After a protracted three minutes, he raised his eyes and spoke.

"Yes, what is it?"

"He claims to have information for you, First Citizen."

Quintus studied the prisoner in silence, sipped from his wine goblet and motioned the captive forward. "Bring him forth, then."

Given a not-too-kindly shove, Deacon Abercrombie staggered forward. "I—I've come to you with a plot for an escape."

Quintus threw back his head and laughed loudly. "Did you now? Would it surprise you to learn that they were captured earlier today and returned to Nova Roma?"

Although quaking internally, Deacon Abercrombie stood his ground. "No. Not in the least. I am not referring to those three men. This has to do with some of my own flock. They are talking about overpowering some of your guards and making a break for it. A young woman, Sister Amelia Witherspoon, is behind it."

Quintus narrowed his eyes. "When is this to happen?"

"I . . . am not certain. Though I would imagine it would be when we are taken to the coliseum tomorrow."

Considering this, Quintus jabbed a ring-encrusted finger at Abercrombie. "And why is it that you have come to me?"

Abercrombie drew himself up, an otherworldly light illuminating his face. "I have reached the conclusion that it is our destiny to be martyred. Our Lord wishes to call us home."

Quintus despised these sanctimonious churchmen for their weakness. He could not keep the sarcasm out of his tone of voice. "How very convenient for your Lord that we have such efficient means to accomplish that. However, I am not clear as to why you slunk off to inform me of this. Hummm?"

For the first time, Abercrombie looked embarrassed. "I—I have come to the conclusion that while martyrdom might be a suitable end for many, and sacrifice for our Lord is always desirable, I—I simply feel that I have much more important work to accomplish during my time here. I have years of good works ahead of me. So, all—all I ask is that I be spared. My wife and I, that is."

Quintus feigned surprise. The jeweled rings on his fingers sparkled and sent off spears of brightness as he moved one hand to his chest in mock distress. "What is this? Do you mean to say you want special treatment?"

"Well . . . yes—yes, I suppose you could say that."

"Oh, you'll get special treatment, all right." Quintus produced a wolfish smile. "You will have the privilege of fighting your way to freedom. After all, the *rudis*—the—ah—wooden sword of retirement—is a cherished custom of the games. Think of it, my dear deacon. If you manage to fight and claw your way over the bloody, broken bodies of your fellow Christians, you will be a free man, a citizen of New Rome and able to do whatever you wish."

A low cry of anguish came from deep in Abercrombie's

chest. His knees sagged, and the men who held him tightened their grip. Quintus gestured to the centurion.

"Take him back. No, take him right now to the coliseum.
Put him in one of the small holding cells alone. It wouldn't
do for him to have pangs of remorse and confess all to his
followers." As the guards frog-marched a stricken Abercrombie out of the dining chamber, Quintus looked across
the room to his son, reclining on a dinner couch. "By the
gods, how I hate such craven villains. They haven't one drop
of the sap of manliness."

Those words stung Phineas Abercrombie, although what
followed utterly humiliated him. "Will he die in the arena,
Father?" young Faustus asked.

"Oh, assuredly. He'll be the last to be chewed by the
lions, because he will cower behind his people. And when he
dies, it will not be with a roar, but rather a whimper."

Word came by way of the slave grapevine. Preacher,
Philadelphia and Buck took the news with grim expressions.
Someone among the passel of Bible-thumpers had started
stirring them up with escape in mind. The time for this attempt would be the next morning.

"And confound it, there's two things wrong with this.
First off, what I hear is, it is a female critter who done the
stirrin' up *and* the plannin'. Whatever she come up with, you
can be sure it won't work. That's for starters. Now, what's it
you heard those guards sayin', Buck?"

Buck, the only one of them who spoke Latin, produced an
expression of contempt and disgust. "It appears as how one
among the gospel group tattled on them to this-here Marcus
Quintus."

"You mean to that ol' he-coon of this whole place?"
Preacher asked.

"The same. Thing is, what can we do about it? They're

due to be thrown to the lions at the games two days from to-morrow."

"Yes," Philadelphia agreed. "That looks like the end for them."

Preacher took over. "Simple. There's little we can do about whatever they have in mind for tomorrow. What we have to concentrate on is to defeat our opponents in the arena, force our way out of there and take these soul-savers along with us."

Philadelphia gave him a blank face. "Oh, you make it all sound so easy, Preacher."

Early the next morning, two small boys splashed and laughed together in the *tepidarium* of the palace private baths. Without their clothing, one could not tell that the blond, curly haired lad wore the purple-striped tunic of a patrician, while the black-haired, shoe-button-eyed kid was his body servant. Master and slave had grown up together and formed a deep bond. Young Quintus Faustus confided all his really juicy secrets to little Casca.

Loyal Casca kept his silence about these revelations. In fact, he often shared in the more entertaining of them. Today, their early morning bathing was energized by their awareness of the looming excitement of the birthday games to be held for Faustus on the last day of September. The birthday boy was beside himself. He jumped and surged in the water, splashed his whole arm, flopped like a seal off the slick tile of the edge, and dived between his only friend's legs.

Casca did the same. Then they swam the length of the lukewarm pool and climbed out with their arms around the shoulders of one another. Light danced in Casca's eyes. "Is it for sure, Faustus? Your father is going to let you be *impera-tor*? All by yourself?"

"Certainly. I will be eleven, you know," he added solemnly.

"Yes. And I will be in two months."

"You're coming to the games with me. I have just decided. You can hand me ices, feed me grapes; we'll sit under the awning and you will have a parasol to shade us both."

"It sounds wonderful."

Faustus put nail-bitten fingers on his servant's shoulder. "It's the least I can do, considering you can't attend the birthday feast as a guest."

Casca produced a brief pout. "Yes. I know. And I understand. I really do."

For a moment Faustus looked like he might cry. "You're a true friend, Casca. You're the best friend any boy could ever have."

"You're my best friend, too, Faustus." His eyes twinkled as he tapped a finger on his friend's wet knee. "Will you—will you sneak me a bowl of your birthday custard?"

"Of course. This time it is a new kind of custard Mother learned about. It is called ice cream."

From an archway of a side entrance, someone cleared his throat in a deeper tone. Marcus Quintus stepped into the damp room, wearing only a towel over one shoulder. "There you are, son. I hoped I would find you here. You may go, Casca."

"See you in the *frigidium*," Casca called over one shoulder to Faustus. After the boy had padded barefoot toward the cold bath, Quintus sat on a bench beside his son.

"How does it feel? It's only two days away now. Are you really ready for it?"

"Yes, sir. I'm so excited. I wish it was this afternoon."

"It will keep. I wanted to urge you to remain stalwart. When you are the honoree master of games, you must retain your poise. Avoid any excessive show of emotion. Listen to Bulbus in regard to giving death to any of the professionals. And, do not flinch at assigning death to those who deserve it. You must show the people that you have the fortitude. Remember one thing. Your performance at the games will show that you either do or do not deserve the title *Princeps Romanus.*"

Prince of Rome! How heady it sounded to Faustus. He got a faraway, glassy look in his eyes as he mentally reviewed past kills he had enjoyed in the arena. His nostrils flared and his breathing became harsh as he answered.

"Don't worry, Father. I *like* to see the blood flow."

Early the next morning, the guards roused the professional gladiators first, and they trooped through a wooden door to the tunnel that connected the school with the coliseum. They would have their breakfast there and spend the morning hours braiding up their hair and oiling their muscular bodies. This was done to prevent a handful of hair from being used against them, and to keep lesser fighters from holding on to them in a bear hug. Too much time and money had been spent on them to allow their defeat by an amateur.

Next, the lesser-trained gladiators were escorted by guards through the underground passage to identical, dank stone cells in the bowels of the large stadium. Preacher judged that an hour passed before the burly, well-armed warders came for him and his companions. As condemned men, they were kept separately from all other participants.

They had only reached the far end of the tunnel when the condemned missionaries got rousted out of their holding pen and directed into the tunnel. Angry shouts rose as Preacher, Philadelphia and Buck were roughly shoved into a cell. The sounds of a struggle came to their ears after the clang of the closing iron-slat door. It appeared the guards had been prepared for this resistance. The hollow, north wind whistle and the crack of whips followed immediately, along with the cries of pain from those who received the lash. Meaty sounds of cudgels on backs and shoulders told Preacher and his friends of the swift end of the brief resistance. So much for their big escape.

Preacher spoke quietly to his companions. "At least some of them Bible-thumpers have got some sand. Maybe we can make use of that when we get out there."

Philadelphia did not agree. "More likely, they got what little spunk they had whupped out of them. Them laddies wield a mean whip," he added, as he remembered the scourging they had received after their recapture.

"With or without them, we're goin' over those walls and out of this place," Preacher declared hotly. "When they come back from practicin' that thing they're supposed to do before the lions, I intend to talk to a few of 'em."

Preacher had his opportunity shortly before the noon hour. The captives were driven back inside the lower levels of the arena and given a chance to slake their thirst. All of the regular gladiators had been released from their cells to be equipped for the practice fights. Preacher had been decked out in the flanged, peaked helmet, net and trident of a *riatarius*. For a while he strutted around the common room, in imitation of the professionals, until the wary guards grew lax. Then he sidled over to the bars of the cage that held the missionaries.

Quickly he outlined his intention to make an escape and reviewed the plans with several of the younger men. He concluded with a logical suggestion. "The more of us that makes the try, the better chance we have of getting away."

A middle-aged Bible-thumper stepped close. "It sounds like you have given this considerable thought. Only, we cannot be a part of it. We're nonviolent. Surely, the government has learned of this dreadful place. They will put a stop to it."

Preacher studied the man like he would a strange insect that had just crawled out of his shirt sleeve. "No man ever got free by whinin' about it until the government gave him freedom as a handout. Government don't give people freedom, they *take it* from them."

"You don't mean that. Our government—"

"Ain't no different in that respect from any other. That's why I spent most of my life out here."

With a self-righteous sniff, the pilgrim announced, "Our trust is with the Lord."

Preacher cocked his head to one side, a twinkle in his eyes. "Might be you need to look a little further into that Bible you're so fond of quotin'. Seems it's writ in there somewhere that the Lord helps them what helps themselves."

Without another word, Preacher turned on one heel of his fighting sandals and walked away. From a short distance off, Sister Amelia Witherspoon looked after him with a longing that was not the least bit sexual. She had been wondering about the whereabouts of Deacon Abercrombie when he had begun to talk with the men. What he said made her completely forget the deacon. She hungered for a man of courage like this one. Someone who would lead these timid souls to freedom. Sounded to her like this could be the one.

15

Two days went by swiftly. Preacher took Buck and Philadelphia aside for a final discussion on their plan to escape
from the arena. His words were as grim as they were low.

"We cain't know when or how we'll do this. I figger we
hoss one another up the inner wall and make a run through
the onlookers. They won't be armed, and most of 'em will
plain panic when we swarm in among them with weapons
drippin' blood. That'll keep the guards away."

Overhead the coliseum was filled with noise as early
spectators filled the rows of stone benches. Concessionaires
could be heard hawking their wears. To Preacher it sounded
like something they would do back East. A Fourth of July
celebration or something.

"I think the best thing is to do it right off. Go after that
brat kid of Marcus Quintus and use him as a shield," Buck
opined.

Preacher slowly shook his head. "No, the guards will be
watchin' right close at first, when we're fresh and all. If we
can string it out until the gospel-spouters are brought in, we

can probably get a half dozen or so to come along. We've all been in enough tussles to know when's the best time. Use your judgment, but keep an eye on me."

The long, valveless trumpets sounded, announcing the entry of the day's master of games. The crowd roared. Another fanfare, and then the other musicians joined in. Metal creaked and grated as the portcullis raised enough to let out a party of clowns. Preacher watched them with divided attention.

They did somersaults and cartwheels, ran into one another, took pratfalls and rolled in the sand. One, with an animal bladder filled with water, pounded on his companions until the thin skin broke and soaked the victim. The crowd howled in merriment. When the last buffoon scampered back inside the dark interior of the coliseum, the attendants went out to smooth off the killing ground. That accomplished, the trainers came to line up the whole company of gladiators and condemned prisoners.

A moment later, the trumpets sounded again, clear and crisp. The gate rumbled upward, and the lead fighters in the Company of the Dead stepped out onto the sand.

Young Quintus Faustus Americus entered the *imperator's* box with the first fanfare. Dressed in a snowy toga, with a broad purple hem stripe, he wore a circlet of gilded laurel leaves, with gold-strapped sandals. Followed by his body servant, Casca, he went directly to the center seat of the front row and raised his right arm. In his hand he held an ivory staff with a gold eagle on the top. He turned from side to side, as he had been instructed, and waved to the cheering crowd.

Some stomped their feet, others cheered and whistled. Led by the paid clique, they chanted his name in a wavelike roar. Eyes sparkling in pleasure, he nevertheless maintained his composure while he seated himself and stared serenely across the sand at the giant portal, behind which the gladiators and condemned prisoners waited. Casca popped a grape between the lips of Faustus. His father and mother joined him and took seats at either side. Bulbus came next, followed by a dozen patrician boys who had been invited by Faustus. When the box had been filled, Faustus rose and elevated the wand. The trumpets roared again.

"The auguries are good! The gods are pleased. Let the games begin!" he called out in his squeaky boy's voice.

Casca handed Faustus a chilled cup of wine as the portcullis squealed open and out spilled the clowns. Their antics delighted the crowd. Their erratic tumbling absolutely captivated the birthday guests. Faustus laughed until the tears ran and he held his sides. Then he suddenly remembered the seriousness of his position today. He cast an uneasy glance at Casca, who winked at him; he then sobered and forced unwilling facial muscles into a placid expression. The *real* fun, he reminded himself, would come later.

When the clowns ended their performance, the trumpets blared again. The portcullis raised the full way, and the Company of the Dead marched forth. In the lead came the ranks of professionals, followed by those in training, and lastly the prisoners. A small smile of expectation flickered on the lips of Faustus. In perfect formation the participants in the games reached the base of the "emperors'" box. They raised their weapons in salute.

"Hail Caesar, we who are about to die salute thee!"

Faustus rose to speak the lines he had prepared. Leaning forward, he addressed them while Casca shaded him with a parasol. "Friends. Thank you for the spectacle you have prepared in honor of my birthday. I am sure that I will enjoy it.

Now it is time to begin. Parade yourselves for my other friends to see, then bring on the first pairs."

It having been spoken in Latin, Preacher did not recognize a word. "Lotta jibber-jabber, you ask me," he whispered to Philadelphia.

Drums and wind instruments struck up, and the gladiators turned smartly to make a circuit of the arena. Behind them came the "accommodators" to smooth the sand. Although the air was cool on this last day of September, Preacher had worked up a sweat from the closeness of the coliseum and the heat of the sun by the time they returned to the cool interior of the underground cells.

At once, the clarions summoned the first two fighting pairs. Four professionals stepped out onto the sand. They faced off, one-on-one, saluted one another and set to. A *riatarius* tested his skill against a gladiator dressed as a Samnite. The long, curved blade in the Samnite's hand danced a blue-white arabesque in the air. The trident man looped his net in a hypnotic pattern before the eyes of the swordsman. He prodded with his three-tined spear. Preacher and Philadelphia stood close to the iron lattice of the portcullis and watched intently.

Beyond the fighters, he saw Faustus lean forward raptly, his mouth sagging open, pink tongue flicking in and out. There was a grunt as the Samnite lunged with his sword. A moment later the crowd roared as the *riatarius* flicked out his net and snared his opponent's blade and right arm. The trident darted toward his exposed, bare belly.

Dancing on tiptoe, the Samnite turned to his right, away from the spear and free of the knotted lines of the net. A mighty shout came from the spectators. Lightning fast, the *riatarius* came after the retreating gladiator. The Samnite's sword slashed through the air and bit deeply into the wooden shaft of the spear.

"Gotta remember to keep from doin' that," Preacher said to himself.

"What's that?" Philadelphia asked.

"I was talkin' to myself. That feller almost got his spear chopped in half. Careless."

"There's a lot to learn for this kind of fighting," Philadelphia agreed.

On the sand, the net flared outward and fluttered down over the head and shoulders of the Samnite. At once, the *riatarius* ran around his helpless opponent and secured him in the snare. Then, with a powerful yank, he jerked the swordsman off his feet. He pounced on the supine body and raised his trident for the fatal blow. He hesitated at that point and looked up at the box.

Faustus, lights dancing in his eyes, leaned forward and shot out his arm. At the last moment, his father reached over and touched him lightly on his bare knee. Disappointment painted the boy's face momentarily. Then he turned his thumb upward. The mob shouted its approval.

When their bedlam subsided, a scream came from the lips of a gladiator with a spiked-ball flail. He had taken his eye off his opponent for a split second. That was all it had taken. With blurring speed, the gladiator with a *gladius* made a diagonal slash from the incautious fighter's right nipple to his left hip. Howls of approval and jeers for the wounded man.

"It's Brutus. Stupid Brutus."

"Brutus has never been any good." More insults came from the audience, though Preacher did not understand them.

"Finish him!" a woman's voice shrieked.

Brutus shuddered as he walked more into Preacher's view. Blood streamed down his torso in a shimmering curtain. He brought up his shield to cover his vulnerable body and began to swing his flail back and forth. The sword came at him again. Brutus blocked it with his shield and converted his sideways motion into a circular one. When the heavy, spiked ball reached a position directly behind its handle, he lashed it forward.

It struck with a clang on the small shield of his opponent. With a powerful yank, Brutus jerked the protective disc out of the other gladiator's grasp. At once he tried to free his weapon. That proved his undoing. The opposing gladiator came at him with a blizzard of varied attacks. It ended with a horizontal slash that opened the belly of Brutus an inch above his navel.

Brutus sucked air deeply and dropped the handle of his flail. He sat abruptly. His eyes grew wide, and he worked frantically to stuff his intestines back inside his body.

"That's dumb, Brutus," a critic directly over Preacher shouted.

Preacher looked over at the box along with the victorious gladiator. Panting in his excitement, Faustus wore the mask of a child demon as he eagerly thrust out his arm and turned his extended thumb downward. The swordsman quickly stepped over and struck the head from Brutus' shoulders. The crowd went wild.

Shoulder to shoulder, the three surviving gladiators marched to salute the young boy in whose honor this display of gore was being held. Then they returned to the gate, which rose to admit them. The trumpets blared and four more professionals came out. A quartet of confused, frightened men followed.

They saluted the *imperator* from the center of the sand and set to it with speed and energy. This round of combats lasted only a short time and the blood flowed freely. Two of the half-trained fighters died within a minute, dispatched by the downturned thumb of Quintus Faustus. The survivors strutted back to the holding pens. Another fanfare brought out the clowns.

Only these were not the same frisky children who had performed first. They appeared to be dazed, uncertain of where they were, or what their purpose might be. Handlers quickly goaded them into fighting one another. Some were armed with tubes of sewn skin, filled with sand, others with air-filled bladders. Another group carried straw-stuffed objects that Preacher could only guess at being animal parts. He watched them with a growing frown as they began to flail away at their companions.

Philadelphia approached him and nodded toward the grotesque performers. "I hear around that those poor folk are captives who have been tormented into states of craziness. They're supposed to whoop it up out there for a while; then comes the really bad part."

"What's that?" Preacher asked him.

"Wait, an' you'll see."

"Sounds grim. Might be you an' Buck can get more cooperation out of those Bible-thumpers. Why don't you go in among them and give them a little backbone?"

"Suits. I'll get Buck." Philadelphia turned away and went to find the teamster. Preacher soon saw them talking earnestly among the missionaries. He looked away, back at the sand, when gales of laughter filled the arena.

"'Pears to me that it's them that's watchin' an' laughin' that's got the sick minds," he grumbled to himself.

The sorrowful clowns had milked their antics for all the laughs they could generate. At a signal from the real master of the games, Bulbus, small gates opened around the arena. Out rushed huge, ferocious, starved mastiff dogs. Screams of terror came from the pitiful, demented clowns as the dogs fell on them. The audience loved it. Preacher made a face of disgust as he looked beyond the slaughter to the small boy in the marble box.

Faustus squirmed in a frenzy of excitement. It made Preacher's stomach churn.

*   *   *

"I tell you, friend, if you don't decide to fight back, you'll get what them poor fellers out there are gettin'. It don't feel nice gettin' ripped apart by a cougar," Preacher told three intently listening young missionaries. "Believe me, I know. I done got mauled by one some years back. If I didn't have a big knife an' a war hawk with me, he'd a-been dinin' on my innards before noon."

One of his audience swallowed hard and made a gagging sound. "If I have something to fight with, I'll fight," he declared shakily. To the angry glare from the son of Deacon Abercrombie, he added, "I have a wife and two children to protect."

"A child has the right to decide for himself," Phineas Abercrombie replied snippily.

Defiance crackled in the words of the young father. "If a child cannot make decisions about property, or his schooling, or anything else, Brother Phineas, I say he cannot properly decide to die for the greater glory of the Lord."

"Careful Brother Fauts, you are close to blasphemy."

Fury born of his protectiveness exploded. *"Damn* your blasphemy! I'll fight, and you would, too, if you had any stones."

Philadelphia left them to further pursuit of that possibility when a burly handler gestured to him with his coiled whip. Buck, too, had been gathered in. Their warders took them to where Preacher stood. Three of the toughest professionals joined them a moment later.

"You will fight in pairs. You condemned men, if you win this match, you will be paired with another gladiator until you are killed. So, fight your best and give the people a good show."

When the last of the demented victims succumbed to the ravenous jaws of the mastiffs, the accommodators cleared the arena. Hawkers moved through the aisles, selling wine, popped corn, slices of melon and other fruit. Others cut shaved-thin slices off roasted joints of meat and built sand-wiches. The spectators ate and drank and talked through their laughter as they recalled their favorite kill by the vicious dogs. It all made Preacher want to drive the three tines of his trident into their guts and twist while they shrieked in agony.

With the clean-up completed, the clarions brayed again, and the six fighters stepped out onto the sand. They advanced in two ranks, with Preacher, Philadelphia and Buck behind the professionals. At the center, they halted and saluted the boy *imperator*. Faustus rose and addressed them, his voice husky with barely suppressed emotion.

"You three who defied the authority of New Rome will die here today. And I will take great pleasure in watching your blood soak into the sand. So, do not slack. Give us a good fight, so we can thrill in your agony." He pointed his ivory wand at Preacher. "Especially you, my magnificent specimen. I expect great things from you. Now, let the fighting begin."

Trumpets shivered the air. All six fighters squared off. Preacher knew he had to make this quick. He began to circle his opponent, the net held loosely in his left hand. He feinted tentatively with the trident. Suddenly, the gladiator opposite him burst forth with a frenzy of furious blows.

Tall, lean, and muscular, Vindix bore in on Preacher with a smooth network of thrusts and slashes. He smiled grimly as Preacher gave ground. He batted the trident aside and pressed forward with a springy right leg. Blinding hot pain erupted in his thigh as Preacher recovered from the beating and drove two of the three tines of his weapon deeply into the flesh of an exposed thigh.

A fraction of a second later, he hurled the net, ensnaring Vindix. With a stout yank, Preacher hauled the gladiator off his sandals. He drew the small dagger from his belt and knelt beside the fallen fighter.

"I'll make this quick, to spare you pain."

Vindix smiled through his agony. "That's what I intended for you. No need for us to provide entertainment for that sick, twisted child."

Preacher looked up at the boy, to see an expression of fury on the soft features. "You were too fast. That's not fair. Spare him," Faustus' squeaky voice commanded.

Preacher replaced his dagger and offered a hand to Vindix to help him come upright. The crowd cheered. Vindix was a favorite. Preacher spoke softly to him. "You live to fight another day."

Vindix gave him a grim smile, face contorted with pain. "More's a pity." He limped away, to be replaced by another gladiator. This one bore the spiked mace. He came after Preacher in a rush.

Philadelphia had been matched with a squat, brawny brute who took particular pleasure in maiming his opponents before finally finishing them off. Despite the lingering discomfort of his old wound, Philadelphia Braddock danced lightly away from the *gladius* that darted before his eyes. Sweat began to trickle down from his temples. He concentrated on the eyes of Asperis and the tip of his sword.

So quickly that Philadelphia almost missed it, Asperis widened his eyes in anticipation of a slash that would sever the mountain man's left arm, leaving him without a shield. With a swift jerk, Philadelphia raised the round metal protector, and the iron blade in his opponent's hand rang loudly against it. Philadelphia swung his right leg forward and pivoted, to smash his armored *caestus* into the point of the left shoulder of Asperis. The triangular blades bit deeply, and blood flowed in a gush when Philadelphia withdrew his *caestus*. He shifted his weight and kicked Asperis in the belly.

Numbed and bleeding profusely from the shoulder, Asperis doubled over, and Philadelphia clubbed him with the armored fist. Unfortunately it left him vulnerable for a moment, during which Asperis drove the tip of his sword into the meaty portion of Philadelphia's side. Fire flashed through the muscles of Philadelphia's torso. Biting his lower lip, he hauled back and rammed the spikes of his *caestus* into the side of Asperis' head. The gladiator went down in a flash.

A low groan came from deep in his chest, and Asperis began to twitch his arms and legs. Philadelphia knew what he had done and wasted no time checking with the pouty-faced brat for the signal to finish Asperis. Behind him, the portcullis clanged again, and another contender entered the arena. Philadelphia turned to see that it would be a *riatarius*.

"More trouble," he grunted.

Buck Sears faced a gladiator done up as a Nubian warrior, complete with zebra-painted shield, towering headdress and assagai spear. Braided elephant-tail hair and feather anklets circled his legs above bare feet. They rippled hypnotically as he bounced and jounced up and down in an advance punctuated by sharp cries from a mouth ringed by a wide smear of black grease paint.

Buck took this all in and lowered the tip of his sword to the sand. He threw back his head and laughed. "Now, ain't you just the silliest damn critter I've ever seen."

The gyrations abruptly ceased. "Huh?"

"I said you look like a fool," Buck called out.

Howling in outrage, the imitation Nubian charged with his spear held over his shoulder in one of the classical positions employed by the Zulu and the Masai, whom the ancient Romans lumped together as "Nubians."

Buck lunged out of the way of the advance. He swung the flat of his blade and smashed it into the ribs of his opponent. Laughter rose from the stands. Buck began to enjoy himself.

Before the Nubian could turn, Buck booted him in the seat of his pants. He stumbled and lowered his shield. Buck thrust with his sword and cut a line along the gladiator's forehead right below the gaudy headdress. A sheet of blood poured out. The mob loved it.

Even that evil-minded brat had started to giggle and clap his hands, Buck noted. He quickly found out he had paid too much attention to such matters. Solis had recovered himself and came at Buck driven by fury. He battered and hacked at the shield Buck carried. Buck's strength wavered momentarily, and Solis seized the advantage. Setting his feet, he slammed his own shield into Buck's face.

Buck's knees buckled, and he dropped onto the left one. Blackness swam before his eyes. He shook his head in an effort to clear it while he fended off the plunging assagai. With a desperate effort, he brought his *gladius* around and drove it through the fire-hardened zebra-print shield. The tip sliced three inches into sweaty flesh. Solis grunted, gasped and loosed a thin wail. Buck pulled back and regained his feet.

Above him, all around the coliseum the throng went wild. They stomped their feet and pelted the sand with greasy strips of paper that had held sandwiches and popped corn. Some threw cushions they had brought along for comfort on the stone benches of the common bleachers. A gray pallor had washed over the face of Solis. He blinked back fear, sweat and blood and tried to focus on his opponent.

Sucking in large draughts of air, Buck found Solis easily enough. His shield arm sagged; the knob-hilled assagai hung in an unresponsive hand. Pink froth bubbled on his pain-distorted lips. Balefully, Buck advanced on him. Deep inside, he did not want to do this. Then he remembered he was supposed to solicit a decision from the *imperator.*

He turned his head upward. Faustus seemed to be on the edge of ecstasy. He rapidly licked his lips and stared fixedly at the bleeding wound in the chest of Solis. At last he regrasped what was expected of him. Solis was a professional. Faustus spared him.

Two arena helpers escorted him out. Another gladiator took his place. The six men—three sapped and worn from their earlier battles, the other trio fresh—faced the box and saluted.

"Awh, hell, we've gotta go through this all over again," Buck muttered. He squared off with the others, and the attacks came immediately.

16

Through the open squares formed by the iron gate to their holding pen, Sister Amelia Witherspoon looked on. At first she viewed the grisly spectacle in horror. Then, as the mountain men and their teamster ally bested one professional gladiator after another, her perusal changed to amorous fascination with Preacher. He had to be the bravest, strongest man ever born.

A shiver of delight ran through her slender body, hidden under the prim, gray dress and her bonnet. If what he did before her very eyes were not so absolutely terrible, she might suspect that she was becoming enamored of him. Possibly even falling in love. *Stuff and nonsense,* she told herself. Cries of trepidation came from others among the missionaries. One of the young men convinced to put up some resistance by Philadelphia spoke quietly beside Sister Amelia.

"Is any of them going to be around to lead the way to freedom?"

An unusual light sparkled in Amelia's eyes. "I'm sure that

one will. Arturus. He has finished off three gladiators so far. Spared the lives of two. He is a true champion."

With an indulgent chuckle, the young man nodded toward Preacher. " 'Arturus' is it? That may be what these crazy folk call him, but the one named Philadelphia told me he is really the mountain man we were questioned about, Preacher."

Amelia's eyes widened. "I knew it! I knew he had to be the best there is. Oh, Preacher, fight for us," she offered up prayerfully.

Out on the sand, it appeared as though Preacher had heard her appeal and responded accordingly. He swung his net, snared another gladiator, and hurtled the hapless fighter toward the deadly tines of the trident. A moment before the barbed spikes entered vulnerable flesh, a high, thin voice barked from above and behind Preacher.

"Hold!" Preacher released his victim. "He has fought well," Faustus continued. "He is free to retire. You will face yet another, more worthy opponent," he told Preacher. "At once."

Looks like the folks in the imperial box have got impatient. Not gonna wait for all of us to finish our fights, Preacher thought to himself as the gate ground open and a huge fellow lumbered out. Taller by a head than Preacher, he was armed with a *caestus* and a twin-bladed dagger. He immediately went for Preacher with a roar.

He swung the *caestus* with practiced ease, and the spectators greeted him by name. "Dicius! Dicius! Dicius!"

Like an elephant attacking a toad, he loomed over Preacher and contemptuously swept aside the net when it hissed toward him. He stepped in and engaged the trident with the dual-bladed knife, gave a mighty twist and yanked it from Preacher's grasp. Preacher tried with the net again and missed as Dicius danced away. Then the muscular gladiator came at Preacher again.

He bounded forward, jinked to his right, tempting another throw of the net. Preacher obliged him. The tar-stiffened, knotted snare fanned out and lofted over the head of Dicius. Before it could descend, Dicius leaped to his left and struck a powerful blow with the *caestus*.

Fortunately for Preacher, the punch landed askew, to glance off the side of Preacher's head. One of the blades cut a ragged line in the hair above one ear. Stunned, Preacher sank to one knee. Dimly he heard the shrill scream as Amelia cried out.

Philadelphia Braddock looked up at the sound of that anguished wail. He saw Dicius poised with his *caestus* raised above his head to deliver a fatal blow. For the moment Philadelphia ignored his own tormentor to grasp his sword in front of the hilt and hurl it like a lance. It flashed in the afternoon sunlight as it sped to the target.

Paralyzed by enormous misery, Dicius emitted a faint moan as the *gladius* pierced his side and sliced through the soft organs in his belly. He rocked from heel to toe for a moment, and the *caestus* dropped without force to land on Preacher's shoulder. Shaking clear of his momentary blackout, Preacher scrambled to retrieve his trident.

He stood over Dicius, who feebly tried to cut the hamstring of Preacher's left leg. With a powerful thrust, Preacher drove the middle tine through his opponents throat. He looked up with a nod and a smile for Philadelphia.

"I reckon they aim to kill us for certain sure. No reason we have to play by their rules," Preacher told his friend as he abandoned his trident. Then he bent, retrieved the *gladius* and tossed it back to Philadelphia.

So astonished by the swift action that he failed to press

his attack, the gladiator contesting Philadelphia only then broke his frozen pose. He came on strong, yet the mountain man managed to elude his darting weapon. Philadelphia gave ground slowly, eyes alert for an opening. While he did, Preacher retrieved the spiked mace of an earlier opponent and looked to the portcullis, where his next enemy would appear.

It turned out to be Sparticus. At the sight of this, Faustus bounced up and down on his chair, thrilled by the prospects. Preacher did not greet it quite so enthusiastically. He gave a tentative swing of the spiked ball at the end of its chain and advanced on the huge escaped slave. A moment later, Philadelphia got too busy to watch.

With catlike grace, the gladiator advanced on an oblique angle to Philadelphia. He prodded at him with the tip of his *pilum*. The slender spear had been equipped with a soft lead collar at the base of the tip to prevent it from being withdrawn from a wound. Altogether a nasty weapon. Philadelphia gave it due respect. His opponent's advance forced him toward where Buck had just dispatched his latest enemy. Weakened by his recent wounds, Philadelphia could not maintain his balance when he backed into the supine body of the dead gladiator.

His knee buckled and he stumbled. At that critical moment, the professional thrust the javelin toward him. Only at the last possible moment, Philadelphia covered himself with his shield, turned the *pilum,* and regained his balance. He hacked at an exposed knee, and the blades bit into flesh at the bottom of the gladiator's thigh. That let Philadelphia recover completely.

Ignoring the threat of the javelin, he pushed in on his opponent. At that moment, Philadelphia would have given anything for a good tomahawk. The short sword would have to do, he decided. At least until he could equip himself with something better. At first he made good progress, his antagonist hobbled by his wound; then Philadelphia planted his foot in a pool of blood while attempting a thrust to the chest.

His feet went out from under him, and he plopped onto the ground. Hoots and jeers rose from the onlookers. Eyes alight with renewed hope, the gladiator moved in on Philadelphia.

Eager to win Sparticus as an ally, rather than having to kill him, Preacher raised his left hand in a cautionary gesture; the net hung limp in his grasp. "It don't have to end here, Sparticus," he prompted.

"Don't talk that talk to me, white man," Sparticus growled truculently.

Preacher ignored him. "I mean it. You can get out of here, too."

Sparticus would have none of it. He came at Preacher with a huge cudgel, a single, long spike protruding through the side of the thick tip. It swished through the air as Preacher jumped backward. Muscles rippled under the oiled black skin as Sparticus planted another big foot on the sand and advanced again.

Preacher whipped the air with his flail. The spiked ball smashed into the boss of the shield on Sparticus' left arm. It made a resounding, thunder-clap sound. Instead of retreating, Sparticus stepped in. The men found themselves chest to chest. The muscles in Preacher's left arm and shoulder strained to hold the powerful arm that supported the cudgel.

To the onlookers they appeared to be dancing as they shuffled their feet to find better purchase. Some began to clap rhythmically. Cries of "Fight! Fight!" rang in the tiers. Preacher spoke quiet reason to Sparticus.

"Even though slavery is the law of the land, it don't amount to a hill of bison dung out here. If you join us in winnin' free, an' takin' them helpless missionaries with us, I'll personally guarantee that you can make a new life for your-self in the High Lonesome, an' live a free man."

Sparticus curled his lips in a sneer and snarled his reply while he cuffed Preacher with a backhand blow with the cudgel. "What do I want that for? I'm due to earn the *rudis* soon. That'll make me a wealthy man, an' free. Why should I risk all of that for a passel of white folk who prob'ly owned slaves before they got captured?"

Preacher gave it another try. "They're Bible-thumpers. Mission folk. Their kind don't hold slaves."

"Knowed me a preacher-man down South. He owned his-self three house slaves. I'll be a big man around here after I kill you an' retire."

Unable to obtain dominance above, Preacher used an old Indian trick. He shifted his weight to one leg, shot the other forward and hooked his heel behind the ankle of Sparticus.

With a swift yank forward, he toppled the big black glad-iator off his feet. At the last second, Preacher rolled away as Sparticus crashed to the ground. Impact forced grunted words from Sparticus' mouth.

"You're good, I give you that. Who are you, anyhow, Ar-turus?"

Preacher decided to gamble it all. He turned his flinty gaze straight into the eyes of his opponent. "They call me Preacher."

An expression of respect, flavored with awe, filled the gladiator's face. "Fore Jesus, I didn't know."

They had come to their knees now. The force of their im-pact with hard-packed sand had knocked the flail from Preacher's hand. He saw the trident only a scant foot from his grasp. Sparticus hefted the club and licked his lips.

"I'll be the richest man around if I finish you," Sparticus declared.

"*If.* I'd think on that were I you."

Sparticus found that to somehow be funny. He threw back

his head to laugh, and Preacher quickly unfurled his net and flung it over the kneeling man. Sparticus flung it off like a mere cobweb. Though not before Preacher could snatch up his trident. Opposite him, Sparticus bounded to the soles of his high-laced sandals. Preacher seemed to react slowly, gathering his net.

With the quickness that made him famous, Sparticus charged. The cudgel led the way. Preacher deflected it with the shaft of his trident and prodded at the chest of his opponent. Sparticus laughed mirthlessly and came on. Forced to give ground, Preacher brought his heel down on the haft of a dropped weapon. Instantly, he stumbled and tottered off to one side.

Sparticus seized the moment. "You gon' die, Preacherman."

Preacher recovered himself as the deadly club swished past his left ear. The heft of the lethal object slammed painfully into the top of his shoulder. Already directed to its target, the trident cut a ragged gash in the lean side of Sparticus. Dizzied by repeated injury, Preacher missed an opportunity to end it.

Pain made his next cast erratic. The net slid from the oiled skin of his opponent and fluttered to the ground. Goaded by the press of time, Preacher hastily gathered it. A blur of movement told him Sparticus had anticipated the miss. The black man bore down on him and forced another retreat.

Feeling the effects of blood loss, Preacher stumbled again. Seized by a frenzy, the crowd howled and stomped their feet. Sparticus acted at once on the tiny break given him. Overconfident now, he stepped in for the kill, only to have Preacher let loose the net again, this time tightly furled. Using a technique he had learned from the instructors, he sent it out like a sinuous snake to coil around Sparticus' ankles.

Immediately he recovered his balance. Preacher ran

swiftly around the black gladiator and bound his legs together. Then, a hefty yank took Sparticus off his feet. In a staggered rush, Preacher closed with him and held the trident poised to drive two tines into the man's thick neck. Slowly, reluctantly, he looked up at the imperial box.

Quintus Faustus had bounded to his sandals moments earlier. He jumped up and down in agitation, his face white, eyes wild, his small, red mouth twisted grotesquely. His breathing came rapidly, and he showed obvious signs of arousal. He cut his pale blue eyes to Preacher's hot, gray orbs as he stuck out his arm.

Slowly, almost lasciviously, he turned his thumb down.

"Last chance," Preacher told Sparticus.

With considerable regret and hesitancy, Sparticus nodded in the affirmative. Preacher relaxed the position of his weapon. Above him, the shrill voice of Faustus held an edge of hysteria.

"Kill him! Kill him!" he wailed.

Calmly, ignoring the willful child, Preacher reached down and unbound the legs of Sparticus, raised him to his feet and disarmed him. Then he turned to the box.

"He yielded," he said simply.

Face clouded with tantrum warning flags, Faustus shoved out his lower lip in a spiteful, pink pout. "I don't care. It's my games, and my birthday, and I want to see men die."

Preacher replied with calm restraint. "I will not kill a man who yields to me."

White froth formed in the corners of Faustus' mouth. He dropped his wand of authority into the cushion on his chair and made small fists of his slim, long-fingered hands. His sallow face flushed scarlet as he stamped one foot like a girl.

"I want him dead! Now! Now! Now!" he shrieked.

To his surprise, Preacher looked on as Marcus Quintus rose from his chair and spoke into his son's ear. At the first words, the boy went rigid, and he shook with the intensity of his childish fury. The more Quintus spoke, the lower the shoulders of Faustus drooped. At last, his tower of rage was reduced to a pitiful bleat.

"But, Father."

"Do it!" His father hissed loud enough to be heard by the men on the sand.

In a show of bad grace, the boy gave a reluctant nod of agreement. He picked up his wand and raised it above his head. The trumpets blared. By then it had become unnecessary. The spectators perched on the edges of their seats in silent expectation. Faustus pointed to the surviving gladiators, one by one.

"Come forward," he intoned.

Preacher, Sparticus, Philadelphia, and Buck did as commanded. They were the only ones. Faustus shook with his barely suppressed outrage, and he stammered as he addressed the four fighting men. He again pointed at each one with the staff of office.

"Since you three are under sentence of death for attempted escape, and you, Sparticus, have made a cowardly surrender and are already a dead man in our eyes, you shall all be thrown in with the Christians and lions. Let the games proceed."

Preacher faced the frightened missionaries in the large holding pen. Arms folded across his chest—a gesture of strength and determination he had picked up from the Indians, rather than one of weakness—he addressed them in a low, hard voice.

"I am only going to say this once. The only way out of here is to fight. There will be plenty of weapons about the arena. I seen 'em puttin' out swords and some spears. They won't be as good a quality as what the gladiators have, but you can kill with them."

"To kill another man is to damn your soul for eternity," Phineas Abercrombie blustered. "Not a one of us will do that."

Preacher cocked his head to one side and eyed Abercrombie with a cold eye. "I was thinkin' on them mountain lions. They're fixin' to eat you before you have a chance to turn a sword on a man. You'd best be willin' an' able to stop them before you go worryin' about facin' a man."

Raising a stubborn chin, Phineas answered stubbornly. "If it comes to that, we'll be martyred with a hymn on our lips."

"Where's your pappy, Sonny? Best be hidin' behind his skirts," Preacher grunted, then turned to the others, ignoring the pompous Abercrombie. "Your best bet is to fight back to back, four of you together. Protect your wimmin an' children inside the squares. That way no lion can come at you unexpected. When the last one is finished off, that's when we go for the walls. Help one another up an' over and then we make a dash for it."

Encouraged by Preacher's positive outlook, Sister Amelia Witherspoon came forward. "Do you think we really have a chance?"

"If you do what me an' my friends say, you have a lot better chance than followin' this feller here who seems hell-bent on dyin' for no reason. Seems to me he's a few straws shy of a haystack. For the rest of you, I reckon you know what to do when the time comes."

"What if we do kill the lions, only to be faced by men?"

Preacher gave them a nasty smile. "Well, there ain't many of them left. Or didn't you watch us out there? But, by damn, if that's the case, you kill them, too. It's the only way."

Tingling notes sounded the final fanfare.

Out on the sand, the missionaries stood in blinking confusion. Boos and insults greeted Preacher and his fellows. Ignoring them, the four fighting men quickly armed themselves. Catcalls and jeers rang down on the terror-stricken Gospel-shouters. Tentatively, Sister Witherspoon began a hymn.

That brought gales of raucous laughter. More mocking retorts came from the audience. One bloodthirsty spectator pointed at Amelia. "Hey, that one's good-looking. Wonder how she'd be in . . ."

"Why aren't they in the buff, like usual?" inquired another.

"Where's that fat one I saw brought in?"

A smaller, low gate swung open, and one of the handlers gave a mighty shove to the back of Deacon Abercrombie. He stumbled out onto the sand, bare to the waist. His pale, bleached-looking skin and flabby condition produced a windstorm of scornful sniggers. His wife ran to him, tears bright in her eyes, face a-flame with embarrassment.

"Cover yourself with my shawl."

Shame encrimsoned the deacon's face. "You might not want to be kind to me, my dear. I—I betrayed you all to that monster Quintus. I only wanted freedom for you and I. I fear I may have prevented your one good chance to escape."

She draped the shawl over his shoulders and patted him consolingly. "There is a strange man, one of the gladiators, who says we still have a way to get out of here."

"Where is he?" Abercrombie asked eagerly.

"Over—over there." Agatha Abercrombie pointed to Preacher.

Phineas Abercrombie scowled. "The troublemaker. I'd not put much stock in him, my dear."

And then they let out the lions.

At once, Deacon Abercrombie began to edge toward Preacher. The spectators cheered and shouted. They rose and clapped their hands in a wavelike motion around the tiers of seats. At first, the cougars seemed as confused and blinded by light as their intended victims. They padded about without direction, sniffed the air and uttered menacing growls. Tension built while the short-sighted critters sought to locate their prey. Two met head-on and traded swats and snarls. Three of the Mobile Church in the Wildwood's women uttered shrill screams.

One big, anvil-headed beast raised up from sniffing and

turned baleful yellow eyes toward the sound. The women screamed all the more. One of the men broke and began to run to the far side of the arena from the deadly animals. At once the golden-orbed puma changed into a study in liquid motion. Flawlessly he streaked through the frightened missionaries, most of whom had remained stock still.

It rapidly closed the ground and launched itself at the back of the running Bible-thumper. Long, curved claws ripped mercilessly into tender flesh and raked along the back of the helpless man. His screams of agony set off a new explosion of yelling, stomping and applauding among the onlookers. At once, Deacon Abercrombie's flock came to life and scrambled as one to put distance between themselves and the ravenous animals.

Preacher turned with all the fluid ease of the deadly cat and hacked through its spine, above the shoulders, with a single blow from the *gladius* he held. It died at the same time as the missionary it had attacked. Instantly, Preacher turned to face another of the beasts bent upon attacking him.

"Dang it," he roared as he split open the nose of the offending puma, "do like I said!"

With Philadelphia on his right, Buck on the left, and Sparticus behind, the four fought off three more cougars. First two, then six more of the missionaries got the idea from this efficient means of downing the snarling bundles of lightning-fast fury. They quickly armed themselves and formed defensive squares. Only Deacon Abercrombie remained alone and exposed. One big cat soon discovered this. While his wife screamed with terror and the deacon made squawking noises, the cougar pounced.

"Stop! I command you in the name of the Lord," Abercrombie found voice to thunder. Then he was shrieking out his life. The sand soon pooled with red. A woman among the missionaries screamed when a mountain lion dragged her out of one formation.

Only a short distance away, Preacher took two fast steps forward and plunged the leaf-bladed *gladius* to the hilt in the animal's chest. It released the woman, shivered mightily, arched its back, and fell dead as Preacher drew out the sword. Fickle as always, the crowd went wild.

Now the spectators cheered the beleaguered missionaries. They had thought to be amused by the pitifully useless antics of the condemned wretches, only to find objects of admiration in the sudden courage displayed by desperate people. Preacher took note of it and spoke to his companions.

"Imagine that. All of a sudden they're on our side. Reckon that'll jerk the jaw of that bloody-minded boy-brat."

Buck answered through a grunt of effort as he split the skull of yet another cougar. "He likes to see blood run, right enough. But I don't think it's that of his prize cats. That one's sick in the head. You can tell by the look in his eyes."

"Best save our breath for fightin'," Preacher advised. "Let's get these folk on the move, form up close together, in two lines. Less target for the cougars that way."

One of the tawny creatures leaped into the air for a high attack. Preacher squatted and split open its belly with his *gladius*. "What good will that do?" Sparticus grumbled as he drove a *pilum* into the chest of a raging puma.

Preacher answered quickly. "We can move around the sand like the hands on a clock. Finish off what's left in no time."

At the shouted urges of the mountain men, the desperate missionaries began to form into two lines, back-to-back. Over his shoulder, Preacher called to those behind him. "Can you walk backwards an' still fight them critters?' When they assured him they could, he issued a loud, if imprecise, command. "Then let's git to it."

The crowd howled in glee as the enraged cougars died one at a time. When only a single pair remained, those on the sand could not hear a word said by anyone beside them. All around them, the last of the big cats could smell the odor of their dead companions. Fangs dripping the foam of their fury, they flung themselves at the wall of human flesh that inexorably forced them to move. A scream emboldened them as an inexperienced missionary went down, his chest and belly clawed open. The cougar that had felled him did not get to savor its victory.

Even before the line had formed, Amelia Witherspoon had taken up a *pilum* and had speared one of the cats. Now she sank the javelin into the side of the blood-slobbering beast that had disemboweled Brother Frazier. The creature screamed like a woman, arched its back and lashed out uselessly with weakened paws. Amelia hung on to the shaft and felt the power of the animal vibrate through her arms. The hind feet left the ground, and she had to let go quickly to keep from being dragged down onto the dying cat.

"Good girl," Preacher said, though no one could hear him over the roar of the mob in the stands. "I knew she had some pluck."

An instant later, he had to defend his life against the last of the beasts. It hurtled at his part of the line with a mighty, bowel-watering roar. Preacher buried his *gladius* in its chest, though not before it had its forelegs wrapped around him and the claws bit agonizingly into his back. Then, half a dozen swords, javelins, and tridents sank into the golden coat to drive the last of life from the animal. Pressure eased in Preacher's back, and he felt the gentle touch of Philadelphia as his friend pried the claws from him.

"It's all done."

"I doubt that, Philadelphia."

Once assured that no more mountain lions lurked to spring upon them, the surviving force turned as one to face the blighted little boy who ran the games. Preacher saw through the haze of pain, and the sting of sweat in his eyes, that Faustus' face had been twisted into a mask of evil. With a sudden-born smile of such sweetness as to melt the hardest heart, the boy made a signal with his imperial baton.

First came the cleaning crew. They hauled off the carcasses of the dead cougars, spread fresh sand over the pools of blood, then exited. It gave everyone time to catch their breath. It also allowed the timid among the missionaries to exercise their imaginations on what might come next. Preacher, Philadelphia, Buck, and Sparticus considered the same thing, though not colored by fear and trepidation.

"I reckon that little monster is going to throw something else at us," Philadelphia opined. "Why ain't we moving?"

"He'll have to do something. He's got his neck stuck a whole ways out sayin' how we would all die," Preacher agreed. "Whatever it is will maybe give us a better opening." Preacher turned to the black gladiator. "What do you figger, Sparticus. And—ah—it'd be kinda nice to know your real name."

Sparticus flashed a white smile. "It's no better'n the one they hung on me. It's—you won't laugh?—Cornelius."

Preacher fought the quirk of a smile. "Then Sparticus it is."

"Obliged. I expect as hows that li'l bastard will send in the whole rest of the gladiators. They'll finish these weaklings fast. Then it'll be up to us."

"Not if I can come up with something better," Preacher promised.

"It had best be good," Buck put in his bit.

Above them, the trumpets brayed. The portcullis raised to admit the twenty remaining trained gladiators. Their weapons were of the serious type. No gaudy costumes or colorful shields. They carried workmanlike swords, flails, javelins, and two had bows. They advanced, their arms at rest, to salute the box. That's when providence handed Preacher a large portion of good fortune.

"I gotta make this fast. All of you sheep listen up. Whatever we do, you do. And that starts now! Run at them," Preacher shouted as he set off at a fast trot toward the unprepared gladiators.

With their weapons aimed more or less at the advancing gladiators, the missionaries followed in the wake of Preacher and his companions. Preacher let out a caterwaul as the unexpected charge closed with the newcomers. It froze them for a vital moment. Preacher smashed one to his knees with the flat of his blade, and shoved through to stab another in the gut. Beside him, the arms of his friends churned in deadly rhythm.

Philadelphia drove a *pilum* into the gut of a burly gladiator who had leaped aside to swing his spiked ball at Preacher. When the tip entered his flesh, he dropped his weapon and doubled over on the shaft of the spear. He clutched it with trembling fingers as he sank to his knees. Philadelphia left the *pilum* in his victim, snatched up the flail and shoved on into the melee of struggling gladiators. The audience lost their minds while the four courageous fighters hacked and slashed their way through the ranks and came out on the other side.

At once, Preacher led the way to the gate, which had not as yet begun to close. He darted under the pointed ends of the portcullis and downed a guard with a sword thrust. Beside him, Buck Sears killed the guard at the windlass that controlled the wooden-framed iron barrier and quickly grabbed hold to secure it.

Behind him came Philadelphia and Sparticus. They made short work of the three astonished handlers who stood gawking at the furious battle. Then they turned back to hold the opening for the missionaries.

Hewing like gleaners in a wheat field, the Mobile Church in the Wildwood's members smashed through the ranks of gladiators. They streamed by ones and twos toward the open gateway. Preacher noticed that the handsome young woman with the spear fought with the ferocity of the men. While he registered this, she poked the iron tip of the *pilum* into the eye of a huge man with a long sword. He fell screaming. The iron-slat gate held motionless while they dashed under its pointed ends.

When the last one cleared the barrier, Buck let it go. It crashed down with a resounding roar. Buck quickly slashed the rope that supported it. Led by Preacher and Philadelphia, the missionaries rushed down the stone corridor, into the bowels of the coliseum. Amelia Witherspoon had dropped her *pilum* and clung to Preacher all the way.

"Where are we going?" she panted in question.

Preacher nodded to the tunnel entrance. "To the home of the master of games."

"But, why? Isn't that dangerous?"

"Not so much as *not* doing it. For one thing, I'm not leaving here without my horses and my shootin' gear. I've got me a pair of Walker Colts I've grown right fond of."

"Walkers? I've not heard of that breed before."

"They ain't my horses, Missy, they's shootin' irons."

"Oh! . . . *OH!*" she squeaked.

Preacher chuckled. Then he thought he had better explain it to these featherheads so they'd know. He slowed his pace, halted them midway in the tunnel and spoke in a low, earnest voice that still echoed off the walls.

"Listen up, folks. This ain't over yet. We're goin' to the storehouse at the games master's house. You can get better weapons, an' you'll need them, and horses to make a quick getaway."

"You mean there'll be more fighting?" Agatha Abercrombie asked in a trembling voice.

"Sure's skunks stink, ma'am. There's the better part of two legions out there."

"Oh, dear, dear, maybe we should not have done this," she wailed.

"You could have always gotten et up by the lions, like your husband," Preacher told her coldly.

"You cruel, cruel man," she chastised.

"*I'm* cruel? What about that devil's spawn brat who ordered all that? I got no more time for you. Keep movin', folks."

Entering the storeroom at the house of Justinius Bulbus from the gladiator school proved easier than the frontal approach. The two guards at the far end of the tunnel had gone down like one man when Preacher and Sparticus unexpectedly appeared. With them out of the way, Preacher had called upon the great strength of Sparticus to help him breach the iron gate.

It gave with a noisy screech, and the refugee missionaries stumbled through. Being empty, the school had an eerie quality to it. Buck Sears led the way to the passageway that issued into Bulbus' residence. Preacher took the point with long strides past the colorful tile murals that lined the hallway. The subjects being gladiators in various forms of killing and maiming, he paid them scant attention. He signaled for a halt when he reached the far end.

A wooden-barred gate closed off the passage. Preacher gave it a try, and it swung open on well-oiled hinges. He found himself again in the courtyard with its tinkling fountain. This time, the steward happened to be out picking posies for his master's table. He saw Preacher and let out a yelp that could have been heard at the Temple of Vesta, had there not been such an uproar from the coliseum. It did serve to summon three burly sentries.

They soon showed that they did not lack the courage to engage the gladiators who boiled out of the passageway to the school. For all their willingness to fight, they did not last long. Their leader, an off-duty *contubernalis* from *Legio II, Britannicus,* took on Preacher—much to his regret as it turned out.

By far not a skilled swordsman, Preacher had nevertheless learned tricks in the gladiator school that were foreign to this stolid soldier. The sergeant lost his sword hand in his first precipitous rush. Preacher nimbly sidestepped him and chopped downward with his *gladius*. The hand, and the weapon it held, appeared to leap from the end of the legionnaire's arm. Desperately he clutched the blood-spouting stump with his other hand while he sucked air in a muted whoosh. With the shield lowered, Preacher got a shot at an exposed neck. A swift cut ended the life of the sergeant. Preacher looked to his left.

Sparticus held one of the guards over his head, straightened out like a man asleep on his back. The startled yelp that came from him broke the illusion of slumber. His scream ended with a loud crack when Sparticus hurled him against the lip of the stone fountain. At once, the huge black gladiator strode across the courtyard to where Buck held half a dozen more sentries at bay in the doorway of the guardroom. Preacher looked the other way to check on Philadelphia Braddock.

To Preacher's right, Philadelphia let go a bear growl and smashed the shoulder of the last guard. Stunned, the man went to one knee, his shield up to protect his head. Laughing, Philadelphia swept the soldier's supporting leg out from under him and crowned him solidly on the top of the head with a heavy cudgel.

"Sparticus, stay there with Buck. We'll bring you weapons, food and a horse."

"Sho'nuf, Preacher." Sparticus grinned and rippled the muscles of his shoulders and arms.

In the arms store, the more aggressive among the young missionaries acted like kids in a vacant candy store. Preacher three times had to caution one or another about taking too many rifles."Takes too long to reload. Tires your horse, too. Take four or six pistols instead."

He quickly found his favorites and loaded them all. He turned to the suddenly belligerent pilgrims and instructed, "Load up every one you take. We'll be needin' 'em to get out of this place."

That prediction proved only too true the moment they reached the street. Two *contaburniae*—twenty soldiers— trotted their way in formation down the Via Iulius. Shields up, their piliae aligned perfectly, the legionnaires advanced, only their shins and grim faces visible. In his insane state as Marcus Quintus Americus, Alexander Reardon had made only one mistake. He had insisted on accuracy in arms and armor, and the Romans had fought long before gunpowder came into being.

Preacher knocked the sergeant of the first rank off his feet with a .56 ball from his Hawken, then laid the smoking rifle across his lap. He let fly with one of his .44 Walker Colts. In rapid succession, three more soldiers fell. His friends, Preacher noticed, accounted for themselves rather well also.

Philadelphia dumped two in the second rank and went for another pistol. A legionnaire yelped, and blood flew from a scalp wound as the .36 caliber squirrel rifle in the hands of Amelia Witherspoon barked to Preacher's right rear. He decided the time had come to depart this place. Setting spurs to Cougar's flanks, he led the charge on the dismounted men.

Their advance became a rout. Shot through the shield and

chest, one soldier staggered to the side to lean on the wall of the gladiator school. He died before the last of the escapees rode out of sight. Panic broke out in the streets. Women screamed and men shouted in angry tones, until they saw the thoroughly armed band that thundered down on them. Then they gave way rapidly.

In seemingly no time, the fugitives reached a gate. Preacher took aim and shot down the guard who wrestled to draw closed the thick, heavy barrier. Then he shouted good advice.

"C'mon, folks, don't dally. We've lots of miles to put between us and them."

18

Confusion and surprise turned to panic when the order to shut the gates was taken too literally by the stadium staff. Spectators swarmed into the aisles, only to find the entrances to the coliseum barred against them. They began to push and shove, then to fight among themselves. In the imperial box, his face a flaming scarlet in childish fury, Quintus Faustus shrieked impotent demands and threats. Robbed of his bloody climax, he lost what tenuous hold he had on his reason.

Marcus Quintus saw the trembling boy with slobber and foam flying from his lips and rose to confront his son. He put a hand on Faustus' shoulder and squeezed gently. Frenetically, Faustus jerked away from his touch. Exasperated and embarrassed beyond endurance, Quintus lost his grip for a moment. He swiftly raised an arm and delivered a solid backhand slap. A red spot appeared on the pallid skin of his cheek, and Faustus bugged his eyes.

"Control yourself," his father snapped.

Faustus sat down abruptly and buried his head in his toga. His thin shoulders shook violently as he bawled like a baby.

Marcus Quintus knew at once that he must take command. He raised cupped hands to the sides of his mouth and shouted over the tumult.

"Open the *vomitoriae!* Clear these people out of here." In stentorian tones, he brayed for his army commanders. "Bring Legate Varras. I want his cavalry after that vermin at once. Bring me Legate Glaubiae! Start a search of the city. Do it now!"

Varras appeared beside Quintus and saluted. "Get out of here, use the private tunnel. Organize your cavalry and get after those people," Quintus screamed at him. Varras saluted again and departed hastily.

Gaius Septimus Glaubiae came next, his face flushed with the effort of climbing the steep steps to the box. Quintus raised his arm casually to return his salute. He leaned slightly forward and screamed in his general's face. "I want the legions organized at once. Outfit them for a long time in the field. They are to search for the escaped prisoners. I want them back. All of them."

"Do you believe they have gotten out of the city?" Glaubiae asked.

Quintus' eyes narrowed. "They will have by the time order can be restored."

Then he began to scream at the panicked crowd. He was still screaming orders when the escaping prisoners swarmed out the southern gate.

Preacher led the fleeing prisoners at a fast pace down the Via Ostia, named for the port to the west of ancient Rome. Why the madman who had created this place had picked that name for the road to the south, Preacher did not know. He doubted that this Marcus Quintus feller knew either. Two miles beyond the corrupt city, he slowed the pace to a quick walk. Elation slowly swept over all but one of the missionaries, he grumblingly noted as they began to chatter among themselves.

"We've lost everything," wailed Agatha Abercrombie. "Our wagons, our portable organ, even the pulpit."

"Be thankful we got out of that place alive," Sister Amelia Witherspoon told her coldly.

That pleased Preacher mightily. That li'l gal had some pluck. She was learning fast. For the first time Preacher looked at her in another way than as a nuisance. Pretty little thing, he mused. Clean her up a little, get some clean clothes on her. . . . He suddenly had to cover his mouth to hide a broad grin and suppress a hearty guffaw that bubbled in his throat as they continued their exchange.

"Excuse me? I am unaccustomed to accepting such criticism from anyone. Especially from my inferiors."

Sarcasm dripped from Amelia's words. "Oh, that's quite obvious. Only I don't see myself as your inferior. I didn't see *you* raise a hand to defend yourself, let alone anyone else back there."

Outrage painted Agatha's face. "How dare you!" She looked around herself for some support, only to see a laughing Preacher. His shoulders shook with his mirth. She redirected her anger. "This is all your fault, you heathen barbarian!" she lashed out.

Nodding, Preacher choked back his hilarity. "Yep. It sure is. An' right proud of it, I am. Weren't but five of you folks got harmed. Might be if you'd lent a hand some of them would be with us now. As fer this fine young woman, she carried her share of the load, fought bravely and did for a couple of cougars, two gladiators an' a soldier. On my tally sheet, that puts her head and shoulders your better, ma'am. Danged if it don't." Preacher's eyes widened, and he screwed up his mouth as though to spit out a wad of chew tobacco. "By damn, there I go speechifyin' like a politician. I'd best put a lid on my word bucket."

He held his peace until the cavalcade crested the saddle notch and halted on the far side. By then he had worked out what needed to be done. He called them together in the shade of a tall old pine that soughed softly in a fresh breeze. "Everybody rest some; drink a little water and eat something." Then Preacher began enlightening them on something that had been bothering him for a long while.

"The way I see it, our best chance lies with splittin' up. That way it thins out them that comes after us. Now, there's somethin' we need to decide on. I declare, that place is the foulest nest of snakes I've ever runned across. Ain't gonna change much, from what I guess. So, this nasty business has to be ended right and proper. To do that, we have to have help." He pointed to Philadelphia and Buck.

"I want you to set off to find any old wooly-eared fellers that's nestin' out there somewhere. Philadelphia, you take the west trails; Buck, you head east. I'll cut down to the southwest, find Bold Pony an' his Arapahos. A couple of those prisoners who died at the hands of Quintus' gladiators were from his band, I learned. That gives him a stake in fixin' this tainted meat. Sparticus, you done good to join us. I want you to stick with these pilgrims. Teach them more about how to fight for when the time comes they need to. Take the big trail south to Trout Creek Pass; it's well marked. We'll all rendezvous there and lay plans."

"Preacher, how do I get any of these mountain men to join us?" Buck asked.

"You tell 'em you're askin' in my name. An' I'll send along a note to that effect. Most of these boys can make out writin' good enough, an' those what can't do know my name an' my Ghost Wolf sign."

"I—I want to stay with you, Preacher," Amelia Witherspoon spoke up.

"Why, the brazenness of that—" Agatha Abercrombie began, to be cut off by a hard look from Preacher.

He shook his head as he spoke to Amelia. "No, it'll be too dangerous."

Undeterred by this logic, she continued to press her issue. "What could be more dangerous than what we just faced?"

To his surprise, Preacher did not have any quick reply for that. He mulled it over a moment. "I can't answer that, Missy. Danged if you don't argue like one o' them Philadelphia lawyers." He shot a glance at his fellow mountain man. "No offense, old friend. But, the answer is the same, Miss Amelia. Where I'm going, the Injuns mightily favor a long lock of yeller hair on their scalp poles."

"Bu—but you're friends with them; I've heard Philadelphia say so."

Preacher smiled to soften his demeanor. "We're friends when they're in the mood for it. Otherwise, they'd lift my hair, too. This time I've got a reason for them to keep right cordial. It wouldn't do, though, to provoke them before I get out my message."

Preacher turned to the rest of them, the subject closed for his part. "So, we'll all rendezvous at the tradin' post. I'll bring in the Arapaho last to prevent a panic."

Preacher took a narrow trail to the southwest when he departed from the others. Leading his packhorse, he made much better time than Sparticus and the missionaries. He was far out on the Great Divide Basin when sundown caught up with him. He made a hasty cold camp and settled in for the night. He doubted he would see anything of the soldiers from New Rome, yet he did not want a fire to betray his presence. No, he'd not see the legions of New Rome again, not until he wanted to. Far off, in the rolling hills behind him, he heard the musical call of a timber wolf.

"Hang in there, ol' feller. We's a pair, we be," he said softly to his distant brother.

That night, Preacher slept well under a blanket of stars that frosted the night as a harbinger of the coming winter.

Marcus Quintus Americus hurled a gold-rimmed wine cup across the room to splinter on the plinth of a bust of Augustus Caesar. Thin, red wine washed over it and stained the first Roman emperor purple. Shocked, Legate Varras of the cavalry watched as the liquid pooled on the marble floor.

"Are you totally incompetent? How can you come to me with a report like this?"

Varras answered mildly. "Because it is my duty, and it is the truth. Beyond the territory of New Rome, we found no trace of them. A large body of the fleeing prisoners rode south on the main trail for some while; then their tracks faded out."

He did not know of the drags that Sparticus had rigged on the last horses in the column, which spread out from side to side on the trail and obliterated every trace of their passage. It was an old trick Sparticus had learned on the Underground Railroad. It would not have fooled a Blackfoot, Cheyenne or a Sioux, but it did confound the inexperienced trackers of the cavalry legion. Quintus fumed a long, silent moment, then turned partly away from Varras. His voice dropped from its previous furious bellow.

"How could four barbarians and that lot of pitiful Christians defeat professional gladiators and outwit my well-trained soldiers to make good this escape?"

Varras was smart enough to remain silent. His first sword centurion stood rigidly at his side, helmet tucked under one arm like his commander. He cut his eyes to Varras and grimaced. Quintus collected himself after his rhetorical question.

"Well, they'll not get away with it. I want you to get out there by an hour after sundown. Best possible speed. Catch up to those vermin, kill only those you must, and bring back the rest. Take what supplies you need and don't leave any area unsearched. Now, leave me. I must talk with the commanders of the other legions."

Glaubiae and Bruno entered together. Quintus eyed them coldly, arms folded over the front of his toga. When they both grew uneasy enough, he poured wine around and handed each general a cup.

"Your health, gentlemen. I must compliment you on the thoroughness of your search of our city. Unlike that incompetent ass, Varras, who lost all trace of the fugitives, you did come up with three escaped slaves. That they were not involved with those from the coliseum is not important. Given that those condemned prisoners had already ridden out of the gates, you did the best you could. Now, I have to ask more of you. I am not convinced that we have seen the last of those miscreants. Here is what I want you to do."

He began to pace the floor as he spoke. "I want you to establish watch towers completely around the rim of this basin. Staff them with enough men to be alert around the clock. Also set up heliographs and signal fires. Have horses so a messenger can reach the city well ahead of whoever comes back." His pacing grew faster. "Set your engineers to manufacturing ballistas, catapults and arbalests."

"You are certain they will attack us?" Gaius Septimus asked.

"Of course," Quintus snapped. "I have learned only this morning that there are enough of these barbarian mountain men with savage allies to form a force that will outnumber us. The important thing is not to let the Senate and the people know that. If we are prepared, if we have advance warning, the quality of the legions and the power of some—ah—weapons I have provided will assure our victory."

That caught the interest of both generals. "What weapons are these?"

Quintus answered guardedly. "Some firearms. Also a few

cannons that will far out-perform our other artillery." A wicked smile illuminated his face.

Septimus and Bruno caught up his enthusiasm. "How many firearms? What sort of cannon?" Septimus urged.

Thinking on it, Quintus answered evasively. "Enough to tip the scale."

Bruno wasn't buying into it. "And when do we train men to use them?"

Quintus surprised him with his answer. "We start this afternoon. Now, get out of here, get orders published for what is needed, and get to work."

Buck Sears had traveled the trails of Texas, driven teams on the Santa Fe Trail, and most recently, had rented his talents to those seeking to take goods overland to the Northwest Territory. It made him fairly savvy about movement where Indians were a factor, and how to repair wagons when the nearest wheelwright or coach shop lay five hundred miles behind. It had not taught him how to find mountain men when sent to round up any who remained in the ranges of the Rocky Mountains. In fact, it was they who found him, more or less.

"You there, stumblin' around in the bush," a voice called out as Buck floundered around in an attempt to find the trail he had been following, which had abruptly disappeared a quarter of an hour earlier. The unknown voice called again.

"If you be friendly, sing out an' let us know who you might be."

"Hello. The name's Sears. Buck Sears. I'm a freight wagon teamster."

A low chuckle answered Buck, then words made soft by amusement. "You're sure an' hell a long ways from any wagon route. C'mon in, set a spell, an' have some coffee."

That completely amazed Buck. "You—uh—you've got a *camp* out here?"

"Shore enough do. Head yourself due north an' you'll run into it."

Buck blundered through the brush, leading his mount, until he came to a small clearing surrounded by ash and juniper trees. Three men sat around a stone-guarded, hat-sized fire over which a coffeepot steamed. Buck ground reined his horse and came forward.

"Well, here I am. Buck Sears."

The one who had called out to him spoke first. "M'name's Abel Williams, but folks most call me Squinty. This here's Jack Lonesome and that other feller is Three-Finger. Git yourself around some Arbuckles," he invited, with a gesture toward the blue granite pot.

"Obliged," Buck responded.

Settled on a mat of aspen leaves, Buck sipped the strongest coffee he had ever tasted, worried for the lining of his stomach, and exchanged incidentals with the three mountain men for several minutes. Then, when Squinty Williams hinted delicately at what business brought Buck into the mountains, he unveiled his story of New Rome.

They listened in amazement, doubt written plainly on their faces. Buck noted this and concluded his personal story to get to the heart of the situation. "The thing is, six years after I was taken by these lunatics, two of you mountain men were captured; Philadelphia Braddock and Preacher."

"Naw. Couldn't be," Jack Lonesome rebutted. "No amount of fellers runnin' around in skirts could best Preacher."

"All the same, it's true," Buck insisted. "He said I might run into some—ah—resistance. Sent along this note." He dug into his shirt pocket and produced the scrap of paper upon which Preacher had scribbled his appeal.

Squinty took it and peered intently at it. At last he nodded. "That's his name, right enough. An' his Ghost Wolf mark. What's it say, Jack?"

Jack Lonesome took the message and read it aloud. *This is to advise any fellers contacted by Buck Sears that we has us a large problem needs solvin' right fast. Buck will explain it to you an' I ask you to come fast to Trout Creek Pass and lend a hand. Yours for old times, Preacher.*

Squinty cocked his head to one side. "Well, I'll be damned. You got our help, Buck. Tell us about this place again; then we'll make use of the rest of this day gettin' out of here."

Buck related the final days in New Rome and what Preacher and Philadelphia were up to at the moment. All three mountain men thought on it; then Squinty came to his boots. "We know where half a dozen of our friends are fixin' to hang out for the winter. We'll go get them and then head for this rendezvous with Preacher. I ain't never seen me a man in a skirt before, but I reckon we can sure put the fear of God in a bunch of 'em."

On his fourth day away from New Rome, Philadelphia Braddock ambled into a camp in the Medicine Bow range occupied by Blue Nose Herkimer. There he also found Four-Eyes Finney, a wild Irish brawler turned mountain man; Karl "Bloody Hand" Kreuger; Nate Youngblood; and, surprisingly to him, Frenchie Dupres. After a few bear hugs, some foot stomping, and a lot of genial cussing, Philadelphia filled them in on what had been happening in the Ferris Range. Bloody Hand Kreuger did not believe it.

"Pferd Scheist! That's all it is, horse shit. I was through there back a ways, and I never saw anything like that."

"How long ago was that, Karl?" Philadelphia asked, using the German mountain man's given name because he knew Bloody Hand did not like it.

Bloody Hand thought on it a moment. "Ten . . . maybe twelve years ago."

"A lot can happen in that time. An' it surely did. That's about the time this crazy feller, calls himself Marcus Quintus Americus, came out here. Boys, I've been there, saw the buildings, took baths in a fancy buildin', and fought for my life in a place where folks come an' watch ya die for the fun of it. Preacher was there with me, like I said. Now, fellers, what'll it be? Are you goin' to join us in doin' away with this place of corruption or not?"

An old and dear friend of Preacher, Frenchie Dupres rose and dusted off the seat of his trousers. "I am ready, *mon ami.* These people sound to be *tres* evil. If Preacher needs our help, I say we give it to him."

"You can count on me," Nate Youngblood agreed.

"I'm with you, Philadelphia," Blue Nose Herkimer added.

Four-Eyes Finney tugged at a thick forelock of sandy hair. "Sure an' it sounds like a fine donnybrook. Count me in."

Although the Kraut mountain man had a long list of grievances against Preacher, Karl Kreuger sighed heavily and nodded in acceptance. "I'll go. What the hell, Preacher is one of us, and no fancy Roman is gonna put down a mountain man."

Philadelphia could not hide his happy smile. "By jing, that shines. Ya can all head out at first light; it's a ways to Trout Crick Pass. I'm leavin' now to see if I can scare up some other fellers."

19

Preacher found Bold Pony and his band settled down in their winter camp in a tidy little valley. He was welcomed with stately courtesy. Then Bold Pony noticed Preacher's injuries. He sent at once for the medicine man.

"I coulda taken care of that for myself," Preacher protested without sincerity. The poultices the shaman put on his cuts and bruises felt cool and soothing. And the Arapaho medicine man could get to the claw marks on his back better than he had been able to.

"Not while you are in my camp, friend," Bold Pony responded. "You will speak of how you received these injuries at the council fire tonight?"

"Yes. I sort of hunted you down for that exact reason. There's some mighty bad people out there that need a lesson taught them."

"We eat first. And drink coffee."

After filling himself with elk stew, Preacher sat back and belched loudly, rubbed his belly to show how much he had enjoyed it, and allowed as how he was ready to talk to the council. They gathered around a modest fire in the center of the village. Bold Pony spoke first, as was his right, then formally introduced the man well known to them. Preacher rose and addressed the council while Bold Pony translated.

He told them of New Rome and what had happened there. "Until some dozen years ago, only the Crows and the Blackfeet roamed through the Ferris Range," he began. He went on to describe the city that had grown there, of the cruelty of the people who lived in it. When he came to the games, Bold Pony used the Arapaho words for "savage" and "barbarian." That amused Preacher. Although he knew the Arapaho tongue well enough to pass the time of day, Preacher wanted to be sure the whole sordid story of New Rome came across clearly. It appeared to him that Bold Pony was doing that right enough.

Angry mutters rose when he described the Arapaho warriors who had been enslaved and killed, and added, "We sang their death songs after the gladiators finished with them." He concluded his account with the escape and an appeal for help in destroying this menace. Buffalo Whip, an aged former peace chief, rose to speak against the Arapaho involvement. "We do not know these people. They have done us no harm. Those men you told about are not of this band. It is not for us to avenge them. It is not wise to take the war trail against people who do not have anger toward us." He rambled on awhile, then repeated the admonition to avoid war.

Preacher rose again. "Thing is, they've got anger toward everyone. They call us barbarians, an' you folks, too. A feller who had been there six years told me they plan on fighting everyone out here. An' he tells the truth."

Another older councilman stood to argue against joining in Preacher's fight. A third followed him. Preacher considered that it wasn't going well. Then came the turn of some of the younger men. Yellow Hawk took his place in front of the assembly.

"There are too many white men out here now. Most are like our friend, Preacher. These men have bad hearts. They hurt women and children. I say we fight them."

Badger Tail agreed. Buffalo Whip spoke again. Two more of the fiery, youthful warriors responded, urging that a war party be organized. The debate raged on into the night. The fire burned low, and young boys, apprentice warriors, built it up again. At last, Bold Pony put a hand on Preacher's shoulder.

"You might as well take some sleep, old friend," he advised. "This will take a while."

Preacher nodded and came to his boots. Stifling a yawn, he ankled off to the lodge where he would spend the night.

Birds twittered in the trees outside the Arapaho camp while the eastern sky turned pink. Preacher emerged from a buffalo hide lodge as the velvet dome above magically turned blue overhead. He wore a huge, relaxed smile on his leathery face. He tucked his buckskin hunting shirt into the top of his trousers and paused. He turned back to wave a sappy good-bye to the occupant, one thoughtfully provided by Bold Pony, and received a very feminine giggle in reply.

After his morning needs had been taken care of, he sat down with Bold Pony to a bowl of mush that sported shreds of squirrel meat. They ate contentedly. Then Bold Pony nodded toward the center of camp, where the debaters had already begun to assemble.

"You must have other visits to make, Ghost Wolf. You may as well tend to them now. This will be a long time deciding. Go to the trading post and wait for us. We will be along, if we are coming, within two days.

* * *

In New Rome preparations for war went on at a fevered pace. The two bold legions—actually their strength compared more realistically with two understrength platoons—conducted mock battles on the Field of Mars. The Campus Martius swarmed with armed and armored troops, their faces grim and set in concentration. Centurions raised their swords in signal, and the sergeants of the *contaburniae* bellowed the command to lock shields and prepare to form the tortoise. The centurions lowered their weapons rapidly.

"Form . . . up!" the leather-lunged sergeants commanded.

At once, the soldiers in the middle of the squares raised their shields overhead, shielding themselves and the outer two ranks as well. Each *pilum* pointed outward, a hedgehog of defense. A shower of blunted arrows moaned hauntingly to the top of their arcs and descended on the shields. They clattered noisily as the brass-bossed, hardened hides shed them. At another command, the ten squads disengaged their shields and faced the same direction.

"Forward at the quick time," came the order.

At once the soldiers stepped off at a rapid pace, their javelins slanted forward. Twenty paces along the base course, the commands came again. With more assurance the formation evolved into the famous tortoise. Standing in his white chariot, its basket supports set off in gold, Marcus Quintus Americus looked on with satisfaction. His heart thundered with excitement. Elsewhere, those men who had proven to be passable marksmen drilled with the rifles. What a shock that would be when those mountain rabble returned. Gaius Septimus rode up on a white charger. The stallion snorted at the scent of its fellows drawing the chariot. Wet droplets of slobber stained the sleeve of the military tunic worn by Marcus Quintus.

"A couple more run-throughs and my legion will be ready for a cavalry charge."

"Excellent. They are learning faster than I expected, and I'm pleased."

"Here's the bad news. Some of your spies have ferreted out the information that the condemned man, Arturus, was in fact Preacher."

Color flared on Quintus' face. "By all the gods! All that while I had my hands on Preacher and did not know it? How could that have happened?"

Septimus looked embarrassed. "I suspected it when I saw him fight at the school. Yet, I had nothing to prove it."

"Who verified his identity?" Quintus demanded.

"Bulbus for one. He overheard one of the other gladiators call him that."

Quintus scowled. "The fool. He should have reported it. We could have kept him in a cell alone, and fought him differently. None of what happened would have been possible."

"And we wouldn't be running around like chickens with our heads cut off trying to prepare for war," Septimus muttered to himself.

"What was that?"

"Nothing, Quintus. I have to get back to my *primus pilus.*" His need to meet with his first spear—his adjutant— was a convenient excuse to avoid the wrath of Quintus.

Half an hour later, a messenger came from Glaubiae to say that his troops were ready for the cavalry. He sent the man on to another part of the Field of Mars, where the mounted troops had been practicing. With whoops of glee, they whirled into attack formation and rumbled across the turf toward the defensive squares of the Thirteenth Legion. A shower of javelins hurtled toward them.

Quickly the spear carriers resupplied the hurlers, and the squares bristled like aroused porcupines. By design, the spears landed short, albeit not *too* short. Marcus Quintus was tickled pink. Not a waver. Not a man broke formation. Those Celtic fools called the plains barbarians the finest light cavalry in the world. Let them come up against the tactics of the legions and see what happens to them. The cavalry whirled and made another approach.

Again the rain of javelins broke their charge. Suddenly the tortoises broke apart and the legionnaires counterattacked, the keen edges of their *gladiae* striking blue-white ribbons from the autumn sun. They descended on the stalled cavalry and began to break into man-to-man duels. Dust became a blinding curtain, from which only sparks from upraised swords could be seen. Quintus knew that Septimus and his officers would be judging the effectiveness of both forces and was not surprised when a *buccina* sounded to end the battle.

Proud of their ability, Varras, the cavalry *legio,* trotted his men forward to salute the First Citizen. Marcus Quintus was beaming with satisfaction, thrilled with how well this mismatched rabble had welded themselves into a disciplined army. That pleasure ended quickly when he recognized his eleven-year-old son, in full armor, in the front rank of cavalry, face begrimed, sweat trickling from under his helmet. It instantly struck him that the boy had been fighting among all the others.

Riveted by that thought, he advanced to the next obvious revelation. *He could have been killed!* For all their well-conducted performance, the legionnaires were only partly trained. One could have gotten carried away, gone farther than orders allowed. And Faustus could be lying on the ground, bleeding, or headless. It chilled his blood and brought an imperceptible shudder to his burly frame. Before he could control himself and rethink the situation, he burst out with a bellow.

"Quintus Faustus, get out of there!"

Faustus could not believe what he had heard "But, Father, I . . ."

Imperiously, Quintus pointed to the driver's position in his chariot. "Get off that horse, come over here, and get in this chariot."

"But, Father, Varras said it was all right, that I would be safe."

Blood boiling, Quintus narrowed his eyes. "There is no such thing as 'safe' in a battle. Even in practice, mistakes happen."

Faustus' voice rose to a near whine. "Father, *please!* I'm not a baby anymore."

"Come here now!"

Faustus swung a bare leg over the neck of his mount and hung from the saddle, to drop to the ground. He walked stiff-legged across the space that separated him from the chariot. With each step his face turned from white to a deeper red. His lower lip slid out in a pout until he discovered it; then he sucked it in and bit it with small, even teeth. The first tears slid down his cheeks as he reached one large wheel of the two-person vehicle. The driver stepped to the ground, and Quintus snapped at him.

"Bring that horse and come with me," he commanded. To a thoroughly frightened Varras, he growled, "I'll see you later at the palace, Varras."

He said not a word while he drove straight to the palace. There he started to lecture Faustus, who bolted and ran off sobbing, to cry his heart out. Still disgruntled by how he had handled the situation, Quintus found little sympathy from his wife.

Titiana Pulcra stared unbelievingly at her husband. Small, slim hands on her hips, she stamped one slender, sandaled foot. "How could you, Quintus? To humiliate the boy in front of all those soldiers like that is unconscionable. It could have a terrible effect on my son. It could even make him into a sissy."

Burning with his own demons, Quintus turned deaf ears to his wife's protests. This impending war would be the ruin of him yet. *Goddamn you, Preacher!* he thought furiously.

* * *

Vickie reached across the darkened room and lightly touched her brother on the arm. "Terry, Preacher's comin' back," she whispered.

"Who told you that?" Terry asked crossly.

"Nobody. I just . . . *know.*"

"You an' your knowin' things," Terry heaped in scorn. "It's like you sayin' he was in real big danger. A body can't know those sort of things."

Vickie defended herself staunchly. "Well, I can. I sort of . . . feel things. Preacher's been hurt, too. I know that, so there."

"How'd he get hurt, smarty?"

Tears threatened in Vickie's words. "Oh, Terry, I can't tell you that. I don't know how I know these things."

Terry pondered that a moment. "What do you suppose we should do?"

The tears leaked through this time. "Don't ask me. That's for you to figger out."

Pausing a long moment in the dark night, Terry turned that over in his head. "Why don't we go to meet him?"

"We don't know where he's coming from," Vickie objected.

"Yes, we do. He went north from here when he left us our new clothes. We'll just go north."

"Really? Do you think it will work?"

"We won't know unless we try. And we can't tell anyone."

"When do we go?"

"Tomorrow."

Sister Amelia Witherspoon stood in the center of camp. Another two days to reach this trading post. She remembered one they had come upon along the North Platte River. Low-slung buildings, with crude thatch roofs, smelly and dirty inside, hardly more than a poor excuse for a saloon. It reeked of stale beer, spilled whiskey, greasy food and human sweat. She had almost gagged when she entered.

If they had not needed supplies so desperately, she would have prevailed upon the new Deacon Abercrombie to pass this pestilential place by. Thought of their former leader, and how he had died, brought a pang to her heart and a lump to her throat. She swallowed hard, hoping she would not break into tears, because she also recalled that he had betrayed them when the first attempt had been made to escape. And that brought her to Preacher.

Oh, how handsome he had looked when he left them on the trail. She remembered him as a shining knight in buckskin on that day he rode off from them, for all his disreputable appearance. She wondered how he would look when he had washed off all that blood, dirt, grease and powder grime, and had a chance to shave. She would find out when he reached the trading post and rejoined them. She could hardly wait.

A sharp report of a pistol from across the campsite drew her away from her favorite subject. Laughter followed. "Brother Lewis, you're supposed to take that thing out of the holster before you pull the trigger."

A thoroughly shaken, crimson-faced young missionary stood with a group of those who had elected to continue to fight. Smoke ringed his knees, and Amelia saw the splintered leather at the bottom of the holster fastened at his waist. Poor Lewis Biggs, she thought. He had always been so clumsy. Only now he could get seriously injured, or even killed, for it. If only Preacher were here to teach them.

That brought back images of the lean mountain man. His eyes normally held a far-off look, as though he saw things a thousand yards away. She really knew so little about him. Though she had heard plenty of wild stories from Sparticus, her practical side found little of it credible. Like wrestling with a bear and killing the beast with a knife. Or leading a wagon train of women from Missouri to the Northwest Territory. No one man, no matter how able and clever, could do that alone.

Which got her to wondering how Preacher had resisted the charms of so many unattached ladies. With a shiver of delight, she thought how much she would like it if Preacher succumbed to *her* charms. Her missionary zeal abandoned, Amelia imagined those strong arms around her, holding her tight, his full lips pressed to hers. She wondered how her somewhat bony, angular body would be fitted to his hard, muscular frame. Oh, when would they reach the trading post? When would Preacher join them?

20

Trout Creek Pass looked mighty good to Preacher when he reached the trading post there three days later. One-Eye Avery Tookes spotted him first and let out a whoop. That brought his partner Bart Weller, Bloody Hand Kreuger, Squinty Williams, Blue Nose Herkimer and Frenchie Dupres. The others were out hunting game for the table. The back slaps, shoulder punches, elbow rib gouges, to say nothing of the general jumping up and down and stomping the ground, went on for a good fifteen minutes.

"We heard you was lookin' for fellers to join a real, ring-tailed mixup, Preacher," One-Eye Avery Tookes declared when the welcoming calmed some and the participants had repaired to the inside of the saloon.

"That I am, Ave." Preacher allowed. "Philadelphia an' me got ourselves in one hell of a fix up north in the Ferris Range."

Three of the mountain men rounded up mugs and dispensed whiskey and foaming flagons of beer while the others pressed close around. Frenchie Dupres spoke for them all.

"We learned some of it from Philadelphia, Preacher, but we would like to hear it from you."

Preacher studied on it a moment, downed half a mug of beer to soothe the trail dust from his craw, then launched into the story of New Rome. "Seems there's this feller, 'bout three beaver shy of a lodge, who's took it in his mind that he's the emperor of Rome. Built him a right accurate copy of the ancient town in this big valley in the Ferris Range." He went on to describe the highlights of the stay he and Philadelphia had endured.

Several times, one or another of the mountain men would interrupt with a question. Through it all, only Karl Bloody Hand Kreuger maintained a skeptical expression. When Preacher concluded, he spoke slowly, through a thick German accent.

"Dot don't zound right. Vhy haff vun of us not seen dis place in der twelf years you zay it has been there?"

Preacher gave him the benefit of a one-eyed squint. "How many pelts have you taken in the past dozen years, Bloody Hand?" he asked mildly. "For that matter, how many of us has been in the Ferris Range in the same time?"

Shaken heads answered him. It urged Preacher to push on a little further. "You all know the fur trade is dead as last year's squirrel stew. There ain't a one of us what has made a living entire off of takin' beaver. Shoot, there ain't even enough beaver for us to harvest them like we used to." He paused to pour off the last of the beer. "Monongahela rye, Duffey," he called to the barkeep. Then he turned back to Bloody Hand Kreuger.

"Now, you listen to me, Bloody Hand. I seened all that with my own eyes. So'd Philadelphia and that young 'prentice, Buck Sears. An' that reminds me. If Buck ain't got him a handle hung on him already, I reckon to call him Long Spear."

That brought hoots of laughter. Blue Nose Herkimer

asked through his chortles, "Is that for what I think it is, Preacher?"

Preacher pulled a face of mock disappointment in his fellow men. "No. It ain't. It's because he done some fierce fightin' with one of them *pilum* things the Roman soldiers use in their army." He downed a respectable swallow of whiskey, smacked his lips and continued. "Buck ain't near as good as some of us; but he's got sand, and he carries his own weight an' then some. He learns quick. And we need every gun we can get for this fight with the crazy Romans."

"Vhy vould anyone lif dot vay?" Kreuger pressed, disbelief plain in his small pig eyes.

Preacher cocked his head to one side, sipped more rye. "Y'know, that's a question I asked myself a good many times. Don't seem that anyone a-tall, with any brains worth countin', would put up with the loco things this feller calls hisself Marcus Quintus Americus expects of 'em. They dress in these outlandish clothes, all robes and nightshirt-lookin' things, and wear sandals, too, like them brown-robed friars come through the Big Empty back in Thirty-one, weren't it? Why, their soldiers even wear skirts."

That proved too much for Bloody Hand Kreuger. "I told Philadelphia that dis vas horse shit, *und* dot's vhat it iss. *Pferd Scheist!* No zoldiers vear zkirts."

Preacher's dark gray eyes turned to flint. "You callin' me a liar, Bloody Hand?"

Kreuger, who had already decided it was a good time to take Preacher to task, barked a single word. *"Fawohl!"*

Preacher downed the last of his Pennsylvania whiskey and dusted dry palms together. "Well, then, let's get to the dance."

"Outside! Take it outside," a nervous Ruben Duffey shouted from behind the bar.

"More'n glad to oblige, Duffey," Preacher told him amiably.

He started to rise, then shifted his weight and lashed out his booted foot in one swift movement. The dusty sole caught the chair in which Kreuger sat at the center lip of the seat and spilled it over backward. Preacher got on him at once. He grabbed the confused and startled German by the back of his wide belt and scruff of shirt collar and made a speedy little run toward the front door. Kreuger dangled in Preacher's powerful arms, feet clear of the floor.

With appropriate violence, the batwings flew outward when Kreuger's head collided with them. Preacher took quick aim and hurled his human cargo into the street. The Kraut mountain man landed in a puddle of mud and horse droppings at the tie rail. Immediately Kreuger let the world, and Preacher in particular, know his opinion of being so used.

"Verdammen unehrliche Geburt!"

"Oh, now, Bloody Hand, you know better than to call Preacher a damned bastard," Frenchy Dupres observed dryly from the porch of the trading post saloon.

A few chuckles went the rounds; then the fight turned serious. Kreuger came to his boots shedding road apples and urine-made mud. Before he could locate his enemy, Preacher walked up from behind him and gave him a powerful shove that sent Kreuger back into the quagmire.

Hoots of laughter ran among the mountain men. Kreuger's face went so darkly red as to look black. On hands and knees he crawled toward the dry, hard-packed ground. Unwilling to lose an important good shot in so critical a battle as the one he visualized upcoming, Preacher determined to go easy on Kreuger. He knew the cause of some of the bad blood between them, yet had not seen the man in some while and could only guess at what other grievances and faults the German had assigned to him. On the other hand, Kreuger sincerely believed this to be the time to tumble Preacher from his high perch, to show him to be no more than any other man. Through the red haze of his fury, he spotted his foe.

Springing quickly to his boots, Kreuger swung a looping left that connected with the point of Preacher's shoulder. Preacher shed it easily, then whanged a hard fist that mushed Kreuger's mouth. Blood flew in a nimbus that haloed Kreuger's head. The huge, bullet-headed German absorbed the force of Preacher's blow and took a chance kick at the mountain legend's groin.

Preacher saw it coming and danced aside. He whooped and jumped in the air, waggling one open hand under his chin at Bloody Hand. Kreuger stared at Preacher uncomprehendingly. On the way down, Preacher enlightened the Kraut as to the purpose of his childish taunt. His target sufficiently distracted, he swiftly jabbed two of those extended fingers toward the man's eyes.

Kreuger recoiled so violently that he tottered off balance. Preacher's boot toes lightly touched when he launched a one-two combination at the midsection of Karl Kreuger. Dust puffed from the buckskin shirt Kreuger wore as the piston fists connected in a rapid tattoo. Grunting, he rocked on back. He went over his center and plopped to the ground on his rump. Anxious to end this before harming even this uncertain an asset, Preacher swiftly stepped in on Kreuger.

Only too far!

A well-aimed kick from Kreuger landed deeply in Preacher's groin. Sheer agony radiated outward from Preacher's throbbing crotch. When the yawning pit of blackness receded from his mind, Preacher recovered himself in time to clap his open palms against the sides of Kreuger's head. So much for going easy, he thought grimly.

Their fight turned deadly serious. Not that Preacher would willingly go so far as to kill Kreuger, so long as the German mountain man would let him avoid it. Howling in pain, Kreuger dived forward and wrapped his arms around Preacher's legs. Digging in with a shoulder, he drove Preacher off his boots. Preacher landed heavily. Dust rose around him as he tried to suck in air.

Kreuger did not give him the chance to fully recover. He climbed Preacher's legs, grunting and growling as he went. Savagely, he bit Preacher in the thigh. Then his forward progress got halted abruptly with a sledgehammer fist. Preacher drove it down on his opponent's crown with all the force in him. A shower of colored lights went off in Kreuger's head. Preacher heaved mightily and sent his antagonist flying. Wincing to hold back a cry of agony, Preacher came upright and stepped over to Kreuger.

"Give it up, Bloody Hand. This ain't fittin'. We got us a whole wagon load of trouble out there we need to be facin' together."

"You go to hell, Preacher."

Their fight might have gone on longer had not the long-expected arrival of the missionaries put a quicker end to it. They streamed in through the stockade gate as Kreuger sputtered out his defiance. In the lead, Sparticus halted them abruptly with a raised hand.

"No need mixin' up in that folks. Preacher, he got ever'thin' in hand."

And indeed it appeared he had. After Kreuger's outburst, sthe German forward while he pile drivered a big right to the broad forehead below an unruly shock of wheat straw hair. The birdies sang loudly between Kreuger's ears. Groggily he tried to get his feet under him. Preacher shook him like a rag doll.

Kreuger pawed at Preacher's arm. Preacher punched him again. Kreuger went rigid, and his eyes rolled up in their sockets. He sighed wearily, and his legs twitched a few seconds before he went still and limp.

Amelia Witherspoon looked on in mingled admiration and horror. She reached out a hand now to touch Sparticus lightly on the arm. "That man? He isn't dead, is he?"

"New, Missy Sister Amelia. I figger Preacher to be a more careful man than that. I also reckon he be mighty glad to see you again."

Amelia flushed. A hand flew to her mouth. "Do—do you think so?"

"Pert' near a certain thing," Sparticus answered with confidence as the downed man recovered consciousness.

Kreuger started to roundly curse Preacher, and Amelia covered her ears with her hands. Her eyes went wide when Preacher treated the swearing man like one would a foul-mouthed boy. The sound of Preacher's backhand slap cracked through the chill, high mountain air.

"Lighten up, Bloody Hand, or you'll be sleepin' with a pitchfork in your hands tonight."

"Go diddle yourzelf, you zon of a—" The hand returned with more punishment.

"I'm gonna leave it at this, Kreuger. Someone dump a bucket of water over this sorehead. It'll cool him off." Preacher turned to walk away, only to stop in surprise. "Well, I'll be. You folks been there long?"

"Long enough," Amelia Witherspoon responded snappishly, only to stop and blush in confusion as she realized how in conflict were her spinsterish words of criticism and the emotions in her heart.

Preacher cut his eyes to a spot on the ground somewhere between them. "I apologize for what you had to witness. That man's got him a mean one like a boil. You folks got here without any trouble?"

"We did," she responded, then gushed out her true feelings, "and I'm so glad you're here."

It became Preacher's turn to be embarrassed. "Aw, that's kind of you to say, but I ain't nothin' special."

Crimson glowed in Amelia's cheeks. "I think you are," she gushed out.

She reached out a hand, and to her surprised relief, Preacher took it. Without another word, the lean, powerful mountain man led her away into the woods behind the trading post.

"I'm cold."

Terry looked at his sister, seated across the small fire from him. "So am I."

"It will be winter soon," Vickie added meaningfully.

"I know that. We've just got to find Preacher."

Vickie offered an unwelcome suggestion. "We could always go back?"

"No, we can't. We stole and lied to those folks. It wouldn't be fittin'."

"They'd understand, Terry. I'm cold and hungry and so tired. Why haven't we found Preacher yet?"

Frustration at his failure goaded Terry. "I don't know. Leave it alone, will you?" He thought it over awhile, forced himself past pride and stubbornness. "I tell you what. We'll wait it out two more days, keep going north. If we don't find Preacher by then, we . . . we can start back."

"But I want to go back now. I'm scared out here, Terry."

Terry sighed off a heavy burden for a twelve-year-old. "All right. I'll take you back. At least until we're in sight of the house. Then I'm headed for the tradin' post."

Over the next day, some ten long-legged, rangy men clustered in the trading post compound. Well accustomed to the rigors of the High Lonesome, they had heard the call for aid for a fellow and dropped what they worked upon and headed to the small settlement. To Preacher's surprised relief, that swelled their number to thirty-five. Now, if only the Arapaho came in, they stood a chance, he reasoned. Amelia Witherspoon provided him pleasant distraction from the preparations for war.

They sat under a huge juniper, redolent with the scent of resin and ripe berries. There had not yet been a sharp frost, so the small, round balls, which served as the base flavor in what the English called geneva, had not turned their characteristic dark blue. Amelia had brought a picnic basket, and they lunched on cold fried chicken and boiled turnips. When the last crumbs of a pie had been devoured, she got to the heart of her purpose in being there.

"I know that those people are simply awful, sinful and terribly vicious. But isn't it up to our army to do something about them?"

Preacher snorted. "I ain't seen a soldier-boy in nigh onto a year an' more. They keeps to their little block-house forts and ride the Santa Fe Trail to protect what folks back east call commerce. Now that Santa Fe, an' all New Mexico, is American, business is boomin'. That's what the politicians will want the soldiers to guard. I hear there's even talk of openin' a stagecoach line. *Civilization,"* he spat. "It gums up ever'thin' wherever it goes."

Amelia smiled and patted him on the arm. "I'm not so sure. People are . . . so much more tranquil in the East."

"Controlled, you mean. I've been there. It's like one great big prison. A feller can't carry a shootin' iron down the street without being gawked at, or even arrested in some places. Folks that live like that ain't free."

"But they are safe, and protected."

Preacher looked long and hard at her. "Miss Amelia, I don't mean to pry, or to offend, but that makes me wonder. If that be the case, then why in tarnation did you folk come out here?"

Amelia tried to find the right tone of answer and failed.

Instead, she laughed and leaned a shoulder against Preacher. "You have me there, Preacher. I could say it was our calling. Or that adventure beckoned. Truth to tell, I suppose it was to be away from the strictures of society." She frowned and returned to her original theme. "Though, when I think of the price to be paid, the terrible things that happened to Deacon Abercrombie and the others, all the blood spilled—and more to come. It makes me question the purpose behind fighting those sick people out there."

Preacher's voice took on an edge. "Because we're the only ones to do it, Miss Amelia. An' it dang-sure needs doing." He bent in the silence that followed to help her pick up the picnic leavings.

Back at the trading post, Karl Kreuger nursed his bruises and aches and avoided eye contact with Preacher. He would go along, he allowed. "Because I giff my vord."

The next day, three more mountain men straggled into the gathering. That called for another whooping, foot-stomping, powerful drinking welcome. The assorted company had hardly settled down when a lone Arapaho warrior appeared at the gate to the compound. Preacher went out to greet him.

"Yellow Hawk, it is good to see you."

Yellow Hawk returned Preacher's sign of greeting and made the one for peace. "It is good to see you, Ghost Wolf. We have come. There are six hands of warriors from the village of Bold Pony and four hands from the village of the people who lost their braves to the Ro-mans."

Fifty warriors, Preacher tallied. Better than he had hoped for. He nodded his acceptance. "We number nearly as many. More will be picked up on the trail. An' maybe some of my Cheyenne friends would like to get in on this."

Yellow Hawk made a face. All was not love and roses between the Arapaho and the Cheyenne. Yet, they had fought together before and perhaps would again. He signed acceptance. Preacher read the thoughts of Yellow Hawk on his stern visage. No matter. They would get along or not. The Cheyenne could always fight alongside the mountain men.

"Bring 'em on in. You can make camp outside the stockade. We leave tomorrow at first light."

A bit after mid-afternoon the next day, Preacher came upon a complication that left his jaw sagging a moment before he let go a low, controlled roar. "What in hell are you doin' here, boy?"

Saucy as ever, Terry Tucker stood at the side of the road, face beaming, while he waved at the man he so admired. "I want to go with you, Preacher."

Preacher's eyes narrowed. "We've been over this before. Where's your sister?"

"I took her back, then come to find you."

'Back? That mean the both of you runned off?"

"Yes, sir. We tried to find you north of here. Saw a lot of fellers dressed like you, but you didn't come along. Vickie got scared and tired and so I took her back. I can come along, can't I?"

"No. Not only no, but hell no."

Terry looked as though he might cry. "I want to join the fight. I can do it, you know that. I—I'm grateful to you for helping Vickie an' me escape a life of crime, and I want to make amends. I can do odd jobs around the camp, care for the horses, that sort of thing."

What a quandary. Preacher removed his old, slouch hat and scratched the crown of his head with a thick fingernail. "I swear I don't know what to do with you. It's more than dangerous where we're going. I've been there onecst an' it ain't no pony ride. Still . . ." he faded off, considering the alternatives. "I can't spare a man to return you. Nor can I trust you to go on your own, given your stubborn outlook. So, I reckon you'll have to come along."

Terry's face came alive, and he gave a little jump of joy. "Really? Oh, Preacher, thank you."

Preacher bent toward the boy. "You'll not be thankin' me five days from now when we run into them Romans. Now, you cain't walk all the way. We got to scare up a horse for you."

With the same coy expression, an impish light in his clear, blue eyes, Terry asked the identical question he had put to Preacher before. "Why can't I ride with you?"

Laughing, Preacher reached for the boy. "I suppose we can make an exception this one time. At least until I can scare up another mount." He swung the boy aboard Cougar, noting that the improved victuals had added to Terry's weight.

Messengers arrived at the palace from the watch towers on a regular schedule. The one that was just shown in to Marcus Quintus brought worrisome news.

"Reporting from Watch Tower Three, First Citizen. We have observed increased movement by the red savages to the east. All appear to be men, heavily armed and moving to the south."

Quintus scowled. That did not sound good at all. "Do you have a count of them?"

"Yes, sir. They number approximately thirty-six."

"Not an exact figure?" Quintus goaded.

Independent service in an isolated command had loosened the reins of discipline for the messenger. "We weren't about to send someone out to parlay with them and count heads, sir."

Anger flared for a moment in Quintus; then he regained control. "No. Of course not. Standing orders remain not to provoke the savages. I wonder where they are heading?"

21

Some ten miles out into the Great Divide Basin, Preacher's small army came upon the advance scouts of the Cheyenne party seeking them. Some grumbling ran through the Arapaho warriors at this, though the two war party leaders, Yellow Hawk and Blind Beaver, kept their men in check. Crow Killer, leader of the Cheyenne, had been a small boy when Preacher first met him. That had been over twenty years ago. He still had the sunny disposition and good sense of humor of his childhood, and greeted Preacher warmly.

"I thought you to be with the Great Spirit by now, Preacher."

"You ain't no spring chicken yourself," Preacher growled good-naturedly.

Crow Killer made a face. "Have you grown as mean as you have old?"

"Dang right. An' fit to wrassel a griz." Preacher let go a big guffaw. "How'er ya doin', Crow Killer?"

"I have a wife now, and three children."

Preacher blinked and cocked his head to one side. "Is that

a fact? You had no more than thirteen summers the last time I saw you."

"It has been a long time, Ghost Walker. I have twice that number of summers now."

"An' three youngins. You got started early."

Crow Killer cracked a white smile. "I went on the war trail first time the summer after you hunted buffalo with our village. I took a wife five summers later."

Grinning, Preacher shook his head knowingly. "Ah, but it is the winters that count in catchin' babies, right?"

Grinning, the Cheyenne motioned his men into the column. "We scout for you, Preacher?"

"Yes, that would be good."

Crow Killer's next words surprised Preacher. "We saw these people you go to fight."

"Did you now? When was this?"

"Three suns ago. We rode past their valley of shining lodges. They make ready to take the war trail. Aha! We have known of it for some time. We did not know how evil these men are, so we left them alone. I will grow much honor fighting at your side."

"The honor is mine," Preacher responded modestly. "What can you tell me from what you saw?"

Crow Killer considered it. "They have built some platforms, like burial racks, put up on the ridge around their basin."

"Watch towers. Reckon they saw you?"

"Oh, yes. We did not try to hide."

Preacher chuckled at that. "That must have given ol' Marcus Quintus a tizzy."

"Who? I do not know that name."

"The he-coon that runs that strange place. Injuns make him nervous."

Crow Killer scanned the ranks of Arapaho and his own Cheyenne. "Then he will soon be very nervous."

Laughing together, they rode on. An hour before sundown, the column pulled into a circle, the Arapaho and Cheyenne on the outer two rings, and settled in for the night. Two of the Cheyenne scouts had taken a small elk, and the savory odor of roasting meat filled the air inside the camp-site. Most of the mountain men had brought along ample supplies of stoneware jugs full of whiskey, and the mood became festive. Not so for Preacher and the more experienced among them, nor for the Indian leaders.

"We can't let any of them Arapaho or Cheyenne get a hand on that likker. We'd have us one hell of a war on our hands if they did. Keep a good watch," Preacher advised the war leaders, Philadelphia, and Frenchie Dupres.

Early the next morning, Terry Tucker rode beside Preacher. Blind Beaver noted this and rode over. "You have a son now, also, Preacher?"

Preacher looked surprised, then embarrassed. "No. Not likely. It—it's just something that growed to me." For all his denial, Preacher gave Terry a wink.

Blind Beaver beamed. "I have two. One is five summers, the other one. The other is a girl. And she is beautiful."

"I'm sure she is." Preacher gave Blind Beaver a hard, direct look. "When we make camp tonight, we will hold council. I want to paint a word picture of how we will attack these bad men."

Grunting in agreement, Blind Beaver made his thoughts known. "It is good. Are they truly Moon Children?"

Preacher considered it. "I don't think so. Ol' Marcus Quintus might be a lot tetched, but he's sane enough to know right from wrong. So do the others. I figger it this way. They're just lettin' themselves go. The pleasures evil can offer can be mighty temptin'."

"Most true, *mon ami*," Frenchie Dupres agreed from the other side.

"Tell me about this boy," Blind Beaver urged Preacher.

Preacher reached out and ruffled Terry's white hair. "He's a stray. Attached himself to me a while back an' I found a home for him and his sister. Now he's run off to help me in this fight."

"You are young for your first war party," Blind Beaver told Terry in Arapaho, with Preacher translating.

"I'm twelve," Terry responded sharply, with only a hint of his usual defiance.

"When I had twelve summers, I still used a boy's bow and hunted rabbits."

"It was meant as a compliment," Preacher added to his translation.

Terry surprised Preacher yet again with his depth of diplomacy. "I'd really rather be."

"You are brave. You will do well," Blind Beaver told the boy. Then, to Preacher he added, "I will go forward, see what has been found."

What the Cheyenne scouts had found would astonish all of them.

Only the day before, one century of Varras' cavalry (actually only fifty-seven men, not one hundred) had at last discovered the tracks left by the fleeing missionaries. They followed it to the southeast now, hungering for contact. Shouted jests as to what they would do to the survivors flew through the air, flung from their mouths by a quick canter. Their concentration so centered on the anticipated targets, they failed to take note of an eagle feather that seemed to flutter incongruously from the center of a large sage bush.

A close study of that out-of-place object would have informed them that the tip had been dyed red. So had the white goose fletchings on the arrows the watcher carried, the shafts of which bore two red bands of paint and one yellow. The watcher's cousins, the Sioux, called them *Sahiela*—which translates loosely into English as "they-come-red"—and the white men called them Cheyenne.

Red Hand had been scouting ahead for hours, and had only swung directly back onto the trail a short while ago. He lived, as did all his brothers, by "Indian time" which took no notice of seconds, minutes, or hours, only of day and night, before high sun and after, of suns (days) and moons (months). So he had no exact idea how long he had ridden forward before his keen hearing picked up the rumble of many mounted men. Alerted, he guided his pony off the trail and dismounted.

His experience quickly led him to the large clump of sage, and he concealed himself there. A hundred heartbeats later, these strange men rode into view. Were they contraries? What odd clothing. That bright red cloth could be seen for miles. And only four hands of them carried bows. What sort of warriors were they? He waited until they had ridden far beyond his hiding place. Then he came out of the brush, gathered dry sticks, and clumps of green grass.

Quickly Red Hand built a small fire. When it went well, he weighted two corners of a blanket with stones, threw the greenery on the blaze and covered it with the square of cloth. He counted heartbeats, then quickly raised the blanket. A large ball of smoke formed and drifted lazily upward. He waited, fed the fire, then repeated the process twice. Crow Killer would soon know.

Crow Killer returned to the mixed column of mountain men and Indians at a gallop. His pony snorted and stamped hooves in excitement at the run when the Cheyenne war leader reined in. He had plenty to tell.

"You weren't gone long," Preacher dryly observed.

"You saw the smokes?"

Preacher nodded.

"There are many. I watched them. Two of my scouts are behind them, to give warning if more come."

Preacher nodded again and spat a blade of grass from his mouth. "That is wise. I'd as leave have half our men behind them, catch 'em in a box. How many?"

"Five two-hands and a hand more and two."

Pursing his lips, Preacher thought on that. "Sure it's the Romans?"

"Yes. All on ponies."

Preacher planned quickly. "Chances one or two will get away from the fight that's sure to come. Wouldn't do for them to know us boys was out here. I hate to turn down a battle with those devils first off, but it's best if they think it's only Injuns. Bold Pony has some good men with the rifle. How about you?"

"I have three hands who are good at it."

"Fine, fifteen more rifles will sure help. I'll get the Arapaho ready, and you set up your warriors. Have 'em try to pot the leaders first off. This ain't for honor, it's for revenge."

Crow Killer's face indicated he didn't think much of that, though he readily agreed. "That is how it will be done."

"Good. Remember, no individual challenges or fights until the leaders are knocked out of the saddle."

After explaining his plan to Bold Pony, Preacher set about convincing the throng of mountain men. "I know this won't sit well with a lot of you. But we've got to keep our intentions hidden from any of the Romans who get away."

Karl Kreuger seized on that. "Vhat are you talking about?"

"There's about fifty-five, sixty Roman cavalry on their way. The Injuns are gonna take them on. Chances are some will get away. They can't take it back to New Rome that we have this large a force. Plain an' simple. We hide over that ridge behind us until the thing is done. No exceptions."

"Who appointed you general?" Kreuger growled.

"I did," Preacher answered simply. "Now, we'd best be moving. Them boys in the red capotes is not far away."

Preacher watched the Roman cavalry approach through his long, brass spyglass. First to appear over the ridge that masked off the swale they had so recently occupied came the horsehair-plumed helmets and tossing heads of the mounts. The men showed next. They rode at a canter, uphill. *Stupid,* Preacher thought.

When the Romans reached the bottom of the reverse slope, the centurion in charge raised his hand in the universal signal to halt. Changing his field of view, Preacher saw the reason why. A dozen Cheyenne warriors had risen out of the tall grass, as though sprang new from the earth itself. They held drawn bows, the arrowheads angled high, to reach for the enemy. *Clever,* Preacher thought.

Sounding like nothing more than the cry of a shrike, the centurion issued his command, echoed by the sergeants. Swords hissed out of scabbards and made pillars of brightness in the sunlight. Another birdlike command and the sergeants separated their squads from the square formation they had traveled in so far. It also identified all of the leaders to the patient Cheyenne. *Idiotic,* Preacher thought.

From hidden locations on the flanks, puffs of smoke rose from the grass. There followed a fraction of a second, and the four sergeants went off their horses, dead before they struck the ground. The crack of discharging rifles followed Preacher's ears. The centurion wavered in his saddle, shot through the breastplate. *Brilliant,* Preacher thought.

Left in confusion, the soldiers milled about, their horses made fractious by the smell of blood. Then they were given something to concentrate upon. The meadow came alive with Cheyenne and Arapaho warriors. Their horses snorted as they rolled upright and came to their hooves. Another volley sounded from the hidden marksmen. Arrows flew from the twelve on foot. Swiftly the Indians mounted their ponies. Before the cavalry soldiers realized it, they found themselves the target of a whooping, hooting, lance-waving Indian charge. *Magnificent,* Preacher thought.

Since the advent of the horse, standard tactics for most plains tribes consisted of swift, powerful charges to ring the wagons of white settlers, or an enemy village, then close the diameter with a gradual inward spiral. Or of individual challenges and man-to-man, vicious hand-to-hand combat. Indians, Preacher had ample reason to know, rarely fought in organized, disciplined ranks. Almost anything could end the fighting: victory, or a perception of bad medicine, or omens like an owl flying in daylight, to a sudden chill wind. Pity the poor pilgrims coming after him, Preacher thought, if this fight today changed all that.

It didn't appear that it would, Preacher acknowledged as he watched, telescope at his side now, while the cavalry formation disintegrated through attrition and the Arapaho and Cheyenne braves picked out individuals to challenge. One by one, the kilted fighting men of New Rome met death at the hands of the Indians. Only seven of them managed to keep their wits long enough to make an escape. One of those lost his chance to a long-range rifle shot. Their commander fared even worse.

Frightfully wounded, he much preferred the peace of the grave to the torture and torment that capture meant. He had heard the stories, of course, and chose the only sensible alternative. He removed his cuirass, reversed his *gladius* and pressed the pommel to the ground, then fell on his sword.

Blind Beaver appeared at Preacher's side. "In the end, he was a woman," he stated scornfully of the centurion. Preacher thought that made a good sum-up of the entire battle, which had not lasted fifteen minutes by his big Hambleton turnip watch.

During the next two days, seventeen more denizens of the High Lonesome wandered in. The word had spread far and wide. Duke Morrison was among them. As was Bunny Tilitson and Haymaker Norris. The Duke approached Preacher during the nooning rest.

"Are you serious about these—"

Preacher cut him off. "Yeah, yeah, them Romans is real enough. D'ya check the trophies our Arapaho an' Cheyenne allies collected off the cavalry?"

"No, but I'll have me a look."

Eyeing the younger mountain man, Preacher reached a conclusion. "Duke, yu'rt purty nigh expert at slippin' an' slidin' around after dark, ain'tcha?"

Modesty commanded that Duke eye the ground beyond Preacher's shoulder. "I've done my share of dark-time stalkin'. You don't intend on *sneakin'* up on these Romans, do you?"

"Yep. On some of 'em at least. Now that you're here, it comes to mind that we ought to do somethin' about these outposts I hear the Romans done put up. Best done at night."

Duke nodded. "You're right on that, Preacher. When do we have a go at it?"

"Reckon you an' me, an' a couple of Bold Pony's boys ought to pull out early tomorrow, get a day or so ahead of the rest. Then we can have a look around and see what can be done."

A broad grin spread the full lips of the big man. "I say that shines. Count me in."

* * *

Shortly before nightfall, two days later, Preacher and Duke Morrison crested the notch that separated them from the New Rome basin by but another valley and ridge. Careful to remain behind a screen of trees, they made a detailed study of the saw-tooth line across the way. After a seemingly long two minutes, Preacher lowered his spyglass. He pointed at a shadowy object partially obscured by tree limbs.

"A watch tower, right enough. I reckon they'll be spread around so's to overlap a slight bit of the view from one to another. I counted six men. Most likely there's some snoozin', an' a couple who act as messengers."

"I saw another tower," Duke revealed. "It looked to have the arms of one of those whatchamacallits—you know, a signal thing."

"A heliograph, or something like it, eh?"

"Yeah. That's it."

"That way they don't waste time sendin' a message, at least in daytime. The thing for us to do tonight is hit enough of these things to make bein' here plain uncomfortable. We want to get these boys all bollixed up. Seein' things that ain't there, firing off reports and alarms to call out the soldiers at all hours."

Duke clucked his tongue. "That won't make the troops very happy."

"Nope. An' it will make them careless. You 'member from bein' a kid the story about the boy who cried wolf? Well, by the time our outfit gets here, that's what the regular soldiers will be thinkin' about these fellers on the ridge. Then maybe we pop up . . ." Preacher went on to outline his plan.

They picked a spot on the far side and settled in among the pines to rest until the best time of night. Preacher and Duke gnawed on strips of jerky and cold biscuits to fill the empty space in their bellies, then caught a few hours of sleep.

* * *

Elijah Morton had quickly become bored with this duty. They could hang a Roman name on him, make him learn Latin, but he knew who he was, or at least who he'd once been. Elijah Morton had been a small-time highwayman who preyed on isolated trading posts along the North Platte. At least until the urge to move farther west, brought on by an increased presence of mounted federal troops, had brought him into the Ferris Range some two years ago. He had been captured and quickly volunteered to join a legion.

Often after that, he had regretted his decision. Not nearly so much as he would this night.

Elijah did not see the dark figures ghosting through the trees toward the watch tower. He had watch and had grown bored with staring into black nothing. Opposite him, Graccus peered toward the distant platform where two others did the same dull task. He sensed at the same time as Elijah the vibration of a footfall on the ladder leading upward. Could it be their relief?

Not likely, Graccus discovered a split-second before bright lights exploded inside his head, to bring excruciating pain for a brief moment, when Duke buried his war hawk in the top of his head. Preacher swarmed over Elijah at the same moment. His forearm pressed tightly against the throat of his victim, which effectively cut off any sound. Preacher leaned close, smelled garlic, onions and rancid, unwashed body, and whispered in one ear.

"You want to live, keep quiet and do as you are told."

The head nodded feebly. Preacher went on. "How many are there up here?"

"Two," Elijah mouthed. Sudden pain erupted under his left ear, and he felt the prick of a knife point.

"Don't lie to me. I counted six men earlier." Preacher eased the pressure to allow for a reply.

"Four are sleeping. There's the messenger down below. Didn't you . . . ?"

"He's tied up," Preacher answered with part of the truth.

Preacher and Duke had closed on the unsuspecting messenger, to find out he was a mere boy, hardly older than fourteen or fifteen. Preacher clapped a big hand over the lad's mouth and yanked him off his feet. They had quickly tied him up, carted him away from the tower and strung him up, head down, in a tree. He prodded again.

"What time is your relief?"

"I don't know. In another hour, maybe."

"What's you name?"

"Elijah Morton."

"You don't have a Roman name, Elijah?"

"Yeah. It's Virgo. I hate it."

"All right, Elijah, if you want to live, you'll answer everything, and then you'll be tied up and gagged. We won't kill you."

"I'll do what I can."

"Good. What's going on in New Rome?"

Elijah talked freely about the preparations for war. He detailed the training exercises of the legions and spoke of the firearms. That came as a nasty surprise to Preacher. They would have to hit at night, spike those cannons and move right into the city. Somehow the idea did not sit well with him.

"Anything else?"

"Oh, sure. The watch towers were built, and we've been in them ever since. Once a week we are supposed to be rotated back to our legion. So far that hasn't happened, and we're gettin' fed up with it."

"Now, that's right interestin'. Well, we're gonna leave those other boys to snooze, lock 'em in that room over there and wait to see what comes of that. I'm gonna turn you loose now. Don't fight me, turn around and put your hands behind your back."

"I hate this place. Can't I come with you?"

"Nope. We've got more of this kinda thing to do. But if you want to ride away from it when you get loose, head due south. When you come to some folks, ask for Philadelphia Braddock."

"I knew some Braddocks back home."

"Where's that?"

"Philadelphia," Elijah answered simply.

Preacher considered that a moment. "Now ain't that interestin'? Turn around."

Elijah complied in silence. After trussing him up, Preacher lowered Elijah to the platform floor. Then he and Duke eased over to the shelter that housed the slumbering sentries. Preacher located a loose piece of wood and used it to wedge the door tightly shut. With that accomplished, they stole off into the night to visit yet another tower.

They completed their jaunt uneasily close to first light. A soft, silver-gray glow hung along the eastern ridge when they rejoined the Cheyennes. Both of them had big grins and six fresh scalps tied to their belts.

"That ain't gonna do them Romans any good when they think about spendin' time out here. Might be we can raise a little more ruckus tomorrow night."

22

A considerable uproar followed Preacher's excursion. The fourteen deaths were attributed to the red savages, and any who had been spared by Preacher and Duke kept their own counsel. It worked so well, Preacher decided, that they would try it on two or three of the other towers the next night. In order to avoid the patrols that had been sent out at first light to search for the perpetrators, he, Duke and the Cheyenne had withdrawn beyond the second ridge out of the city.

"Heck of a thing," Preacher announced when they returned after nightfall. "Looks like our funnin' with them has backfired on us." He referred to the neat rows of cooking fires that spread around the meadow outside the walled city.

"What's that?" Duke Morrison asked.

Preacher gave a short, sharp grunt. "That's the legions. They've taken to the field. Changes our plans somewhat. But that can wait until the rest git here. Now's the time to shake them up a bit more."

Things had changed on the final rim also. Two sentries guarded the base of the first tower Preacher and Duke approached. It took them only slightly greater stealth to close on the alert guards than it had the unsuspecting messengers of the previous night. From the moment he had learned that the towers operated independently, Preacher had been working on fateful decisions for those who occupied the ones they would visit tonight.

No more sparing of lives. To create the maximum of fear and terror, all would die. It didn't make a problem for the Cheyennes, albeit he and Duke went to it grimly, taking no pleasure from the task. The two guards died swiftly and without a sound. The slumbering messenger awakened in time to see the blade of a war hawk descending toward his head. His scream died along with himself. The moccasins of the two mountain men made only the softest of whispers as they ascended the ladder to the platform.

One of the watchmen, more attentive than his partner, sensed more than heard the silent approach. He turned, his hand going to the heft of his *gladius*. Preacher bounded up onto the boards of the platform and turned off the source of such commands with his tomahawk. The blade sank to the hilt in the soldier's forehead. Before he could wrench it free, Duke joined him and finished off the other sentry.

Preacher spoke softly. "There's two more in there, most likely."

Duke nodded, and they moved cat-footed to the door. Duke pointed to his chest and then the closed portal, indicating he would go through first. Preacher dipped his chin a fraction of an inch and yanked open the crudely made panel. Duke went through with Preacher at his heels. The scuffing motions of their moccasins awakened a light sleeper. Duke's big Hudson's Bay Company knife sank into the unfortunate legionnaire's chest and trashed his heart.

He died with a soft sigh. Preacher swung to split the skull

of the dead man's companion, only to find his wrist in a grasp like iron. The big man grunted, but did not cry out. The coppery tang of blood in the air told him there would be no one to hear. He tried to rear up, but Preacher's weight bore down on him and pinned him to the straw mattress. Preacher used his free hand to draw his Green River knife and plunge it into soft tissue below the rib cage. He was aware of the amazing rubbery tension of skin for a brief moment, before the tip sank into muscle and angled upward.

The soldier convulsed as the blade pierced his diaphragm and sped on to his heart. His tremors became more violent, and then he went rigid and lay still. Preacher took a deep breath.

"Time to get movin'," he told Duke.

Cassius Varo stared into the night. Had he seen slight movement in Tower Seven? If so, it could only be the men on watch, he told himself. Bored by long, fruitless hours of this static activity, he paced the two sides of the plank square for which he was responsible. Time went by so slowly. Varo's eyelids had started to droop when a sudden, very wet *thok!* came from below.

Suddenly alert, he touched his partner on one shoulder, then leaned over the railing to call softly to the guards on the ground. "Titus, Vindix, what's going on?"

His answer came in the form of a broad-head arrow that drove into his forehead. His single, violent convulsion sent him crashing over the rail. By then, Preacher had ascended the ladder and had only to swing smoothly to smash the brains from the other sentry with his war hawk.

Duke quickly joined him, and they finished off the sleeping pair without even a stir. Outside, Preacher nodded to the tall, black bulk of another tower, standing out against the starlight. "Two down, one more to go."

* * *

At mid-morning the next day, the mountain-man-and-Indian army arrived beyond the third ridge from New Rome. Preacher and Duke greeted them and called for a parlay of all leaders. Bold Pony, Blind Beaver and Philadelphia attended. Terry Tucker hovered at Preacher's elbow. Most of the former fur trappers stood around in a loose circle. Their long lives of independence gave them license to eavesdrop, or so they believed. Having done it enough times himself, Preacher made no further notice of them.

He got right down to business. "Things have changed. We shook 'em up a little an' they put their legions out in the field. They's camped all around the city. So we'll not be scalin' any walls right off. Put your men to makin' ladders fer it, anyway. We'll need 'em after we deal with the soldiers, I reckon."

"How do we do that?" Philadelphia inquired.

Preacher gave him a smile. "I thought you'd never ask. First thing is we've got to draw them out. I see you brought along a couple dozen more than we had at our last camp together. That's good."

"We're more than a hunderd an' fifty strong now, Preacher," Philadelphia announced. "An' that could git bigger by tomorrow."

"Even better. Cold camp tonight. We don't want our Roman friends knowin' we're here. I know it'll be hard not gettin' in some drummin' an' singin', Bold Pony, Blind Beaver, but you've both done some war trail sneaks before, I'm sure. We can all dance up a storm oncest this is over." The war leaders nodded solemnly. "Now here's how we get them to come to us. First off we have to get rid of all those watch towers they've built. Then, the morning after that's done, we show up in a double line on the last ridge. That'll make us ringtailers and the Cheyenne."

"Vhat about the Arapaho?" Karl Kreuger asked nastily from the sidelines. "You goin' soft on dem vor a purpose."

"Nope. Not at all. Matter of fact, they've got the hardest part of all. Before we show ourselves to the Romans, they've got to sneak down into that valley durin' the night . . ." Preacher went on to describe where the Arapaho warriors would go and what they would be doing.

"Sounds complicated," Philadelphia Braddock observed.

"It ain't. Not if ever'one does what he's supposed to. If all of us keeps our place and not act on our own, we can have this over before nightfall."

"You said they had cannons," a voice came from a mountain man Preacher did not know.

"Those we take care of the same time we empty the watch towers. Which reminds me. Duke an' me learned a whole lot about how they are run. After the soldiers are tooken care of, we leave two men in each tower to make the morning signal. Then those boys can join the rest of us. As far as the cannons go, I found these little things in one of the towers we hit last night. Must be used for holdin' somethin' together. Thing is, they'll serve our purpose." Preacher unwound from his squat on the ground and went to his saddlebags.

From them he took a buckskin bag about six inches long. From it, he removed three dull, grayish objects. They had been flattened on one end, and the opposite one tapered to a fine point. He raised his arm to show them around.

"While the towers are being silenced, Duke an' me and a couple others will slip in among the Romans and spike the touch holes of those big guns."

That didn't sound too good to Philadelphia. "Won't they hear you doin' that?"

Preacher gave him a confident smile. "Not if we use padded wooden mallets. A couple of pops on each, then break them off. Those tired soldier-boys will think it's just horses stompin' in the night."

"If you say so," Philadelphia relented, still unconvinced.

"I want to go with you, Preacher," Terry pleaded.

"No. You'll stay on the ridge with them towers. An' that's final."

"When do we get all this started?" another mountain man asked.

Preacher swept his arm in an inclusive gesture. "We'll git us a little rest now. Then, when it is good and dark tonight, it all begins. Them Romans will never know what hit them."

Prudence, as much as good luck, guarded Preacher and the five mountain men with him as they glided across the tall grass of the central meadow. For some reason, he had noted, the cannons had been left outside the temporary palisades of the nightly encampments of each cohort. He had no way of knowing that the cause was ignorance and laziness—twelve-pound Napoleons weighed over a ton, and were hard to move around.

The generals had decided where they would fight the enemy when he came, and so the long guns had been laid to provide the maximum effect. There they would stay. Coincidentally, that put three cannons on each flank of the supposed Roman main line of resistance. Well and good, Preacher figured. Shortly before sundown, Haymaker Norris, who claimed to have put his trapping aside for two years to serve in the Mexican War as an artilleryman, instructed the sabotage party in the proper way to spike a cannon. Along with the mountain men who were to take out the watch towers, they set out on foot at midnight.

Leaving a cold camp, their night vision was not affected in the least. Those who used tobacco chewed on sweetened leaf or, like Preacher, chomped on the butt of an unlighted cigar. They moved with astonishing speed and silence. No one spoke; not a loose item of equipment or clothing clattered or rattled. Not even a clink came from the Roman plumb bobs—for that's what the lead spikes were identified as by Four-Eyes Finney, who had been an apprentice carpenter before he ran away to the Big Empty. It seemed no time until they had crested the first of three ridges that separated them from New Rome. Preacher called a short halt there to catch their wind. Funny, neither he nor any of them had needed to do that in the past, even packing around some respectable wounds.

He eased over to each of the men with him and repeated whispered advice.

"We'd best be givin' some time for those boys up ahead to do their dirty work."

"Another ridge to cross," Four-Eyes Finney reminded him.

"Then we'd best be gettin' there," Preacher declared as he set off along the trail. The others followed at once without having to be told.

When Preacher and his companions reached the watch tower beside the main southern trail, not a living person remained there. The other force of mountain men had done their work well and vanished into the night to their next objective. Preacher again ordered they take a breather. They had made it this far without another stop, which pleased him. Now the hard part would begin.

"We'll take the cannons on the right flank first. That's our left," he added for the benefit of Blue Nose Herkimer.

"I know that," Blue Nose whispered back in mock irritation.

"You do *now*," Preacher responded through a low chuckle.

They began their descent five minutes later. Avoiding the roadway in order not to be seen, the mountain men angled across the basin, through the tall grass nearly invisible even to one another. Preacher's long, meticulous survey of the valley paid off. He had a fairly accurate map of the terrain in his head. It took not the least effort to direct the spiking party to a wide, deep ravine that cut diagonally across to the Roman right flank.

At five minutes after three in the morning, they arrived at their objective. The perfect hour, when the circadian rhythm of human life ebbed lowest. It was the time of deepest sleep, when dreams formed and the body became sodden with relaxation. Working two to each gun, the mountain men placed the spikes, then rapped on them with padded mallets. The soft thuds that accompanied each blow did indeed sound like the stomp of a hoof. Preacher had insisted that they not strike together or too rapidly.

His precaution paid unexpected dividends. When the last spike had been broken off, they entered a small gully on hands and knees. Preacher's keen hearing picked up soft voices speaking in English from the main gate to the camp as they passed it.

"Lazy cavalry. Picketed their horses outside the camp," came a scornful remark.

"All right with me," the other sentry answered. "I don't like the smell of horse crap at breakfast."

A soft chuckle rose for a moment. "Considering what they feed us, how can you tell the difference?"

Like soldiers anywhere, Preacher thought as he crawled away.

They reached the second trio of cannons without incident. Preacher squared off on the flattened top of a lead plumb bob and gave it a whack. Ice shot down his spine a second later when an inquiring voice came from behind the palisade.

"What'cha doin' out there with horses?"

Preacher thought fast. He'd have to make some response. Fortunately the question had been in English. "Early patrol. The generals are getting nervous." He could speak as correctly as any man when he chose to do so.

"You horse soldiers have it made," came an envious response.

"Don't we though?" Preacher hoped the man would shut up with that. He did not like the idea of chatting away with the enemy when there were so many so close.

"Good luck," served as words of dismissal. Preacher let go a soft sigh of relief.

Plop! came from another cannon touch hole. Then again. Then it was Preacher's turn. He took a swat, then glanced nervously at the stockade. Two more followed his. He suddenly realized he was sweating bullets. Much of this could take years off a life. He tugged at the spike to check its set, then hit it on the shaft. It bent but did not break off. Damn. He did not dare risk another. Preacher raised his hand to signal the others, and they stole off into the darkness, their task completed.

Preacher's small party, and those who had attacked the watch towers around the rim, waited out the rest of the night on the intermediate ridge. Their horses would be brought up to them. Elated, and relieved that they had encountered no difficulties in the night's activities, Preacher chose to spend his wait on a good snooze. He reckoned as how he would need every bit of alertness and stamina he could recover during the day to come. An hour before dawn, the main force arrived. Preacher roused himself to speak with the leaders.

"Yellow Hawk, I want you and your warriors to take your place where I told you about now. Have 'em keep low and be danged quiet. They must stay complete out of sight until I give the signal."

Preacher had brought along six fat, greasy, paper-wrapped sticks of blasting powder from the trading post. He had caps and fuse for them in his saddlebag. Some would be used to distract and confuse the enemy, or to blow down the gates to the city. The first one would be to signal the Arapaho to attack.

"Have them take plenty water gourds, too. Wouldn't do for 'em to get too thirsty to fight proper."

Yellow Hawk nodded his understanding. "You have fought many more battles than I, Ghost Wolf. It is good to have wise counsel. Only one thing worries me. That we are not to fight in the open, pick our enemy and count coup before we slay him and go for another. We have never fought this way before."

"Let's hope you never have to again," Preacher said fervently, recalling his earlier thoughts on the subject. "But this time it is important. The way the Romans fight makes it so. Now, if you please, go on and put the braves in the right places."

Preacher turned his attention to the others. "Philadelphia, you'll lead our boys in this fracas. I'll be quarterin' the field between you an' the Cheyenne. It's gonna be pure hell to keep them dog soldiers from breakin' ranks and countin' coup before we can spring the trap. So I'll mostly be with them."

"Think they'll listen to you?" Philadelphia asked with an eye on the patient Indians who remained with their mountain men allies.

"They'd better, if they want to stay alive. In the right hands, them javelins have might near the range of a Cheyenne arrow. They ain't like a head-heavy flint lance point. Timin'. Everything in this counts on timin'. We're outnumbered, sure's hell. But if we do this right, there won't be enough Roman soldiers left to form one of those . . . what do you call them ten-man outfits?"

"Contaburnium," Buck Sears supplied.

"Yeah. That's the one."

Buck scratched his head. "You seem so sure of this, Preacher. Did you learn it from some army feller?"

"I'll tell you about it later, Buck. Right now, I want to go convince Blind Beaver to keep a lid on his men." Before he could do that, he had one more task to complete. He squatted before Terry and put a big, hard hand on one slim shoulder.

"You do right like I said. Stay here on this ridge tomorrow. Don't move a muscle."

Shortly after the sun rose two fingers over the eastern rim of the valley, the mountain-man-and-Indian army crested the ridge to the south. Not a signal went out to announce their arrival. Below, in the camps of the legions, the soldiers went about their morning fatigue duties of taking down the stockade and tents. The approaching host had ridden halfway down the reverse slope when someone first noticed them.

Brassy blasts on the long, straight, valveless trumpets sent the men hastily to their weapons. Tent mates helped one another into their breastplates and greaves. Bawling NCOs brought order to the ranks, which formed in the traditional Roman squares. By then, the bandsmen had been assembled.

While the invaders walked their horses onto the floor of the meadow, the *buccinae* hooted and the *clarinae* tooted, while the *timpanii* throbbed and rumbled in fine martial style. Lastly, the legates of the legions appeared, dashing on their powerful chargers, the cavalry legion of Varras swinging into the traditional position in the order of battle. They took their reports from their adjutants and began to exhort the legionnaires to do their utmost in battle. The enemy rode inexorably closer.

At about two thousand yards, their double line began to change shape. The flanks, two ranks deep, curved inward, while the middle, consisting of three ranks, hung back slightly. When they had molded in a bison-horn formation, they halted. All of this brisk human activity had frightened the small animals and birds to flight or silence. When the invaders halted, an eerie silence enveloped both sides. Curious eyes studied the "barbarians."

Equally curious eyes took in the boxlike formations of the legions from the other side. Squinty Williams nudged Philadelphia in the ribs. "What they all bunched up like that for? They're just askin' for a shower of Cheyenne arras."

"We'll find out soon enough, I reckon, Squinty," Braddock replied. "Accordin' to Preacher, the old-timey Romans were real mean fighters. Whupped ever'body they went against."

"Wull, they didn't never come against *us* fellers, I bet."

Philadelphia stifled the laugh that rose in his chest. "No, Squinty, they didn't."

Abruptly the drums opposite them began to throb. Bull-roar voices bellowed orders. In full regalia, complete with cavalry and band, the Roman legions began to march forward like a single man, rather than nearly nine hundred.

Marcus Quintus Americus gazed over the ranks of his brave legions. Pride swelled his heart. They were ready. They surely were honed as fine as any soldiers could be. They had about a thousand *stadia* to cover, and then the cannons would open up. The legions had heard them fired enough not to falter when they blasted away. And then the cohorts would pick up the pace to a trot, pilae slanted forward at eye level to these unprotected barbarians.

Riflemen would open up at the same time. This should be over soon enough that he could be back in the palace for a soothing bath and a light lunch. How tedious these matters could be. It would bloody the legions, which they would need. Knowledge of New Rome had undoubtedly become wide-spread outside the valley. Secrecy could not be maintained forever, he knew. Yet, he had hoped to keep the true enemy ignorant of his power and intentions for a while longer. A sudden shout came from ahead of him at the left-hand battery. It was repeated by stentorians until he could make meaning of the sounds.

"The cannon have been spiked! The cannon are useless!"

Those fateful words chilled Quintus. Everything hinged on the artillery. He looked about him in serious despair. He had to act. He must do something, and it had to be right.

23

It wouldn't do to start off with all this fanfare and then re-treat in the face of a determined, if small, hostile force. There could not be more than a hundred and fifty of them, Marcus Quintus made a quick, inaccurate tally. *Be decisive.* The words mocked him. Yet, he must do something. Marcus Quintus turned to the trumpeter beside him.

"Sound for the legates," he commanded.

With a nod, the signalman put the mouthpiece of his instru-ment, one which had been coiled to compact it, to his lips and blew. It produced a mellower note than the straight trumpets. At once, Glaubiae, Bruno and Varras turned the heads of their mounts and cantered to the center. They saluted formally.

Quintus spoke brusquely, not meeting their eyes. "I am sure you heard the disastrous news. Somehow those barbar-ians had the wit to infiltrate our encampment and spike the cannons. That places the burden of victory more directly upon your soldiers. We will advance within range of our archers and pilae. The cavalry is to divide and take positions to sweep those thin flanks back on the main body."

"First Citizen," Varras spoke urgently. "I recommend against splitting my force."

"Why not?" Now Quintus glared directly into the black eyes of Varras. "Given a good shower of arrows and javelins, these unarmored louts will break ranks and flee. You will be able to slaughter them at your leisure."

"Need I remind you that they all have guns. Even most of the red savages."

Quintus found that a subject for contempt. "Savages cannot hit what they shoot at. See that it is done as I have said. I will take the center in my chariot."

He dismounted and climbed to the platform of the gold-chased chariot. There he drew a silver inlay *gladius* and held it at the ready. Disgruntled, yet keeping their tongues silent, the legates of the three legions of New Rome rode back to their commands. There they conveyed the orders of their supreme commander, and the cavalry departed for the flanks of the mountain men's formation.

When they reached the desired location, Quintus raised his sword and ordered his troops forward. The band began again, and the soldiers stepped out with a steady, measured tread. They came right on until a distance of only fifty yards separated them from the invaders. Not unlike an exercise on the drill field, the commands barked from centurions to sergeants to the men. Javelins hissed through the air while arrows arched above and moaned their eerie song.

"Now ain't that obligin' of them to come in so close?" Philadelphia Braddock drawled.

Preacher agreed with him. "Sure enough is. Steady on, boys," he added as the Romans halted, their formation still perfect.

Then came the commands to fire. The projectiles seethed through the air. Unlike the static squares of the Roman soldiers, the mountain men and Cheyenne allies were free to move at will. Which they did by jumping their horses forward enough to be missed by the missiles. A split second after recovering from the movement, they fired a ragged volley.

Bullets punched right through bull-hide shields. Even the brass ornaments on them yielded to .56 caliber lead balls. Preacher had taken aim at a fancy dude in a glittery uniform who seemed to be in command. His slug shattered the breastbone of Yancy Taggart and ended the career of General Gaius Septimus Glaubiae. The gaudy uniform became a heap of lifeless clothing at the feet of the *primus pilus* of the Thirteenth Legion. At such short range, not a one of the mountain men and Indians could miss. One hundred fifty-seven Roman soldiers went down in that first volley.

Marcus Quintus Americus stared on in horror as he saw his senior general slain with casual indifference. Another flight of arrows and javelins answered the fire, only to be avoided while men rapidly reloaded. The air turned blue with powder smoke once again.

Preacher made quick note that the discipline of the troops they faced had begun to falter. With a little luck, he might not even need to use the Arapahos. He drew a .44 Walker Colt, and the mountain men around him went to pistols also. The more rapid fire had a withering effect on the legions.

It had even more on the fancy-dressed fellow in the two-wheeled cart, Preacher realized as that one—it must be that Marcus Quintus—shouted an order. Another shower of arrows and then the Romans began to withdraw, marching backward, long rows of leveled javelins pointed at the men whom they left in command of the field.

"Well, if that don't just beat all," Preacher declared wonderingly. "Don't know what to make of that."

"Me neither," Philadelphia remarked. "A feller gets himself all worked up for a fight like they did, it usual lasts a spell. They sure's the devil had us outnumbered."

"They may be back. Best pull back a ways and stand fast. I mark that Quintus feller to be a tricky bastard."

While the archers let fly another deadly flock and the soldiers hurled their slender javelins, Marcus Quintus Americus looked around him in confusion. Another ragged volley came from fifty yards off. Why weren't his own riflemen firing? For a moment, it plagued him; then he recalled that he had assigned them to cover the cavalry, which as yet had not engaged the enemy. Another thought struck him.

He would have to get a replacement for Gaius Septimus. His first spear had all the imagination and initiative of a stone post. Who could it be? Rufus Longinus of the Second? Yes. He had almost as much knowledge of military matters as Glaubiae had possessed. Bruno could get himself a new *primus pilus*. But this was hardly the place to hand out promotions. He turned to right and left, bawling out the most bitter order ever given by a commander.

"Fall back on the camp. Make it in good order and keep an eye on the enemy."

Trumpets sounding, the order was relayed by the adjutants of each legion, one in temporary command of his. Slowly the tramp of thick-soled military sandals sounded, and the century squares became a retrograde movement. Dust began to rise in thick clouds. Not enough, though, to mask, let alone protect, potential targets.

Although puzzled by the retreat, the mountain men and Indians kept up a steady fire into the dwindling ranks of the legions until they maneuvered out of range. Quintus ordered his chariot to turn and get around the formations of troops. He wanted to be calmed and refreshed when he met with his generals to promote one man and offer advice. Tomorrow would be a far better day, he convinced himself. Besides, the omens had not been all that promising at the morning sacrifice.

Four-Eyes Finney seemed mightily pleased with himself. "He who hits and runs away . . . ," he quoted.

"Is a yellow-bellied cur," Jack Lonesome added his own version to the end.

"Naw, that ain't it, Lonesome," Four-Eyes corrected. "It's about livin' to fight another day."

"Why'd they run? Why didn't we just finish them here an' now?" the grizzled mountain man pressed his point.

"Tell you what, Jack," Preacher began diplomatically. "We got 'em whittled down some, and it's for certain sure those cannons don't work. But there's at least five of them for each one of us. What say we pull back to the base of the ridge and settle in. They'll do somethin' 'fore long."

Preacher turned out to be right on that. An hour later, three officers, one with a white flag, rode out from the Roman camp. With them came a number of soldiers and a line of wagons. The one with the truce flag advanced to where the mountain men lolled on the ground, eating and sharing some scarce whiskey.

"Which one of you is the general in charge?"

Preacher came to his boots and tucked the stick of jerky he had been gnawing on in a shirt pocket. "I reckon that would be me. But I ain't no gen'ral."

"What do you call yourself?"

"Folks around these parts call me Preacher."

"By Jupiter and all the gods," the young Varras blurted. "Gaius told us you were the one we saw fight in the arena." His tone turned rueful, and his expression became wry. "No one but you could have made good on that escape." He saw that his flattery had no effect on Preacher. That decided him to come to the point.

"We came to ask permission to recover our dead and wounded."

"He'p yourselves. We've got no quarrel with them."

"But you do with us?"

"Somethin' like that. There's those among us who don't take kindly to having our friends made into slaves and forced to fight to the death.

The trio of officers exchanged glances. The one in the middle, with the flag of truce, looked back at Preacher. "What's wrong with that? It's a good way for a barbarian to make a living." They all laughed.

Preacher instantly developed a thunderous expression. "You keep that up an' you'll be joinin' those you came to get."

Varras' protest came at once. "Bu-but we're under a flag of truce."

Preacher reached up and yanked the white flag from the astonished general's hands. "Funny, I don't see a damn thing."

Youngest and the most nervous of the junior officers, the one on his left spoke in a soft, quiet voice. "Legate Varras, I think he's serious."

"At least *you've* got it right, Sonny," Preacher snapped.

Touching a lightly trembling finger to his lips, the youthful general pushed his point. "Let's—uh—get on with it, shouldn't we?"

To their stiff backs, Preacher said, "You can come back for this rag when you're done." To the others he spoke in a low tone. "We're gonna have to do somethin' about that rudeness."

By the time the dead and wounded had been retrieved from the field, darkness hovered on the ridge to the east.

Westward, magenta and gold washed over the pale blue of the sky. Preacher had men busy making objects from the thorns taken from the underbrush and rawhide strips. While they worked, he went among them, explaining what would happen.

"When it gits good and dark, we're gonna take these things out and scatter them in front of those little movable forts of theirs. Really sew the ground with them. Then some of us is gonna pay a visit to the big city."

"How do ve get past dose soldiers?" Bloody Hand Kreuger asked in a surly tone.

"*Ve* don't. You'll be with the others spreading these here caltrops. Horses don't like 'em much and men don't either. Messes up their walkin' right smart. I'll pick those goin', and everyone eat a good meal. We'll start out at midnight."

True to his word, Preacher led an expedition out from their camp at midnight. He and eleven others would penetrate into the city and cause what havoc they could contrive. Another party, under charge of Philadelphia Braddock, set off to scatter the deadly four-point caltrops in the tall grass outside the Roman camps. Preacher's picks had smeared soot and grease on their faces, and all wore dark clothing.

They had a variety of flopped hats and animal-skin caps to break up the regularity of the shape of their heads. All carried pistols and knives, a few tomahawks. Rifles would only hamper them. At Preacher's direction, fire pit trestles had been heated and one end of each bent into a hook. Ropes had been attached and knots tied along their length. Preacher had remained secretive about the purpose of these.

When they reached the walls, the fires burned low behind the palisades and everything lay in silence. Preacher wrapped his hook in cloth and shook out a length of rope. He gave it a steady swing, moving his hand and arm faster with each circle. At last he let it go and it sailed upward. It struck a foot short with a soft thump. When it dropped back, Preacher tried again. Once more he failed.

"This one'll do 'er," he assured the others in a whisper.

It didn't.

At last, on the fifth toss, the hook sailed over the wall and stuck fast when Preacher pulled on the rope. Quickly the others with hooks began to throw them at the battlement. When the sixth one caught, Preacher leaned back and went up his hand-over-hand, feet braced against the outside of the rampart. More men quickly followed until all twelve had scaled the barrier.

"We're here, now what?" Squinty Williams asked.

"I'd say a visit to the baths," Preacher offered.

"Me?" Squinty squeaked out. "I've done took my summer bath."

"I was thinking of breaking a few things in there and flooding the streets," Preacher responded. "You won't even have to take off those ripe-smellin' moccasins, Squinty."

"Don't you be doin' that to me, Preacher. I'll have to swim for it if you break that place apart."

"Not if you run fast enough. Now, let's go."

The twelve-man party made it to the baths without the *vigilii* spotting them. Inside, they subdued the night watchman and spread out through the series of pool rooms. Buck Sears led the way to the confluence of the underground waterways. There they plied crowbars and mauls to break the plaster away and penetrate the brick walls.

In no time after that, they were walking ankle deep in swift-flowing water. It spread through the baths and headed for the front door. Enough done here, Preacher thought. He directed them to split up into pairs and go do mischief.

"Keep a sharp eye for those watchmen," he cautioned. He and Squinty headed for the central square, the forum.

"What are we going to do there?"

Preacher chuckled as he explained. "We're gonna wake up some ladies and scare them out of their nightshirts."

Squinty cocked his head, then shook it. "You actual thinkin' about dallyin' with some wimmin in a place as dangerous as this?"

"Nooo. Just scare the Vestal Virgins a mite. Stir up some hullabaloo."

Portia Andromeda awakened to something that she had not believed possible. A man in the cloisters of the Temple of Vesta! Not only a man, but a brute-ugly one at that. He had a hairy face, gaps in his teeth, which were too dark to be healthy, eyes too close together and squinched up. The shock of it robbed her of immediate speech.

"What are you gawkin' at, you ugly old prune?" a raspy voice asked her.

By the gods, are those animal skins he is wearing? Portia asked herself. In all of her years in service to Vesta, she had never seen such a creature. As senior priestess, she must maintain her composure, her brain reminded her.

"Get out of this cell," she demanded coldly, finding her voice at last.

A shriek came from another cell down the hallway. Had the barbarian army defeated the legions and entered the city? No. That was too preposterous to believe.

"How about a little kiss first, Sister?"

And then, Portia herself screamed. It seemed to come up from her toes to ululate through wide-stretched lips that trembled from more than the force of her wail. When she again opened her eyes, the man had disappeared.

"Where we headed now?" Squinty asked Preacher after they left the cloisters in shrieking feminine confusion.

"To the gladiator school," Preacher told him simply.

"You joshin' me, ain'tcha?"

"Nope. I told Buck and the others to meet us there."

"What do you want to go there for?"

"Simple, Squinty. There's bound to be about fifty highly trained fighting men locked up in there. We're gonna let them out. If they wants to join us, they'll be welcome."

"I can see that. We need more on our side, right enough. Only, what if they want to stay right there and are willing to fight to do it?"

"We can leave those locked up. Down that street there, the Via Julius."

Fires had drawn all of the watch away from seeking those who had started them. The twelve mountain men reached the gladiator school within five minutes of one another. Preacher advised speed.

"We've got to do this quick-like. Go in, free the ones want to come with us, and get out. Then it's for the walls."

Two guards at the entrance to the cells died swiftly, downed by .44 bullets from one of Preacher's Walker Colts. A quick twist of key in lock and the men beyond began to yell in confusion and some in rekindled hope. Preacher and his band moved rapidly along the corridor, snapping back the wooden bolts that held the cell doors. Forty-seven wanted to join in the fight against New Rome.

"There's all sorts of firearms in a storage room I'll show you in the house of Bulbus." They cheered him loudly as Preacher and Buck set out to lead the way.

All of the noise in the streets had awakened Bulbus. He looked wistfully at the trim posterior of the young slave girl in his bed, gave the bare buttocks a pat and climbed from his bedclothes. Once fully dressed, he headed for the atrium. He got there at the same time the mountain men swarmed into the central courtyard garden.

Swords and javelins proved no hindrance to the blazing

pistols of the wild and wooly men of the High Lonesome. T hey brought down the five guards in as many seconds and surged toward the stores. Suddenly angry beyond any vestige of fear, Bulbus went for them with a *gladius* flashing in his pudgy hand. Preacher turned in time to see the blade poised to strike his head from his shoulders.

Having practiced long ago to speedily unlimber a six-gun, he filled his hand in a blur of controlled movement. The hammer came back and he squeezed the trigger. The small brass cap went off flawlessly, and the powder charge instantly followed. The .44 ball smacked into the thick middle of the master of games. A second ball went higher, through his heart, and flattened against his spine. Bulbus dropped the sword and staggered toward the fountain.

With a mighty cry, which sounded of regret more than pain, he pitched over the lip of the basin and splashed face-first into the water. Preacher watched Bulbus' right foot jerk spasmodically for a second and then turned to the men.

"Right through there. Pick the best, there's plenty of it. An' bring along all the powder, shot and caps you can haul. We have to beat these Roman mongrels to the wall."

Preacher soon found that they had lost the race to the parapets. Helmeted soldiers lined the southern and western ones. He veered his much larger band into a darkened street and plunged along it toward the east wall.

Only a dozen men topped that bastion, Preacher discovered when they reached it. Easy as anything. He picked out five of the ex-gladiators who had taken helmets from the fallen guards and sent them up the stone steps.

"Tell 'em you've been drafted to help defend the city," he instructed.

Halfway up the stairway, the "relief" force had attracted the attention of all but one of the soldiers. That was when

thirty shots cracked in sharp echoes off the walls of buildings and the stone barrier. Thirty balls sieved the defenders,
who pitched headfirst off the parapet or lay where they had
fallen. Preacher led the way up after the decoys.

At the top he found a determined sergeant holding the
two former gladiators at bay with a *gladius*. Preacher looked
at the other man for a second, then clucked his tongue as he
fired a fatal shot to the forehead of the sergeant. Then he
studied their surroundings.

"Too bad we didn't get back to our ropes. We'll have to go
back down and get out through that little bitty gate."

Several looked at Preacher as though he were mad. "We
can't make it," one protested.

"I say we can. Now, git movin'."

With trusted mountain men to serve as rear guard,
Preacher started the freed gladiators through the low, narrow
gate toward the outside. He cautioned them to remain quiet
and stay close to the base of the wall. They might not know
about the movable forts of the Romans. Nearly half of the
escapees had disappeared into the tunnellike passage through
the thick base of the stone rampart when others discovered
their presence.

Some sixteen of the *vigilii* rounded the corner nearest the
portal and stopped abruptly. These watchmen carried javelins
in addition to their swords, Preacher noted at once. Made
edgy by the sudden uproar within their city, and so far unable to account for it, the men of the watch reacted quickly.
They all rocked back, and each hurled a *pilum*.

One whistled past the left ear of Preacher, even as he
drew his left-hand Walker Colt. He eared back the hammer
the moment the weapon came clear of the holster and quickly
aligned the sights. The big .44 bucked in his hand, and one
of the watchmen cried out in pain. Other pistols fired a moment later. Eight of the watchmen had gone down in the first
exchange. Preacher aimed at another and fired again.

In such an unfair contest, there could be no doubt of the outcome. The remaining eight died in a hail of bullets. Unfortunately, it served to announce the presence of the invaders to those on the walls. Hard sandal soles scuffed on the stones of the parapet as other sentries called to one another and closed in on the knot of men at the gate below.

"The main gate! Open the gate! Barbarians in the city," one leather-lunged soldier bellowed.

While legionnaires poured in through the slowly opening portals, Preacher urged all speed and left New Rome at last. Behind him, the sky glowed orange from the fires in the buildings and gardens of New Rome. Alarmed shouts rose to the stars. Women and children were trampled by panicked citizens and the confused legions who hunted for a phantom enemy. Now all they need do was get past the legion camps and safely back to the ridge. Yeah, that was all.

24

Once again, daylight found the legions drawn up outside the bastions of New Rome. With blaring brass and throbbing drums, they formed their battle squares and began a slow, stately advance toward the distant collection of what Marcus Quintus Americus referred to as rabble and gutter-born barbarians. Like before, those he held in such disdain spread out in a long, double line and came forward. Following their strategy of the previous day, they deployed into a bison-horn formation. Only this time they were nearly fifty stronger. That had caused some dispute, and not a little discontent, among the generals.

All was not well in New Rome, they maintained. The turmoil of the past night had left deep marks on many. The senior Vestal Virgin and the Chief Priests of Jupiter and Mars had argued against resuming the battle so soon. The dawn auguries had foretold misfortune, they explained. One of the doves had been missing a heart, and the sheep had a large tumor on its liver. Furious at the insult handed him by the barbarians within his own walls, Marcus Quintus Americus scoffed at the omens for the first time since he had begun his childhood sacrifices at age ten.

Since then, he had completely forgotten his identity as Alexander Reardon. Like his son, he had been fascinated by blood as a child, and had taken an exhilarating, sensual pleasure in tormenting, killing, and examining the entrails of small animals. Now, enraged by the humiliation he felt, he turned his back on that and ordered the legions forward. Although still deprived of his cannons, the process of clearing the touch holes long and tedious, and requiring precision, he went forth with high expectations. The forces of New Rome still outnumbered the enemy by better than five to one. He sent the infantry against the center of the enemy line, now three ranks deep.

Riflemen opened fire first. He had included a number of them with the infantry this time. Poorly trained at best, they had little effect beyond causing a few of the scruffily dressed barbarians to duck with exaggerated motions, which elicited raucous laughter from their fellows. The steady tramp-tramp of sandals made a hypnotic rhythm as the infantry continued to advance. This would be easy! The legions would roll over this ragtag collection like a giant wave, Quintus thought to himself. He had instructed his generals to have the men take as many prisoners as possible. The games that would follow would be quite amusing.

"When they git to a hundred yards, open up on them," Preacher ordered in a calm voice.

Obediently, the mountain men raised their rifles and took aim. The pretty boys in the band would get the worst of it, Preacher considered, pleased that there were noticeably less of them today. When the heads of the musicians rested in the buckhorn rear sights of the long guns of the mountain men, a ragged volley erupted along the line. The first rank knelt to reload while the second immediately fired over their heads.

Down went a third of the band and one centurion behind them. The range had closed to seventy-five yards. Another crash of weapons from the third rank. By then the first rank had reloaded and discharged their rifles from the kneeling position. With each man who dropped in the front rank of the advancing cohorts, another took his place from behind. At fifty yards, there was no longer a band, and the last volley barked from the rifles. From here on it would take too long to reload.

At fifty yards, the first flight of arrows hissed from the Roman squares. Three men among the ex-gladiators went down with slight wounds. Two in the front file, intent on readying their pistols, died for their incaution, transfixed by Roman arrows. The flat reports of handguns filled the air. The Roman enemy kept coming.

With all ranks firing and the flanking "horns" of the formation engaged also, the legions began to falter and slow. Preacher bellowed loudly to his army.

"Hold fast. Just a little longer now. An' watch out for them spears."

A flight of javelins seethed through the blue morning to rattle and quiver when they struck only grassy turf. Another flock of deadly, feathered shafts took flight. To be answered by the roar of a hundred pistols. Cheyenne shafts answered them. More javelins arched in the sky and moaned through their descent. The shield wall of the Romans had closed to within twenty feet. Spear tips darted like the tongue of a rattler, probed all before them. Another bark of pistols brought down thirty soldiers.

Preacher emptied one Colt six-gun and drew the other. Soon now. He eased up the stick of blasting powder from behind his belt and made sure it would come free easily. Three legionnaires brought down as many among the ex-gladiators. They launched a final cluster of spears and drew their swords.

Suddenly the Cheyenne wavered and began to give ground. Soon the entire middle did the same. Menaced by the darting blades of the legionnaires, they appeared to have entirely lost their nerve.

Marcus Quintus saw it at once. He pointed out the faltering lines to Rufus Longinus at his side. "See? The savages flee in disorder from my magnificent legionnaires," he smugly brayed. "They won't last long now."

Inexorably the Roman center was drawn deeper inside the tips of the "horns," something which held not the least significance for Marcus Quintus. His chest swelled with pride as he saw for the first time a litter of barbarian and Indian bodies on the ground, rather than only his soldiers. Aware now that the one commanding his enemies was the living legend, Preacher, Marcus Quintus took extreme pleasure from watching the destruction of the invaders. He turned to Longinus again.

"Send a messenger to Varras. Have his cavalry sweep the field obliquely. They are to try to get around behind the enemy and prevent any escapes."

"As you wish, First Citizen." Privately, Rufus did not like this the least bit. The evolution of the battle plan had a hauntingly all too familiar appearance. Something they had studied at West Point, he recalled, back in another lifetime, but not the name of the engagement or its outcome.

Stubbornly, the three ranks, minus the Indians, continued to hold, though now bowed in slightly. Then the cavalry began their charge. They had ridden only a few lengths, enough to be within the limits of the "horns," when the buckskin-clad Preacher raised his arm and arched his body sharply. He hurled an object with all his strength.

It exploded a foot off the ground and disintegrated four legionnaires. A dozen more received injuries. Then, before the horrified eyes of Varras, the Arapaho, who had been hidden in a deep ravine to the left rear of the battle formations, rose up and fell upon the horsemen and the backs of the advancing cohorts.

Preacher timed the throw perfectly. With scant seconds left of the fuse, he hurled the blasting powder with all his might. "Let 'er rip!" he shouted to those around him.

With the roar of the explosion fresh in their ears, the mountain men steadied their line, and as the Arapaho seemed to materialize out of the very ground, the Cheyenne turned back to face the enemy. They laughed and hooted to show their complete lack of intimidation. It had a disastrous effect on the Romans. So did another stick of blasting powder that landed in the midst of a battle square.

Bodies flew through the air, and parts sailed higher. Dust cloaked everything, and the screams of men dying to their rear demoralized the front ranks. The tight, disciplined Roman formations dissolved into swirling masses of men, desperately engaged in hand-to-hand fighting.

A terrible slaughter began. On a low hill nearby, young Terry Tucker danced from foot to foot in anxiety. The night before, he had won his contest with Preacher to be allowed closer to the battle. He had not seen *anything* from the tower on the ridge. Even here, the dust had grown so thick he could no longer distinguish Preacher from the other fighters.

The conflict lasted for hours as the Arapaho and Cheyenne took revenge for their murdered brothers. Reduced to tomahawks and big, wide-bladed fighting knives, the mountain men hewed through the struggling legionnaires with deadly accuracy. The scent of blood thickened the air in a cloying, coppery miasma. Unremittingly, the numbers diminished for the Romans. Preacher's men were able to fall back and take time to reload pistols. Their addition to the fray took a brutal toll.

At last, the bedraggled survivors among the legions broke off and fled the field for the imagined safety of New Rome. Preacher called out to halt pursuit.

"Hold back now! We gotta get organized. Then we go after them. I want a tally of how many we have fit to fight."

Subordinate leaders, appointed by Preacher, and the war chiefs of Arapaho and Cheyenne made quick head counts. It turned out that only forty had been killed—less than the number who had joined from the gladiator school. Another sixty had been wounded, ranging from serious to cuts and scrapes. It left Preacher mightily pleased.

Blue Nose Herkimer swaggered up to Preacher, who was cleaning his revolvers and Hawkin rifle with little Terry Tucker standing proudly at his side. Herkimer had a big smile plastered on his face. He clapped Preacher on one shoulder. "That was sure something, I declare. Never seed the like. How come those fellers was so dumb as to fall for it?"

Preacher thought on that a moment. "They failed to scout the battlefield. And, I reckon they never had much use for old fights fought a long ways off."

"How's that?" Herkimer asked. "An' more to the point, how'd *you* know what to do an' that it would work?"

An enigmatic smile bloomed on Preacher's face. "A little reading I did a while back," Preacher informed him. "About a feller named Hannibal and the Battle of Cannae."

With his forces rallied now, Preacher went about laying siege to Nova Roma. The palisades of pointed-tip lodgepole pine saplings came down first, then the gaudy tents of the officers and plain ones of the enlisted men. From the bastions, the defeated Roman legions looked on in numb disbelief. How had it happened? How *could* it happen?

More than one asked that of his comrades. Meanwhile, given the distance between the camps and the city, they could retaliate against their primitive enemy only by hurling a few stones and large darts from ballistae and arbalests. Preacher had even considered it safe enough to allow Terry Tucker to join him. With night coming on, the destruction was completed. Fires were kindled and the invaders enjoyed sumptuous hot meals from the supplies of the officers of the legions. At least, the demoralized legionnaires consoled themselves, there would be no more fighting this day.

Early the next morning, their respite ended. Under cover of the most expert marksmen among the mountain men, Preacher rode to the large southern gates and buried the last four sticks of blasting powder under one pivotal corner. He tamped it down firmly, and wedged a big, flat piece of limestone between the ground and the wooden portal. Then he lighted the fuse and swung atop Cougar to race away without a scratch.

Moments later, the explosion shook the ground and threw gouts of dirt higher than the walls. When the smoke and dust cleared, the gate panel hung drunkenly on its upper hinge, canted sharply inward. The scaling ladders would not be needed. A superstitious mutter rose among the Indians. A couple of mountain men made the sign of the cross.

"Awesome," Squinty Williams breathed softly.

Preacher was not done yet. "Let's go!" he shouted, waving a Walker Colt in the sign for an attack.

With a roaring shout, mingled with war whoops, the small army rushed the gate. Boiling water poured down on the assault force until sharpshooters picked off the soldiers who dumped it. Rocks rained down, along with a shower of arrows and javelins. Men fell screaming, yet nothing slowed them.

Mountain men swarmed through the opening and spread out in the streets. They left the legionnaires behind them for the Arapaho and Cheyenne to deal with. Those able warriors did so with grim efficiency. Far better trained, since childhood, they kept three arrows in the air to each one fired by the Romans. Those arrows hit their targets, tumbling legionnaires from the walls in a continuous spill. Shouts and the screams of the dying became a constant bedlam.

In a swirl, the battle turned into house-to-house fighting as the legionnaires abandoned the exposed positions on the wall and rallied in small numbers to resist the invaders. Leading a dozen stalwarts, Preacher made for the half-finished Imperial Palace. From the forum he had seen the distinctive figure of Marcus Quintus Americus disappear in that direction.

Twenty well-armed soldiers held them at bay half a block from the front of the marble structure. Their rifles cracked in irregular volleys. Preacher and the others spread out and returned fire. Two of the guards died. Another one screamed hideously when he discharged an inadvertently triple-loaded rifle. Three times the normal powder load ripped the breech plug from its threads and drove it into his mouth. It mushed his lips, shattered teeth, and embedded itself in the back of his head.

His scream changed to a gurgle that ended as he died. That broke the nerve of two others, who rose from behind the low wall and ran toward the building. Three quick shots dropped them. A deeply appreciated lull followed.

"I'm goin' around back. I got a feelin' that feller Quintus has got a lot of rabbit in him."

Preacher had the right of it about Marcus Quintus Americus. While the legionnaires fought and died outside to buy him time, the First Citizen of New Rome hastily stuffed large panniers full of gold bars and shouted for servants to hurry in packing his clothes. His wife, Titiana Pulcra, stood in one corner of the treasure room and dithered.

"Why are you doing this, Marcus?"

"Shut up, woman, and help me."

Shocked at his tone, Pulcra gathered her past store of grievances and responded hotly. "Alexander Reardon, don't you dare speak to me like that."

Shocked at that, Quintus paused with one ingot in each hand. His voice held an artificially calm tone. "I don't believe this, Pulcra. You have always obeyed me. Please do so now."

Pulcra began to weep. "It's all coming apart, isn't it? We are destroyed, I feel it in my heart." With a soul-wrenching sob she ran from the room.

Taken aback, Quintus stared after her, then recovered. "Faustus, come in here," he yelled. "Quintus Faustus, come to your father."

Woefully lacking in training, the two guards at the rear of the palace fired at the same time. It had been easy for Preacher to trick them into doing so. He had simply jumped into sight at the edge of a marble column, shouted and popped a round into the air. At once they brought up the rifles they carried and cut loose. By that time, Preacher had disappeared behind the pillar. Not even his great experience as a fighting man could prevent him from wincing when the fat balls smacked into the opposite side of the stone plinth. Then he came out with a .44 Colt blazing.

Down went one soldier, who had bent over his weapon to reload. The other died a second later. Preacher advanced when a voice came from behind him.

"Want some company?"

Buck Sears and Philadelphia Braddock grinned broadly

as they approached. They found trouble the moment they entered the column-supported hallway. More *gladius*-waving soldiers awaited them. With hoarse shouts, the fighting men of New Rome came at the invaders.

"Dang," Preacher quipped. "What is it with these fellers who don't bring the right tools to a gunfight?"

He shot one in the chest, cocked his Walker Colt, and put his second .44 ball through the hand holding another *gladius*. The iron blade rang noisily when it hit the stone floor. Time to change. His second Colt brought down a third who moaned and rolled on the floor, clutching his belly.

Beside Preacher, Philadelphia took aim at a sergeant who lunged at him with a *pilum*. The javelin went wild as the mountain man discharged both barrels of his pistol at once. Slammed backward, the sergeant grew a shocked expression, his eyes wide, mouth round, while he clattered against a wall in numb shock and darkness settled over him.

Wisely, those remaining fled. Preacher sent a shot after them and hastily reloaded his pistols. That accomplished, they started toward the central core of the building.

A trembling messenger stood before Marcus Quintus Americus. Helmet tucked in the crook of his left arm, his face smeared with blood, dirt, and sweat, he panted out his litany of doom. "General Varras and what was left of the cavalry have been surrounded and destroyed by the red savages. General—er—Legate Longinus has fallen in street fighting near the forum. You already know about Legate Glaubiae."

Trembling from the effort to restrain himself, Quintus spoke with heavy sarcasm. "Is there any good news to tell me?"

"N-no, First Citizen. I mean, we continue to fight, and the enemy is taking losses . . ." his voice trailed off.

Bitterness colored the words of Quintus. "Only not so

many as we, eh?" In a moment of clarity and sanity, he added in a tone of sorrow, "I am afraid the only advice I have is for you to find your way out of the palace and get as far from Nova Roma as you can."

Relieved not to have been summarily executed as the bearer of bad news, the young centurion nodded his agreement, saluted, then turned to make his departure. That was when Preacher, Philadelphia and Buck stormed into the room.

Preacher let out a roar when he recognized Marcus Quintus. His first shot went wild, but sent the centurion with the First Citizen to the floor in an ungainly sprawl. To his regret, the young officer had already learned that a *gladius* had little use against firearms. He hugged the marble floor, feigning death, until a boot toe dug painfully into his ribs. He grunted in discomfort and rolled over, intending to hack at a leg with his sword, only to find himself staring down the barrel of the oddest weapon he had ever seen.

It had a round part with holes in it that revolved when its owner pulled back on the spur at the rear. Beyond the extended hand and arm, a powder-begrimed face grinned at him.

"The Mezkins has got a sayin', feller," Preacher told him. "It's addyose."

And the centurion learned one final fascinating fact about the strange weapon. Flame spat from its mouth a moment before excruciating agony and utter blackness washed over him and the back of his head flew off. He never heard the bang. Preacher checked on his companions and found them otherwise occupied, each engaging four guards who had rushed into the treasury room at the sound of the Walker Colt. Grinning now, Preacher turned to Marcus Quintus.

"Looks like you're mine," he declared. "Reckon that's sort of fittin', you bein' the bull elk of this place."

"Quite fitting indeed. You really are Preacher, aren't you?"

"Yep. That's what folks call me."

"Then prepare to die like a man."

To the utter surprise of Quintus, Preacher threw back his head and laughed. "I don't allow as how it's gonna be me does the dyin'," he brayed.

Quintus snatched up his *gladius* from the table where he had laid it and charged Preacher. The mountain man held his ground until the distance between them closed to ten feet. Then he raised his arm and squeezed the trigger of his .44 Colt.

Nothing happened. Only a loud click. In the heat and speed of battle, Preacher had forgotten to count the number of rounds he had fired since last reloading. He jumped aside as Quintus made a mighty swing with his sword, and drew his second Colt. The heft of it in his hand told him that it, too, had been fired dry. Quintus came on, and Preacher nimbly jumped over a table, putting it between himself and the Roman tyrant.

"That will not do you any good," Quintus spoke in precise English.

It gave Preacher time to draw his tomahawk. Over the years, the old war hawk had stood him well. He hoped it would again. Quintus lunged over the small table. Preacher batted the leaf-shaped blade of the *gladius* away with the iron head of his war axe. Quintus developed an expression of surprised appreciation. A truly worthy opponent. He maneuvered to get past the barrier that kept him at a disadvantage.

Preacher countered it. A sharp scream punctuated by a gurgling gasp told of another legionnaire on his way to his Maker. Preacher did not break his concentration as Quintus reached a low commode beside a desk. His left hand darted out and snatched up the bowl of pine nuts resting there. With a bellow intended to freeze his opponent, he hurled the confection at Preacher. Quintus followed it.

A spray of roasted pine nuts hit Preacher in the face. The sthe tabletop and execute a horizontal slash with his *gladius* that cut through the buckskin shirt and opened a fairly deep line across Preacher's pectoral muscles. Blood flowed in a curtain. Quintus had little time to savor his brief victory.

Ignoring the pain and accompanying weakness, Preacher swung his tomahawk, and the keen edge bit into flesh in Quintus' left shoulder. The Roman grunted and staggered precariously close to the edge of the table. In the last moments, he righted himself and leaped to the larger counter where the gold reserves had rested earlier. Fire throbbed in his deltoid muscle as the blade of the war hawk tore free. Quintus made another pass at Preacher as he gained the storage shelf.

Preacher batted the *gladius* aside with the flat of the 'hawk and did a fast, two-step shuffle forward. When Quintus brought his arm up for an overhand stroke, Preacher aimed for the Roman's exposed knee. The tomahawk bit deeply, with a loud *plock!* that turned heads in other parts of the room. Face squinched in overwhelming pain and mouth open in a soundless howl, Quintus dropped to his good knee. With a kneecap split, his *gladius* became as useless as his other leg.

He abandoned it for the double-edged dagger on the belt at his waist as Preacher came at him again. Bright steel flashed in the air, and Quintus made a fortunate cut on the right forearm of his opponent. Preacher was forced to drop his tomahawk as blood streamed from a severed vein. Only then did Quintus remember the small .50 caliber coach pistol he had concealed in the folds of his battle cloak. He reached for it eagerly.

"Preacher, here," Philadelphia Braddock shouted when the deadly little pistol appeared in Quintus' hand.

Preacher caught the double-barreled pistol Philadelphia had tossed left-handed and fired it the same way.

"No!" Quintus shouted in useless denial as first one, then a second .60 caliber ball smashed into his body. His eyes went wide as they sought to capture some of the fading light in the room. His body would no longer obey his commands. Slowly he sagged down, his death rattle loud in the silence.

A sudden disturbance at one entranceway drew the attention of the mountain men from the dying man. *"Father!"* young Quintus Faustus shrieked as he dashed through the archway, a dagger held high.

He hurled himself at Preacher, intent on burying the slim blade in the man's heart. Seemingly from nowhere, little Terry Tucker darted into the room at an oblique angle to Preacher and flung himself between the man and the Roman boy.

His exposed chest took the full brunt of the blow aimed by Faustus, though not before he triggered a round from a small pistol he held. The ball blew the brains out of Quintus Faustus before Terry collapsed into the arms of the man he admired above all others.

"I—I got him, didn't I?" Terry gasped. Then, at Preacher's wooden nod, he slumped into unconsciousness.

Blood dripped from his fingertips as Preacher gently brushed the hair from Terry's face as he cradled the lad in his arm. "Awh, Terry, Terry-boy, didn't I tell you to stay clear of the fightin'? But you saved my life, certain sure. Today . . ." The words would not come. Preacher swallowed hard. "Today you became a real man. One I'd be proud to call friend. Go with God, Terry Tucker."

Terry must have heard him, for a small smile froze on his peaceful face as he quietly died.

Preacher took a deep breath and allowed himself no further time to grieve for the boy who had saved him. He brushed a knuckle at the moisture that stole stealthily from his eyes, cleared his throat, and came to his boots.

"What now, Preacher?" asked Philadelphia, reluctant to intrude on the mountain man's sorrow.

"I'd be obliged if you would bind this arm and my chest, Philadelphia. An' you, Buck, round up the rest. Tell them to clean up this abomination, pull down the buildings, and burn everything. Free any slaves, and any who want can he'p them down to Bent's Fort and a chance to return to a normal life."

"What about you, Preacher?" Philadelphia and Buck asked together.

"Me? Why, I'm off for my winter home. Got myself a nice, blond bed warmer a-waitin'."

"What?" a startled Philadelphia demanded. "You mean that frisky young gal what took up arms and fought her way out of the arena with us?"

Preacher sighed through a spreading grin. "Yeah, that's right. The once-upon-a-time Bible-thumper."

BLOOD OF THE
MOUNTAIN MAN

Dying is a very dull, dreary affair. And my advice to you is to have nothing whatever to do with it.

—*W. Somerset Maugham*

1

Sheriff Monte Carson swung down in front of the mountain home and petted several of the many dogs that lived around the place. Properly stroked, they scampered off to resume their playing. Monte looked up as the front door opened. The sheriff had never gotten used to how big the man was who stood in the doorway. The man was inches over six feet, and with the weight to go with it. His shoulders were door-wide and hard-packed with muscle. His hips were lean and the muscles in his legs strained his denim jeans.

"Smoke," Monte said.

"Monte," the West's most famous gunfighter said. "You're just in time for breakfast and coffee. Come in."

Monte took off his hat and stepped into the lovely home of Smoke and Sally Jensen. He howdied and smiled at Sally, just as beautiful as ever, and took a seat at the kitchen table. Sally turned to the stove and cracked three more eggs and added another thick slice of ham to the other skillet.

"What's up, Monte?" Smoke Jensen asked, pouring the sheriff a cup of coffee.

"Smoke, how long's it been since you heard from your sister Janey?"

The question took Smoke by surprise. "Why . . . years. I thought she was dead."

"She is," Monte said bluntly, as was the Western way. He reached into his jacket pocket and took out a telegraph. "This came in early today. It's from the marshal of a little town up in Montana. Right smack in the middle of the Rockies. A mining town called Red Light."

Smoke looked at the man and Sally turned from the stove, arching an eyebrow at that.

Monte smiled. "I know. Strange name for a town. You'd better read the wire, Smoke."

Sally put the sheriff's ham and eggs and home-fried potatoes in front of him and Monte took knife and fork to hand and fell to eating, after buttering a hot biscuit.

The telegraph read: JANEY JENSEN, DIED RECENTLY OF NATURAL CAUSES AND LEFT EVERYTHING TO HER BROTHER. IMPORTANT THAT MR. K. JENSEN COME TO RED LIGHT AS SOON AS POSSIBLE TO LAY CLAIM TO ESTATE, WHICH INCLUDES BUSINESS IN TOWN AND RANCH IN VALLEY.

It was signed, CLUB BOWERS, SHERIFF, RED LIGHT, MONTANA.

"I knew a Club Bowers," Smoke said. "He was an outlaw."

"Same one," Monte said. "I know him, too. That might give you an idea what kind of town it is."

"Just where is Red Light?" Sally asked.

"In the middle of nowhere," Monte said. "It's a mining town, and it is isolated. Nearest town of any size is a good hundred miles away. There's talk of changing the name from Red Light to something else, but so far it's just talk."

Smoke sipped his coffee and stared at the sheriff.

"Monte, you're walking around something. Come on—what is it?"

"This is one of those freak strikes, Smoke. It's in a place where gold and silver shouldn't be. But they were found, and it's a good vein. It's slowing down some, but it'll probably be producing for a good many years to come. I know about Red Light. I had a friend killed up there a couple of years ago. The town is set up in the mountains, above one of the prettiest valleys you ever put your eyes on. Valley runs for miles and miles. River runs right through the entire length of the valley. The ranchers down there supply the beef for the miners. Tell you the truth, in a situation like that, I'd rather have a ranch than a gold mine. You'd best get up there. If you tarry long, you just might not have a ranch left."

"The other ranchers might take it?"

"You betcha. And you'll notice the wire read 'K. Jensen.' That tells me your sis never let on about your nickname. You bet those other ranchers will try to horn in. They'll be fightin' like coyotes over a scrap of meat."

"I wonder what the business in town is?"

Monte shrugged.

"Janey," Smoke said. "All these years I thought she was dead. I would have sworn she was dead. I heard she was." Smoke snapped his fingers. "I *know* she's dead. Then . . ."

"Her daughter, honey?" Sally said, putting his plate in front of him and sitting down with a biscuit and a cup of coffee.

"That all you're eating?" Smoke asked with a frown.

"I'm on a diet. Her daughter?" she repeated.

"Maybe. She did have a daughter by that gambling man she took off with back in Missouri. She pulled out in '64 and heard she had the child in '67. She wouldn't be out of her teens."

"She had a daughter, Smoke," Sally said. "I remember

some of the women talking about it back in Idaho Territory—before I met you. Jenny was her name."

"Monte, can you wire back and see if this is Janey or Jenny who died?"

"Sure."

"I'll be in town this afternoon and stop by your office."

Monte finished his breakfast and headed back to town. Over a second cup of coffee, Sally said, "This is bringing back bad memories for you, isn't it, Smoke?"

"Some." He smiled at her. "But I'll survive them."

"This girl, if it is Jenny, would be no more than a child. Seventeen at most."

"What do you remember about her?"

"Nothing. I never saw her. The ladies of the town said that she was at school back East.

"We'll know more after I go into town."

"Saddle my pony for me. I'm riding in with you."

"Sidesaddle, of course, Smoke said with a straight face.

Her reply would not have been printable in those times.

"Here's the whole story, Smoke," Monte said, handing Smoke several pages of telegraph paper. "I wired a sheriff I know up in Montana Territory. He knew all about it."

Smoke opened the envelope. MISS JANEY JENSEN DIED OF FEVER TWO YEARS AGO. WAS PROMINENT BUSINESSWOMAN IN TOWN. OWNED BUSINESSES AND RANCH IN VALLEY. IS BURIED IN RED LIGHT, MONTANA CEMETERY. HAD ONE DAUGHTER, JENNY. JENNY RETURNED TO RED LIGHT AND IS LIVING ON RANCH. ENTIRE ESTATE LEFT TO JENNY. NO ONE KNEW WHERE TO FIND JANEY'S BROTHER, A MISTER K. JENSEN. UNDERSTAND HE WAS FINALLY LOCATED IN COLORADO AND NOTIFIED. TELL HIM TO BE CAREFUL. DON'T TRUST

ANY LAW OFFICER IN COUNTY. K. JENSEN IS RID-
ING INTO A DEN OF SNAKES. ANY RELATION TO
SMOKE? IF SO, TAKE HIM ALONG. JUST KIDDING.
TAKE CARE OF YOURSELF, MONTE.

"Man lays it right on the line, doesn't he?" Smoke said.

"Tom's a good man," Monte replied. "Is Sally going up
there with you?"

"No. Not initially. I might send for her later on. Jenny
vanished. I don't like the sound of that. Damn it, Monte,
she's my only kin. Except for some folks in Iowa that I have
never seen and who fought against my father in the war. I understand they harbored such bad feeling toward those Jensens
who fought for the south that they changed their name to
Jen*son*."

"That war tore up a lot of families, Smoke. Mine included. When are you pulling out?"

"Tomorrow, probably. I'll ride the trains as far as possible. It's been awhile since ol' Buck and I hit the trail. We'll
both look forward to it."

"Not taking one of your appaloosas?"

"Not this time. Buck's a mountain horse and better than
any watchdog in the world. And meaner, too. I want him to
see some more country before I retire him. Lord knows, we
have seen some trails together."

"You really love animals, don't you, Smoke?"

"Yes. And I respect them. I don't trust a man who doesn't
like animals. There's a flaw in his character . . ." He smiled.
"Although some of Sally's highly educated friends say that is
not true."

"They called you a liar to your face?"

"Only once."

Buck was a mountain-bred buckskin that was just about
too big and too much horse for the average man. But Smoke

was not an average man. He had gentle-broken the animal and was the only one who could ride it. Truth be known, he was about the only one who *wanted* to ride the mean-eyed animal.

"Now, you change into your suit when you reach the rails," Sally told him, handing him a sack of food for the trail.

"Yes, dear," the most famous gunfighter in all the West replied.

"And you button your collar and fix your tie properly."

"Yes, dear."

"And if your suit is rumpled, you have it brushed and ironed at the nearest town."

"Yes, dear."

"And as soon as you are settled up there, send for me."

"Yes, dear."

"And you will *not* let anyone know that you are Smoke Jensen unless it becomes absolutely necessary."

"Yes, dear," he said with a smile, towering above her outside the house. He closed his big hands around her arms and gently picked her up with all the ease of picking up a pillow. He kissed her lips and set her back down, then chuckled.

"What is so funny?" she demanded.

"Knowing my sister, what if it turns out the business she owned in town is a whorehouse?"

Sally narrowed her eyes. "If that is the case, *Mister* Jensen, you are in a world of trouble."

"Yes, *ma'am!*"

2

Smoke Jensen was a known gunfighter, though not by choice. Dozens of books—penny dreadfuls—had been written about him, ninety-nine percent of them pure crap and nonsense. Songs had been sung about him, and at least one play was still being performed about the life and times of Smoke Jensen. Smoke had read some of the books, or as much of them as he could stand, and he usually used them afterward to light fires in the stove or fireplace. The songs were terrible and the play was worse. But for all his fame and notoriety, relatively few people knew what he looked like. He seldom left his horse ranch, called the Sugarloaf, in the mountains of Colorado, and when he did venture out, it usually was not for long. Since so many would-be toughs and gunslingers had taken to wearing their guns as Smoke wore his, that trademark was no longer a giveaway.

Smoke rarely buckled on two guns anymore, doing so only when he knew he was riding into trouble. He was content to wear one gun, right side, low and tied down.

He was a ruggedly handsome man, but not in the pretty-boy way. His face was strong, his jaw firm, and his eyes cold as winter-locked fjords. He loved children and animals, and attended church on a regular basis, even though the preacher in the town of Big Rock, Colorado, knew Smoke would never pay much attention to the New Testament, since he was strictly an Old Testament man.

He raised appaloosas on his ranch, running only a few head of cattle now.

His wife, Sally, was of the New England Reynoldses, and enormously wealthy. She was a strong-willed woman, not one to mince words and certainly not someone to ride over. Sally was a strong supporter of women's rights, was very outspoken on the subject, and would not back down from a grizzly. She had strapped on pistol and picked up rifle and sent more than one thug to Hell in her time. She was also a loving mother and a faithful companion to her husband and a sweet person . . . just as long as you didn't mess with her man.

Smoke rode to the rails and boarded the train. At rail's end, he signed the hotel registry as K. Jensen and no one paid any special attention to him, except for the men commenting on his size and the ladies on how handsome and how well mannered he was.

Smoke had stabled Buck, curried him, and told the boy to grain him and not mess with him. It was doubtful Buck would hurt a child; he never had, but one never knew. The horse was a killer, and he bonded only with Smoke.

Smoke carefully bathed and shaved, and dressed in a dark suit, white shirt, and black string tie. He belted his gun around him and tied it down, slipping the hammer thong free of the hammer. It was something he did from habit, like breathing.

The large hotel, fairly fancy for the time, had a separate bar and dining room, connected by a door that was guarded on the saloon side by a man who looked like he ate wagons for lunch. Smoke entered the bar and ordered a whiskey. Not much of a drinking man, he did occasionally enjoy a drink before dinner, sometimes a brandy after dinner, and a beer after a hard day's ride.

Saloons were a meeting place, where a man—women were not yet allowed—could find out road conditions, trouble spots where highwaymen lurked, the best place to buy horses or cattle, what range was closed, and where good water could be found. Smoke leaned against the bar, sipped his whiskey, and listened.

"I heard Smoke Jensen got killed down in Mexico," a man said. "Gunfighter name of Jake Bonner got him."

Smoke hid his smile.

"What'd he do, back-shoot him?"

"Outdrew him."

Smoke tuned them out. Jake Bonner was a two-bit punk who had been making brags for several years that if he ever came upon Smoke Jensen, he was going to kill him.

"Bonner's in town." That remark brought Smoke back to paying attention to the gabby citizens.

"And he's sayin' he killed Jensen?"

"He's talkin' big about it."

'Well, by God. I knew he'd been gone for several months. I heard he hired out his gun. Say, now, this is news."

"Says he's got proof. Says he's got Jensen's boots, just jerked off his dead body. Fancy, engraved boots. Got the initials *SJ* right on the front of each one."

"You don't say?"

By this time, twenty men had gathered around and were listening to the bull-tossing.

"Say, stranger."

Smoke realized the citizen was talking to him, and he turned slightly. "Yes?"

"Didn't you come in on the 4:18 train?"

"That's right."

"Thought so. Did you hear anything about Jake Bonner killing Smoke Jensen?"

"No. I haven't heard anything about that."

"Funny. Seems like the news would be all over."

"If it's true," Smoke replied, sipping a bit of whiskey.

"Mister, you're a big'un, but I'd not call Jake Bonner a liar if I was you. Jake's a bad one."

"Every town has one."

"Not as bad as Jake. The man's cat-quick with a gun. Why, he's got five notches carved in his gun handle."

"Tinhorn trick," Smoke said.

"You callin' me a tinhorn?" the voice came from the boardwalk batwings to the saloon.

Smoke turned slowly. The man facing him from about thirty feet away was young, no more than twenty-two or -three. He wore two guns, pearl-handled, in a fancy rig. His coat was swept back, his hands by his side.

"Anybody who carves notches in his gun-handles is a tinhorn," Smoke said, placing his shot glass on the bar. "If that fits you, wear it."

"I'm Jake Bonner. The man who killed Smoke Jensen. And you'll take back that remark, mister. Or you'll drag iron."

"What if I decide to do neither?"

"Then you're a yeller dog."

"I've known some nice dogs in my time. As a matter of fact, I've known a lot more nice dogs than nice humans."

Back in a corner of the big room, a faro dealer sat with a smile on his lips. Of all the men in the room, he alone knew who the big man in the black suit was. He'd seen him several times, once in action. And he knew that if Jake Bonner didn't close his mouth and do it real quick, he was either dead on the floor or stomped into a cripple.

Jake walked closer to the bar, his fancy spurs jingling. "Mister, I think you're a liar and a coward. What do you have to say about that?"

"I think you'd better go home before I decide to change your diapers."

The bar cleared, the men leaving as of one mind. Only the faro dealer remained in the direct line of fire. He knew that if Bonner was dumb enough to draw—or attempt to draw— he'd never get a shot off. The faro dealer figured he was in the safest spot in the saloon.

"Before you *what?*" Jake's words were almost a scream.

Smoke was getting angry, but his was never a hot anger. It was a cold fury. "Are you deaf as well as stupid?" He knew he was pushing, but punks infuriated Smoke. Especially one who walked around making the claim that he'd killed him.

Jake walked closer, and Smoke knew then that Bonner was no gunfighter. No gunfighter wanted action this close up. The odds were too great that both men would take lead.

"You're a dead man, mister," Jake hissed the words.

"No," Smoke said slowly. "But you're sure a hurt one." He backhanded Jake with a hard right that knocked the man spinning. Jake fell against a table, the table collapsed, and Jake landed on his butt on the floor in a state of confusion.

Things weren't supposed to work out this way. Every time he'd try to get up, the big stranger would knock him back down. Jake felt his lips pulp and knew he'd lost a couple of teeth. The big man hauled back a huge fist and busted Jake right on the nose. Jake screamed in pain as his beak busted and the blood poured. In a fog of hurt, Jake felt himself being jerked to his feet and hurled through the air. He crashed against a wall and the air left him.

When Jake could catch his breath, he reached for his guns, but his holsters were empty. He blinked a couple of times and saw his guns, on the bar, in front of the big stranger. The stranger was calmly sipping at his whiskey.

Smoke unloaded the matched .45s and lined up the cartridges on the bar. "Children shouldn't play with guns," he said. "You might hurt yourself, Booper."

"The name is Bonner," Jake gasped.

Smoke nodded gravely and finished his drink. "You all through trying to play tough boy, Bonehead?"

Jake struggled to his feet and stood swaying for a moment. Then, with a curse, he reached behind him and jerked out a knife.

"I really wish you hadn't done that," Smoke said.

"Jake!" the faro dealer shouted. "Don't do it, boy. You don't know who you're messin' with."

Jake sneered at the dealer. Smoke stood facing the bar, both hands on the polished mahogany.

"I'm gonna gut you like a fish, mister," Jake panted, the blood dripping down from his busted nose and smashed lips.

The batwings flipped open and a man wearing a star stood there. "Put it down, Jake," he ordered. "Do it now, or I'll shoot you where you stand."

Jake slowly lowered the knife. The marshal walked around to face the young would-be tough. "What the hell ran over you, Jake? A beer wagon?"

Jake refused to answer.

"Put the knife up, Jake. Right now."

Jake sheathed the big blade and with something that sounded like a sob, abruptly turned and lurched from the saloon.

"These are his guns, Marshal," Smoke said. "I took the precaution of unloading them."

The marshal walked up to Smoke and the counterman placed a cup of coffee in front of him. "Jake's a pretty salty type, mister. Not many men around here would have tried to disarm him."

"He's a two-bit loudmouth," Smoke replied. "Nothing more."

"You got a name?"

"Doesn't everybody?" Smoke turned and walked out of the bar and into the dining area. He was seated and a menu was placed in front of him.

The marshal was irritated and his face showed it. He turned to follow Smoke and the faro dealer said, "Leave him alone, Jeff. He's a good, decent man who was pushed, that's all. Believe me when I say that is the *last* man in the world you want to crowd."

"You know him, Sparks?"

"I've seen him a time or two, yes. He just wants to have a meal and a good night's sleep, that's all."

Jeff thought for a moment, and then nodded. "All right, I'll take your word for it. But you know Jake's not gonna stand for this."

"His funeral, Marshal."

"Yeah, that's what I'm afraid of."

Smoke ate his meal and had coffee, then stepped out onto the porch for a cigarette and a breath of night air. He had not forgotten Jake Bonner. That would have been a very unwise thing to do. For the Jakes of this world, once humiliated, would never forgive or forget, and Smoke was careful of his back.

He looked across the street and saw the marshal sitting on the boardwalk, watching him.

The marshal knows Jake isn't going to forget what happened in the saloon, he thought. And he's thinking Jake just might decide to do something tonight.

Smoke sat down in a chair that was shrouded in darkness and finished his cigarette. He was tired, but not sleepy. He knew he should go on up to his room and lie down, but he didn't want to do that. He was more irritated than restless. He would have liked to walk the main street of the town. But to do that would only bring him trouble. Hell, he thought, sitting here will probably bring me trouble.

In my own way, I am a prisoner.

Come on, Jake, he reasoned, his thoughts suddenly savage. Come on. If you're going to do something foolish, do it now and get it over with.

The marshal stood up and walked to his office. He stood for a moment in the open door, then stepped inside and closed it behind him.

I'm a stranger here, Smoke thought. I'd better have witnesses.

He stood up and walked through the hotel lobby to the bar, a tall, well-dressed man in a tailored suit. In the saloon, he ordered coffee and stood by the bar, waiting for it to cool. The place was doing a brisk business. But when Smoke elected to stand at the bar, the long bar cleared, the men choosing tables instead.

That amused Smoke, in a sour sort of way. He was conscious of the faro dealer watching him. I've seen that man somewhere down the line, Smoke thought.

The batwings pushed open and Jake Bonner stood there, his bruised face swollen now. He'd found him more guns and his holsters were full.

"I'm callin' your hand, mister," Jake said, his voice husky with emotion. "Now turn around and face me."

Smoke turned, brushing back his coat as he did. "Go home, Jake Bonner. There is no need for this."

"Do what he says, Jake," the faro dealer called. "He's giving you a chance to live. Take it."

"Shut up, gambler!" Jake yelled. "This ain't none of your affair. I'm the man who killed Smoke Jensen. No two-bit stranger does to me what this one done."

"You didn't kill Smoke Jensen, Jake," the dealer said. "Smoke Jensen is standing in front of you."

The saloon became as hushed as a church. Jake's face drained of blood and he stood pale and shaken.

"Go home, Jake," Smoke told him. "Go home and live. Don't crowd me."

"Draw, damn you!" Jake screamed, and grabbed iron.

Smoke's draw was perfection, deadly beauty. As Jake's hands closed around the butts of his guns, he felt a hammer blow in the center of his chest. He stumbled backward and fell against the wall, then slowly slid down to sit on the floor. His guns were still in leather.

"No," he said. "This ain't . . . this ain't right. This ain't the way it's suppose' to be."

"But it is," the faro dealer said.

"You go to hell!" Jake Bonner screamed.

It was the last thing he said.

Smoke holstered his gun and stood by the bar. He picked up his coffee cup with his left hand and took a sip. Just right.

"Jesus God!" a man breathed. "I seen it but I don't believe it. It was a blur. Hell, it wasn't even that!"

The marshal stepped in, gun drawn. He looked at Jake, then at Smoke, and holstered his .45. "I knew it was going to happen," he said. "I thought about lockin' Jake up until mornin'. Now I wish I had."

"Jake called him and drew first," a man said. "Or tried to. That's Smoke Jensen, Marshal."

"The poor dumb fool," the marshal said. "Not you," he was quick to add, looking at Smoke.

"You have any questions for me?" Smoke asked.

"Only one. When are you leavin' town?"

"First thing in the morning."

"Good. Somebody get the undertaker and get Jake fitted for a box." The marshal looked at Smoke. There were things he wanted to say, but he was wise enough not to say them. It wasn't that he blamed Smoke, for he was sure that Smoke had been pushed into the fight. "Good night, Mister Jensen," was all he had to say.

Smoke nodded and left the room.

He was gone before dawn the next morning.

3

Smoke had a long ride ahead of him, but it was one he was looking forward to. He had wanted to provision up at the town that was now miles behind him, but felt it best to move on. There might be more like Jake Bonner in town.

He shot a rabbit and had that for lunch, then caught several fish and had them for his dinner. The next day he rode up to an old trading post and after looking it over from a distance, decided to provision there. He stepped inside and knew immediately he had walked into some sort of disagreement. There were six men besides the owner in the dark and smoky room that served as a bar—cowboys, from the look of them. Three stood facing three, and their faces were dark with anger. The owner or manager or whatever the hell he was stood behind the rough plank bar.

"Beans and bacon and flour and coffee," Smoke said, walking up to the bar.

"Mister, this ain't a real good time for doin' no grocery shoppin'," the man told him.

"It's as good a time as any, Smoke replied. "Fill the order."

"I reckon Dupree hired you, too, mister" a cowboy said to Smoke.

Smoke looked at him. "Nobody hired me to do anything. And I never heard of any Dupree. Just passin' through is all. You boys carry on with your business and let me do mine." His gaze returned to the man behind the bar. "And toss in a box of .44s while you're at it."

One of the cowboys had looked out the window at Smoke's horse. "I never seen that brand before."

"Now you have," Smoke replied. "A can of peaches, too," he added to his order. "You have any food cooked?"

"Beans and beef," the man said. "Mister, ride on. This ain't no time for . . ."

"Dish me up a plate of it. A big plate. I'm hungry.

"Are you hard of hearin'?" a cowboy asked. "You was told to ride on."

All in all, Smoke thought, this trip is turning out to be a disaster from the git-go. "Buddy, I don't know what your problem is. But I do have a suggestion. Leave me the hell alone and stick to your own knittin'!"

The cowboys, obviously working on opposite sides of the fence, and probably arguing over range or strayed beef or water rights, looked at one another and silently decided to band together against this stranger who, it appeared, was not taking either side very seriously.

The bartender shoved a plate of food at the tall stranger and Smoke stood at the bar and went to eating, ignoring the cowboys.

"Well, if that don't beat all!" one said. "Just turns his back to us and starts feedin' his face."

"Fill the order," Smoke told the man behind the bar.

The man sighed.

"You fill that order, Smith," a puncher said, "and you'll get no more business from the Lazy J."

"And none from the Three Star," the other side warned.

"Fill the order," Smoke told him.

"Man," the bartender said. "You have put me in one hell of a bind. You know that?"

"It's a free country," Smoke told him. "If you don't want to sell me the goods, then do so of your own choosing. Not because of threats from this bunch of saddlebums."

"Saddlebums!" one of the men shouted.

Another walked to the bar and leaned against it, staring hard at Smoke. He took a closer look at the man nonchalantly eating his meal. Feller sure was big. He looked at the man's wrists. Bigger than most men's forearms. But he figured the six of them could handle him without much trouble.

"Mister, I think we'll just clean your clock."

Smoke turned and hit him with a left that seemed to come out of nowhere. The impact sounded like a melon hit with the flat side of an ax. The man's boots flew out from under him and he was slammed to the floor, flat on his back. He did not move.

"Now leave me the hell alone and let me finish my meal," Smoke said, without looking at the remaining five.

They looked back at him, then at the motionless puncher on the floor. One side of the man's face was rapidly swelling and they knew his jaw was broken.

One punch. One broken jaw. No one among them seemed especially eager to step up to the bar.

"Close your mouth and fill my order," Smoke told the man behind the bar.

"Yes, sir," the man said softly.

"You as good with that gun as you are with your fists, mister?" a cowboy from the Lazy J asked.

"Better," Smoke told him.

"You just might have to prove it," he said.

"Then that makes you short of sense," Smoke replied. "I'm passing through, nothing more. You boys are on the prod, not me. You pushed me, not the other way around. Think about it."

The man on the floor still had not moved, except for his swelling jaw.

"You got a name?"

Smoke put down his fork and turned, facing the five. It was then that several of them noticed the hammer thong had been slipped from the big stranger's six-gun. No one had seen him do it, so that meant it was done when his boots left the stirrups and hit the ground. All of them noticed that he was facing five-to-one odds and showing no fear, no excitement, nothing except dead calm.

"Smoke Jensen."

The bartender slowly sank to the floor, behind a beer barrel. Somewhere within the confines of the trading post, a clock ticked loudly.

Of the five punchers, one found his voice. "Feller down the way claims to have killed Jensen in Mexico."

"He lied. Jake Bonner is dead. I killed him night before last. I didn't want to. But he crowded me. Just like you're doing."

"I ain't crowdin' you," a Three Star rider said. "I'm sittin' down and stayin' out of this."

"Me, too," a Lazy J man said.

"That makes three of us," another one said.

The men moved out of the line of fire and sat down and very carefully put their hands on the rough tabletop. It was by no means an act of cowardice. It was just showing exceptionally good sense. "Sit down, Luke," one of the three said. "You, too, Shorty. This is stupid. The man ain't done us no harm. I'm big enough to admit we was out of line and pushy."

"I ain't takin' water from no killer," Luke said stubbornly.

"Me, neither," Shorty said. "And I ain't real sure this is Smoke Jensen. I think he's a tinhorn."

"I'll turn around and finish my meal." Smoke offered an honorable way out of a bad situation. "You boys sit down and have a beer on me. How about that?"

"I say you go right straight to hell," Shorty said, his voice thick.

"It won't be me who takes that trip today, boys," Smoke told them. "Think about it."

"You can't take both of us," Luke bragged.

"Yes, I can," Smoke said quietly and surely. "But I don't want to."

"Now I *know* he ain't Smoke Jensen," Shorty said. "He's yeller."

The front door opened and two men stepped in. Both quickly sized up the situation.

"Shorty," one said. "Sit down."

"Luke," the second man said. "You do the same. Right now."

"This tinhorn braced me, Boss," Luke said.

"No, he didn't," one of the men seated said. "We all started this. Dixie there," he looked at the man on the floor, "he stuck his face in the stranger's and got stretched out with one punch."

"This hombre says he's Smoke Jensen, Boss," Shorty said.

The men, obviously the owners of the Lazy J and the Three Star, stepped between Smoke and the two riders. One faced the punchers, the other faced Smoke.

"Is that right?" Smoke was asked.

"That's right. I came in here for a meal and supplies. Nothing more. And I'll ride if given the chance. But no more mouth from your boys."

"We pay the men for work. What they do or say on their own time is their business."

"Then I hope you have room in your cemetery for two more." Smoke was blunt.

The bartender had stood up. "Jensen's tellin' the truth. He didn't do nothin' 'cept come in here and ask for supplies."

"I think you better ride," the rancher facing Smoke said.

"Is that an order?"

The rancher's smile was thin. "Just a suggestion, Mister Jensen."

Smoke nodded his head. "Sack up my supplies," he told the man behind the bar. "And total up my bill. I'll be moving along."

"Just like I said," Shorty popped off. "Yeller."

The ranchers stepped out of the way. That was the final straw and they both knew it. No man would stand for that.

Luke sat down.

Smoke looked at Shorty. The man was scared and sweating. He had worked himself into a corner and didn't know how to get out of it. Shorty was probably a pretty decent sort; it was not a crime to be young. Smoke took a chance and took a step toward the puncher.

Shorty looked confused and stood a step back, bumping into a table. Smoke kept walking toward him.

"Are you crazy?" Shorty said, a shrill sound to his words. "Hold up, man."

Smoke kept walking.

The others in the room wondered what in hell Jensen was up to.

Smoke walked right up to Shorty and jerked his six-shooter from leather. He tossed the gun to a puncher seated at a table. The puncher caught the .45 and held it like he was holding a lighted stick of dynamite.

"Sit down, Shorty," Smoke said. "And I'll buy you a drink. The trouble is over."

Shorty sat, then looked up at the man. "That took guts, Mister Jensen. I acted the fool."

"We all do from time to time. You sure don't hold a corner on the market."

Smoke walked the room, introducing himself and shaking hands with all the men. Whatever friction might have been between the punchers had vanished. The men had gotten Dixie to his boots and the man wobbled over to the table and sat down. Turned out his jaw wasn't broken, but it damn sure was badly bent.

"I had a mule kick me one time; wasn't that hard," Dixie mush-mouthed.

The ranchers sent their men back to home range and they sat and had coffee with Smoke.

"So Jake Bonner finally got himself six feet," Three Star said. "It's overdue."

Lazy J said, "You lookin' for land up this way, Smoke?"

"No. I'm heading for a place called Red Light. Can you tell me anything about it?"

"It's a damn good place to stay away from," Three Star replied. "It's a den of snakes and they're all poison."

"It's a hard four-day ride from here," the other rancher said. "Figure on six unless you want to wear your horse out. But," he added with a smile, "if that's your buckskin out yonder, it don't look like he ever gets tired."

"He's a good one," Smoke acknowledged. "And the best bodyguard I ever had."

"I can believe that. He gave me a look that caused me to give him a wide berth," the rancher said. "Thanks for givin' Shorty a break. He's a good boy, but hot-headed. This might cool him down some."

The men chatted for a time, the ranchers telling Smoke

the best way up to the rip-roaring mining town of Red Light, and then Smoke packed his supplies and rode north.

"I always figured Smoke Jensen for a much older man," one rancher said.

The other one bit off a chew and replied, "Killed his first man when he was about fourteen. Then he dropped out of sight for a few years. Raised by mountain men. Ol' Preacher took him under his wing. When Jensen surfaced a few years later, he was pure hell on wheels with a gun. Nice feller once you get to know him."

The West was being settled and tamed slowly, but it was getting there. Smoke avoided the many little towns and settlements that were cropping up all over the place. Most would be gone in a few years, some would prosper and grow.

At the end of the third day, Smoke was beginning to feel a little gamy and wanted a hot bath, a bed with clean sheets, and a meal that someone else had cooked. He topped a ridge and looked down at a small six-store town, about a dozen homes scattered around the short main street. He rode slowly down the rutted road. As he entered the town, he was conscious of the eyes on him. He swung down in front of the livery and told the man he'd stall and curry Buck himself.

"I damn sure wouldn't touch that hoss," the liveryman said. "That beast has got a wicked look in his eyes."

"Gentle as a kitten," Smoke said.

"What kind of a kitten?" man asked. "A puma?"

Smoke smiled and spent the next few minutes taking care of Buck while the big horse chomped away at grain.

Taking his kit and his rifle, Smoke walked across the street to the combination saloon, cafe, and hotel. It was mid-afternoon and the town was quiet. He registered as K. Jensen and went to his room. Taking fresh clothing, he walked to the barbershop and ordered hot water for the tub while he had himself a shave.

"Passin' through?" the barber inquired.

"Yup," Smoke told him. "Seeing the country. Thought I'd head up to Red Light and see what's up there."

"Trouble," the barber was blunt. "That's a bad place to head for, mister."

"Oh?"

"Yes, sir. You're a hard day and a half from Red Light. Over the mountains. Used to be a decent place. Lots of small miners. Then Major Cosgrove moved in with his pack of trouble-hunters and before you knew what had happened, he owned the whole kit and caboodle. Them that tried to hold on to their claims suddenly got seriously dead. They tried to get their dust out, and they was robbed. I ran a shop up there for a few years. I made good money, but man, it got chancy, so I pulled out and settled here. The money ain't so good, but the peace is nice. Except when Red Lee and his boys come to town."

"Red Lee?"

"Owns a ranch east of here. Likes to think he owns everybody around here, too. Know the type?"

"Sure."

"A couple of his boys is over to the saloon now. You'd best walk light around them. They like to start trouble, and they fancy themselves gunslicks."

"I'll certainly take that under advisement," Smoke said.

He bathed carefully and then ordered more hot water to rinse off in. Dressed in clean clothes, while his others were being laundered, Smoke walked back to the hotel and into the saloon for a whiskey to cut the trail dust. It was just a little early for supper.

He ignored the three men sitting at a table and walked to the bar. But he immediately pegged the men as rowdies and trouble-hunters. Nowhere had he seen any sign of a marshal or a marshal's office in the small town.

Smoke was beginning to have bad feelings about this trip. All he'd set out to do was settle his dead sister's affairs, and so far all he'd had was trouble. He really wished he was back on the Sugarloaf, with Sally.

"Whiskey," he told the bartender. "From the good bottle."

"Well, now," one of the rowdies said. "Looks like we got us a dandy come to town, boys. *From the good bottle,*" he mimicked mockingly.

Smoke looked at the bartender as he poured the whiskey. There were warning signs in the man's eyes, but Smoke ignored them. He was tired from the trail, wanting only a drink, a hot meal, and a warm bed. He was in no mood to be pushed around by the likes of those at the table.

He despised that type of man and always had. He'd helped Sheriff Monte Carson run more than one of 'em out of town, and he'd personally killed his share of 'em over the years. They were, as the good folks in the Deep South called them, white trash.

Smoke took a sip of his whiskey and carefully sat the glass down. He turned to face the men. "You have a problem with that, loudmouth?"

The men fell silent, their mocking smiles suddenly gone from their faces. The bartender moved back, away from the tall stranger. Two locals at a table looked at each other and wished they were somewhere else.

"Are you talkin' to *us*, mister?" one of the trio said.

"I don't see anyone else in the room who stuck his lip into my business."

"You just bought yourself a whole mess of trouble, mister," another of the three said.

"You got it to do," Smoke told him. "Fists or guns. It doesn't make a damn bit of difference to me. Step up here and toe the mark."

4

The three looked at each other and smiled. "You know who you're about to tangle with, drifter?" one asked.

"Three braying jackasses."

The men flushed as anger overtook them. "You want him, Carl?" one asked.

"Let's put a rope on him and drag him," another suggested.

"Fine idea, Shell."

Smoke looked at the third man. "You have a name, or did your mother just throw you out with the garbage and forget about you?"

"Why, you! . . . Yeah, I got a name. Ned."

"Well, come on, Ned. Don't be shy."

The men again exchanged glances. They'd been riding roughshod over people for years. At no time had they ever run up on anybody like this tall stranger.

The locals were doing their best to hide their smiles. And it did not go unnoticed by the three rowdies.

"You think it's funny now, citizens," Shell told them. "But when we finish with this yahoo, we'll settle your hash, too."

"You won't be able to do anything in about five minutes," Smoke told him. "None of you. Now either shut your damn mouths or step up here. What's it going to be?"

Ned cussed and walked up to the bar. Smoke hit him in mid-stride, his left boot still off the floor in a half-step. Smoke hit him with a solid left that pulped the man's lips and knocked him flat on his butt on the floor.

Shell and Carl rushed him. Smoke turned, picked up a chair, and splintered it across Shell's face. The blood flew and Shell joined Ned on the floor.

Carl's eyes widened and he did some fast back pedaling, but it was too late. Smoke stepped in and began hammering at the man with both fists, the lefts and rights landing like small bombs, and sounding like them.

Carl swung a wild blow and Smoke grabbed the man's forearm and tossed him over the bar. He landed on the ledge amid dozens of bottles of whiskey. The mirror jarred free of its braces and fell on him, shattering in hundreds of pieces. Ned was staggering to his feet just as Smoke grabbed him by the neck and the seat of his jeans and propelled him toward one of the big front windows. Ned started hollering as soon as he realized what Smoke had in mind. His bettering was cut short as Smoke tossed him through the window. Ned sailed over the warped boardwalk and impacted against and wrapped around a hitchrail. Ned did a little acrobatics around and around the rail and landed on his back in the street, the wind knocked from him.

Carl was staggering around behind the bar, trying to figure out what had happened. Smoke cleared it all up real quick by grabbing the man by the bandanna and brutally hauling him over the bar. Carl's eyes were bugged out and he was making choking sounds. Smoke began spinning him around and around in a circle, Carl impacting on tables and chairs and knocking them in all directions. Smoke released his hold on the bandanna and Carl went sailing across the room, right through the second large window and out into the street. Carl was thrown up against a horse and the animal reared in fright and kicked out with its hind legs. The steel-shod hooves caught Carl right in the butt and the would-be tough went sailing across the street. He landed on his face in the dirt, out cold.

The citizens in the saloon were enjoying every minute of it, wide eyed and smiling.

"Oh, hell!" Shell said, getting to his feet and facing a mean-eyed Smoke Jensen.

Smoke smiled at him and then reared back. Shell bounced off a wall and very unwillingly came toward Smoke. Smoke stepped to one side, grabbed the man in the very same manner he'd done with Ned, and threw him out into the street. Shell landed in a horse trough and wisely decided to stay there.

A very startled Red Lee and his foreman had just ridden up and stared in amazement at the sight before them.

"Who is that out there?" Smoke asked the locals who were still sitting at a table.

"Red Lee and Jim Sloane," he was told. "Big rancher and his foreman."

"Is that right?" Smoke said. He found his whiskey, downed what remained of it, and walked out to the boardwalk, using the batwings, about all that was still intact at the front of the saloon.

Smoke stood on the boardwalk and looked at the two men for a few seconds. The big, rough-looking man with red hair returned the stare.

"I suppose you're Red Lee," Smoke said.

"That's right. What the hell is going on around here?"

"Some of your boys decided to get lippy. One of their suggestions was to rope and drag me. I didn't like the idea."

"Damn shore didn't," Shell muttered from the water trough. "It was a really bad idea."

"Shut up," Red told him. He returned his gaze to Smoke.

Smoke said, "You obviously enjoy the notion of your hands riding roughshod over people. So that makes you responsible for whatever happens. The saloon needs to be swept out and straightened up. You do it."

The whole town had turned out. At least thirty-five people now stood on the boardwalk, silent and listening and watching.

Red's expression was priceless. It took him a moment to find his voice. "You want me to do *what?*"

"Swamp out the saloon."

"When Hell freezes over," Red said.

"Oh, it'll be before then." Smoke's hand flashed and his .44 came out spitting fire and lead. The bullets howled and screamed around the hooves of Red's horse. The animal panicked and reared up, dumping Red on his butt in the street. The foreman was frantically fighting to get his own horse under control.

Smoke could move with deceptive speed for a man of his size. He was off the boardwalk and in the street in the blink of an eye. He jerked the foreman out of the saddle and threw him down in the dirt on his belly, momentarily addling the man. He turned and planted a big fist smack on the side of Red's jaw. The rancher went down like a brick.

Smoke jerked their guns from leather and tucked them behind his own belt. Jim got to his boots just in time to feel a hard hand gripping his neck and another hand gathering up denim at the seat of his pants. The foreman felt himself propelled out of the street, up on the boardwalk and then through the broken window. He slid on his face for a few feet before his face came to rest against a full cuspidor.

Jim looked up to see his boss come sailing through the other broken window. Red Lee landed hard on his belly and slid a couple of yards, coming to an abrupt halt when his head banged against the front of the bar.

The bartender had long since exited out the back door and hastily beat it over to the barbershop. He and the barber were standing by the front window, watching.

"Who is that man?" the bartender asked.

"Damned if I know," the barber replied. "But he's sure a one-man wreckin' crew."

Over at the saloon, the bulk of Smoke Jensen filled the pushed-open batwings. His hands were filled with guns taken from the still addled hands of Red Lee. "Find some brooms and dustpans," he told the men on the floor. "And get busy."

"You're a dead man," Red Lee said, his voice harsh and filled with hatred.

Smoke tossed him a pistol. The six-shooter landed on the floor, inches from the rancher.

"You want to try your luck, be my guest," Smoke told him.

Outside, Ned had climbed out of the water trough and was slopping around. The liveryman ran over and whispered in his ear, and Ned damn near fainted. He squished up to the boardwalk and over to a busted window.

"Boss? Dyer just read the brand on that stranger's horse. That's Smoke Jensen, Boss."

The saloon had never been so clean. Ned, Shell, and Carl pitched in and the five of them worked at it until it shone. Smoke sat at a corner table and ate supper while the men worked.

"I'll be back through here from time to time," Smoke said, having no intention of ever returning to this town. "Chances are you won't know I'm around, but I will be. If I hear of you or your men ever crowding another citizen or drifter, I'll hunt you down and kill you, Red."

"This wasn't none of your affair, Jensen," Red said sullenly, pushing a broom across the floor.

"Not until your men started crowding me. That made it personal."

"They was just havin' fun."

"I didn't see the humor in it."

Other area ranchers and farmers had drifted in and were enjoying the scene. The saloon was nearly full. Red and his men had been throwing their weight around for years, and payback time was long overdue and much appreciated.

Smoke was under no illusions about what Red was going to do. Just as soon as Red got a chance, he was going to try to kill him. Ned and Shell and Carl were cowboys, not fast guns. They rode for a rough brand, but they were not killers.

But Jim Sloane was another matter. Smoke felt he would side with his boss when it came down to the nut-cuttin'.

Red finally threw down his broom and turned to face Smoke. "That's it, Jensen. No more."

"Your choice," Smoke told him, a fresh pot of coffee on the table before him.

"You'd kill me over a bunch of people you never laid eyes on before today?"

"I don't want to."

"That don't answer my question."

"You figure it out."

"I come in here first, Jensen. I fought . . ."

"I don't want to hear that crap!" Smoke said harshly. "I'm sick of hearing it from men like you. Yes, you fought Indians and outlaws. Yes, you settled this land. But it's 1883 now. And time has passed you by. The old ways are all but gone. It won't be long before this territory will become a state. With a state militia and maybe even a state police force. You think they'll put up with the crap you've been pulling? The answer is no, they won't. Look around you, Red."

Red did, and saw a half a dozen ranchers and their foremen, all armed, all staring back at him. Suddenly, all because of one man, Red knew his days of being top dog were over. The people had become united against him. And he hated Smoke Jensen for that.

"You still lookin' for hands out at your spread, Mister Jackson?" Shell asked a rancher.

"Still lookin', Shell. You interested?"

"I sure am."

"Me, too," Ned said.

"And me," Carl was quick to add.

"You're all hired."

"You yellow bastards!" Red told his former riders. "You'd best watch your mouth, Mister Lee," Shell told the man. "You can insult me all you like, but leave my family out of it." He looked at his friends. "Let's get our gear from the ranch. See you 'bout dark, Mister Jackson."

"The grub will be hot and waitin' on you, boys." The three punchers left the saloon . . . after nodding respectfully at Smoke.

Red Lee cursed the men until they were out of sight. Smoke waited, well aware that the man was hovering near the breaking point.

"Go home, Red," another rancher told the man. "Go home and cool off."

"Don't you tell me what to do, you goddamn rawhider."

"We all were rawhiders when we first came here, Red," another rancher said. "Even you. So you got no call to insult us."

"I'll do just as I've always done," the man popped back. "And that is whatever I damn well please."

"Them days is over, Red," a farmer spoke up. "You're the only rancher in the area that don't buy my vegetables and bacon and hams, and whose men still ride roughshod over my place. It'll not happen again. I tell you that face to face."

Red pointed a finger at the farmer, dressed in overalls and low-heeled boots. The finger was shaking and his voice was thick with barely controlled emotion. "You don't talk to me like that, Jergenson. I don't take lip from a goddamn squatter."

Smoke sat and listened. With any kind of luck he would not have to draw on the hair-trigger-tempered rancher. He felt that the locals were just about to deal with Red Lee. And maybe he'd been wrong about the foreman, Jim Sloane. The man was slowly edging away from his boss, occasionally looking pleadingly in Smoke's direction.

Smoke sat drinking coffee, waiting. He hated two-bit tyrants like Red Lee. He'd had a gutfull of them as a boy, back in Missouri, working their hard-scrabble rocky farm from can-see to can't-see while his daddy was off in the war and his mother lay dying.

Red suddenly stopped his cursing and shouting and turned on Smoke. "Stand up, gunfighter," he said.

"Don't do it, Red," Smoke told him. "Just settle down and be a good citizen from now on. Can't you see that the others are willing to forgive and forget?"

"I said get up, damn your eyes!"

"Try me, Red," the rancher named Jackson said.

Red turned, disbelief in his eyes. "You, Jackson? You want to try me?"

"I reckon it's come to that, Red, the rancher said calmly, standing with his feet spread and his right hand close to the butt of his six-gun.

"I'm out of this, Jim Sloane said. "Red, man . . . come on. Let's go home."

"You're fired, you son-of-a-bitch!" Red shouted.

"You're hired," a rancher told Sloane. "You're a good cowboy, Jim."

"Draw, damn you!" Red shouted to Jackson.

"I'll not start this," the rancher said.

Red's temper exploded and he grabbed iron. He got off the first shot, the lead splintering wood at Jackson's feet. Jackson didn't miss. His shot took Red in the center of his chest and the man staggered back, an amazed look on his face.

"Why . . . you shot me," he said.

Smoke poured another cup of coffee.

Red tried to speak again but his mouth was suddenly filled with blood. He slowly sank to his knees on the fresh-mopped floor and his gun slipped from his fingers to clatter on the boards. Red knelt there, looking at the pistol.

"It didn't have to be," Jackson said.

"Yes, it did," another rancher disagreed.

The words were very faint to Red Lee as the world began darkening around him. This just couldn't be happening to him. Not to him.

"I tried to tell him," Jim said. "Over the past months I've tried and tried to talk sense to him. He just wouldn't listen."

"I know you have," Jackson said.

"The day of the tyrant is over," Jergenson said. "I knew it had to happen."

"You be sure and save me a couple of them hams come this fall," a rancher told the farmer. "They was mighty fine eatin'."

"I will," Jergenson said.

"Hams?" Red Lee gasped.

"Has he got any kin?" the barber asked.

"Not that I know of," Jim Sloane replied. "His wife took the kids and run off years ago. Right after he beat her real bad."

"She had it . . . comin'," Red said.

Jackson punched out the empty and loaded up. "I don't have much use for a man who'd beat a woman," he said.

Red Lee fell over on his face.

"Hell, now I got to mop the damn floor," the bartender said.

5

Smoke rode out just as the sun was beginning to peep over the ragged crags of the mountains. He had not looked forward to this trip in the first place, and so far his feelings had certainly proved accurate.

He was glad to put the little no-named village behind him as he rode north toward the mining town of Red Light.

By the end of the day, he was deep in the mountains and climbing higher through the twisting and winding passes. He'd been here before, back when he was a boy, roaming the wilderness with the mountain man, Preacher. He remembered a quiet little stream and was looking for it. Smoke loved the high country. It was here amid the splendor of the mountains that he felt most at home, most at peace with himself and his surroundings.

He did not dwell on the death of the rancher, Red Lee. To Smoke's way of thinking, the deaths of bullies and those who took from society more than they gave were no more meaningful than the hole a man leaves after sticking his finger into a quiet creek. Nothing.

Smoke Jensen did not know how many men he himself had killed. He knew the figure was very high. If he never had to draw a gun on another man, it would suit him just fine. But if he had to kill again, a bully, a rapist, a murderer, a man who rode roughshod over the rights of decent people, it would not cause him to lose a second's sleep.

Courts were fine and dandy. A needful thing, he supposed, to protect those who could not protect themselves. Smoke needed no such protection. He could take care of himself, his loved ones, his property. And if anyone violated anything he loved or protected or owned, they would have to face him, and courts be damned. His was a simple code, one if followed by all men would make the world a simpler place in which to live: You leave me alone, I will leave you alone. You have a right to a personal opinion, just as I do. But no more than I do. If you violate my space, you will have to fight me. Smoke knew he was an anachronism. He knew that courts and lawyers and judges were responsible for making the world a safer place, but a much more complicated one. And he felt it didn't have to be.

Smoke rode his own trails, followed his own code of conduct, and tried to live a good life. And he did not give a damn whether others liked it or disliked it.

He found the spot where he and Ol' Preacher had camped so many years ago, and to his delight it had not been disturbed by the destructive hand of man. He made his camp and fished for his supper and was just washing up the skillet when a man helloed the camp.

"I'm friendly," the man called. "I done et, so you don't have to feed me, but I sure would like a cup of that coffee I smell."

"Come on in," Smoke called.

The man was not young, probably in his late sixties, Smoke guessed. A miner, to judge by the equipment his mule carried. Smoke pointed to the coffeepot and the man squatted down and poured himself some, using his own tin cup, which had certainly seen better days.

"Leavin' Red Light," the miner volunteered, "'tain't no fit place to be no more. Done gone lawless and mean. If you're headin' that way, mister, I'd suggest you give it a second thought."

"I was thinking about checking it out."

The miner shook his head. "Then you're headin' into trouble." He eyeballed Smoke. "Although I'd allow as to say you look like a man who could handle 'bout anything that was throwed at you." He looked at Smoke's Colt. "That ain't new, he remarked. "But it's seen some use," he added dryly.

"Some."

"I ain't never gonna go back up yonder, so I can tell you who to look out for and what's wrong with the place," the miner said. "And that's easy. Everything is wrong. Don't trust the sheriff or none of his deputies. They're all in the pocket of Major Cosgrove, who's a thief and a murderer and an all around no-good. He talks fancy and lives in a fine home. But he's no-'count. Red Light's a boomin' town now, and mean to the core. Must be seven, eight hundred people all crowded up there. It'll stay that way 'til the gold is gone. Then there won't be fifty people left. Jack Biggers is the big rancher in the area. He's just as mean and no good as Sheriff Bowers and Major Cosgrove. As are the men who work for him. It's just not a good place to tarry, son. I'd give it some thought."

"How about other ranchers in the valley?"

"You know about the valley, huh? They ain't but two other ranchers. Jack Biggers and Fat Fosburn. Jenny Jensen and an old man named Van Horn is holdin' the kid's ranch agin' long odds. The powers that be want the girl's ranch. The other ranchers was burned out, run out, or killed. I fear for the girl's life, I do. For them men would as soon kill a girl as shoot a snake. She come into all her ma's property. But most of it ain't fitten for a decent girl to be associated with."

"Oh?"

"No, sir. It ain't. All but the ranch. It's a beautiful little ranch in that valley. And my, my, it do have good water and graze. But Jack Biggers wants that property for hisn. And what Jack Biggers wants, he gets." He finished his coffee and stood up, moving toward his horse and mule. "Well, I thank you for the hospitality. I got me a favorite place 'bout three, four miles down the way. But I smelled that coffee and got to salivatin'. See you, young feller."

Before Smoke could ask another question, the miner had swung into the saddle and was gone. Smoke went to his pack and began removing what he felt he might need, including a ten-gauge Colt revolving shotgun that he had had for many years. He had sent it back to the factory in Hartford to have it reworked and refinished and they'd done a bang-up job. It was originally a 27-inch barrel and he'd sawed that off to within a few inches of the forestock. At close range it could clear an entire room of all living things. The cylinder held five rounds, and Smoke had loaded them and a sackful of other shells himself.

He took his pistols and cleaned them carefully loading them up full. For the time being, he would not wear his left hand holster but instead tuck the second pistol behind his gunbelt. He had a hunch—unless somebody recognized him, he could, for a time, ride in and be known as K. Jensen with nobody the wiser. At least it was worth a try.

He cleaned and loaded his rifle and rolled up in his blankets and went to sleep. He wondered what kind of business his sister might have had that would not be "fitten" for a young lady to go near.

* * *

Smoke topped a rise and looked down at the town of Red Light. He took an immediate dislike to the place. The streets were crooked and twisty and narrow, the buildings all jammed up against one another. Like most boom towns, it was a mish-mash of buildings and tents and wagons. Even from where he sat above the town, he could hear the shrill and false laughter of hurdy-gurdy girls, busy separating miners from their gold dust and nuggets, and behind it all the banging of tinny-sounding pianos.

Smoke had deliberately not shaved his upper lip since leaving the ranch, and his mustache was nearly grown out, since he had a naturally heavy beard. The mustache made him look several years older and a hell of a lot meaner. The mustache was beginning to droop down toward his chin and made Smoke look like he'd just come off the hoot-owl trail.

"All right, Buck," Smoke said. "Let's go check out this dump."

The livery was on the edge of town and Smoke reined in and swung down. A young boy of about thirteen came out and pulled up short at the sight of the huge, mean-eyed horse.

"I got a stall for you, mister, but you're gonna have to handle that hoss yourself."

"What's the matter, Jimmy?" a loudmouth hollered from a boardwalk so new, some of the boards had not yet lost their sawmill color. "You want me to show you how to handle a hoss?"

"Nick Norman, Jimmy whispered. "He's a really bad one, mister. A bully."

"Tell him if he thinks he's man enough to handle this horse, come on and try," Smoke returned the whisper. "Don't worry about him coming back at you. He'll be so stove-up he won't be able to walk for six months. If he lives."

"Well, why don't you come show me, then, Nick" Jimmy called.

"I'll do that," the loudmouth said, stepping off the board-walk. "And then I'll give you a thrashing for being smart-mouthed with me."

Nick looked at Smoke and said, "Get out of the way. I'll larn your horse some manners."

Smoke smiled and pointed at the dangling reins.

Nick jerked up the reins hard and said, "Come on, you ugly son-of-a-jerk."

Buck bit him, clamping down with his big teeth. Nick screamed as the arm was lacerated and the blood flowed. Nick jerked out a pistol to shoot the horse and Buck butted him, knocking the man to the ground, the pistol sliding away in the mud. Nick grabbed up a heavy board and got to his feet. He reared back to strike Buck and Buck reared up and came down with both shod feet. One hoof made a terrible mess of Nick's face and the other smashed a shoulder, the sound of the breaking bones clearly audible. Nick lay in the mud, badly hurt and unconscious.

A man came running up, pushing through the gathering crowd. He wore a star on his chest.

Smoke pointed to the bloody and broken Nick and said, "You'd better get your resident loudmouth to a doctor, deputy. He's hurt pretty bad."

The deputy started to say something about the best thing to do would be to shoot the damn horse. But he bit back the words and closed his mouth. He didn't like the look in this big stranger's eyes. And to make matters worse, that damn big horse was looking at him, too, ears all laid back and wall-eyed mean. The deputy had seen a few killer horses in his time, and this was definitely one of them.

Smoke petted Buck for a few seconds and then picked up the reins, starting inside the huge barn.

"Where do you think you're goin'?" the deputy called.

"To stable my horse," Smoke called over his shoulder. "You have any objection?" Before leaving town, Smoke had wired a friend of his, a judge down in Denver, and asked if his Deputy U. S. Marshal's commission was still valid.

"That was a lifetime appointment, Smoke. You think you might need that badge soon?" he'd asked him.

"Maybe," Smoke wired back.

"You have the full weight of the United States Government behind you, my boy," the judge had wired.

"All the weight I need I carry on my hip," Smoke closed the key.

"By God, I might!" the deputy hollered, losing his temper. "I don't like your attitude, mister."

Smoke dug in his saddlebags and pinned on the badge before stripping off saddle and bridle and pouring grain into a feed trough.

"Did you hear me, damn it?" the deputy yelled as the crowd outside the livery swelled, the small mob making no effort to assist the unconscious Nick Norman. "I said," the deputy shouted, "do you hear me, you damn saddlebum?"

Smoke hesitated for a moment, then took off the U. S. Marshal's badge and put it in his pocket. Might be more fun without it, he thought.

"Git out here and look at me!" the deputy shouted, now reenforced by two other badge-toting men.

Smoke made sure his second gun was hidden by his coat and then he walked out of the gloom of the livery to face the three so-called lawmen.

"All right," Smoke said, as the mob of men and painted women fell silent. "I'm looking at you. But if I have to look at you for very long, I'll lose my appetite." He glanced at the other two. "And that includes you, too."

The three men looked at each other, not quite sure how to handle this situation. As deputies under Sheriff Bowers, they were accustomed to bullying their way around the area, and having people kowtow to them. But this stranger didn't seem a bit impressed by their badges.

They didn't realize that Smoke immediately knew that the three of them combined wouldn't make a pimple on a good lawman's butt.

"We're deputies," one of the three said.

"Wonderful," Smoke told them. "Go get a lost cat out of a tree."

Jimmy the stableboy could not hide his grin.

One of the deputies noticed it and flushed. "I'll slap that smirk offen your face, boy."

"You'll do it when Hell freezes over," Smoke told him.

The deputy cut his eyes to the big stranger. "You don't talk to me lak 'at, mister. I got me a notion to put you in jail."

"Why don't you try?" Smoke said softly.

"All right!" a voice shouted from behind the crowd. "Get out of the damn way and let me through."

The crowd parted and a big man stepped into the small clearing in front of the livery. He was about the same size as Smoke and did not appear to have an ounce of fat on him. He was clean-shaven and smelled of cologne. He wore a very ornate star pinned to his coat and at first glance appeared to be a man used to getting his own way. He wore two guns, low and tied down.

"I'm Sheriff Bowers," the man said, fixing his gaze on Smoke. "What's going on here? What happened to Nick?"

"Nick got rough with my horse," Smoke told him. "My horse didn't like him or the treatment and let him know about it. Then this loudmouth piece of crap wearing a badge showed up and I don't like him. He threatened this boy here." He pointed to Jimmy. "That tells me what type of sorry trash he is. So, Sheriff, if you own him, you'd better put a leash and a muzzle on him." Smoke was feeling the old wildness settle on him. It was a cold sensation. He had felt the same emotion when he'd entered the old silver camp years back, hunting the men who had raped and killed his wife and killed his baby son. Smoke had left some fourteen-odd men dead in the streets.

This trip had turned sour from the git-go and Smoke was feeling more and more of the old wildness fill him.

Sheriff Bowers read the warning in Smoke's eyes and took in the man's boots and clothing. The boots were hand-made and expensive. The coat was handmade to fit the man's huge shoulders and arms. The .44 he wore at his side was old, but well-cared-for, and it had seen a lot of use. It was not fancy, and that spoke volumes to the sheriff.

There was something about this big stranger that was un-nerving to the sheriff. He did not like the sensation. "A few of you men carry Nick to the doctor's office. The rest of you people break this up and go on about your business."

"That son-of-a-bitch called me trash," the deputy in question said. "I'll not stand for that."

"Shut up, Patton," the sheriff said harshly. "Just close your mouth and keep it closed." He turned his attentions back to Smoke. "You mind walking with me?"

"Not at all, Sheriff," Smoke said. "You object to my checking in at the hotel?"

"Not a bit. We'll talk on the way over there."

Patton stepped toward Jimmy. "I'll take a buggy whip to you, boy. Teach you to sass me. I'll strip the hide right offen your back."

Smoke hit the man, suddenly and unexpectedly. The blow made an ugly *smushing* sound in the air. Patton's boots flew out from under him and he landed on his back in the mud, his mouth leaking blood. He did not move.

The sheriff, the deputies, and the crowd stood in shocked silence. Smoke looked at Jimmy. The boy's clothing was patched and his shoes were held together by faith and rawhide. Smoke handed the boy two gold double eagles. Jimmy stood in open-mouthed shock.

"You go get you some new clothes and boots, boy. Then come back here and take care of my horse. If any of these badge-wearing trash bothers you, you come get me. They won't bother you again. All right?"

Jimmy looked at the money in his hand. More money than he had ever seen. "Yes, *sir!*"

"You come over to my store, Jimmy," a merchant called. "I'll fit you right up and treat you fair."

Smoke looked at the man. "You be damn sure you do just that." He started walking toward the hotel.

"Somebody carry Patton to the jail and lay him on a cot," Sheriff Bowers said, his voice suddenly filled with weariness. He had just noticed the pinholes in Smoke's shirt, made by the badge. Invisible warning lights flashed in the sheriff's head. Something was all out of whack here. Go easy on this, he cautioned himself. Real easy.

Patton moaned in the mud and sat up. Smoke stopped and turned around, his right hand close to the butt of his gun. Patton cursed him and struggled to his knees in the mud. He pulled out his pistol and jacked the hammer back. Only then did Smoke draw.

No man or women in the crowd had ever seen such a draw. Most didn't even see it, it was so fast. A blur of speed and a report of fire and gunsmoke. Patton fell back, a hole right between his eyes.

"Smoke Jensen!" a man shouted. "I knowed I'd seen him afore."

"Oh, my God!" Sheriff Bowers said. "That's Janey's brother."

6

It was all out in the open now, so Smoke registered at the hotel using his real name. The desk clerk stood goggle-eyed as he wrote his name.

"I want the best room you have," Smoke told the man.

"Certainly, sir! I'll give you the Eldorado Suite. And may I say it's a pleasure having you here? We'll do everything we can to make your stay as relaxing as possible."

"Fine. While I have a cup of coffee in the restaurant, you make sure the sheets are changed on the bed and a tub of hot water drawn. I want lots of towels and a fresh bar of soap."

"Oh, absolutely, sir. Right now."

Smoke turned to look at the bulk of the sheriff, standing in the door. "Have some coffee with me, Sheriff?"

Sheriff Bowers nodded. Damned if he knew just what to do about this situation. Jensen guns down one of his deputies, then calmly turns and walks off without even so much as a fare-thee-well.

Club Bowers opened his mouth to speak, but Smoke was already walking into the dining room. Getting more irritated by the second, Club followed along behind and flopped down in a chair when Jensen finally chose a table in a corner of the room and called for coffee.

"Do you understand that you just killed one of my deputies?" Club blurted.

"He was trying to kill *me,"* Smoke replied. "Is there a law in this town against defending yourself?"

"Patton was an officer of the law!"

Smoke said a very ugly word and smiled sarcastically at the sheriff. "But not much of one."

"What do you mean by that?"

"The way I get it, Bowers, is that you and your men are in the pocket of Jack Biggers and a Major Cosgrove."

"That's a damn lie!"

Smoke smiled up at the waiter. "I'd like some pie, too, please. Apple, if you have it. Sheriff?"

"No. I don't want any damn pie! Who told you that crap, Jensen?"

"A fellow I met along the trail. He wasn't very complimentary toward you and your department. Or Cosgrove and Biggers, for that matter."

"Who was he?"

"I didn't ask his name. Who's the attorney handling my sister's estate?"

"Dunham. His office is over the assayer's place." He leaned back in his chair. "I didn't know Janey had a brother."

"Where is her daughter?"

"Jenny? Out at the ranch, I suppose. When you see her, tell her to sell. She's bucking a stacked deck."

"Biggers want the spread?"

"It butts up against his. Hell, Jensen, Jenny's just a kid. She can't run the place."

Smoke ate his pie, conscious of the sheriff's eyes on him.

"You worn a badge from time to time, Jensen?"

"I've worn one before."

"I should remind you that you're way out of your jurisdiction here."

Smoke smiled at him and pushed his pie plate to one side. "I have a lifetime U.S. Marshal's commission, Bowers. And Judge Francis Morrison knows I'm here and *why* I'm here. Don't crowd me. Don't crowd my niece. And above all, don't interfere in my business. You got all that?"

Never in his life had Bowers been talked to in the manner in which he was now being addressed. For a few moments he could but sit and stare at the man across the table from him. He was under no illusions about Smoke Jensen. He knew all about the man, or thought he did. Jensen operated under his own strict code of ethics. And no matter how the law read, he did not deviate from them. Less than ten minutes had passed since Jensen had shot one of his deputies right between the eyes, and now the man sat calmly, finishing up his apple pie. Incredible.

Bowers would be the first to admit he was no match for Jensen when it came to gunplay. The thought of facing Jensen eyeball to eyeball and dragging iron had not even entered his mind. He did not think there was a man alive that could match Jensen's speed and unbelievable accuracy with pistol or rifle. Few men were as strong as Jensen. And Bowers also knew that Smoke Jensen's courage was matched by few, if any.

Bowers knew all the stories about the legendary gunfighter. He'd heard them for years, no matter where in the West he happened to be. He'd been raised by mountain men, killed his first man when no more than a towheaded boy. Had faced alone up to twenty men and emerged victorious. His exploits were known worldwide. Books had been written about him. Songs had been sung. Plays had been staged. But he didn't know how much was true and how much was pure balderdash.

He suspected it was all true.

Club Bowers was unable to find his voice. He shoved back his chair and stood up, still staring open-mouthed at Smoke. He knew he should say something, but he didn't know what. He shook his head and walked out of the dining room. At the archway he stopped and turned, looking back at Smoke Jensen. The man was rolling a cigarette while the waiter filled his cup with coffee.

"Incredible," Club muttered.

Smoke slept well that night and awakened refreshed and ready to face the day. He dressed in jeans and a black-and-white checkered shirt. Since his identity was known and there was no need for any charade, he'd shaved off his mustache and strapped on both pistols, the left hand pistol worn high and butt-forward. Sally made his shirts for him, since store-bought shirts were usually too tight across the shoulders and too small for his massive arms. He usually carried four or five extra shirts. He made sure all the loops in his gunbelt were filled with .44s and then checked his big-bladed Bowie knife. It was razor-sharp. He stepped out to meet the day.

After breakfast, he strolled over to Lawyer Dunham's office, the townspeople giving him a wide berth as he walked, his spurs jingling.

Smoke pegged Dunham as a shyster immediately. And he suspected that Dunham knew he had, for the lawyer attempted no tricky legal maneuvering when Smoke told him to produce the will.

"Since Jenny is young," Dunham said, "Miss Janey left everything to you until the girl comes of age. I . . ."

"Where is my sister buried?"

"Just outside of town, sir. It was a lovely funeral. The headstone has just been set in place. Quite an elaborate monument, I might add. The local minister and some of the good ladies of the town were, ah, upset at the inscription, but Miss Janey was quite clear as to what she wanted on the stone."

Smoke stood up. The lawyer was obviously in awe at the bulk of the man. "You get all the papers in order. I'll be back after I pay my respects to my sister."

"Certainly, sir. I shall have them ready."

At the livery, Jimmy was decked out in new duds and boots. A nice-looking boy. He'd even had his hair trimmed. "I got money left, Mister Smoke," Jimmy said.

"Keep it. As long as I'm in town I'll pay you to look after my horse."

Smoke saddled up and rode to the windswept and lonely graveyard. Janey's monument was the largest in the cemetery. He was amused at the inscription, and could see why the local, so-called "good ladies" might be offended at the words.

Carved deep in the expensive stone, under Janey's name and date of life and death, were the words: I PLAYED LIFE TO THE HILT AND ENJOYED EVERY GODDAMN MINUTE OF IT.

"There never was any love lost between us, Sis," Smoke spoke the words softly. "But I understand you raised a good girl. I'll see to it that she makes out all right."

He put his hat back on his head and walked out of the graveyard. A time-weathered old cowboy was waiting at the entrance to the cemetery.

"I'm Van Horn," the man said. Smoke guessed him to be in his late sixties or early seventies. But tough as wang-leather and no backup in him. "I worked for Miss Janey at the ranch. Miss Jenny is there now. She's waitin' to see if you're gonna throw her off the place."

"Why would I do something like that? I don't want the ranch or any of my sister's property. It all goes to Jenny when she comes of age. I intend to see that it does."

Van Horn grunted. "I figured Miss Jenny was being fed a

line by Biggers and Cosgrove and Dunham. I know your reputation for being fair and told Miss Jenny what them others
was sayin' was all a pack of lies."

"Ride with me," Smoke said. "Let's go settle this at the
lawyer's office."

Smoke read the documents carefully and then signed the
papers. He then stared at Dunham so long the man began to
squirm in his chair. "Did you tell my niece that I was going
to throw her off the ranch and take all of the property?"

"Why, ah . . ."

"Do you represent Biggers and Cosgrove?"

"Why, ah . . ."

"Did you encourage her to sell to Biggers, all the while
knowing that she could not legally do so?"

"Why, ah . . ."

Van Horn stood leaning against a wall, enjoying the
lawyer's discomfort. He didn't know what Smoke Jensen
was going to do, but whatever it was, he wasn't going to
miss a second of it.

"You are a lowlife shyster son-of-a-bitch lawyer," Smoke
told the pale and shaken barrister. "Playing both sides against
the middle and trying to cheat a young girl out of her inheritance."

"You can't talk to me like that!" Dunham protested.

"I just did." Smoke reached across the desk and got a fist-
ful of Dunham's shirt. He hauled him over the desk and then
proceeded to throw him out of the second-story window.
Dunham went squalling and shrieking through the glass. He
bounced off the awning and fell into the mud of the street,
landing squarely in a big pile of horse droppings. He wasn't
badly hurt, except for his dignity, which was severely bruised.

Sheriff Bowers stood on the boardwalk in front of his office and shook his head at the sight.

The hearse carrying the body of Deputy Patton rattled by,
heading for the cemetery. Doc White had told Club that he

didn't know if Nick Norman was going to make it. That killer horse of Jensen's had fractured the man's skull. Jensen was going to have to be dealt with, but damned if Club knew how to go about it. Biggers and Cosgrove were due in town this morning. He'd lay it all in their laps.

Club watched as Smoke and Van Horn mounted up and rode out of the town, heading for the ranch out in the valley.

"You own that, too," Van Horn said, pointing to two-story house on the edge of town. It was a fancy and well-kept place. The sign on the lawn proclaimed it to be The Golden Cherry.

"What is it?" Smoke asked.

"You don't know?" the old cowboy asked.

"No."

"It's a whorehouse."

Jenny Jensen was quite the young lady, very pretty and petite and well mannered. She seemed in awe of her Uncle Smoke.

Smoke put her at ease quickly and Van Horn left them alone in the house. As she made coffee and set a platter of doughnuts on the table, she smiled at Smoke shyly.

"I can't do much," the girl admitted. "But I can cook. That's one of the things taught us at finishing school in Boston."

The girl was lovely, with a heart-shaped face and a figure that would turn any man's head. Smoke smiled at her. "How long have you been out here, Jenny?"

"About a year. I came out when I learned of my mother's death."

"How did she die, Jenny?"

"There was an outbreak of fever. Mother and her . . . girls nursed the sick miners. Mother caught the fever and died. It took Lawyer Dunham almost a year to find me."

"He knew where you were, Jenny. He was just stalling for

time. He and Biggers and Cosgrove couldn't figure out a way to cheat you out of your inheritance, that's all. Then I entered the picture and that really shook them up. What do you know about this ranch?"

"More than most men think I do. I *really* have a very good education and understand business. I've gone over the books and the ranch is paying its way. I don't have many cowboys left, not nearly enough to efficiently run the ranch. And no one will come to work for me."

"I'll get you hands, Jenny. Don't worry about that. Do you want to stay out here?"

"Oh, yes. I love it. I've had entirely enough of cities."

"Then here is where you'll stay. Do you object to my moving in here?"

"Oh, no! Not at all."

"I'm going to send one of the hands to the nearest telegraph office and get my wife up here pronto." Smoke smiled. "I'd better let her know that I now own a, ah, house of ill repute."

Jenny laughed and it was a good laugh, full of life and good humor. "The Golden Cherry. Yes. And the Golden Plum, too."

"What is that? The will only stated that I owned all of Janey's businesses in town and the ranch."

"A saloon in town. A very profitable one. I've never been inside either establishment. Van Horn won't let me. He's the foreman. He's really a nice man."

"Do you ride?"

"Oh, yes. But when I came out here I swore I would never again ride sidesaddle. It's not very comfortable. I'm afraid I shocked some of the so-called good women around here by wearing a split skirt and riding astride."

"You and my wife will hit it off, Jenny. You both think very much alike. Can you shoot?"

She shook her head. "I never fired a gun in my life until a few months ago. Van Horn is trying to teach me. But I'm afraid I'm not very good."

"We'll work on that." Smoke rose from the table and walked through the house, and it was a nice home, the rooms large and airy. The place was a bit too feminine for his tastes, but since a woman had owned the ranch, he didn't find that unusual.

Smoke paused at a gun rack and took down a double-barreled twenty-gauge shotgun. He checked it and handed it to Jenny. "You practice with this, Jenny. My wife will be here in about a week, and the two of you can target-shoot together. Can you trust all your hands?"

"Absolutely. Van Horn ran off those he felt were not loyal. Even the younger men are afraid of him."

Smoke nodded. "They should be. He was one of the very first gunfighters. I remember my mentor speaking of him. Can you get me some writing paper, please?"

He sat down at a desk and wrote: "Sally, you'd better get up here fast. Among other things, I just inherited a whorehouse. See you soon."

Smoke called for Van Horn, handed him the note and some money and said, "Give this to your most trusted hand and have him ride for the nearest telegraph office. Wait for a reply."

The old gunfighter read the note and smiled. "Be good for the girl to have a decent woman to associate with. I'll get a rider out now. You going to stay out here on the place?"

"Yes. I'll want to see the spread first thing in the morning."

"I'll see to your horse." He turned to go, paused, and looked back. "Preacher done a good job with you, Smoke. I'm right proud to have you here. The girl might stand a chance now."

Van Horn gone, Smoke said, "Let's take a look at the

books, Jenny. That's something I hate to do, but it has to be done. Then we can sit down and you can tell me about your mother."

"I don't know that much."

"Whatever you know is more than I do. I've only seen her a couple of times since she ran off back in '64 or '65." Smoke smiled. "She tried to have me killed both times."

7

The spread was not a huge, sprawling one, but it was certainly large enough to provide a family with a very good living. The graze ran from ample to lush and the water was plentiful. The cattle were fat and sleek.

"Any problems with rustling?" Smoke asked.

"Once," Van Horn replied. "I caught two of Biggers's no-'count hands usin' a runnin' iron and shot them both."

Smoke noticed but made no comment about Van Horn's strapping on two Remington hoglegs and tying them down. If just half of what Preacher had told him about Van Horn was true, the old man was a pure devil in a gunfight. Preacher had said that Van Horn had once faced six men in a trading post down in Colorado and when the gunsmoke had cleared, Van Horn was the only one standing, and he had four bullet holes in him.

"Fat Fosburn owns the spread north of this one," Van Horn said as they rode. "He's the mayor of Red Light. Biggers owns the land south. They got us boxed for a fact."

"Fosburn? That name is familiar."

"Used to be an outlaw. Rode with Bloody Bill back in the sixties. He's as mean as a skunk and will stop at nothin' to get what he wants. He's said that if he has to, he'll kill Jenny to get the land."

"Real nice fellow."

"Yeah. Just dandy. Yonder comes Ladd. He's been ridin' the south fence. Good boy."

Ladd was a man in his early twenties, stocky and with a go-to-hell look in his eyes.

"Ladd," Van Horn said. "This here's Miss Jenny's uncle, Smoke Jensen."

Ladd's eyes widened.

"He's gonna be with us for a time, seein' that Miss Jenny gets her due. You go on to the house and get you some breakfast. Then you and Ford stay close to home."

"Yes, sir," the young puncher said. "Pleased to meet you, Mister Smoke."

"Now you've met all the hands we got," Van Horn said. "Ladd, Ford, and Cooper. We need at least three more."

"We'll get them. Parcell has a cabin somewhere in these mountains."

"Wolf Parcell?"

"That's him."

"Hell, Smoke, he's older than me, and I'm near 'bout as old as God. I didn't know he lived around here."

"Over there," Smoke said, looking toward the towering mountains. "I'll find him. And there is a kid in town at the livery, Jimmy. He'll do to take care of things around the house."

Van Horn smiled. "Little Jimmy Hammon. His folks had a small spread west of here. Biggers and Fosburn burned them out and killed the boy's parents 'bout seven or eight years ago. You're right. Jimmy's a good boy."

"We need one or two more good men."

"You got anything against Mexicans or Indians?"

"Not as long as they do their work. Knowed some fine Mex punchers in my time."

"There's one in town. I saw him."

"Pasco? He come in here as a sheepherder. No rancher will hire a sheepherder."

"I will. I know Pasco's cousin. He's a gunfighter. Carbone. He spoke highly of Pasco. One more."

"There's a half-breed Injun roams the valley. But he's a surly one. Don't seem to like nobody."

"Has anybody ever given him a chance?"

"You do have a point."

"What's the Indian's name?"

"Bad Dog."

"We have a crew."

It took Smoke two days to find the cabin of Wolf Parcell. The old mountain man was standing in the door when Smoke rode up.

"I heard you was in the area," Wolf said. "Figured you'd be about, pesterin' me." The old mountain man was still rock-solid tough and had a mean look in his eyes. He wore two pistols belted outside his buckskins and a huge Bowie knife. "I'll have to say that Preacher done well with you. What do you want?"

"Get your kit together, you worthless old coot. You're going to work for me."

"Work! Wagh! I ain't worked for nobody but myself in fifty year."

"I need you," Smoke said simply.

"That's good enough for me," Wolf said. "Light and set. Coffee's hot and strong. I'll be a few minutes."

Fifteen minutes later, the two men rode out.

That afternoon, with Wolf leading the way, they rode to the camp of Bad Dog, a half-breed Cheyenne.

"Dog," Wolf said, "this here is Smoke Jensen. His little niece is in trouble down in the valley, and I aim to help her."

Bad Dog looked up at Smoke. "Heard of you. My people say you are a fair man. You fight Biggers and Cosgrove and Fat?"

"Yes."

"Me, too."

And the three rode out.

Van Horn had sent Ladd into town, and he returned with Little Jimmy and the Mexican, Pasco.

"You got any objection to working with cows?" Smoke asked the Mexican.

"If it means a fight with Biggers, Cosgrove, and Fat, I'll work for the devil," Pasco replied.

"I've been called that," Smoke said.

"So I've heard," Pasco smiled his reply.

"Stow your gear in the bunkhouse."

Over coffee, Jenny said, "That is the most disreputable-looking crew I think I have ever seen. Except for Jimmy."

"They'll stand to the last man, Jenny. They're tough as rawhide and meaner than pumas. Right now, I want you to bake a half dozen pies and fry up a tubful of doughnuts. Then I want you to bake a dozen loaves of bread and cook up the thickest stew you ever made in your life. Can you do that?"

"You bet I can, Uncle Smoke."

"After this evening's supper, Jenny, you won't be able to drive those men off with a shotgun."

The men spent the rest of that day getting set up in the bunkhouse, mending shirts or socks, looking over the remuda, and loafing. Young Jimmy Hammon was in for a quick education, bunking with these salty ol' boys, but most of what he would learn would be vital and stand him in good stead for the rest of his life. And Smoke also knew that the older men would look after the boy.

Soon the aroma of baking began to fill the house and Smoke had to leave before his mouth got to watering so bad he'd look like a drooling fool.

He got a couple of carrots and an apple from the kitchen and walked to the corral and picked out a horse to ride, sparing Buck. The horse was a big black with a mean eye. He and Smoke took to one another right off.

Van Horn strolled up and leaned against the railing. "He's a bad one, Smoke. Nobody rides Devil. He's a pure killer."

Smoke smiled and whistled softly. The big black came right to him, the other horses giving him a wide berth. Smoke had quartered the apple and the black took the pieces as gently as a baby.

"I knew one man tried that and lost part of a finger," Van Horn said.

"We understand each other," Smoke said, rubbing the velvet of Devil's nose. "We're alike and he senses it."

"He ain't been cut, Smoke. He's dangerous."

"No, he isn't. He's just misunderstood, that's all." Smoke stepped inside the corral and walked around, the big black following along behind him, just like a puppy, occasionally reaching out to nibble at Smoke's shirt, but with only his lips, not his teeth.

The other hands had gathered around the railing, watching Smoke and the big horse. After a time, Smoke put a blanket on him and walked him around, then saddled him and the black took the bit with no fuss.

"Damnedest thing I ever did see," Van Horn said.

"Open the gate," Smoke called, swinging into the saddle, and he and the black went out of the corral at a gallop. The black loved to run, and Smoke let it go until it tired. Several miles from the house, the big black slowed and Smoke reined up and swung down, letting the animal blow.

"We're going to get along just fine," Smoke told the horse

named Devil. "I might even buy you from Jenny and take you back with me."

Smoke looked all around him, in this valley surrounded by mountains. Fine spread, he thought. I can see why the others want it. But they're not going to get it . . . not the way they plan, anyway.

Back in the saddle, he walked Devil back to the ranch. Rather than risk Jimmy getting hurt, he rubbed the black down himself and turned him into the corral. He forked some hay for the animals and finished just as Jenny started ringing the supper bell. The men started lining up and Smoke smiled at them as Jenny waved them into the house.

"We all eat together, gentlemen," the girl informed them. "So come on and fill your plates."

And fill them and eat they did, all of them with one eye on the mound of doughnuts she had fixed and covered with a cloth. Then she started taking apple pies out of the oven and Smoke thought the men were going to stampede the stove.

The hands drank at least two gallons of coffee, and were so stuffed with stew and freshly baked bread and pies and doughnuts, Smoke hoped the ranch was not attacked that night. None of the men seemed capable of moving, much less fighting.

He gave them an hour to rest after so much food and then walked over to the bunkhouse. "You boys get enough to eat?"

Bad Dog rubbed his belly and smiled. "The young lady has a cowboy here forever, if she chooses."

"Same goes for me, Pasco said. "For one so young, she sure knows her way around a kitchen."

Wolf Parcell was stretched out on his bunk, sound asleep and snoring softly. Jimmy was also asleep.

But Smoke wasn't fooled about Wolf. The old mountain man would come awake instantly at the first sign of trouble, a pistol in one hand and a razor-sharp Bowie in the other, cutting and slashing and shooting. Smoke knew from experience and observation that young trouble-hunters who tangled with old men usually came out much worse for wear, for old men have no illusions about fair fighting: they fight to win.

Smoke was raised by old mountain men, and he shared their philosophy: there is no such thing as a fair fight. There is only a winner and a loser. If you're in the right, it doesn't make any difference how you win or what you use to win in defending yourself. Just win.

Van Horn came out of his small private quarters into the main bunkhouse and said, "All right, boys. Wake up and listen up. By now, Biggers, Fosburn, and Cosgrove will know we've hired a crew. Up to now, they haven't made any raids on our property. But that might change. What you boys can expect is for their hands to try and catch you off this spread and stomp you or shoot you or drag you." His eyes touched young Jimmy. "And that includes you, boy. For the time being, Jimmy, your job is take care of the ranch grounds and the barn and so forth. You're mighty young to be totin' a six-gun, but no younger than me or Smoke here. So startin' tomorrow, you pack iron like the rest of us. I'm gonna put a rifle in the barn, the shed, and the outhouse. There'll be an ammo belt with each one. Things are gonna get real bad real quick, I'm thinkin'. Try not to do no lone ridin'. Always buddy up if you can. We got to have supplies, so tomorrow I'm gonna send a wagon into town. Smoke here said he'll ride in with it. Ladd will drive, Cooper will ride flank. One of us will always be here on the ranch, or no more than five minutes from it. Jimmy will be here all the time. The next day we start a cattle count, as close as we can, that is, and brandin'. We got to sell about five hundred head, and that means we got to move them into Red Light to the holdin' pens. Smoke, when are you expectin' your wife to arrive?"

"In a couple more days, three at the most. I've arranged for the Pinkertons to escort her up from track's end."

"Good move. She'll be safe along the way, then," Pasco remarked. "No one around here wants to get the Pinks down on them."

"I'm counting on that. With Sally here, that will free another man to work the herd. My wife will put lead into a man faster than you can blink. And she'll have Jenny shooting well in a few days. One thing we have to do tomorrow is stock up on ammunition. Enough for a siege. I suggest we take two wagons into town and stock up enough staples to last several months."

Smoke eyeballed the men. "Might as well tell you now, Jenny wants to ride into town with us."

Van Horn started cussing.

Smoke let him wind down. "I don't like it either. But she's a young woman and she wants to pick up some lady-things and just shop for a time." He smiled. "Besides, she is the boss."

Wolf Parcell belched, grinned, and patted his belly. "Damn shore is that."

8

Sheriff Monte Carson had handed Sally the telegram and stepped back while she was opening it. He was expecting Sally to explode, and she didn't disappoint him.

"A *whorehouse!* Sally yelled.

"Now, Miss Sally," Monte said. "It ain't as bad as . . ."

"A *whorehouse!* Sally yelled. "My husband owns a whorehouse!"

"He says you better get right on up there."

"You can bet your boots and spurs I'm going up there." She went to the door and yelled for the foreman. He came at a flat run.

"Yes, ma'am?"

"Get my horse ready for travel. I'm pulling out first thing in the morning. You run things here until we return."

"Uh . . . yes, ma'am."

Sally turned to the sheriff. "When you get back to town, you get me passage on the train. Rent a car. I'll alternate between passenger car and staying with my horse."

"Uh . . ."

"Do it, Monte!"

"Right! Consider it done, Sally."

The sheriff gone, Sally packed swiftly. Just a couple of dresses; mostly jeans and work shirts and an extra pair of boots. She paused. And a pair of shoes for the dress, if she elected to wear a dress. She tossed in a gunbelt and her .44. Walking to the gun cabinet, she took down her .44 carbine and put it in the saddle boot.

"A *whorehouse!* " she said.

The next morning she was on the train, heading north.

Not yet trusting Devil around people he was not familiar with, Smoke saddled up Buck for the ride into town. Jenny climbed up beside Ladd and off they went, rattling down the road.

Just before leaving, Smoke told Van Horn, "I'm expecting trouble in town. It's just a feeling I have in my guts."

The old gunfighter nodded in agreement. "So do I." He toed out his cigarette butt. "Ladd and Cooper are good boys. They'll stand. Don't worry about things here. You just be careful. We don't have many friends in Red Light."

That was evident when the man at the big general store insulted Jenny and refused to sell her anything. Ten seconds later, after looking into the cold eyes of Smoke Jensen and almost soiling his drawers, he apologized profoundly for his remark and began filling the large order as fast as he could work.

Several cowboys appeared in the door. Smoke had seen the Biggers brand—a Triangle JB—on a dozen horses lining the narrow street. "Shopkeeper, you was told not to sell to them," one of the men said.

"It's a free country," Smoke replied, turning from the

counter to face the men. "And who the hell asked you to stick your mouth in this matter?"

"Jensen," the spokesman for the group said, "you may be a big wheel down where you come from. But around here, you ain't jack-crap. I'd bear that in mind, was I you."

"You're not me," Smoke told him. "Now why don't you just shut your face and wander back to wherever the hell it is you came from?"

"That's all!" Sheriff Bowers said, walking up and stepping into the store. "Seems like you can't even come to town without startin' trouble, Smoke."

"I didn't start this. But I will finish it, if I have to. We came into town for supplies, that's all. These yahoos tried to stop the store owner from selling to us. Now, what do you have to say about that?"

Club Bowers was silent for a moment. Everything would have been real easy if Smoke Jensen hadn't showed up. Everything was working out to plan . . . until he rode into town. Now everything was all fouled up. Taking a ranch away from a seventeen-year-old girl and an old has-been of a gunfighter was one thing. Pulling iron against a U.S. Marshal was something else. Especially when that marshal was Smoke Jensen. He knew the Marshals' Service had a nasty habit of avenging their own. And they didn't always do it according to a law book. What the powers that be in the town didn't need right now was for a bunch of U.S. Marshals to come riding in, hell-bent for revenge. But, Club thought, if I ain't in town, I can't be held responsible for what happens.

"You boys go on back to the saloon and cool down," Club told the JB riders.

"The boss said to . . ."

"Did you hear me?" Club's question was loudly and harshly spoken. "Move." When the men had gone, Club turned and walked swiftly to the livery.

"He's ridin' out," Cooper said.

"Well, we're in for it now," Smoke said.

"That was Dick Miles doin' all the talkin'," Ladd said. "He's a bad one, Smoke. All of Biggers' men are drawin' fightin' wages."

Smoke smiled. "I forgot to tell you boys—so are you."

The punchers smiled. That extra money would go a long ways toward a new saddle or a gun or a handmade pair of boots to wear on special occasions.

"There go the deputies," Cooper said. "All of them. High-tailin' it right after Club."

"And here comes Dick and a whole bunch of others," Ladd added. "They ain't even waitin' 'til the law gets out of town."

Smoke walked to the gun racks and took down three double-barreled shotguns, tossing one each to Cooper, Ladd, and Jenny. He broke open a box of shells and said, "Load them up. I'm going to open the dance. Stay inside and when I yell, if I yell, open fire."

"Mister Jensen?" the shopkeeper said. "I heard that Major Cosgrove has offered a thousand dollars to anyone who kills you."

"Is that all?" Smoke asked. "That's an insult. I've had a hundred times that amount on me." Smoke pulled both guns and stepped out onto the high boardwalk, cocking the .44s. He'd been doing this since he was a boy, and Preacher had taught him that when somebody's huntin' you, why hell, just take it to them and open the dance.

"Is it a good day to die, boys?" Smoke called, lifting his .44s.

"Jesus!" one of JB hands said, a rifle in his hands and the words drifting to Smoke. "This ain't gonna be no tea party."

"You can believe that Smoke said, and opened fire without warning.

The street was suddenly filled with rolling thunder, twelve rounds fired so close together it sounded like one long, ragged volley. Smoke jumped from the boardwalk and jerked his rifle from the saddle boot. But there was no one left standing in the street, only a bloody pile of dead and dying and badly wounded Triangle JB hands.

Cooper and Ladd and Jenny stood in the store and stared open mouthed at the carnage before them. Smoke calmly punched out empties and reloaded, holstering his .44s. A half dozen men, all with guns in their hands, had come after Smoke Jensen. Only two would live past that bloody morning in Red Light, Montana. Dick Miles had taken a round in his rifle butt, the slug's impact driving the stock into his belly and knocking the wind from him and putting him on the ground, otherwise unhurt. His ridin' buddy, Highpockets Rycroft, was only slightly wounded. But neither of them wanted any more of Smoke Jensen on this day.

A doctor ran out into the street and began ministering to the wounded as best he could, but their wounds were fearsome ones, all belly and chest shots.

Dick struggled up on one elbow. "You won't get away with this, Jensen" he called. "This is one time when your fancy name don't mean nothin' to nobody."

"Yeah?" Smoke said. "Why don't you carve that on the tombstones of your buddies?"

"I tell you, boys," Cooper said, relating the day's events to the crew, "I ain't never seen nothin' like it in my life. Smoke just walks out on the boardwalk, says, 'Is it a good day to die, boys?' and started tossin' lead."

"That's the only way to do it," Van Horn said. "If you know somebody's comin' after you, don't give 'em no breaks. Just plug 'em.

"I wish I'd a seen it!" Jimmy said, sitting wide-eyed on his bunk.

"You'll see a lot more than that 'fore this battle's done, son," Van Horn promised. "Jack Biggers will pull out all the stops now. He don't have no choice in the matter. This is gonna be a fight to the finish, and Smoke knew it today. That's why he done what he done."

"Well," Wolf Purcell said, rising up from his bunk. "That's four gunhands we won't have to deal with. Let's go have some of Miss Jenny's grub. I'm hongry."

Jack Biggers couldn't believe his eyes or ears. Four of his best men had been brought back to the ranch tied across their saddles. Dick was out of it for a few days because of a horribly bruised stomach, and Highpockets had lost the use of his left arm for a time.

"Jensen just opened fire?" the rancher asked. "He just started shooting? Why, that's against the law!"

The two survivors exchanged glances at that comment. "He asked us if it was a good day to die, and started shootin'," Dick said.

"I don't think any of us even got off a shot," Highpockets admitted. "I never heard a man work no .44s like that. This wasn't no fast draw. Jensen had his hands full of iron when he stepped out of the store. And I never in my life seen no man that rattlesnake cold."

"Oh, I have," Biggers said. "I know several of them. I'll send a wire and have them here within a week. If this is the way Jensen wants to play it, I'm just the man to show him a thing or two."

The two toughs again exchanged glances. Maybe so, maybe not, they were thinking. But you might change your mind if you ever see Jensen in action.

"I'll have that girl's spread," Biggers said, after shouting for a rider to get the hell over to the house. "And I'll have it soon."

Highpockets thought: I wouldn't count on that, was I you. I really wouldn't.

Sally rode into town, accompanied by three Pinkertons who looked as though they would relish the idea of a little trouble, just to liven things up. No one bothered them, for the word had spread from track's end.

Deputy Brandt called for Club as soon as he saw the three men and one woman ride in.

"Leave them alone," Club said. "Trouble with Pinks is the last thing we want." His eyes appraised Sally as she swung down from the saddle. Quite a looker, he thought. But something told him that Smoke Jensen's wife would be just about as tough to handle as Jensen himself. Sally was one hundred percent a lady, Club had no doubts about that. It was evident in her bearing. But she also had a pistol strapped around her waist and a short-barreled carbine shoved down in a saddle boot. Club had no doubts as to her ability, and willingness, to use both weapons. Club decided to play the gentleman. He walked over to the group and introduced himself, being sure to take off his hat.

"If I may be so bold, ma'am," Club said. "Are you Mrs. Jensen?"

Sally turned to put cool eyes on him. She was a lovely lady, Club thought again, and she sure do fill out them jeans. But them eyes is remindful of the eyes of Smoke Jensen. This woman would kill a man just about as quick as her husband would. Biggers, he mused, you better back off and re-think your plans. All of you better do that.

"I am," Sally said.

"I'm Sheriff Bowers, ma'am. Pleased to meet you, I'm

sure. The Circle Cherry is just a few miles outside of town. That's where your husband is. Take the right fork at the end of town and you'll ride right to it."

"The Circle . . . *Cherry?*" Sally gasped.

"Yes, ma'am," Club replied. "Like the little fruit with a circle around it. It's kind of an . . . unusual brand."

"I saw the Golden Cherry riding in."

"Ah . . . yes, ma'am. But that's something that's not fitten for a man to discuss with a good woman."

"You mean it's a whorehouse, don't you?" Sally laid it out bluntly.

The three Pinks all looked everywhere except at Sally. The blue of the sky suddenly held a lot of interest for them. Club had not blushed since childhood. But blush he did now. "Ah . . . yes, ma'am. You are certainly right about that."

The mayor, Fat Fosburn, walked up to take a better look at this beautiful woman dressed in men's britches.

"Mayor," Club was quick, "this is Smoke Jensen's wife."

Fat looked first at Sally, then at the three heavily armed men with her, and then swept off his hat.

"My escorts," Sally said, lifting a gloved hand toward the Pinks.

"Gentlemen," Fat acknowledged.

"We'd better be riding, Miss Sally," one of the Pinks said.

"Yes," Sally said. She nodded at Club and Fat and swung into the saddle. Looking down at them, she said, "I'm certain we'll be seeing each other again. My husband and I plan on spending a great deal of time around here. Good day, gentlemen." She lifted the reins and was gone down the street.

"It just keeps gettin' worser and worser," Club said glumly.

"It's a game to Jensen," Fat said. "He's played this out before. I know about Sally Jensen. Comes from one of the wealthiest families in New England. Railroads and banks and newspapers and all sorts of businesses. She could buy this whole damn town if she wanted to. She could have a hundred of them damn Pinks in here if she wanted to. Five hundred of them. Send one of your men with a message to Biggers and Cosgrove. We've got to have a meeting. Tonight. At my place. What started out as something simple has suddenly become very complicated."

"It might be too late to stop it," Club said, nodding his head toward two men riding slowly into town.

"What do you mean?"

"Yonder comes Whisperin' Langley and Patmos. Biggers told me he was hirin' him some guns."

"All hell's fixin' to break loose around here," Fat said.

"Yeah," Club said. "Everything's complete now."

Fat looked at him.

"The Devil's already here. His name is Smoke Jensen."

9

Sally and Jenny hit it off immediately and before the afternoon was over, they were good friends. The Pinks stayed the night and were gone the next day. One more hand was hired, a quiet man in his late forties or early fifties who came riding up. Van Horn had hired him on the spot.

"Name's Barrie," Van Horn said. "I hadn't seen him in years. Used to be a town-tamer down in the southwest."

"I've heard of him," Smoke said. "I thought he was dead."

"Nope. He just got tired of it. But he's pure hell with that .45. He's a cowboy at heart. I heard that there was a big meetin' at Fat's house night before last," Van Horn abruptly changed the subject. "I got me two, three sources in town. Club Bowers wanted Cosgrove and Biggers to back off and leave us alone. But they wouldn't hear of it."

"What's so special about this ranch, Van Horn?"

"That's a good question, Smoke. There sure ain't no gold. It's up yonder in the mountains. It boils down to greed, I reckon. Pure and simple. But it ain't just the ranch. Red Light will boom for six months, a year, maybe two years. Then it will quiet down or just maybe die out, like a lot of other gold and silver towns out here. They just want it 'cause it's here and they can't have it. Then, too, as long as the town booms, the, ah, house of ill repute and the saloon will bring in tubfuls of money from the miners."

Smoke had arranged with the local banker to make sure that Jenny's money was deposited daily from the "businesses" in town. And even though Cosgrove owned the bank, he knew better than to dicker around with the girl's money. With Sally now in town, and being from one of the oldest and most respected banking families in all the nation, Jenny could consider her money as secure as if it had been surrounded by a division of armed guards. Cosgrove was wealthy, but he knew that Sally Jensen could have him ruined with no more than a stroke of a pen. And he also knew that she would not hesitate to do so. All parties aligned with Major Cosgrove were in a bit of a quandary. Biggers had arranged for hired guns to come in, over the objections of Sheriff Bowers and Fat Fosburn. But so far, Smoke had not left the ranch since his wife had arrived. And attacking the ranch was not in anyone's plans . . . yet.

"We're bein' watched," Van Horn said, as the men leaned against the corral railing and smoked.

"Yes. I know. I plan on doing a little hunting tonight. Pull all the boys in and keep them close until I get back."

"You goin' alone?"

"All by myself."

Just as it was getting dark, Smoke stepped out of the rear of the house after kissing Sally goodnight. He was dressed all in black, with moccasins on his feet and a dark bandanna tied around his head. He carried a length of rope wound across his chest, and precut lengths of rawhide tucked behind his belt. He carried no rifle, just his six-guns and a knife.

"Don't wait up for me, Sally," he spoke from the darkness of the backyard.

"I won't. But I'll leave coffee on the stove for you."

"And a piece of pie, too."

"Maybe. You're getting a little chubby around the middle."

Smoke chuckled. There wasn't a spare ounce of fat on him, but that was a standing joke between them. Smoke disappeared into the gloom of early night.

"Don't you worry about him, Aunt Sally?" Jenny questioned.

"No. I'll worry about him if he starts visiting that whorehouse in town."

The teenager giggled. She knew there was no danger of her Uncle Smoke ever doing that. Sally and Smoke were in love, and it was evident to anyone with eyes.

"Times are slowly changing out here, Jenny," Sally told the girl, as she cut slices of pie and placed them on the table for any hands who might want a late snack, and they all would. Then she covered a platter of doughnuts with a cloth. She placed both on a counter by the back door so the cowboys could find them without waking the whole house. "But for now, in many areas, the lawless rule. Men like Smoke are the only thing that stands between those who would obey the law, and those who would make a mockery of it and stamp on the rights of the just and the decent."

"It's changing back east."

"That is one of the reasons why I left. It isn't changing for the better. People will tell you it is, but it isn't. Instead of the lawless being put in an early grave, many courts are now handing down very light sentences and the criminal element is back on the street within a year or two. And most of them are just as savage, or more so, than when they went behind bars. Prisons without adequate rehabilitation facilities are no more than a college for the lawless. And it will worsen, Jenny. Even my own family, who, even though they are bankers and monied people, are champions of the downtrodden, agree with that. I shudder to think what it will be like for our great-grandchildren."

"What is Uncle Smoke going to do out there tonight, Aunt Sally?"

Sally smiled and put up the dish that Jenny had just dried and handed to her. "I suspect he's going to make life miserable for those working against you, Jenny."

"Kill them?"

Sally shook her head. "Not unless they get hostile with him. Those men in town approached him—us—with drawn guns in their hands. Their intentions were perfectly clear. Tonight is different." Again, she smiled. "To Smoke, it will be fun. To those spying on us here at the ranch, it will not be fun."

The gun-for-hire, who had hired on with Jack Biggers' Triangle JB, felt himself suddenly jerked from the saddle and thrown hard to the ground. He landed on his belly and the air whooshed from him, rendering him, for a moment, unable to move. A gag was tied around his mouth and his hands were tightly bound behind him by what he assumed, correctly, was rawhide. Then someone possessing enormous strength picked him up and toted him off like a sack of grain. A few hundred yards later, he was dumped to the ground, on his butt, his back to a tree.

"Shake your head for no, nod your head for yes," the big man said softly. "Do you understand?"

The gunhand nodded quickly.

"In a moment I'll remove the gag and you can whisper. Do you know what I'll do if you yell?"

The gunhand again nodded. He didn't know for sure, but he had a pretty good idea.

Smoke asked him a few more simple questions and then removed the gag. The hand spat a time or two and then looked at the bulk of the man squatting before him in the darkness. No doubt in his mind who this was. Jesus, the guy was big.

"How much is Biggers paying you?"

"Seventy-five dollars a month," the hand whispered.

"That's a lot of money to wage war against a seventeen-year-old girl."

"Seventeen?"

"Yes. My niece, Jenny. She's seventeen. You must be real brave to want to kill a young girl."

"I don't want to kill any kid!" the hand protested. "Nobody said nothin' to me about no kid."

"Who did you think you were fighting?"

"You. If you're Smoke Jensen."

"I am. But why are you fighting me? What have I done to you?"

The question seemed to confuse the hand. "Well . . . I guess nothin'. Except you're squattin' on land that belongs to Jack Biggers."

"He told you that?"

"Yeah."

"Now let me tell you the truth. My sister died. She owned this spread, all legal and proper. She left it all to her daughter, Jenny. I'm here to see that Jenny keeps it. That's the top, bottom, and middle of it all. You ever heard of a man named Wolf Parcell?"

"Who hasn't? Mean old bastard. He'd as soon shoot a man as look at him."

"That's him. He works for me. You ever heard of a man named Barrie? B-A-R-R-I-E."

"Hell, yes. Town-tamer from down in the southwest."

"He works for me, too. There's an old gunfighter called Van Horn. Ever heard of him?"

"He's near abouts as famous as you."

"Well, he's foreman of my niece's spread. How about a breed called Bad Dog?"

"Sure. Don't tell me he's workin' for you, too?"

"Yes, he is. Now, you're not a real gunslick. You're a cowboy drawing fighting wages. Have I got you pegged right?"

"You have. I ain't no fast gun. I just ride for the brand."

"How many more like you over on the JB?"

"Maybe . . . four or five. The rest of them comin' in are hired guns, some of them out-and-out killers. Back-shooters. They damn sure ain't cowboys."

"Name them."

"Patmos. Val Davis. Dusty Higgens. Bearden. Whisperin' Langley. Ned Harden. Kit Silver. I damn shore ain't in their class. I damn shore don't *wanna* be."

"You know a man name of Will Pennington, down in Wyoming?"

"Heard of him. Runs the Box WP."

"That's him. He's hiring men. You and your buddies pull out and ride down there. Tell him I recommended you. Do that, or stay here and die. What's it going to be?"

"I'm gone first light. But I ain't alone out here this night, Mister Smoke. There's others that I don't know their names. Just Jack and Paul and Red and Blackie and so forth. But they ain't punchers, I can tell you that."

"Known guns?"

"They think they are."

Smoke untied the man and helped him to his feet. He

gave him back his gun. The cowboy looked at it, then grinned and slipped it into his holster. "I never was worth a damn with it noways. As soon as the main house goes dark, me and the others will be gone to Wyoming, Smoke. Much obliged."

"Take off and good trip."

"They're waitin' on you, Smoke."

"Good. I sure wouldn't want to disappoint them."

Smoke waited for a full sixty count after the hand had gone. Then he began following the wide creek toward the south end of the spread. He felt sure the hand would leave as he said he would. Smoke wanted no innocent to be caught up in this battle, and a battle it was about to become. He also had him a hunch that when the cowboy he'd talked to laid it on the line to his friends, they would all soon be gone. Since it was near the first of the month, they had been paid, so there was nothing to keep them around.

He saw his second rider of the evening over on the other side of the wide creek. In some parts of the country, it would be called a river. Smoke picked up a rock and gave it a chuck, the stone hitting the horse on the rump and frightening it. The horse reared up suddenly and started bucking. The rider fought to stay in the saddle. While he was bucked and jumping and snorting, Smoke crossed the creek and knelt about thirty feet from the horse and rider. Then Smoke coughed like a puma and the horse had had quite enough of that area. He put his rider on the ground and took off.

"You hammer-headed no-'count!" the rider now on foot yelled. "I'll take a club and a chain and beat you bloody when I catch up with you."

That made things easier for Smoke. He had no use for a man who would abuse any animal.

Smoke slipped up behind the man and tapped him on the shoulder.

The man spun around, a hand dropping to the butt of his gun. Smoke smacked him in the mouth with a gloved fist and the man dropped like a rock, stunned but not out. Smoke reached down, hauled him up by the front of his shirt, and popped him again, this time on the side of the jaw. The man's eyes rolled back in his head and he was out.

Smoke stripped him down to the buff and tossed his clothes and boots into the creek and left him lying on the dewy grass. The man's drawers needed a good washing anyway.

He heard another rider before he could spot him. "Dewey?" the rider called in a hoarse whisper. "I got your horse, man. What's the trouble?"

Smoke waited.

"It's Frankie, Dewey. Answer me, boy."

Smoke suddenly screamed like a panther, and Frankie's horse went crazy. Frankie left the saddle and landed on his back in the grass. Smoke could almost hear the air leaving his lungs at the impact. Smoke was all over the man before he could even think of recovering. One savage blow to the jaw put Frankie in dreamland for a while. Then Smoke gave him the same treatment he gave Dewey, slinging the man's gunbelt over one shoulder. He caught up Frankie's horse and talked to the animal for a moment, calming it. He looped the gunbelts over the saddle horn and rode south, toward the Triangle JB. He hadn't gone half a mile before he was hailed.

"Frankie! Over here. It's Teddy. Let's have a smoke." He was going to have a Smoke, all right—but not the kind he was hoping for. "Have you seen Dewey?"

Smoke rode right up to him and hit him with the coiled-up rope he'd brought. Fifty feet of stiff rope is a formidable weapon, and the rider was knocked out of the saddle to the ground, his mouth and face bleeding. Smoke stepped down and popped him. Teddy sighed and went to sleep.

When Teddy woke up, he was buck-assed naked and a good eight miles from the ranch.

10

Jack Biggers was mad to the core and his face beet red as he stood in front of Club Bowers' desk. "Now, damn it, Club. I ain't gonna take no more of this. Three of my top guns come staggering up in the middle of the night, nekked as the day they was borned, feet all bleedin' and cut, and you're sit-tin' there tellin' me you ain't gonna arrest Smoke Jensen?"

"Settle down, Jack," Club told him. "If we pull a district judge in here, he's gonna want to know how come your men, on a night with no moon, and so black it was like a mine pit, could identify Smoke Jensen. Now, Jack, times are changin'. He'll turn Jensen loose—providin' I ever get him to jail in the first place—and put your hands in jail for perjury. Times ain't like they used to be. Them days are over."

"Now what?" the voice came from the front door.

Biggers turned around to face Major Cosgrove. The man was approximately the same size as Jensen, but carrying just a bit of fat around the jowls and belly. He was in his mid-forties. Behind him stood his mine foreman, Mule Jackson. A huge bear of a man, with arms and hands and shoulders even more heavily muscled than Smoke Jensen, and a cruel face.

Jack, slightly embarrassed, told Cosgrove what had happened.

Major (that was his real name, not a military title) shook his head in disgust and said, "Forget about bringing charges. Any judge, even a bought one, would have to throw it out. Were the men on Jenny's property?"

"Well, yeah. Just like we agreed to do."

"That land is posted. Forget it." Major sat down. "Coffee, Mule."

Mule lumbered across the floor and poured his boss a cup, carefully sugared it, and set the cup on the desk.

Major sipped the hot brew cautiously and said, "We have to proceed very carefully on this, gentlemen. Jensen is a rich man in his own right. Very few people know that he has a freak vein of gold on his ranch, the Sugarloaf. But it's a deep vein. He could tap into that anytime he wished and hire an army. His wife, Sally, has more money than the King and Queen of England. Her family is the richest in all of New England."

"So what do we do?" Biggers demanded. "Give up?"

Major shook his head. "No. We just wait. Only we four and Fat know those mountains on the west side of Jenny's spread, which she owns—or rather, Smoke does, until she comes of age—contain the richest ore deposits of this strike. No, we do what we should have done from the outset. We act like civilized men and buy her spread. Not for the paltry sum we originally offered, but for what it's worth plus the cattle on it. Whatever amount we offer, there is a hundred, a thousand times that in gold in those mountains. That much money will set the girl up back East and we'll be rid of her. Sally Jensen is a businesswoman, very sharp, very astute. She will see the sense in our offer. Bet on it."

* * *

"Riders comin', Mister Smoke!" Jimmy yelled from the yard. "Three riders and a buggy. It's Major Cosgrove in the buggy."

Smoke stepped outside, buckling his gunbelt around his waist. Sally stood by a window, her short-barreled carbine at the ready.

Major stepped down from the buggy and knocked the dust from his dark business suit. He smiled at Smoke. "Sir, I am Major Cosgrove, owner of the Cosgrove Mine Company. Might I talk some business with you?"

Smoke looked at the huge man on the huge mule. Mule Jackson and Smoke Jensen took an immediate dislike to each other.

Smoke knew the type well. A bully, a head-knocker, a man who liked to hurt people. A man who was stupid and didn't know it.

"Certainly, Mister Cosgrove," Smoke told him. "Come on in the house. We have fresh coffee."

Seated in the living room, Cosgrove sipped his coffee and complimented Jenny and Sally on its flavor. The women smiled and said nothing.

"I'm afraid," Major said, "I have been cast in a bad light by some people. As a businessman, I must make a profit to stay in business. But not at the expense of innocent people. Jenny, you have had some trouble out here on your ranch, but none of that trouble came from me. You may believe that, or not believe it, but it is the truth. It is no secret that I wish to buy your ranch. But only at a fair price, both to you, and to me."

Smoke had ridden the ranch and knew approximately how many cattle were on the spread. He knew the price of beef and the price of land this lush. And so did Sally. They both listened to the offer Cosgrove made, and both knew it was a fair one.

Mule waited outside, squatting like a great ape by the buggy. Hands came and went and his eyes took them all in. There was not a man among them who would last a minute with him in a fight. Not even Smoke Jensen.

But Major Cosgrove, no stranger to toe-to-toe fighting, thought differently. Jensen was quite another matter. Major had seen eyes like that before, but not often. They were the eyes of a man who walked through life with supreme confidence. A man who took no water from any man. Mule was bigger and stronger than Jensen, but in a fight, Mule would lose because Jensen was smarter and would play on Mule's stupidity.

Major wondered if he could take Jensen in a fight. It would be interesting, at best. At worst, he would get his brains kicked out by the gunfighter many called the last mountain man.

"That certainly is a fair offer, Major," Smoke said. "And I assure you that Jenny will give it some thought. But I must tell you that at the present time, she is not interested in selling the ranch."

Major Cosgrove smiled. Thinly. He had been sure they would jump at the offer. He kept his anger under control, but it was with an effort. He was a man accustomed to getting his own way. All the time. Failure was not a part of his plans.

Too much money, Sally thought. I've gone over the books carefully and know what this place is worth. He's offering too much money. Why? She cut her eyes at Smoke and he nodded in understanding and agreement.

"Well," Major said, carefully placing his cup and saucer on a table. "It's been an enjoyable first meeting and I hope a mutually profitable one. Will you two be staying long?" He directed the question at Sally.

"Just as long as it takes," she replied.

And that didn't set well with Major Cosgrove either. This Sally Jensen was an uppity woman who needed to be slapped down into her place. This was a man's world, and women didn't belong in business. Before this was all over, he felt he just might have to show Sally Jensen a thing or two.

After Cosgrove had left, Sally said, "His offer was far too high. He offered nearly twice what the place is worth."

"Yes," Smoke said. "But Van Horn tells me there is no gold on the spread." He got up and walked to the window and stared out at the mountains to the west. "It's up there," he said softly. "Bet on it. Just like back on the Sugarloaf. The veins are spotty but run deep." He went to the desk and got out the deed to the ranch, going over it carefully. "No question about it, Jenny. You not only own those mountains to the west, you own the mineral rights as well."

"You mean there is gold there?" the girl questioned.

"Yes. Probably a lot of it. But up there, it would take a lot of capital to get set up. Cosgrove has that capital. One person, working alone, could probably dig out enough to make a fair living. No more than that. That's just my opinion."

"So what do we do, Uncle Smoke?"

"Sit back and wait. But while we wait, we round up some cattle and sell them to get some money to operate on."

"Not that we don't have ample funds," Sally added. "And that's something you can bet Cosgrove knows."

"True. Which is why he won't wait too long before making his next move."

"And that will be?" Jenny questioned.

"Unpleasant," Smoke said flatly. "And soon."

"Are you certain you want to do this?" Smoke asked Sally.

The morning after Major Cosgrove had visited the ranch and made his offer, Sally was putting the finishing touches to her dressing, tying a bandanna around her throat.

"Positive."

"I wish I could talk you out of it."

"No way, husband dear."

"Don't you trust me?"

"With all my heart. I just don't trust those chippies at the Golden Cherry." She shook her head. "What a name for a place like that."

Smoke turned his head to hide his smile. But Sally caught it.

"You find something amusing, dear?"

"Not a thing, dear."

"Who runs this . . . establishment?" Sally asked.

"Van Horn tells me the madam is a lady called Clementine Feathers."

Sally muttered something under her breath. Smoke did not ask her to repeat it. He really was not looking forward to meeting his . . . employees, so to speak. "Jenny wants to ride into town with us."

Sally gave him a look that would wilt cactus.

"Ah, right!" he said brightly. "Not a good day for her to do that."

"Van Horn and Barrie will be riding in with us," Sally said, pulling on her gloves. "Barrie says he wants to look over the town. Get a taste of us, in his words."

"That warhoss wants to check out any possible trouble-makers and mark them down in his mind," Smoke said. "But I sure wonder why, all of a sudden, he showed up here."

"Van Horn is mysterious about that, too," Sally said. Her slight anger was gone. "But I get the feeling that they both might be hiding something. And before you ask, no, I have no idea what it might be." She smiled. "Ready to ride for town?"

Smoke always worried when that smile appeared, for Sally was not a woman bound by the dictates and constraints of the time. She did what she damn well wanted to do, when-ever she damn well wanted to do it.

And Smoke had him a hunch that today she just might decide to do something.

To surprise him.

The town had a feel to it that they all sensed when riding in. The streets were deserted, with not so much as a dog nor a cat present. All the horses had been stabled, and the hitchrails were all vacant.

"Something's up, Van Horn said.

"We been watched," Barrie said. "Those that want the ranch has got people constant on all sides. I was tempted to shoot one out of the saddle the other day. I resisted the temptation," he added dryly.

Since it was a miner's boom town, there were as many saloons as other stores on both sides of the twisting street. And the four riders were very much aware of eyes on them as they rode up the street.

"I ain't felt a friendly eye on me since we rode in," Van Horn said. "I'm gettin' the feelin' I ain't welcome in this place." He spat a stream of tobacco juice. "I just can't imagine why that would be."

Smoke was riding Buck today, since the big horse had nearly torn down his stall in his irritation over Smoke daring to ride another horse.

The unknown voice, calling from concealment in a whisper, reached them. "It's a setup, Smoke. Watch out."

"Miss Sally," Barrie spoke with hardly any lip movement. "I hate to say this, but the safest place for you just might be in the Golden Cherry. And we're right here on it."

"Go, Sally," Smoke said firmly. Softening his tone and with a smile, he added, "Just remember, what's mine is half yours."

Both Van Horn and Barrie struggled to suppress a chuckle at that. They couldn't contain it.

Sally noticed the expression on the men's faces and smiled. "Just for that, I might bar you men from entering this pleasure palace."

Van Horn laughed. "Ma'am, at my age, that ain't no threat at all."

"Be careful," Sally said, then turned her horse into the half-circle drive of the Golden Cherry.

A henna-haired woman stepped out onto the porch of the two-story home. "Honey, you get in here quick. Moses will take care of your horse. This damn town is about to explode."

Sally stepped out of the saddle and handed the reins to the huge, heavily muscled black man with any easy smile on his lips.

"You go on up to the house, Mrs. Jensen," he said. "You'll be as safe here as in a church."

"I'm Clementine Feathers," the bottle-redhead said, taking Sally's arm. "I run this joint. That husband of yours is some man, ain't he?"

"He is that," Sally said, looking around her. "My showing up here should give the good women of the town something to talk about, shouldn't it?"

Clementine laughed. "Honey, when the lamps are turned down and the covers pulled back, there ain't no such thing as a good woman."

Sally smiled. "Would you by any chance have some tea?"

"Honey, I've got the best tea this side of 'Frisco. Come on in and meet the girls. We've all been wondering when you'd show up. Jenny is a fine little lady. We all like her."

"That there's a hell of a woman you got, Smoke, Barrie said. "She'll do to ride the river with."

"Believe me, I know. Let's head over to the Golden Plum and have us a beer. I need to look the place over."

"You haven't been there yet?" Barrie asked.

"No. But I think now is a dandy time to visit. I feel like there must be a hundred guns pointed at me."

"Cosgrove didn't wait long, did he?" Van Horn asked, as the men reined up in front of the saloon and swung down.

"I guess he figures it would be a lot easier to deal with Jenny than with me," Smoke replied, stepping up onto the boardwalk.

About a dozen locals were seated around tables, and five men stood at the far end of the bar. Smoke knew only one of them, a hired gun out of Utah who called himself Stoner.

The interior of the saloon was as fancy as anything Smoke had ever seen, with heavy drapes and polished brass spittoons. The long bar was gleaming. Gambling tables of all descriptions were spaced across the floor. The place was unusually quiet for this time of day.

"Remember me, Barrie?" one of the five men at the bar asked. He had an ugly-looking knife scar running down one side of his face.

"Can't say as I do," the ex-town tamer replied. He looked at the barkeep. "Beer."

Smoke ordered coffee and Van Horn asked for rye.

"You gunned down my brother in New Mexico Territory some years back," Scarface said.

"Do tell. I don't remember it, so he must not have been very hard to handle. Or very important," he added.

Barrie was on the prod and Smoke wondered about that. Everything he had ever heard about the man added up to the picture of a careful man, not one to push or crowd.

There's more here than I know, Smoke concluded.

"Hey, old man," another of the five called to Van Horn. He was young, not more than twenty-four or -five, and very foolish if he was seeking trouble with Van Horn. Van Horn was as much a legend as any man who ever strapped on six-shooters.

"There's one in every crowd," Van Horn muttered.

"The famous Smoke Jensen," Stoner said, sarcasm thick in the words.

"What's your interest in this affair, Stoner?" Smoke asked. "Other than making war on seventeen-year-old girls, that is."

"You ain't no seventeen-year-old girl."

"You want to make war on me, Stoner?" Smoke lifted the coffee cup with his left hand and took a sip.

Stoner stepped away from the bar, both hands hovering over his guns. "I never did believe all that crap folks say about you, Jensen. You can die just like any other man."

"But not this day," Smoke said, then shot the man in the belly.

11

Stoner folded over and took a step backward. He straightened up, a terrible look on his face, and managed to pull one .45 from leather. Smoke gave him another .44 slug and the man sat down in a chair, the .45 clattering to the floor.

"Now, Barrie!" Scarface hollered.

Everybody pulled iron, the bartender hit the floor, the locals flattened out under tables, and the Golden Plum erupted in gunfire.

The loudmouth who just had to try Van Horn didn't even clear leather before the old gunfighter's Remingtons roared fire and smoke and lead. The kid took two in the heart and was dead before he stretched out in front of the bar, his eyes wide open in death.

Smoke put one in a tall, lanky gunhand and the man sat down hard, hollering in pain.

Van Horn and Barrie finished off the remaining two and the saloon began quieting down.

Outside, somebody began beating on a bass drum and another person started tooting on a trumpet.

"The local temperance league," Van Horn explained, re-loading. "Led by Preacher Lester Laymon and his wife, Violet. But she ain't no violet. She's got her a mouth that'd put a champion hog caller to shame."

"Forward into the fray, brothers and sisters!" a woman shrieked. "Into the den of sin and perversion we shall march."

"That's her," Van Horn said.

"Hell, I'd rather put up with another gunfight than have to listen to her," the barkeep said, standing up and brushing off his apron.

"I need a doctor," one of the gunhands moaned.

The sounds of marching feet hammered on the board-walk. The batwings were flung open and a crowd of men and women marched in. A tuba had joined the bass drum and the trumpet.

"Good God!" Smoke said.

Violet Laymon was slightly over six feet tall and rawboned. She looked like she could wrestle steers. She marched up to Smoke and damn near met him eyeball to eyeball. The man beside her was maybe five-feet-five and about as big around as he was tall.

"Help!" one of the gunmen on the floor hollered.

"Are you saved, you poor misguided wretch?" a woman hollered at the man. "Have you been washed in the blood?"

"Hell, he's got it all over him," Van Horn said.

"Shut up," the woman told him.

"Yes, ma'am."

The tuba player oom-pahhed, the bugler tooted, and the drummer pounded the skins.

Club Bowers and one of his deputies stepped into the sa-loon. "I'll handle this!" the sheriff said.

"You shut up, too," a woman told him.

Violet Laymon looked Smoke square in the eyes and thundered, "Are you the infamous Smoke Jensen, the man who has cold-bloodedly killed five thousand men and who had a place reserved in Hell by the time he was fifteen years old?"

"I really don't know how to respond to that," Smoke told the woman.

"I do!" Sally yelled from the batwings. She stepped inside, followed by Clementine Feathers and half a dozen other soiled doves from the Golden Cherry. "That's my husband, and a better man you'll not find anywhere!"

"Cover yourself with proper attire for a lady," Violet yelled at the jeans-clad Sally. "You shameless hussy!"

"Oh, hell," Smoke muttered.

"Somebody get me a doctor!" a wounded gunhand moaned weakly.

Doc White came pushing and shoving through the crowd, followed by Major Cosgrove, Jack Biggers, and the mayor of the town, Fat Fosburn.

The band started up again, a sort of ragged rendition of "A Mighty Fortress." "Sing it with vigor!" Preacher Lester shouted.

A dozen voices lifted in song.

Smoke looked at Van Horn. He was holding his glass of rye in one hand and leading the choir with the other, humming along.

Another badly wounded gunhand lifted himself up on one elbow and pointed a shaking finger at Cosgrove. "You said . . . you said it would be . . ." He fell back and died, his statement unfinished.

"I hope you didn't tell him it would be easy," Van Horn said, over the singing of the choir.

"I didn't tell him anything," Cosgrove snapped. "I never saw that man before in my life."

"Of course, you didn't," Barrie said. "He surely mistook you for someone else."

"Yeah," Van Horn said. "Maybe he thought you was some sort of an angel."

"Jeff," Madam Clementine Feathers said, "get the swampers in here and clean this place up."

"Yes, ma'am."

Cosgrove cut his eyes and found the eyes of Smoke Jensen hard on him. It was not a particularly enjoyable sensation. Major turned abruptly and left the saloon.

"Knock off this damn singin'!" Sheriff Bowers hollered. "This ain't no church. Brandt, Reed, get these people out of here. Where the hell is the undertaker?"

Violet Laymon huffed past Sally, still standing near the batwings, and hissed, "Hussy!"

Sally replied with a smile. Her reply sounded similar to "hitch."

"Well!" Violet threw back her head and marched out, her husband, the choir, and the band right behind them. "Oom-pah-pah, toot, boom!"

"What the hell happened in here?" Club Bowers asked, when the place had quieted down.

"We'll never know from this side," Doc White remarked, standing up. "The last one just died."

At the Golden Cherry, Smoke and Sally sat in the comfortable and spacious kitchen and drank coffee and ate pie. Van Horn and Barrie sat in one of the "receiving" rooms, talking with a group of soiled doves.

"Some of the girls don't do anything more than talk to the men," Clemmie said. Clementine was too formal, she told Smoke and Sally. "A lot of these miners are happily married, with families hundreds of miles away, and they just want to talk to a woman. But those girls still get tarred with the same brush as the others, unfortunately."

Sally had quickly gone over the carefully kept books and found that the Golden Cherry and the Golden Plum did a fantastic business. Jenny was a very well fixed young lady.

"I'm known from 'Frisco to St. Louie," Clemmie said with a smile. "And I'm known for running the cleanest and the most honest places to be found anywhere. No shanghaiing allowed. No foot-padders allowed. No rough stuff with the girls. You seen Moses? Believe me, not even Mule Jackson wants to mess with Moses. Nobody gets rolled in any of *my* places. And nobody gets cheated. The wheels at the Plum are honest, and so are the dealers. I find out they aren't, they're gone."

"How much of a cut does Sheriff Bowers get?" Smoke asked.

Clemmie smiled. "He gets his share."

"Not anymore. Divide what you used to give him among the girls and yourself here, and among the employees at the Golden Plum," Smoke told her. "All payoffs have ceased. You ladies stay here and chat. I'll go tell Bowers personally."

Van Horn and Barrie tagged along.

Smoke saw Jack Biggers and Major Cosgrove leave the sheriff's office, both men walking with their backs stiff with anger. Cosgrove's shadow, Mule Jackson, looked back and spotted Smoke. Major and Jack stopped and turned around. They watched as Smoke entered the sheriff's office, while Van Horn and Barrie waited outside.

Club and his four deputies were sitting around the office. Smoke was met with very unfriendly glances from the five men. "All payoffs to you from Jenny's estate have now ceased," Smoke told the man. "Try to shut down the businesses and I'll kill you. Try to force more money from Clemmie and I'll kill you. If the establishments mysteriously burn down, I'll kill you. If the employees are hassled by you or your men, I'll kill you. Do you understand all that, Club?"

Club Bowers was so mad, he could not speak. He and his men were salting away a good bit of protection money each week from the Golden Cherry and the Golden Plum. Now all that was over.

Brandt stood up, his face mottled with fury. "Why, you goddamn . . ."

Smoke took two steps forward and hit him. The blow took the crooked deputy right on the side of the jaw and the man dropped like an anvil. Brandt lay motionless on the floor, a slight trickle of blood coming from his mouth.

Club Bowers sat behind his desk and stared hate at Smoke. But he was wise enough to keep his hands in plain sight and his mouth free of threats or cussing.

The other deputies, Reed, Junior, and Modoc, sat quietly. They were not afraid of Smoke. They knew that if they all pulled iron together, some of their bullets would nail Jensen. But they also knew that the odds of any of them coming out of it unscathed were very, very slight. At best, two or three of them would die under Smoke's lead. At this range, the carnage would be terrible.

Club Bowers, beneath all his anger, knew that Jensen could not stay in this area forever. Even if all the imported gunfighters that were here and still on their way did not kill the man, he had to leave sometime. He and his wife both had businesses to run back in Colorado. Taking a deep breath to calm himself, Bowers slowly nodded his head.

"That was just common business practice, Jensen," the sheriff said. "It goes on from New York City to San Francisco. But if you want it stopped, it's stopped.

"Fine," Smoke said, then turned his back to the men and stepped out onto the boardwalk. Biggers and Cosgrove were still standing on the boardwalk, Mule Jackson a few feet from the men. Fat Fosburn had joined them. Smoke walked up to the men.

"The payoffs to the sheriff and his men from the Cherry and the Plum have just stopped," Smoke informed the men. "One of them had something to say about that. He's still out on the floor. Do any of you have objections to that?"

"I do," Mule said. "I just flat don't like you, Jensen. And I think I'll tear your meathouse down right now." He stepped forward, and for a big man, he was surprisingly swift.

But of all the men present on the boardwalk, Smoke had suspected Mule would be the one to offer up a fight. Smoke sidestepped, then stuck out a boot, and Mule tripped. A little shove from Smoke and the huge man fell off the boardwalk and landed face-first in the mud of the street.

Smoke unbuckled and untied, handing his guns to Van Horn. He pulled leather riding gloves from his back pocket and slipped them on while Mule was cussing and spitting out mud and dirt and getting to his feet. Mule was spewing and spitting out just what he was going to do to Smoke. None of it was pleasant.

"You watch that brute," Van Horn cautioned. "He's killed men with those fists."

"So have I," Smoke replied.

Clemmie and Sally came at a run, as did most of the town's citizens, many of them climbing onto awnings and running up to second-floor landings to get a glimpse of the upcoming fight. Mule Jackson had never been bested in a fight, and while Smoke Jensen was a known gunfighter, and a very well-put-together man, most believed he stood no chance at all against a wicked brawler like Mule.

"Five hundred dollars on Mule!" Fat Fosburn hollered.

"I'll take that bet," Clemmie Feathers shouted.

"Fifty dollars on Smoke," Van Horn said.

"You're on," Club said.

The betting became hot and heavy.

Violet and her band of followers raced up, pushing and shoving through the crowd. "This is disgraceful!" Violet shrieked, while her husband was jumping up and down, trying to see what was going on. He finally perched on top of a water barrel by the corner of a building.

Store owners locked their doors and hung CLOSED signs on the doorknobs. No one wanted to miss this fight.

"One thousand dollars on Mule Jackson!" Major Cosgrove shouted above the din.

"I'll take that bet!" Sally yelled. "And go five times more. Five thousand dollars on Smoke. You want to put your money where your big fat mouth is, Cosgrove?"

Major's face flushed a deep crimson as his eyes met Sally's. She and Clemmie and a couple of the Golden Cherry's soiled doves were standing in the bed of a wagon.

"I'll take that bet, Little Lady," Major yelled.

Sally nodded her head. "I'm a lady most of the time," she said to Clemmie. "But I can be just about as mean as my husband when I choose to be."

"I don't doubt that for a second, honey," Clemmie replied.

"Come on, you lard-butt!" Smoke yelled to Mule, still slipping and sliding in the mud of the street. "Are you going to fight or dance all day?"

With a roar of rage, Mule charged.

12

Mule slopped up onto the boardwalk, muddy and wet to the skin and mad to the bone. Before he could get set, Smoke hit him flush in the mouth with a straight right that snapped the man's head back and bloodied his lips. Mule stood for a couple of seconds, shaking his big head. Before he could clear out all the little chirping birdies and ringing bells, Smoke crossed a left that landed on the side of the man's jaw and buckled his knees. Mule covered up and took a staggering step back. The bully knew at that moment he was in for the fight of his life. Smoke Jensen was no ordinary man, and he could punch like a sledgehammer! There was a roaring pain in his head that Mule had not experienced since childhood. He was going to have to end this brutally and quickly, and he knew he was going to have to kill Smoke Jensen. He could not let the man beat him. His reputation would be ruined and he'd be a laughingstock. He couldn't let that happen. All that went through his mind in the course of two seconds. When the third second ticked past, Smoke followed him in and hit him twice in the stomach with a left and right that hurt.

Smoke pressed and clubbed the man on the neck with a balled fist, then stepped back, out of reach of Mule's powerful arms.

Deputy Modoc stuck one boot out to trip Jensen. He felt the muzzle of a pistol jam into his ribs and he pulled back his boot and cut his eyes. He was staring into the cold eyes of the town tamer, Barrie. "Do that again," Barrie said, "and I'll kill you."

Club Bowers looked over at Sally. She had taken a rifle from someone's saddle boot and was holding it, hammer back. He sighed and shook his head. He'd never before met a man like Smoke or a woman like Sally. They were made for each other.

Mule screamed like an angry bull and ran at Smoke in an attempt to lock his arms around the man and crush the life from him. And Smoke knew the man was capable of doing just that. Smoke stepped to one side and smashed a right into Mule's face, flattening the man's nose and sending blood spurting. Mule stopped as if hit with an iron stake, his boots flying out from under him. He landed on his back on the boardwalk, the breath momentarily knocked from him.

"Stomp him, Smoke!" someone in the crowd yelled. "He'd do it to you."

"You shut your damn mouth!" Major yelled, his eyes searching the crowd for the citizen.

"You go to hell, Cosgrove," the citizen yelled.

Smoke let Mule slowly lumber to his muddy, low-heeled lace-up boots. Mule could not believe this was happening to him. He had yet to land a punch on Smoke Jensen. The damn man just stood there waiting.

"Stand still and fight!" Mule said, blood leaking from his mouth and nose.

"Well, come on," Smoke told him. "I'm right here." Smoke was under no illusions. He knew he had been awfully lucky so far in this fight, and that just might be subject to change at any time if he got careless.

Mule lifted his big fists and came at Smoke slowly. The man had seen the error of his ways and realized that brute strength alone would not win this fight. Smoke had hammered him some terrible blows, and those blows had taken some of the steam out of Mule. He could not recall ever getting hit as hard and as many times as he'd been hit this day.

Mule had never had to rely on fighting skills to win fights. He could take a punch with the best of them, and if he ever got his hands on a man, the fight was over. Mule liked to crush bones, to hurt men, cripple them. He'd killed a dozen men with his hands over the years, and made cripples out of twice that number. And he had no doubts about the outcome of this fight.

But he should have.

Mule flipped a left at Smoke and Smoke ducked it and went under, driving his right fist into Mule's belly, about two inches above his belt buckle. The air *whooshed* out of the man and Smoke followed that with a jarring left to the side of Mule's jaw that damn near crossed Mule's eyes. Smoke smashed a left and a right to Mule's ribs and then slammed a big right fist over Mule's heart.

Mule staggered back, hurt.

Major Cosgrove cut his eyes to Sally. She was looking straight at him, smiling.

Damn the woman! Major thought. Damn her! She'd never had a doubt about who would win the fight. And damn Smoke Jensen, too.

Club Bowers watched the fight and thought: Mule is finished. Smoke is going to maul him, humiliate him, and maybe bust him up real bad.

Those citizens who supported the power structure in Red

Light had fallen silent. They all knew that some professional fighter could probably whip Mule, someone like Jem Mace or that new up-and-comer John Sullivan. They could have beaten Mule, fighting by the rules. But to have some gunfighter come in and do it . . . that was, up to this point, unthinkable.

"Give it up, Mule," Smoke told the man. "Just give it up. I don't want to have to kill you."

"You, kill *me?*" Mule was visibly shaken. "Why, you two-bit gunslinger. I'll tear your head off!" Mule bored in, and that got him a left and right to the face, the left smashing his already flattened nose and the right pulping his lips.

Screaming in rage and pain and almost total frustration, Mule plowed ahead, roaring curses at Smoke, slamming lefts and rights at him. Smoke backed up and took the blows on his arms and shoulders, and they hurt, but did no damage. When Mule grew arm weary and out of breath, he stepped back, and Smoke jumped in close. Mule thought he was swinging for his head and covered up. Smoke instead back-heeled the huge man, sending him crashing to the board-walk.

When Mule tried to get to his feet, he made the mistake of momentarily presenting his big backside to Smoke, and Smoke couldn't resist it. He planted one boot on Mule's butt and shoved, sending the man off the boards and sprawling into the mud. Mule landed with a mighty splat and buried in the mud.

"Now, that's it, Mule" Smoke called. "The fight is over. If you get up, I'm going to hurt you. Stay down, man."

"A thousand dollars if you'll get up and fight, Mule!" Major shouted. "A thousand dollars, Mule."

Smoke looked at the man, contempt in his eyes. Cosgrove was even sorrier than Smoke had first suspected. He returned his gaze to Mule Jackson.

The man was struggling to get to his feet.

"Don't do it, Mule," Smoke called. "Stay down."

But Mule was furious, that rage shining in his eyes. There was a maddened look on his muddy face. He pulled himself out of the mire and crawled back up to the boardwalk. Slowly, he lifted his fists.

Smoke did the same.

The crowd was now totally silent, so quiet that Mule's ragged breathing could be heard.

Then Mule made the worst mistake he could possibly make. He grinned at Smoke and said, "When I finish stompin' you, gunfighter, I'm gonna snatch that wife of yours out of that wagon, tote her to a bed, and peel them jeans offen her down to her shinin' bare butt. Then I'll show her what pleasures a real man can give a woman."

Killer and no-'count that Club Bowers was, he could but shake his head at that remark. Fat Fosburn put his hands to his face and stifled a moan. Jack Biggers' mouth dropped open. And Major Cosgrove gasped at the stupidity of the man. Men had been hanged for saying less.

Smoke's eyes turned as cold as the frozen Arctic. He slowly walked the distance between them and kicked out with one boot, the point of the boot catching Mule square in the balls. Mule screamed and doubled over. Smoke brought his knee up and the crowd could hear the bones crunch in Mule's face.

Grabbing the man by his long greasy hair, Smoke straightened him up and began battering the man's face and body with savage fists. He smashed the man to the boards, now slick with Mule's blood, half a dozen times, each time dragging him back up and smashing him down again.

"He's unconscious, baby," Sally called from the wagon, just as Smoke drew back his bloody-gloved fist to strike again.

Smoke let Mule fall. He stood, this big last mountain man, his huge chest heaving with exertion and his eyes savage with killing fury. He turned and took a step toward Major Cosgrove.

"You hit me and I'll sue you!" Major yelled.

The crowd exploded in laughter and Major's face drained of blood, then filled to a high crimson of embarrassment.

Smoke nodded his head and stripped off his gloves. "You bet my wife five thousand dollars on this fight," he panted the words. "Pay her. Right now, Cosgrove."

"I don't have that kind of money on me!"

"Then get it, you son-of-a-bitch!" Smoke shouted at him.

"You can't . . . call me that!" Major said.

"He did," Van Horn said. "Mayhaps you'd better strap on iron, Cosgrove. And just in case Smoke don't feel up to meetin' you, I'd be glad to take his place."

"Look at me, Cosgrove!" Sally said.

Major cut his eyes. Sally's rifle was to her shoulder, the muzzle pointed straight at Cosgrove's chest. "Send someone for my money or you're a dead man."

"Whoooeee!" Clemmie hollered. "Sally, you are my kind of woman." She cocked her head. "Well," she amended that. "Sort of."

13

Sally was five thousand dollars richer when she swung into the saddle and the four of them rode out of Red Rock to the cheers of most of the citizens of the town. Van Horn and Barrie had money in their pockets from betting on the fight, and all of them were still smiling over the public humiliation of Major Cosgrove. Mule Jackson still had not regained consciousness when the four rode out of town.

"It's going to be all-out war now," Smoke said, putting a damper on the high humor. "Cosgrove will have to come out fighting if he's to regain any of his power."

"I should have shot him," Sally said.

"You're mighty right about that," Barrie said.

"Don't encourage her," Smoke said with a smile. "She's getting as notorious as I am. She'll start packing two guns tied down if this keeps up."

Sally smiled at the good-natured kidding. But she knew her husband was right about Major Cosgrove; he would have to come out fighting if he were to maintain any semblance of his old power. Now, more than ever, Jenny was in danger. But there was no way the girl would consider leaving for her safety. She had that Jensen strain of courage coursing through her veins. And stubbornness, Sally added.

"I hate Mule Jackson," Jenny said, after sitting enraptured, listening to the news of the day. "He gives me a spooky feeling, the way he looks at me."

"He won't be doing much looking for at least a month, Sally said. "I have never seen a man beaten that thoroughly."

"But he'll be more dangerous now," Smoke said, soaking his hands in warm salted water to keep down the swelling. "He'll be carrying a powerful grudge against me."

In the bunkhouse, Barrie was holding the floor. "I never seen nothin' to compare with it," he told the hands. "Mule didn't even get one good lick in on Smoke. Smoke tore him down and whupped him to a fare-thee-well."

"Mule had it coming," Pasco said, sitting on his bunk, mending a tear in a shirt. "He killed a friend of mine with his fists. Killed him for no other reason than that he was Mexican."

"Boys, this is shapin' up to be a bad one," Van Horn took the floor. "Up to now, it's been mild. Now it's gonna turn rough. You all ride with a spare six-shooter in your saddlebags and extra ammo. And you ride wary at all times. Cosgrove has got to come back at us for this day. So we might as well get ready for it."

"You reckon he'll hire more gunslingers?" Ford asked.

"Bet on it. He can't afford to lose. If he does he'll have to leave the country."

"Smoke really called him a son-of-a-bitch?" Ladd asked.

"Flat to his face."

Ladd shook his head. "Smoke musta really been mad."

"You could say that," Van Horn's reply was dryly offered.

* * *

Doc White stepped out of his small clinic into the outer office and faced Sheriff Club Bowers. "Mule Jackson has received the most thorough beating I have ever seen given a man. It's a miracle the man isn't dead. While he was unconscious, I had the dentist come over and extract several teeth that were broken off. He is very nearly a total bruise from his face to his waistline. He has several cracked ribs, and if he didn't sustain some type of internal injuries, I'll be very surprised. I put so many stitches in his face I lost count. Oh, one other thing: that man who was kicked in the head by Jensen's horse? He's dead."

Muttering under his breath, Club walked back to his office to find a very angry Major Cosgrove and an equally angry Jack Biggers there. The mayor, Fat Fosburn, sat calmly drinking coffee.

"Five thousand dollars!" Major stormed. "That damn uppity woman took five thousand dollars from me. At gunpoint. And you didn't do a damn thing to stop it, Club."

"Half the town heard you make the bet, Major," Club told him. "It would have been worser had you tried to welch on her."

Cosgrove did some more cussing and stomping around, then finally sat down. He threw his expensive hat on the floor. "And the man dared call me a son-of-a-bitch," he wound down.

"Nick Norman just died," Club told the men.

"Who cares?" Biggers replied. He stared at the sheriff. "I got Lonesome Ted Lightfoot ridin' in this week. He's bringing some of his friends with him."

"I didn't know Lightfoot had any friends," Club said. "But thanks for telling me. Who's comin' with him?"

"Les Spivey, for sure. Maybe Curtis Brown."

Club nodded and turned to the window facing the muddy street. He had had a good deal working here. Plenty of money and plenty of power. But he could sense that it was all coming to an end. It didn't make any difference how many gunslicks Major and Jack and Fat brought in. Not any difference at all. The big three, Cosgrove, Biggers, and Fosburn, were beaten men. They just didn't know it yet. But they were whipped.

The best thing for me to do, Club thought, is just pack up and pull out. Just get the hell gone from here. If I stay, I'm going to die.

"What are you thinking about?" Fosburn spoke to the sheriff's back.

"Pullin' out," Club said honestly.

"Pulling out!" Major said, jumping to his feet. "Have you lost your mind? We've got a gravy train here. In a few years we can all be enormously wealthy men."

Club turned to face the town's power group. "We don't have a few years. I don't 'magine we have even a few months. Not if we continue buckin' Smoke Jensen."

"Jensen won't be around in a few weeks," Biggers said, sticking out his chin belligerently. "I got twenty-five of the best guns in these parts on my payroll with more coming in. There ain't no way Jensen can survive all that."

"Jensen's had a hundred men chasin' him before," Club said, "includin' friends of mine who will swear to this day they'll never tangle with Smoke Jensen again. You forgettin' a couple of years back when all them people were chasin' him up in the mountains. He must have killed fifty of them, and Sally Jensen put lead in ten or twenty. You 'member last year, I think it was, that German feller, Count something-or-the-other, hired all those gunslingers to help him hunt down Smoke Jensen? Well, they hunted him until he got tired of it and made his stand. Do you know how many men died durin' that foul-up? You couldn't stack their bodies in these two rooms here and all them cells yonder. Listen to me, people. I know Smoke Jensen. He probably don't remember me, but I *damn* sure remember him. Let me name you some men who had the bad judgment to brace him. Slick Finger Bob, Terry Smith, Tom Ritter, One-Eye Slim, Warner Frigo, Canning, Felter, Kid Austin, Grisson and Clark, Curly Rodgers, Curt Holt, Ed Malone, Boots Pierson, Harry Jennings, Blackjack Simpson. Richards, Potter, Stratton. Smoke Jensen killed *nineteen* men by himself in a ghost town over in Idaho. Then there's Greeny, Lebert, and Augie. There was Dickerson, Brown, and Necker. Joiner and Wilson and Casey. There was Jack Waters and his three brothers. Then there was Lanny Ball and four of his friends. I think their names was Woody, Dalton, Lodi, and Sutton. Dad Estes had himself and his whole gang wiped out by Jensen. Cat Jennings and Barton and Mills and no-'count George Victor. Utah Slim—*everybody's* heard of him—faced Smoke one day. That was the last thing he ever did. Pig-Face Phillips and a gunhand named Carson called Jensen out. They died in the dirt. You want me to name some more? Hell, I ain't even scratched the surface yet!"

Club Bowers walked the floor, eyeballing each man there. "People, understand something: Smoke Jensen was raised by mountain men. He don't fight like nobody you or me know. And when you get Smoke Jensen riled—and I've seen him riled—he's like . . . well, a whole room full of grizzly bears. He's . . ."

Jack Biggers waved him silent. "You're lettin' your imagination run away with you, Club. Jensen is a tough man. We all saw that when he fought Mule. But he's still just a man. He ain't got no supernatural powers."

"Injuns say he does," Fat Fosburn said. "I used to have some Injuns ridin' with me in my gang, both breeds and full redskin. They were all scared slap to death of Smoke Jensen. You see, Smoke was sort of raised up by a mountain man called Preacher."

That got everybody's attention.

"Yeah," Fat said with a smile. "Preacher hisself. The most famous mountain man of them all. Mean as a snake and tough as an oak tree. And he brought Smoke Jensen up to be just like him. And done a damn good job of it, too. Now you know why he's so damn mean. Club's right about Jensen to some degree. What we got to do, I'm thinking', is get us a good back-shooter in here."

"You know one?" Major asked.

Fat smiled. "I've already sent for him."

The man Fat had contacted despised Smoke Jensen with a hatred that bordered on insanity. Preacher had killed his father with a knife back in the mid-fifties, after he'd caught the man trying to steal one of his horses. Peter Hankins had been a boy in his teens when it had happened. A boy who was already an accomplished thief, liar, pickpocket, murderer, and just about anything else evil he was big enough to be. Trappers had brought the elder Hankins back to the trading post and dumped him at Peter's feet, telling him what had happened.

"Out here, boy," a mountain man told him. "You don't steal a man's horse. A lot of times, that's like givin' a man the death sentence. Your pa got what he deserved. Let it lie. You go after Preacher, and he'll kill you."

Peter Hankins drifted East and joined the Union Army at the start of the War Between the States. He had always been expert with a rifle, and he was made a sniper. He loved it. He loved to kill from a distance. He especially loved to kill Southerners. He'd won medals for it. When the war ended, he drifted back West, joined a gang of scum and ne'er-do-wells, and a few years later was caught up in a completely unexpected fight with Preacher and a young man named Smoke Jensen. Smoke got lead into him, although Peter doubted the young man knew it at the time. His hip still bothered him because of that fight. So after that, he shared his hatred of Preacher with hatred of Smoke Jensen.

Now he had a chance to kill him and make a couple thousand dollars in the process. It was too good to pass up.

As soon as he received the wire, he bought a train ticket and was on his way, sleeping in the car with his horse and his Sharps "English Model" 1877 .45-caliber rifle. Peter hand-loaded his own ammunition (2.6-inch casing) and knew almost to the inch what distance they would carry, and they would carry accurately for more than fifteen hundred yards, providing the wind was not kicking up.

Peter would kill man, woman, or child. He made no distinction. He was a man utterly without morals. And he was looking forward to this job.

Smoke stepped out of the house for a breath of night air after another of Sally and Jenny's excellent suppers. The men had staggered off to the bunkhouse, all of them full as ticks. Three days after the fight, and his hands were no longer sore or swollen. There had been no trouble from Biggers, Cosgrove, or Fat. Smoke was not expecting any from Club Bowers. Scoundrel that he was, he was also a man who had been around and could read signs. Smoke had him a hunch that Club would pull out of this fight given just the slightest opportunity.

Van Horn walked up and stood silent for a moment, rolling a cigarette. "When you figure they're gonna hit us, and how do you figure it?"

"Just as soon as they get everyone in here that's coming in."

"You know of a person name of Peter Hankins?"

"Peter Hankins?" Smoke mused. "Yes. I do. He's a long-distance shooter. He uses a special made Sharps .45. Sharps made the rifle for about a year, I think. Made it for target shooters. It had something to do with English marksmanship rules, I believe. I've never seen one. Hankins, huh? My mentor killed Hankins' father. Preacher caught him stealing horses and carved him up. That was years before I knew Preacher. I've known for a long time that Hankins hates me."

"How old a man would he be?"

"Probably in his early to mid-forties. He was a teenager when Preacher killed his father back in '55 or so. I have no idea what he looks like or where he lives. He's a loner. He comes in, bodies fall, he leaves. Usually without anyone ever seeing him. How'd you find out about him coming in?"

Van Horn smiled. "Oh, those sources of mine I told you about."

Smoke chuckled. "You mean the girls at the Golden Cherry, don't you?"

Van Horn laughed quietly. "Not much gets by you, does it, Smoke?"

"I can't afford to let much by me, Van. I have too many people who want to see me dead."

"I do know the feelin'," the old gunfighter said. "But if they attack this ranch, they're gonna be in for a tough fight of it. That's a salty bunch yonder in the bunkhouse."

"They'll attack. It's coming. That's why I sold off most of the cattle, except for the good breeding stock, and had you bunch the rest in that box. Will the girls tell you when Hankins gets into town?"

"Within the hour."

"Let me know. Tomorrow we all work close to the ranch. We've got to get ready for anything that might come our way."

"See you in the morning."

Smoke was up before dawn, as usual, and with coffee in hand, stepped outside to meet the dawning, about a half hour away. Wolf Parcell had been waiting on him.

"What's on your mind, Wolf?"

"Let's take the fight to them. Kill them all," the old mountain man said coldly and bluntly. "End it. Then the girl-child can live in peace."

Smoke smiled in the darkness. Mountain men were not known for their gentle loving nature toward anyone who had openly declared themselves an enemy. And for the most part, that philosophy was shared by Smoke. But he had learned to temper his baser urgings . . . to a degree. "Those days are just about gone, Wolf. Besides, we've got to keep public sentiment on our side."

The old man *harrumphed* at that but said nothing in rebuttal for the moment. He drained his coffee cup and stuffed a wad of chewing tobacco into his mouth. He chomped and chewed and spat and finally said, "Two Injun friends of mine come to the bunkhouse last night. Told me a whole passel of gunslingers rode into town 'bout ten o'clock."

"I thought I heard something about one."

"Figured you would. Injuns asked about you. I told 'em you wasn't near 'bouts ugly as Preacher, and you was sizable bigger and somewhat smarter."

Smoke chuckled. And waited. He knew Wolf had more on his mind and would get to it in his own good time.

"Said they was a double handful of the gunslingers," Wolf said, after he spat. "They didn't know no names."

"The odds are getting longer, aren't they?"

"Yep. But we can handle them come the time. You'll cut your puma loose soon enough I reckon. And we'll be right there with you."

"You're looking forward to this, aren't you?"

"I'd be lyin' if I said I wasn't. That's a good girl in yonder. I like her. I ain't got no use for people who'd hurt a girl like that. Riles me up considerable. I take it personal. Bad Dog feels the same way. So's the rest of the fellers. When they come, Smoke, I ain't offerin' no quarter to none of them. I just want you to know that. I'm speakin' for me, Pasco, and Bad Dog. Cain't talk for none of the others."

"Try not to take scalps," Smoke said dryly.

"I'll think about it." The old mountain man got up as silently as a stalking cat and moved into the darkness. He stopped and turned around. Smoke could see the faint smile on his lips. "You're a fine one to tell me not to take scalps, Smoke."

"That was a long time ago, Wolf."

Wolf chuckled. "You ain't old enough for it to be that long ago, boy. You got more of Preacher in you than you think. And I think this here fight's gonna turn real interestin'. For a fact I do."

14

Smoke saddled up, secured his bedroll, and rode out alone, taking a couple of sandwiches with him. He had told Sally, "I'll be back."

She did not question him. He might be back by noon, or he might return the next day; He might be back in three or four days. Sally knew they were in a fight to the death now, for her husband never tried to shield her from the truth. Hired guns were riding in from all over a three-state and territory area. By stage, by train, by horse. They were coming to Red Light to accept the fighting wages of Biggers, Fosburn, and Cosgrove. They were coming in to attempt to kill Smoke Jensen.

And this teenage girl, Sally added, cutting her eyes to the young girl standing at the kitchen counter, kneading dough for bread. They have no right to do that, Sally mused, her thoughts turning savage. She has harmed no one. She has a right to live on the ranch her mother left her, and to live in peace. Damn those men who would harm a child . . ."

"When you finish with that, Jenny," Sally said, "get your guns. We're going to practice awhile."

"Yes, ma'am. Won't Uncle Smoke be alarmed at the gunfire?"

"No. I told him about it. Sally went to the front door and looked for Van Horn. The old gunfighter was by the corral, Wolf Parcell and Bad Dog with him. She walked down to him. He turned at her approach, taking off his hat.

"Jenny and I will be down by the creek for a time, shooting. I want Jimmy to come with us. I want to see how he handles a gun."

Van Horn smiled. "Yes, ma'am. I'll come down, too. Smoke say where he was goin'?"

"No. I didn't ask him. He'll be back when he finishes what he set out to do."

"I thought he was gettin' a mite riled when I spoke with him."

"He's given those who want this spread fair warning. In his own way. Now, I suspect, he's taking the fight to them."

"But he's all alone," Jimmy Hammon said, walking up.

"No, he ain't, boy," Wolf said. "He's got the spirits with him. Preacher's with him. And so is Griz and Nighthawk and all the rest of 'em. Five hundred years of fightin' and ridin' alone is with Smoke this day. Everything about survivin' that could be taught a man was taught to Smoke by them that took him as a kid and saw to his needs. Mayhaps we—and I was a part of lookin' after him—mayhaps we didn't do him right. Our time was endin' when Ol' Preacher took the boy under his wing. We didn't teach him no gentle ways. He'd done been taught that by his ma and pa. And they done a good job of it. Smoke's got a good mind to what is right and what is wrong. What we done was teach him the gun and the knife and the fight. I allow as to how it was fate that brought the boy to the High Lonesome and to us." He smiled down at young Jimmy. "I'd take you under my arm and tote you up to the High Lonesome, son, and I'd larn you the ways of the mountain men. But I'd be doin' you a disservice if I did. Them fancy-pants Eastern ways is rapid movin' out here. All talk and no action is the way it'll be in a few years. 'Fore long, any man'll be able to walk up to you and spit in your face. And if you gut him or shoot him, the law'll put you in prison for it. You mark my words: this country is in for a turrible time of it."

Sally put a hand on the boy's shoulder. "Jimmy will receive a formal education. Smoke and I will see to that."

"You mean I got to go to school?" Jimmy blurted.

"Yes," Sally said firmly. "You will go to school."

Van Horn looked at him. "Don't say nothin' 'ceptin' yes, ma'am, boy."

"Yes, ma'am, Miss Sally," Jimmy said.

Smoke sat his saddle on the north side of the fence, facing three of Jack Biggers' hands, who sat their saddles on the south side. The three had known it would someday come to this. They had just hoped it would not be this soon.

"We ain't doin' you no harm, Jensen," one finally spoke. "And we're on our own range."

"That's right," Smoke replied. "And it is a mighty pretty place to be buried."

"Huh?" another said.

"What are you talkin' about?" the third asked.

"You ride for Jack Biggers. He's paying you seventy-five dollars a month for your guns. Jack Biggers has sworn to take my niece's ranch even if he has to kill her. That makes all of you an enemy of mine. So fill your hand or ride."

The three Triangle JB riders wanted to exchange glances, but they dared not take their eyes from Smoke Jensen. In a time when the average cowboy made about thirty-five dollars a month, that seventy-five Biggers had offered had looked awfully big. Now they weren't so sure of that.

"I'm giving you all a chance, boys," Smoke spoke softly but firmly. "Take a moment and think about it."

"Jensen," one said. "I'm gonna put both hands on this here apple and keep them there. Okay?"

"Fine. Do it."

The men carefully placed his gloved hands on the saddle horn and gripped it, one hand on top of the other, the reins under the hand holding the apple.

"Me, too," another said, and slowly followed suit.

"I'm not," the third hand said.

"Think about it, Jess," the first hand to show some sense told him.

"I ain't takin' water from Jensen."

"I am," the second man said. " 'Cause it's mighty scarce in Hell."

"Make your play, Jensen," Jess said.

"After you," Smoke told him.

Jess grabbed for iron and Smoke's .44 boomed. Jess fell backward out of the saddle. Neither of his buddies had taken their hands off the saddle horn. Jess tried to get up, the front of his shirt stained with blood. His gun had fallen from the holster.

"Ain't no human person that fast," Jess gasped, unable to get any further than to his knees.

"You boys take care of the burying and then ride out of this country. Get you a good job punching cattle and leave the gunfighting to someone else," Smoke told the remaining two.

Jess fell over to lie in the tall grass.

"Can we climb off these hurricane decks to see about him?" the first hand asked.

"Of course, you can. Just don't try anything stupid."

"Believe me, Mister Jensen, that didn't even cross my mind."

Jess cried out, "I'd like to live to see you get plugged, Jensen!"

"You'd be at the end of a long list," Smoke told him. "You'd best start making your peace with God and tell these boys where to send your saddle."

"You go to hell!" Jess said.

"Jess," one of his buddies said. "Hush now."

"You go to hell, too!" Jess told him. "As a matter of fact, both of you can just go to hell!"

Smoke watched as Highpockets Rycroft and Dick Miles rode up, both of them still looking sort of peaked from their last encounter with Smoke Jensen. Highpockets favored his left arm and Miles wore a pained expression on his face. Obviously, his stomach was still tender.

"What do you two want?" Smoke asked.

"We're on our side of the damn fence!" Highpockets protested. "We ain't botherin' you."

"I find you both offensive to look at," Smoke replied. "I don't want to see either of you again."

"Well, what are you gonna do if you do see us after this?" Dick asked.

"Shoot you."

"Shoot us?" Highpockets hollered. "Now, wait just a minute!"

"What about me?" Jess said.

"You done been shot!" Dick said. "Shut up."

"Or I might decide to hang you," Smoke added.

"Now, just hold on here," Highpockets protested. "We're just cowboys. We push beeves. And that's all. You got my word on that."

"Since when?" Dick blurted before he thought.

"Since right now!" his buddy told him. "And shut your damn mouth, you fool!"

Smoke lifted his .44 and cocked the hammer, pointing it at Dick.

"Whoa!" Dick bellered, throwing both hands into the air. "I ain't touched no gun, Smoke."

"You implied you hired out your gun against me," Smoke told him. "That's good enough for me."

"I didn't do no such a damn thing!" Dick yelled. "I don't even know what that means."

"I'm dyin' and don't nobody seem to care," Jess moaned.

"Well, do so quietly," Highpockets told him. "I got troubles of my own here."

"Shuck out of your gunbelts," Smoke told them.

"Huh?" Dick asked.

Highpockets looked at him. "Dick," he said, unbuckling his belt and letting it fall. "I always knowed you was slow, but you ain't gettin' me killed 'cause of it."

"Oh!" Dick said, and let his guns fall. "Uh, Mister Jensen—are you gonna kill us?"

"Nope. At least, not this time around. But I really think you boys should stop wearing guns. Now, that's not an order. But it *is* a suggestion. However," Smoke slowly let the hammer down on his .44 and all in front of it relaxed, "I might also suggest this." He looked at two standing over Jess. "What are your names?"

"Howie and Biff. I'm Howie. This is Biff."

"That . . . is reasonable," Smoke said. "All right, what I'm about to suggest goes for you two, as well."

"What about me?" Jess whispered.

"Shut up, Jess," Howie told him. "You're supposed to be dyin'."

"I want words spoke over me!" Jess said.

"Do I have to kick you in the head to shut you up?" Howie whispered. "Hush! You were sayin', Mister Jensen?"

"It might seem strange for you men to suddenly stop wearing guns. So if you decide to stay around here, you may wear your guns. But everytime you see me, you throw your hands in the air. If you don't, I'll just have to assume that you're unfriendly. And I'll shoot you."

"Throw . . . our hands in the air ever'time we see you?" Dick questioned.

"That's right. Can you do that?"

"I can do that!" Howie said. "Can you do that, Biff?"

"I can do that!" Biff said quickly. "Yes, sir."

Highpockets raised his hands. Swiftly. "Like this, Mister Jensen?"

"Just like that."

Dick threw his hands into the air. Biff and Howie did the same. They all looked kind of silly.

"We're just cowboys, Mister Jensen," Biff said. "That's all. We ain't gunfighters."

"Fine. When this is all over, if—*if*—you men behave and do like I tell you, you can all go to work for Miss Jenny. She is going to be the new owner of the Triangle JB."

"She is?" Highpockets asked.

"She is. Lower your hands. You'd like working for my niece. She keeps a tubful of doughnuts around all the time. And she bakes pies one day and cakes the next. She's a fine cook."

"I'm hungry now," Biff said.

"I'm dyin'!" Jess hollered. "Don't nobody care about me?"

"You want to take him into town?" Smoke asked.

"He wouldn't make it," Dick said. "He's about done for now."

"Oh, Lord!" Jess cried.

"You'd actually hire us to work for your niece after we rode for Biggers?" Highpockets asked.

"Sure. Just as long as you boys stick to punching cows

and not punching or shooting at me," Smoke said with a grin.

"We're out of it," Howie said. "From now on. And that's a promise, Mister Smoke."

"Fine. See you boys." Smoke rode away.

"That's a nice feller there," Howie said. "I sure had him pegged wrong."

"He seemed right sure about Miss Jenny goin' to own the Triangle JB," Dick said.

"I damn sure believed him," Howie replied. "I am a changed man, boys. Believe it."

"What are we gonna do about Jess?" Highpockets asked.

Biff looked down at the would-be gunhand and shook his head. "Get a shovel."

Smoke rode toward the eastern slopes of the mountains that ringed the valley. He felt the men he had left alive by the fence would keep their word. He was a pretty fair hand at judging people, and those men had the appearance of being nothing more than good, working cowboys who'd had the misfortune to sign on with the wrong outfit.

He put the ranch out of his mind. Van Horn and the others would protect it—and Sally and Jenny—with their lives. Smoke had no doubts about that. For now, he had to concentrate on staying alive. He felt that those men by the fence were probably all the real working cowboys Jack Biggers had left on the payroll. All his other hands would be thugs, toughs, hired guns, or men who felt they were good with a gun. And there was a great deal of difference between the two.

Jess had found that out the hard way.

The terrain began to slope upward now, as the valley ended and Buck started the climb upward. The timber was thick here, and Smoke stayed in it. This was his type of country. It was here that he felt most at home and here that, if he had a choice, the fight would begin and end. Smoke was not called the last mountain man without good reason. He was hell on wheels in any type of fight, under any type of circumstances, in any terrain, but in the mountains, he was most effective. He understood the wilderness, the high country, and used it all to his advantage.

He swung down from the saddle, ground-reined Buck, and squatted for a time, building a cigarette and thinking, his eyes never stopping their searching for any sign of trouble.

He decided he'd given the Triangle JB people enough grief for the time being, climbed back in the saddle, and headed north, for Fosburn's spread. He'd see what kind of trouble he could get into up there.

Jess had been a hothead and not much of a cowboy. Jack Biggers summed up Jess's worth and then dismissed him. But it rankled him that Smoke had gunned down another of his men with the ease of stepping on a bug.

And Highpockets and Dick, Biff and Howie were all behaving strangely since their return to the ranch. But Jack didn't want to chastise them too much; those four were the only real cowboys he had left, and somebody had to do some work around the place. Not that there was that much to do, especially this time of the year. The mountains provided a natural corral for the herds, and the Triangle JB's part of the valley was lush enough to sustain a herd three times the size.

But Jack wanted it all. He even wanted Fat's northern range, and he intended to get it. What he didn't know was that Fat wanted Jack's part of the valley and Major Cosgrove wanted all of it. Each of the partners had their own little schemes all worked out. Or so they thought.

Jack got a fresh mug of coffee and walked out to sit on

the front porch. He spotted Highpockets and Dick, Biff and Howie, and watched them for a moment. He frowned at them. What the hell were they doing?

The four men would walk a few steps, then stop and throw their hands into the air.

"Waco!" he called for his new foreman. His old foreman was one of those who had died in the street in front of the general store when the half dozen or so JB hands had come after Smoke.

"Boss?" Waco said, appearing by the side of the porch.

"What in the hell are those men doing over there by the bunkhouse?"

Waco looked, blinked, took off his hat and scratched his head, and took another look. The four men sure were acting strange. Looked like some sort of a dance to him. He'd never seen cowboys act like that before.

"Well, Boss . . . I can't say as I rightly know. Some of them saloons in town just got in a whole new batch of girls from St. Louis. Maybe that there's some sort of new eastern dance step those boys are tryin' out."

"Well, have them stop it immediately. They look plumb foolish to me. Looks like a bunch of schoolgirls doin' the do-si-do. Silliest thing I ever seen."

"Yes, sir."

Waco waited until Jack had gone back into the house, then, after taking a slow, careful look all around him to be sure he was not observed, he took three steps, stopped, and threw up his hands. He was not aware that Whisperin' Langley and Val Davis were watching him from a bunkhouse window. "I kinda like it," Waco muttered.

"What the hell is that man doin' over yonder?" Whisperin' said.

"I don't know," Val replied. "But them four over there is doin' it, too."

"Didn't Biff and Howie go into town last night?"

"Yeah. To the saloon where them new gals from St. Louis is workin'. I heard 'em talkin' about it."

"It's a dance. That's what it is. Them gals done brought a new dance out here with 'em. Let's watch so's we can do it, too."

"I ain't much on dancin'."

"That looks easy to me."

Two of the West's most feared and formidable gunslingers looked around the bunkhouse. They were alone. Whisperin' took three steps forward, stopped, and threw up his hands.

"Try it, Val. It's easy."

Val, spurs jingling, took three steps forward, stopped, and threw up his hands. "Yeah. It is, ain't it?"

Kit Silver had started into the bunkhouse. He paused at the doorway, stared for a moment, and then carefully backed out. He waved for Patmos to join him.

"What's up, Kit?"

"You better watch Whisperin' and Val," Kit warned. "I think they done fell in love. With each other!"

15

The man felt the rope settle around him and tighten, pinning his arms to his side. He didn't even have time to yell before he was jerked out of the saddle. He landed on his butt, on the ground, the wind ripped from him. He felt himself jerked to his boots and slammed against a tree, and the rope wound around him. When his head stopped spinning, his vision cleared, and he could see and comprehend what was happening, he knew he was in serious trouble.

"You like to make war on young girls, huh?" Smoke asked him.

"Not exactly," the rider gasped. "I just ride for the brand."

"You think you're going to continue doing that?"

"Not if you give me a chance to get gone."

"That might not be necessary," Smoke told him.

"Huh?"

"Did you hire out your guns or your skills with cows and horses?"

"I ain't no fast gun, Mister Jensen. Last time I tried that I damn near shot my foot off. I punch cows and mend fence and brand and . . ."

"I get the picture. How many working cowboys on Fat's spread?"

"Me and two others. The rest is hired guns. My name's Luddy. My buddies is Dud and Parker."

"Lud and Dud?" Smoke said with a smile.

The cowboy tried to hide a grin. "We been together since we was kids. Parker's all right, too."

Smoke loosened the rope and let it fall. As he was looping it back, he asked, "Step away from the tree. Keep your hand away from your gun."

"You can have it if you want it, Mister Jensen."

"Keep it. Is Fat paying you fighting wages?"

"No, sir. Thirty-five dollars a month and found. I could make more in the mines, but I ain't never liked caves and tunnels."

"Name some of the guns Fat hired."

"Tom Wilson, some guy named Chambers, Dan Segers, Russ Bailey. Then there's Al Jones, Paul Hunt, and some feller named Pell."

"Jim Pell?"

"Yes, sir. That's the one."

"First rate gun-handler. Anybody else?"

"About ten more. I don't know their names and stay out of their way. Then there's Bobby Jewel."

"He's a bad one, all right. Luddy, you tell your buddies to stay out of my way. The same goes for you until this mess is over. And it will be over, and then you can go to work for my niece."

"That's right nice of you, but her place ain't big enough to support no whole bunch of punchers."

"It will be when *I'm* through."

There was something in Jensen's eyes that told Luddy

this man planned to take the whole damn valley for his niece. Luddy figured he could do it, too.

Smoke rode straight onto Fat Fosburn's range, staying just out of the timber, but close enough to reach it in a hurry, should the need arise. He hadn't ridden a mile before he heard a shout, and that was followed by a gunshot. He stopped and wheeled Buck around. The fools were shooting at him with pistols from about a quarter of a mile away. Six of them. Smoke waited for a moment, then turned Buck and rode into the thick timber. He found a game trail and stayed with it for a few minutes, until coming to a tangle of brush. He circled around it, found a place in the back where he could push through, and swung down from the saddle, taking his rifle and a bandolier of ammunition. He stripped the saddle and bridle from Buck and let him freely roam the small clearing. There was some graze and a few puddles of rainwater gathered. Plenty for as long as Smoke planned to be gone.

He took off his spurs and put them in his saddlebags, took a long drink of water, and slipped out of the tangle, squatting and listening.

Smoke knew immediately these were not manhunters. This bunch was blundering around the woods, making enough noise to raise the dead.

"Over here, Willie!" one shouted.

Smoke sighed. Amateurs.

"What'd you find, George?"

"His trail. Come on. We'll get that bounty money and have us a high old time with the ladies."

George and Willie came a-blundering through the timber. Smoke slung his rifle and picked up a good-sized club and hefted it. Then he stepped behind a tree and waited. He didn't know whether it was George or Willie who came foggin' through the brush. Whichever it was got yanked out of the saddle and the club laid up alongside his head. Then he sighed once and went to sleep.

Smoke trussed him up and tossed him in the brush, then caught up the spooked horse and quieted it down, leading it off the dim trail and loosely tying the reins to a branch.

The second half of the pair came up as fast as he could in the brush and timber and yelled, "Where are you, George? Sing out, man!"

Smoke stepped out just behind and to one side and laid the club across the would-be tough's back. The blow knocked him clean out of the saddle and landed him on his face on the rocky ground. Smoke dragged him off the trail and trussed him up beside his careless friend.

"Jackie!" he heard the shout. "Here's Willie's horse. And I ain't seen hide nor hair of George since he shouted out. Ride back to the ranch for more men. We'll keep Jensen pinned down 'til you get back."

"Sure you will," Smoke muttered. "But only if I get careless and you get real lucky."

"Mister Fosburn says no bringin' him back alive," another voice drifted to Smoke. "He's to be cold dead. Then we hit the kid and them old wore-out bassards with her."

That's all I need to know, Smoke thought, then hauled out the two .45s he'd taken from George and let them bang. For a few seconds, the timber trembled with the sounds of rapid-fire pistols. Smoke heard one man holler, but didn't know if it was from a hit or a close slug.

Smoke quickly changed positions and unslung his rifle, earing back the hammer. He waited.

There had been six, maybe seven men who had spotted him. George and Willie were out of it. One had ridden back for reinforcements. Three or four hired guns left. He waited.

His cover was not the best, but Smoke stayed put. His clothing was earth-colored, blending in well with the surroundings. He moved only his eyes, knowing that any movement attracts more attention than small noises. His rifle was in a position where he could fire it one-handed, like a pistol, if need be.

His captive came to and began thrashing about and hollering. The guns of Smoke's pursuers roared and the thrashing ceased.

"You kilt George!" the voice screamed out from where Smoke had left the pair trussed up. "Oh, my Lord, you blowed half his head off."

"Willie?"

"Yeah."

"You stay put, now. Don't move around none. More men's a-comin'."

Smoke spotted a flash of a red-and-white-checkered shirt and fired, instantly changing position. He heard a cry and the sounds of a man thudding into a tree or log. Smoke knew he'd made a righteous shot.

"I'm hard hit!" a man groaned. "Oh, God, he's shot me in the belly."

"Stay down and quiet. We'll get you out. The boys will be here in a little while."

But by then, I'll be gone, Smoke thought.

On his belly, Smoke began inching his way in a long, slow half circle. As he crawled, he listened to the voices calling back and forth in frustration.

"Cain't nobody see him?"

"I ain't seen him yet."

"I have!" Willie yelled. "Sort of. He's big as a mountain and meaner than a puma."

"He's just a man," another voice added, and this one was so close to where Smoke had crawled it startled him.

"Are you sure George is dead, Willie?"

"Sure? Hell, yes, I'm sure. Half his head is gone."

The man only a few yards from him grew impatient and

shifted his weight. Through the thin brush, Smoke could see the man, half-turned away from him. He waited with the patience of a stalking Apache. He man turned his head and Smoke could see his profile. Lucky Harry, a gunfighter from California. Fat had imported some pretty good talent. Willie and George had chosen the wrong profession at the wrong time. But only one of them was left to question the choice . . . if question it he did.

Willie answered that. "I'm loose!" he hollered. "Damn you, Jensen. Me and George was pards. I'm gonna kill you, do you hear me?"

"Idiot," Lucky muttered. Then he was gone, moving silently and swiftly out of Smoke's sight.

Smoke knew that Lucky, and men like him, were as wary as an old wolf. They would take no unnecessary chances. That was why they had stayed alive after years in the manhunting and gun-for-hire business.

"Damn your murderin', ambushin' heart!" Willie yelled, his voice filled with rage. "Stand up and fight me like a man, Jensen."

Nitwit! Smoke thought. You won't last in this business, boy.

"Git down, you damn fool!" a man called.

Smoke wasn't interested in putting lead in Willie; at least, not at this point. The other men were the dangerous ones, and they weren't going to make any rash moves. Only if Willie threatened him directly would he gun him down.

A slight movement caught Smoke's eyes. Slowly he lifted his rifle. A man's arm came into view. Smoke sighted in the arm and squeezed the trigger. The gunhand screamed in pain as the slug ruined his left elbow. He would go through life with limited use of the arm. Smoke rolled from his position as the lead started whining all around him.

He rolled down into a natural depression and stayed there until the lead stopped singing its deadly song. He groaned loud and long, knowing that surely no one would fall for that old ruse.

But Willie did.

"Got him, by God!" Willie shouted, jumping to his feet. "I'll gut-shoot that sorry no-good."

"Damn!" Smoke muttered, rolling over on his belly and peering over the lip of the depression.

Willie was running toward his position, a rifle in his hands and a wild look on his face.

Smoke knocked a leg out from under him, the slug striking the young man just above the knee and sending him crashing and hollering to the rocky ground. Willie's rifle clattered on the rocks as he grabbed at his leg with both hands. He scooted and hunched for cover, bleeding all the way.

"You better hunt you another line of work, boy," a man's voice called out from behind rocky cover. "You just ain't suited for this one."

Smoke stayed where he was, but shifted a few feet to get behind a bush, scant cover but better than nothing.

The man with the busted elbow could not contain a groan of pain. "I'm bleedin' bad," he called out. "And Boots is dead. This ain't no good."

"All right," the man who seemed to be the leader of this bunch called after a few seconds. "Start backin' down toward where we left the horses. Jensen can't get out. We'll just wait."

"Don't bet he can't get out, Walt," Lucky called. "You don't know Jensen like I do."

Has to be Walt May, Smoke thought. I put lead in him ten years ago. So this will be highly personal for Walt.

"I'm clear," Lucky called. "I got Chookie with me. Willie, you can ride Boots's horse. He ain't got no more use for it."

Chookie must be the one with the busted elbow, Smoke thought.

"I'm a-comin'," Willie called out. "I got to drag this busted leg. I'll kill you someday, Jensen!" he screamed out. "Damn you, I'll kill you."

Smoke reloaded his guns and waited. The sounds of galloping horses drifted to him and he slipped down and picked up the rifle Willie had dropped, taking it with him. He walked over to Boots and took his guns, slinging the gunbelt over one shoulder and picking up his rifle. He looked at the dead George. A slug had entered the man's head from the side, just above the temple area, and made a real mess when it exited.

Smoke saddled up and rode out, but he headed north, not south, staying in the timber. Fat's ranch would be, for the most part, deserted, the men riding hard for the timber. Smoke would see just how much chaos he could cause there, and then ride into town to check on Jenny's "business" interests.

Smoke sat his saddle and watched the dozen or so men ride south, toward his last position. Smoke figured he had maybe thirty minutes, forty at the most, to do his mischief at Fat's ranch. Plenty of time. He loaded up all the pistols and kept the best rifle he'd picked up, discarding the other one.

"All right, Buck," he said. "Let's go be neighborly and pay a visit to Fat's spread."

He stayed on the ridges and in the timber until he was within a half mile of the ranch complex. He could see no one working or loafing around the buildings. Fat was not married, so there was no danger of any women or kids getting hurt. Biggers and Cosgrove were also bachelors. Smoke studied the layout for a few seconds, then smiled.

"Let's go, Buck," he said.

He walked Buck slowly down the ridge and onto the flats. A rider who did not appear to be in any rush attracted little attention. Just another wandering cowpoke riding the grub line.

Smoke swung down in front of the bunkhouse and was

greeted by a man wearing a stained apron. "Howdy," the man said. "Coffee's hot and you can fix you a sandwich, if you like."

"That's neighborly of you. Folks down the way told me to avoid this place. They said it was an unfriendly place."

"It is. That's why tomorrow's my last day. I got me a job down South. You best eat 'fore those no-'count riders Fat hired gets back. That's the surliest bunch I ever seen in all my life."

"Why not leave now?" Smoke suggested.

The man looked at Smoke for a long moment. "Oh, my God!"

"That's right."

"I'll be packed and gone in five minutes!"

"You do that."

While Smoke was busy wrecking everything in the main house, the cook galloped away. Smoke dumped out and mixed flour and salt and sugar and coffee and beans. He smashed plates and threw pots and pans outside into the dirt. Using his knife, he slashed feather ticks and ruined blankets and easy chairs. He tore down drapes and curtains and threw them into the dirt of the front yard. Then he set about smashing every window in the house by tossing chairs and benches and footstools through them. He hadn't had so much fun since he was kid. When there was nothing left in the ranchhouse to smash, break, turn over, or throw in the fireplace, Smoke set fire to the outhouses, tore down the corral and set the horses free, then tossed a flaming torch into the bunkhouse. He decided he might as well burn down the barn, too. So he checked the barn for animals, freed the horses from their stalls, and fired the place.

Back in the saddle, he surveyed all that he had done and sat his saddle for a moment, chuckling. There was going to be a lot of very irritated hired guns in about half an hour. And Fat was going to be as mad as a man could get.

440   *William W. Johnstone*

Smoke decided he'd ride into the Golden Plum and have him a drink and something to eat.

He'd worked up quite an appetite, and it wasn't even noon yet.

16

Stopping just outside of town, Smoke washed up in a creek and brushed the last bits of flour and sugar and so forth, from his shirt and jeans. He rode slowly up the twisty street and made sure Sheriff Bowers saw all the gunbelts hanging from his saddle. Bowers' eyes bugged out at the sight. He didn't need a professor to tell him that the men who had worn them would no longer be needing them.

"Morning, Sheriff," Smoke called cheerfully.

"It was," Club said sourly.

Smoke laughed and rode on. He stabled Buck and walked to the Golden Plum. He took a table at the rear of the place, his back to a wall. "A beer and something to eat, Jeff," he told the bartender.

"Right, Boss. Comin' up."

"How's business been?"

"Not good. Major Cosgrove ordered his men not to come in here."

"Did he now?"

"Yes, sir."

"You send your swamper to fetch Cosgrove. Tell him Smoke Jensen says for him to haul his big butt over here. Right now. If he doesn't, I'll come personally and drag it through the mud in the street."

Jeff grinned. "Right away, Boss. This I gotta see."

The swamper left at a trot, just as Club Bowers was walking up. He went to the bar and ordered a beer.

"You'd better not do that, Club," Smoke called. "Your master has forbidden all his slaves not to patronize this place."

Bowers turned around slowly. "Nobody tells me where I go, Jensen."

"Oh, well. If that's the case, by all means drink up and enjoy yourself. I just didn't want you to get into trouble with your lord and master."

"You're pushin', Jensen. Where'd you get all those guns hanging around your saddle?"

"I found them on the road. If their owners show up here, send them out to the ranch to claim them."

"You found them on the road, huh?"

"That's right. Just piled up there. Maybe they're broken. I haven't tried to fire any of them."

"You expect me to believe that?"

"Personally, Club, I don't much give a damn what you believe."

Club did not take exception to that. Smoke Jensen was a study to him. He knew Smoke's history and knew that Jensen was not a trouble-hunter—or had not been, up to this point. You had to push him and then he pushed back. But this time the man had ridden into Red Light pushing from the git-go. This kept up, Jensen would be taking scalps before it was all said and done. Club had heard that the man had done it before. He suppressed a shudder at the thought.

Club turned his back to Smoke and sipped at his beer.

Heavy bootsteps pounded on the boardwalk and the

batwings were suddenly slammed open. Major Cosgrove's bulk filled the space. Club turned to look at the man. Major was madder than the sheriff had ever seen him. Jeff stood behind the bar, smiling. Major pointed a finger at Jensen. He was so angry his finger was shaking.

"You, Jensen," Cosgrove's words were almost a yell, "you do not give me orders. You do not send bums over to my office giving me ultimatums."

"You came, didn't you?" Smoke spoke softly.

Cosgrove cussed Smoke, calling the man every filthy word he could think of. Smoke smiled. He had finally succeeded in making the man blow his top.

Club watched Smoke. The smile baffled him. Jensen wanted a fight with Cosgrove. Not a gunfight, but a fistfight. Club was sure of that. But if Jensen thought Major would be easy, he'd best think again. Major Cosgrove was a skilled boxer, not a stupid mass of muscle like Mule Jackson. Jensen could probably whip Major, but both men would be a bloody mess when it was over.

"Major," Smoke said, after taking a sip of coffee. "You tell your workers they can patronize any business in this town they choose to. This is America, not some dictatorship. And you are not king in this town. Nor am I. But I'll tell you what I am. I'm a man who despises those who would make war against a young girl. Physically or financially. I'm going to stay in town until after the first shift ends at the mine. This place better fill up, Major. Because if it doesn't, I'm coming after you. And if I have to do that, one of us will be the guest of honor at a burying. Do you understand that?"

Major Cosgrove stood rock still for a moment. He was so angry he could not speak. He opened and closed his mouth half a dozen times, but no words came out. With an effort that was visible to all in attendance, he began calming himself. It was showdown time, and he knew it. And he could not afford to go into it so angry it overrode logic.

"Major . . ." Club started to protest, as he realized what the man was about to do. He cut his eyes at a movement on the second-floor landing. Moses stood there, a double-barreled sawed-off shotgun in his hands. At the other end of the landing, Clementine Feathers and several of her girls had gathered, all with rifles. Behind him and to his right, Jeff the bartender stood with a ten gauge sawed-off Greener.

Smoke still sat at his table, a strange smile on his lips. Outside, the sounds of hard-ridden horse thundered up the street and the rider jumped off in front of the mayor's office.

"Mister Fosburn!" the shout was heard. "That damn Smoke Jensen done ruined your ranch and killed George and Boots. He wounded two, three more and burned down the barn and the bunkhouse and all the outhouses. He tore down the corral and scattered the horses all to hell and gone."

Major's face tightened and he clenched his big hands into big fists. Running boots were heard on the boardwalk and the batwings slammed open. Fat Fosburn stood there, his face red with anger. He spied Smoke.

"You! You . . . God damn you, Jensen. Club, I want that man arrested immediately."

Club got all tight and cold inside as Smoke cut his eyes to him. Now it was down to the nut-cuttin'.

"Did you hear me, Club?" Fat hollered.

"I heard you." Club was thinking hard. "Who saw Jensen do this?"

"Why . . ." That brought Fat up short. "Hell, I don't know. Somebody must have."

"Naw," the rider who brought the news said, standing just outside the batwings. "All the men was gone up on the ridges after Smoke. And the cook packed his kit and took off to Lord knows where."

"Well, why in the hell did you say it was Jensen, then, Parker?" Fat hollered.

" 'Cause he was the one the boys was after, that's why. I was out working cattle with Dud. I don't know where in the hell Luddy is. I seen the smoke from the fires come a-foggin'. Willie was there with a bullet in his leg, and Chookie's arm is busted."

"Then nobody saw Jensen do anything?" Club questioned, waves of relief washing over him. It was not fear of the man—just plain ol' common sense.

"I reckon not," Parker said, slipping in and walking to the end of the bar. He then got his first good look at Smoke Jensen. Lord, the man looked awesome.

Major removed his tie and collar and dramatically rolled up his sleeves.

Smoke stood up and took off his gunbelt.

Major did a couple of deep kneebends and fired some lefts and rights into the air. He held his arms out and shook them a time or two.

Smoke waited.

"Nobody gives me orders in this town, Jensen," Major said. "I run Red Light."

"Not after today," Smoke replied.

Major stopped his jumping around and shadow boxing. "I'm not Mule Jackson."

"You're going to resemble him when I'm through with you."

Fat Fosburn eased himself to the edge of the bar and stood beside Parker. He signaled to Jeff for a beer.

"Get it yourself," Jeff told him.

"No one will interfere in this," Major said, his voice firm. "You hear me, Club?"

"I hear you."

"Fat?"

"I hear you, Major."

He returned his eyes to Smoke. "Are we going to fight like gentlemen, Smoke?"

"Nope."

"I suppose it was foolish of me to expect that from someone of your caliber."

"You're not going to make me mad, either, Major. But if I were you, I wouldn't brag too much about how high-class you are. I've never made war against young girls."

Major flushed deeply, but he held any comments. This was a fight he had to have, and a fight he had to win. He had humiliated himself in front of several hundred people by shouting that he'd sue Smoke if the man struck him. That had been a foolish thing to do, since Major felt he was a much better boxer than Jensen, and infinitely more intelligent.

He was wrong on both counts.

Deputy Reed stepped in and quickly sized up the situation.

"Stand over here by me, Reed," Club said. "And don't interfere. Them's Mister Cosgrove's orders."

Smoke stood a step toward Major, pulling on riding gloves as he walked.

Major smiled. "No need for that if you soak your hands in brine, and I did back East when I was a young prizefighter. And I was a very good prizefighter."

"You fight your way, I'll fight mine," Smoke told him. "But your hands look mighty soft to me."

"You'll soon find out they are not." Major Cosgrove lifted his fists and assumed the stance.

"Then come on, Major. Show me. Prove it. You're about to put me to sleep with all this talk. That's about the only way you could win it. Talk me to death."

Major tucked his chin down toward his shoulder and advanced. Smoke thought he looked ridiculous, one arm all stuck out and the other pulled back. And with his head jerked down like that, he looked all cockeyed.

Smoke laughed at the man. "You're about the silliest-looking thing I believe I ever did see."

Major lunged at him and tried to fake him out. Smoke didn't fall for it. Major snapped a left at him and Smoke flicked it away. Still he did not attempt to land a blow against Cosgrove.

The two big men circled each other. Smoke said, "I win, you call off the boycott against this saloon."

"Agreed," Major said, then swung a wicked right that just missed. "I win, you leave town."

"Agreed," Smoke said. "But don't get your hopes up too high." Then he knocked the living hell out of Major.

The blow seemed to come out of nowhere and staggered the big man backward. It was not unlike being kicked by a horse. The blow had caught him flush on the mouth and bloodied his lips, sending pain coursing through his head. Before he could get set, Smoke pressed and hit him four times, two lefts and two rights to the head that hurt.

Major Cosgrove felt his jaw beginning to swell and knew one eye would soon be closing from the terrible blow. He backed up, shaking his head. The blood flew with the effort.

Outside the saloon, a huge crowd had gathered, threatening to collapse the boardwalk. About fifty men had run around to the rear and entered through the back door of the saloon, lining the walls, most of them thinking that this was much better than a gunfight. It lasted longer.

Major Cosgrove knew now that he was in for the fight of his life. Smoke Jensen was no common brawler. The man had studied boxing and knew the moves.

Smoke certainly was no common brawler, although he could brawl with the best of them. He knew kick-and-gouge, boxing, rough-and-tumble, and Indian wrestling. And he was going to show Major Cosgrove a little bit of all of it.

Smoke pushed in and took a right to his head. The blow

had power behind it and it hurt, splitting the skin. But it didn't slow him down. Ignoring a hastily thrown left from Cosgrove, Smoke plowed in, hooking a half dozen blows to the wind of the big man, bringing gasps of pain and backing him up. Major dropped his guard for just a second and Smoke seized the moment. He reared back and busted Major flush in the chops, scoring the first clear knockdown of the fight.

Major landed heavily on the floor and lay there for a moment, looking dazed and disbelieving that something like this could happen to him.

"Stay down and catch your wind!" Fat hollered.

Smoke backed up and gave the man a chance to climb to his boots.

Major glared balefully at the man. "I thought you weren't going to fight like a gentleman," he panted, blood dripping from his busted lips.

Smoke shrugged his shoulders and waited, letting his hands hang to his sides.

Major struggled to his boots. The entire front of his white shirt was now stained with blood. One eye was closing and his face was bruised.

Club picked up a pitcher of water from the bar and walked to Cosgrove, pouring it on his head. Major shook his head and bloody water flew in all directions. The men lining the saloon walls were silent.

"Thanks, Club," Cosgrove said. "That helped." He wiped his eyes on his sleeves of his shirt and lifted his fists. "I'm ready, Jensen."

"I'll call it off and we'll shake hands, Major," Smoke replied. "Then you leave Jenny alone and everybody will be friends. How about it?"

"I haven't even got my first wind yet, gunfighter," Major replied.

"Then that makes you a fool," Smoke flatly told him. "I'll not give you another break."

"I know how you fight now," Cosgrove said.

Smoke smiled and lifted his fists. "Then come on, big-shot. Take your lickin' like a man."

With a curse and a roar, Major Cosgrove charged Smoke, both big fists windmilling.

17

Smoke was forced to back up under the savage, almost mindless onslaught. He caught two blows from the windmilling Major. One big fist struck him on the side of the head and knocked him back. Another slammed into his side and brought a grunt of pain from his lips. Smoke quickly recovered and ducked and sidestepped the wildly charging man, still shouting curses and dumping dire verbal threats on Smoke's head.

Smoke smacked Major on the jaw with a left and stopped him in his tracks with a right to the mouth that further pulped the man's lips and brought a dazed look to his eyes. Seizing the opportunity while it was available, Smoke set himself and hammered at Major's face. The blows drove the man back, his backward movement knocking over chairs and shoving tables aside.

Smoke pursued the man, relentless in his attack, while Cosgrove's supporters stood by and watched their boss get the crap kicked out of him, all of them well aware of the rifles and shotguns ready to crack and boom should they make any attempt to interfere.

Many of the miners in the town stood in the street and listened to the smacking of fists against flesh and the cracking of chair legs and made no attempt to hide their smiles. Most had no love for Major Cosgrove.

Major grabbed up a chair and splintered it over Smoke's shoulders. Smoke had turned just in time to prevent the chair from taking him in the face. So much for Major conducting himself as a gentleman. The chair had torn Smoke's shirt and bruised and cut the flesh on his shoulders and upper back.

Smoke backed up, picked up a chair, and hurled it at Cosgrove, the chair striking the man in the face and chest and knocking him off his feet. He hit the floor with a mighty crash that shook the walls and windows. Smoke backed off and let the man get up. Major was much slower getting to his feet this time. Blood dripped from his nose and mouth. His breathing was ragged. Each time he exhaled, he sprayed blood.

"Give it up, man," Smoke urged.

"To hell with you, gunfighter!" Major spat the words mixed with blood.

Smoke stepped in close and drove a big right fist through Major's guard that connected solidly with the man's jaw. Major swayed on his feet for a second and then called on his deep reserves of strength and recovered. He pressed in, stumbling as he came.

Smoke hit the man in the belly and drove a savage left hook into his ribs. Major cried out and turned. Smoke pounded his kidneys and Major crawfished back, his bloody face a mask of hurt.

Smoke did not let up. He pressed hard, driving both fists into Major's face, smashing his nose and further pulping his lips.

"Go down, Major!" Fat called out.

But Cosgrove only shook his battered head and stayed on his boots.

But not for long.

Smoke stepped up and swung a wicked right, the fist colliding against Major's jaw. Part of a tooth flew out of the man's mouth and he cried out as he went to his knees. Club Bowers winced at just the sound of the blow. The sheriff knew that after this fight, no one in his right mind would challenge Smoke Jensen to toe the line with fists. Mule Jackson still lay battered and broken in bed, and within moments, Major Cosgrove would probably be in the bed next to his foreman.

Major Cosgrove gripped the side of a sturdy table and slowly pulled himself to his feet. The man cannot be faulted for lack of courage, Smoke thought. On his boots, Major lifted his fists and advanced. His face was bruised and torn, and one eye was closed. The man's expensive shirt was in bloody tatters, his suspenders hanging down, ripped and flopping. His britches were torn and dusty from the floor of the saloon. Still he pressed on.

Smoke feigned and Major bought it. That was all Smoke needed. He smashed at the man with wicked blows to the face, driving Cosgrove back, stumbling and staggering. Smoke hit the man in the belly with everything he could put behind a punch, and Major doubled over, his face white with sickness. Smoke gave him a savage uppercut that straightened Major up to his toes. Smoke stepped in and hooked to the side of the jaw, and Major went down. This time, he did not move.

Smoke stepped to the bar and picked up a pitcher of water, pouring it on his head. Jeff handed him a bar towel and Smoke dried his face. "Club, tell the men outside to come in and have a drink on me. This place is now open for business to all who want to come in."

* * *

Major Cosgrove did not show his face on the streets of Red Light until one week after the fight in the Golden Plum. Even then, his face was still mottled with fading bruises and marked with healing cuts. He walked slowly because of several still badly bruised ribs. His anger had now been replaced with a savage hatred for Smoke Jensen and everything and everybody connected with him. Which came as no surprise to Smoke when he was informed of it. He was well aware that men of Cosgrove's ilk are not rational people. He had given Cosgrove the opportunity to shake hands and live and let live. The man had refused it. Smoke knew now that the killing fields were fertile and would soon blossom blood-red with the flowers of death.

"You two do not leave the ranch," he told Sally and Jenny. "Cosgrove has got to make a move against us here. His long-distance shooter, Hankins, has been in this area for several days. Right now he's up on the ridges mapping out the best places to shoot from. Indians have spotted him and told Bad Dog. It's all down to the wire now."

Smoke walked the grounds of the ranch complex. All fire barrels were full. The area had been cleared of excess brush and anything else that might burn. Smoke had worked along the others, cutting the tall grass for several hundred yards all around the complex and then burning what was left down to the roots, leaving the area void of hiding places. Sneaking up on the ranch would be nearly impossible.

One week after the fight in the Golden Plum, Sally told Smoke they had to have supplies.

Smoke nodded his agreement. "I'll take Wolf, Bad Dog, and Barrie with me. We'll take two wagons. The rest of the men will stay here."

She stared up at him. "It's close to the end now, isn't it?"

"A few more weeks and it'll be over. Surely no more than

a month. You know I've never held back from you, Sally. There'll be an all-out effort to kill me now."

"That's been tried before, honey."

"I seem to recall a few times, yes." Smoke kissed her. "You better see to bandages and alcohol and ointments and so forth. I have a hunch we're all going to get bloodied before this fight is over."

"Then why don't they come on out here and try to run me off?" Jenny said, considerable heat in her young voice.

Smoke and Sally turned. The youngster stood with a .45 belted around her waist and a rifle in her hands.

"Now you just calm down," Sally told her, walking to the girl's side.

"No, Aunt Sally. I won't calm down. My mother left this ranch to me. And the . . . businesses in town. I have a *right* to live here and be safe. I won't let Fosburn and Biggers and Cosgrove and their hoodlums interfere with my life another time. But I have no right to ask somebody else to fight and die for me." She walked to an open window. "Mister Van Horn!" she hollered.

Van Horn was standing just outside the window and nearly jumped out of his boots. "Yes, ma'am, Miss Jenny?"

"See that my horse is saddled. I am going to town and handle my own affairs."

"Yes, *ma'am!*"

Smoke tried to hide a grin but failed miserably. He wanted to tell his niece that it would be extremely dangerous for her to ride into town. But the girl had Jensen blood flowing in her veins, and to the best of his knowledge, no Jensens on his side of the family had ever shirked their duty, at least, as they saw it. Even his sister Janey, no-'count as she might have been, had done her best to raise a good girl and see to her future. That counted for something.

Van Horn led a dainty-stepping paint pony up to the house. The mare was not a big horse, but it had a heart as big as any horse on the spread and it loved its master. Jenny had fallen in love with the paint at first sight and had gentled it herself.

Jenny went outside and booted her rifle and swung into the saddle. Sally looked at Smoke and together they laughed softly.

"She's a Jensen, all right," Sally said. "Well, I shall have a roast prepared for this evening's meal."

"With plenty of carrots and potatoes and a big bowl of thick gravy?" Smoke asked hopefully.

"Why, of course." She thumped his big chest with a small fist. "And if you're late, and supper gets cold, you will, Smoke Jensen, answer to *me!*"

"Yes, *ma'am!*" Smoke said.

Wolf and Bad Dog rode the wagons, Jenny rode beside Smoke at the head of the procession, and Barrie rode rear guard. The town-tamer had grown thinner in the few weeks since he'd signed on, and Smoke suspected the man was seriously ill and wanting to go out in a blaze of glory. Even though Barrie had not let up on his working around the ranch, Smoke had noticed he always kept a bottle of pain-killing laudanum handy.

"I'm going to ride back with Barrie for a time, Jenny," Smoke told his niece. "You lead this parade, okay?"

"Yes, sir."

Barrie looked at him as he swung back and fell in beside him on the bumpy road. "How far along is your cancer, Barrie?" Smoke asked.

Barrie grunted. "How'd you know?"

"Just a guess."

"Doc down in Butte said I might last out the summer. But that the end would be no way for a man to go. I don't intend to go out screamin' in pain."

"Not much I can say, is there?"

"Not a thing, Smoke. I'm just proud to have had the

chance to ride with you and to help out that young lady up yonder. My own daughter would have been about three years older than her."

"Would have been?"

"Outlaws killed her when she was just a baby. And after they had their way with my wife, they killed her, too."

"I do know the feeling."

"Yeah. I know the story. Summer of '72, wasn't it?"

Smoke nodded, the memories rushing back.

"Something like that tears a man wide open," Barrie said. "It leaves a terrible invisible wound that don't never really heal. You got the ones who done it to your wife and baby. I got the ones who did it to mine. And now, you and me got the same opinion of outlaws."

"For a fact, we do. Does Van Horn know?"

"Oh, yeah. Me and that old *pistolero* go way back. He learned me about guns. I'd appreciate it if you wouldn't tell no one else"

"I won't."

"You know where that ol' lightnin'-blazed tree is up on the east slope, above that little spring?"

"Yes."

"Plant me there. I want to listen to the winds blow and the wolves howl. I always liked wolves. Never had no quarrel with them. I like to think they'll come down an' visit me from time to time. Jenny will come see me now and then, too. I know she will; she's a good girl. Makes a man feel good to know his final restin' place will have visitors ever' now and then."

"You sound like you're telling me good-bye, Barrie."

"Pain's gettin' worser. I can near 'bouts control it with laudanum, but I don't know for how much longer. I may not get another chance to say my farewells."

"I'd ride the river with you anytime, Barrie," Smoke said simply.

"That's mighty high praise, comin' from you, Smoke. Now you go back up yonder and ride beside that little niece of yours." He smiled. "She's got spunk, that one. She'll do. Van Horn thinks the world and all of her. So do I."

Smoke rode ahead to join Jenny. She looked at him. "Everything all right, Uncle Smoke?"

"It will be, baby. It will be."

Smoke knew they were in trouble the instant they rode into town. The boardwalk in front of every saloon, and gambling house was lined with strangers, each wearing one or two tied-down guns. Smoke knew some of them. Cosgrove, Biggers, and Fosburn had sent for the best they could find within a week's ride of the town. He spotted the man called Keno. Standing beside him was the Texas outlaw, Burt Nevins. Sitting down was Amos Mann, from over Nebraska way. Directly across the street were the King twins, Vern and Eddie. They smiled at Jenny and tipped their hats.

"Goddamn worthless trash!" Both Smoke and Jenny heard Wolf mutter hotly. "I hope they has the audacity to speak direct to that girl. I'll gut both of them."

Jenny grinned and looked back at him.

"Don't pay no nevermind to that pair of white trash, girl," Wolf said.

"Old man," Vern called, his face red from the remark. "You'd best watch your mouth before I take a notion to jerk you off that wagon and stomp your guts out."

Wolf whoaed the wagon and hopped down, leaving the wagon in the middle of the street. He walked over to the boardwalk, stepped up on it, and knocked the gunhand smooth off the boards and onto the ground. Turning, he smashed one huge, gnarled old fist into the gut of Eddie, doubling the man over and putting him gagging and puking on the boards. Vern crawled to his knees and tried to reach for a gun. With no more emotion than he'd feel stomping on a scorpion, Wolf kicked the man in the face, then reached down, pulled their guns from leather, and tossed them into a watering trough. Then, without looking back, he climbed back to the wagon seat and clucked the team.

Chuckling, Smoke lifted the reins and moved out. Jenny looked back and winked at Wolf.

The old mountain man blushed.

"Don't you be actin' brazen, now, girl," he called to her. "It ain't comely."

While others of their ilk were trying to get the King twins up on their wobbly feet, Smoke and the small procession were entering the next block on the twisty street. Smoke's eyes narrowed as he spotted Rod Ivey standing beside Lonesome Ted Lightfoot. On the other side of Lightfoot stood Sam Jackson, one of the most worthless men ever to pull on a pair of boots. Standing behind him was Clayton Charles.

"They're sure scrapin' the bottom of the barrel with this crowd, ain't they?" Wolf called.

"For a fact," Smoke called over his shoulder. "Back-shooters, the whole bunch of them."

"All these men gathered against us," Jenny said, her voice small. "I don't understand it."

Barrie had ridden up even with Bad Dog. "I have never seen so much human garbage in one place. Look there," he said, cutting his eyes. "Jesse Griffin and Kell Duffin. Those two are the scum of the earth."

Bad Dog nodded his head. "I saw Louie Devine and Ossie Burks, too. One thing bothers me, Barrie. If the men fighting this one very nice little girl have so much money they can afford to hire all this scum, why do they want one small spread?"

"Power, my friend," the dying town-tamer said.

"The white side of me understands that," the breed said. "The Indian side of me does not understand the yearning for more than a person needs to live comfortably."

"It's a mystery, for sure."

The wagons were pulled in behind the large general store. Smoke told Jenny, with a firmness to his words that the girl knew better to cross, to stay inside the store. He smiled at her to soften his words. "You pick out something pretty for Sally. Some cloth, maybe. Something. It's going to take a good hour to choose and load these supplies. Barrie will stay with you. I'll be about."

"Are you going to start something, Uncle Smoke?" the girl whispered.

"I might as well begin cutting the odds some, Jenny. Just remember this: all those men out there came here to kill you and me, and to help some very ruthless men to take something that doesn't belong to them. This is pure black and white, Jenny. There is no gray."

Smoke checked both guns and loaded up full. He walked behind the counter and took down a sawed-off double-barreled shotgun, broke it open, and loaded it up. He put a handful of shells, in his jacket pocket. "Put this on my bill," he told the very nervous shopkeeper." He looked at Barrie. "Stay with Jenny. For sure they'll try to kill her this day."

"They got to go through me to do it," the town-tamer said. "And that ain't no easy task."

Smoke looked at the shopkeeper. "How do you stand in all this?"

"Neutral!"

"That figures." Smoke stepped out of the store and onto the boardwalk. He looked at Bad Dog, standing a few yards away. The man had found a chicken feather on the street and had stuck it in his hair. The halfbreed Cheyenne had a strange sense of humor.

"Count plenty coup today," Bad Dog spoke in broken English, a smile playing on his lip. "Take heap scalps." Then he laughed out loud.

"I happen to know that you graduated the eighth grade and had offers to go to college," Smoke said drily.

"Don't spread it around," Bad Dog said. "It would destroy the image I've worked so hard to cultivate."

"Right, Clarence."

Bad Dog groaned. "Especially don't let *that* get out. How did you discover my real name?"

The faint sounds of a trumpet reached the center of town. Within seconds, the booming of a bass drum came to them.

"Here come them damn Bible shouters," Wolf said, walking up. "Man over yonder at the assayer's office told me they was gonna hold a parade and a meetin' today."

The sounds of "Onward Christian Soldiers" rolled up the street.

"Wonder where the sheriff and his deputies are," Smoke said.

"They was all called out of town for some reason or the other."

"How nice for them."

The tooting and the drumming and the singing grew louder.

"Hey, old man!" Vern King shouted, walking up the boardwalk, his brother beside him. "This is your day to die, you son-of-a-bitch!"

The old mountain man didn't bat an eye or change expression. He just one-handedly lifted and leveled his Winchester model '73, .44-.40, thumbed the hammer back, and let it bang. The big slug caught the twin in the belly and doubled him over, dropping him screaming to the boards. His brother jumped for cover and the fight was on.

Vern rolled off the boards to land in the dirt, both hands holding his punctured belly.

Smoke saw a two-bit would-be tough who rode for Fat jerk both .45s from leather. He leveled the shotgun and gave the punk both barrels from across the narrow street. The charge lifted the thug off his boots and sent him crashing through a store window.

"Behind you, Uncle Smoke!" Jenny screamed from the store.

Smoke turned to see a wild-eyed man with a knife in his hand coming up fast. He reversed the heavy shotgun and smashed the man's skull with the stock, splintering the wood and rendering the express gun useless. Smoke pulled iron and went to work.

Two of Cosgrove's toughs jumped onto the loading dock of the general store, rifles in their hands. They made it as far as the back door before running into Barrie. The town-tamer gave them .45-caliber frontier justice, the slugs knocking them back and sending them tumbling off the dock and onto the ground. Barrie twirled his .45s and waited.

Jenny lined up a rifleman on the roof of a store across the street and plugged him through the brisket with her short-barreled carbine. The sniper fell over the side, crashing through the awning and bouncing off the boardwalk.

Bad Dog took out two in just about as many seconds. His guns left the pair motionless in the street, both shot through the heart.

The temperance parade was briefly halted as the paraders jumped for cover, but the shouting and singing was only momentarily silenced. "Sing, brothers and sisters!" Violet shrieked from her station behind a horse trough. "Play, musicians!" she hollered.

The tooting and the drumming began. The choir was only a tad ragged.

Paul Hunt found Smoke Jensen and lined him up in his sights. Before he could pull the trigger he saw fire and smoke erupt from the muzzle of Smoke's .44. A heavy blow struck him in the belly and he sat down hard, his .45 slipping from numb fingers. His last living thought was that this couldn't be happening to him. It just couldn't.

But it did.

Paul Hunt fell over in the dirt and closed his eyes for the last time.

"Help me, Eddie!" Vern hollered.

Eddie ran out to help his brother and jumped very quickly back behind cover as lead howled all around him. Wolf Parcell shoved cartridges into his .44-.40 and waited, crouched behind a barrel.

Pony Harris galloped his horse up the street, the reins in his teeth and both hands on pistols. Smoke shot him off his Triangle JB mount and the gun-for-hire rolled in the street. He rolled up onto the boardwalk and crashed through a window. He died in front of the receiving counter of Chung Lee's laundry, with Mister Lee shrieking Chinese curses at him.

Several Fosburn men charged the rear of the general store and were cut down by withering rifle and pistol fire from Jenny and Barrie. The young girl and the sick town-tamer stood side by side and stacked up the bodies. The shopkeeper and his wife had hit the floor behind the counter and stayed there.

Fat Fosburn, Jack Biggers, and Major Cosgrove lay on the floor of the mayor's office and wondered how the battle was going. Outnumbered fifty-to-one, surely Smoke and his crew and that damn snip of a girl would be dead before long.

The general store was across the street and just kitty-cornered from the mayor's office. Jenny had a wicked look in her eyes as she left Barrie to guard the rear and punched rounds into her carbine as she walked to the front of the store. She took down several rifles from the rack, loaded them all up, and stacked them beside her. Then she started methodically putting .44-caliber holes in the mayor's office.

"Jesus Christ!" Biggers hollered, as the lead began howling and shrieking all around them. A round struck the stove, whined off, and just missed Fosburn's head. Fosburn started hollering in fright. Major Cosgrove lay on his still-bruised belly and cursed the unknown rifleman.

Smoke was crouched in the alley between the general store and an empty building. He carefully chose his targets and seldom missed. Wolf Parcell and Bad Dog had chosen good cover and were making each round count.

Most of the hired guns had elected to stay out of this pitched battle. It had started out bad for their side and was getting worse. The singing and the drumming and tooting stayed constant from the far end of town.

The second block of Red Light was littered with the dead and the dying. The gunfire gradually died down, and then silence filled the street.

Cosgrove, Biggers, and Fosburn crawled to their hands and knees and peered out the shattered window of the mayor's office. They stared in disbelief at the body-littered street. A few of the less severely wounded were attempting to crawl to the boardwalk. Doc White was in the street, along with some volunteers, picking up the wounded and carrying them off.

Smoke had reloaded and was walking down the center of the street. He stopped in front of the mayor's office. "Cosgrove! Biggers! Fosburn! Let's settle it now. The three of you against me alone. In the street. Come on, you yellow-bellied mice. You're eager to fight a seventeen-year-old girl. Try me. Here's your chance."

"Kill that son-of-a-bitch!" Cosgrove screamed from the office. "That's what you men are getting paid for."

Smoke jumped to one side and rolled into an alley as the street once more erupted in lead and gunsmoke.

Jenny took aim at the office and pulled the trigger, her slug sending wood splinters into Cosgrove's face. He hollered in pain and hit the floor, Biggers and Fosburn right behind him.

"Here come my boys!" Biggers yelled, as pounding hooves began echoing along the narrow street.

Fosburn peeked over the bullet-shattered window sill.

"And my crew, too!" he hollered. "By God, it'll soon be over for Jensen now."

I'll believe it when I see it, Cosgrove thought. But he stayed on the floor. That damn girl over there in the general store was too good a shot.

Biggers had his hat blown off his head and he quickly joined Cosgrove on the glass-littered floor. Fosburn yelped in fright as one of his men was blown out of the saddle by a blast from a shotgun and the bloody body was flung onto the boardwalk. It rolled up to the bullet-shattered door, which was hanging by one hinge, and into the office. The blast had very nearly torn the man in two.

Across the street, Moses reloaded his Greener and let it bang. One of Biggers' men was tossed out of the saddle as if hit with a giant fist.

"Somebody kill that goddamn nigger!" Lonesome Ted Lightfoot yelled. He stood on the stoop of a dress shop.

Moses turned and pulled the trigger just as Lonesome hit the boards. The charge went over his head and blew a hole the size of a water bucket in the wall. Lonesome jumped into the dress shop and ran into a fully gowned mannequin. Lonesome and the mannequin hit the floor, his spurs all tangled up in the gown. Miss Alice, owner of the shop, ran out of a back room just as Lonesome was getting to his feet. She hit him on the back of the head with a flatiron and Lonesome sighed and hit the floor. He was out of this fight.

Smoke and Bad Dog fired at the same time, the pistol slugs slamming a Triangle JB rider out of the saddle and to the ground. One of his own men rode a horse right over him.

Jenny screamed and Smoke dived through an open side window of the general store. Barrie was down, blood streaming from a cut on his head, and Jenny was grappling with Lucky Harry.

Lucky was grinning at her and holding both her hands in

one of his, his other hand roaming over her body, touching her in places that made her face redden.

Lucky's luck was rapidly leaving him.

Smoke closed the distance, jerked Lucky from the girl, and savagely broke the man's right arm, popping it clean at the elbow. Lucky screamed from the pain and passed out. Smoke bodily picked him up and threw him through the one remaining store front window. The unconscious gunhand bounced off the boardwalk and fell into the path of a galloping horse.

Lucky's luck had run out.

The band had stopped playing and the singers ceased their singing and everyone had sought better cover. The temperance parade was over for that day.

Barrie's wound was not a serious one, and Smoke got him back on his feet while Jenny stopped the bleeding with a compress.

"Get in here!" Smoke called to Wolf and Bad Dog. "This thing is far from over."

The men dashed for the cover of the solidly built store.

"They got us cold, Smoke," Bad Dog said. "Must be fifty or sixty men still on their feet out there. They're all around the place."

The storekeeper and his wife had fled for the safety of another part of town.

"Are we trapped, Uncle Smoke?" Jenny asked.

Smoke's eyes had found several wooden crates stacked off to one side of the store. He smiled. *"They* think we are," he said.

18

"Out the back way, quickly!" Major said. "We can end this today if we seize the moment."

The three men behind the drive to kill Jenny Jensen and lay claim to her ranch and the gold that was in the mountains gathered a few of their most trusted hired guns and laid out their plans.

Inside the general store, every available rifle, pistol, and shotgun in stock was loaded up full and placed close to hand. Clemmie Feathers had gathered up her soiled doves and barricaded them on the second floor of the Golden Plum. They were armed with the rifles and pistols Moses had picked up from the fallen gunhands. Moses and Clemmie remained on the first floor of the saloon, along with Jeff the bartender and a few citizens who had the nerve to come out against Cosgrove, Biggers, and Fosburn.

The Red Light, Montana, Temperance League had wisely decided to give up their plans for a parade that day. When the shooting stopped, they had left their rather precarious cover and taken refuge in the livery, just down the twisty street from all the action.

In the general store, the small band of defenders had erected barricades of barrels and sacks of feed and Smoke had told everyone to grab something to eat while they had time. He was sitting on the sack of feed, calmly eating from a can of peaches.

Wolf Parcell shifted his wad of chewing tobacco and said, "This reminds me of the time me and Frenchy Ladue and Lobo and Powder Pete and Preacher was trapped in a cabin with about two hundred angry Kiowas outside. It got right chancy there for a time, but we held 'em off to a standstill. We had plenty of powder and shot and vittles. But we did get on each other's nerves there toward the end."

"How long were you trapped in there?" Jenny asked.

"Five days, as I recall," Wolf replied. "Them Kiowas finally just give up in disgust and rode off. We must have kilt a hundred of 'em."

Smoke tossed his empty peach can into a garbage barrel and stood up. Barrie and Bad Dog were defending the rear of the store. Smoke, Jenny, and Wolf stood by at the front.

"I can't believe they'll try a charge," Jenny said.

"They'll try one," Wolf said. "We ain't dealin' with the most intelligent folks in the world. Them's hired guns out yonder. Too damn lazy to work and too stupid to realize that ridin' the outlaw trail is harder work than near 'bouts anything else they might do. They're cowards, most of 'em. Almost all bullies is. But what worries me is, ain't none of us seen hide nor hair of that back-shooter, Hankins. He could be out at the ranch right now, worryin' the fool out of our people."

"I have a hunch that's exactly where he is," Smoke said, earing back the hammer on his Winchester and pulling the stock to his shoulder. "But that house is a fort, and he can't get much closer than five or six hundred yards. Besides, we'll be out of this bind in a few hours and back at the ranch an hour later." He sighted in and gently took up slack on the trigger. The Winchester barked and a man screamed a second after the slug shattered his ankle.

"You got a plan, Smoke?" Barrie carried, a bloody bandage around his head.

"Ten cases of dynamite over yonder in the corner," Smoke replied. "Plenty of caps and fuses. The street is narrow, and that makes for an easy toss. We'll liven up their day when the time is right and then make our break for it. One man with a rifle can hold off an army at the curve of the mountain road coming into town." He smiled. "Then I'll blow it closed and catch up with you before you reach the ranch."

Bad Dog chuckled his approval. "It is a good plan. But no," he contradicted. "I shall hold off the men and blow the pass. You need to be with Jenny and the wagons."

"He's right, Smoke," Barrie called.

"Suits me." Smoke listened for a moment. The street had grown very quiet.

They're gettin' ready to make a charge," Wolf said. "They'll come all at once, front and back. Get set."

Smoke looked at Jenny. The teenager had tossed her hat to one side and tied a bandanna around her forehead. Her face was sooty from the gunsmoke, but her hands were steady holding the short-barreled carbine. A bandolier of cartridges was slung across her chest and she had belted a second gun belt around her slender waist.

Wolf caught Smoke's eyes and grinned and nodded his shaggy head. Then he spat a stream of brown juice, stopping a scurrying roach cold on the floor, pulled his rifle to his shoulder, and said, "Here they come."

The men charged with a roar, and with a roar ten times as deadly, those inside the store fired, working the levers on their Winchesters as fast as they could. Smoke dropped his empty rifle and filled his hands with deadly .44s. Twelve rounds sounded as one long booming. When the shooting stopped, a dozen men lay dead, dying, or badly wounded in the street.

Reloading, Jenny asked, "Uncle Smoke? What will happen to Moses and Miss Clemmie and the girls once we leave?"

"Nothin', child," Wolf said. "All they've done so far is protect their interests. Right now, if news of them out yonder attackin' you was to reach the outside, they'd be five hundred Montana cowboys in here 'fore the week was over, all with knotted hangropes in their hands, lookin' for Biggers and Cosgrove and Fosburn. And not even the U. S. Army could stop 'em from stringin' them men up. Western justice is harsh at times and unfair at times. But out here, you lay anything but a gentle hand and a kind word on a woman, you're most likely dead."

"But they're soiled doves," Jenny said.

"That doesn't make any difference," Smoke said. "You own the establishment, so that makes it a war against you. They'll be all right."

"Let us drag our wounded in to tend to them!" the shout came from across the street.

"Go ahead," Smoke called out. "And while you're at it, check the buildings close by and make sure no women or kids are in danger, and then clear the street of any stray horses."

Several hired guns exchanged glances at that and silently came to the conclusion that that was a fair man over there in the general store. They holstered their guns and slipped away, heading for the livery. They wanted no more of this.

The others watched them go and thought them fools. But they kept their opinions to themselves.

While the street was being cleared of the wounded,

Smoke and Wolf took that time to charge the sticks of dynamite.

"This is gonna come as a right nasty surprise to them ol' boys across the street," the old mountain man proclaimed, a wicked glint in his eyes.

"That's what I'm counting on. How about the wagons and the supplies?"

"We got nearly all of it loaded," Barrie called. "The horses are still hitched up and all right. They're in the alley to my left."

"You mean we're actually going to take the wagons?" Bad Dog asked.

"Damn right," Smoke told him. "We came into town for supplies, didn't we?"

Wolf laughed in anticipation. "When we start tossing this giant powder, they'll be so much dust and confusion and crashin' of ruined buildin's and hollerin' and moanin' and groanin', it'll take those varmits over yonder ten minutes to figure out what the hell happened. By that time, we'll be clear of the pass and home free."

"Bad Dog, you and me to the second floor with the dynamite. We can get a better angle from up there. Jenny, to the back."

Bad Dog grabbed up a case of capped and fused dynamite and was gone up the stairs. Smoke turned to Wolf. "When I tap on the floor three times, you get the hell gone from the front of the store, Wolf. Just as soon as the dynamite blows, open up with rifle fire and get to the wagons. We'll blow the rear on our way out."

Wolf nodded and grinned.

Upstairs, Smoke went to work passing out the tied-together dynamite. Three sticks to a bundle.

"The street's all clear, Jensen," a man shouted. "No women or kids or animals close by."

Smoke did not reply, not wanting to give away his new

position overlooking the street. He tapped three times on the floor as he and Bad Dog were lighting the first bundles of dynamite.

"Clear," Wolf called.

Smoke and Bad Dog hurled the sputtering lethal charges. Just seconds before the center part of town started blowing up, someone yelled, "Jesus God! That's *dynamite!*"

In the rear of the store, four rifles started barking.

Then the mayor's office, a keno joint, one empty building, and Major Cosgrove's office erupted in a million pieces of mud, dust and dirt, splinters, bits of paper, busted spittoons, broken coffee pots, pieces of glass, the ragged remnants of four or five pairs of dirty long handles, shredded boots and shoes, and no small amount of various body parts.

Lester Laymon jumped up in the livery and flung out his hands. "It's the mighty hand of God!" he cried. "Bringing retribution to this earthly Sodom and Gomorrah."

Violet jabbed him in the butt with a pitchfork and Lester shrieked and jumped. "Sit down, you fool!" she admonished him. "That's Smoke Jensen blowing the crap out of the place with dynamite."

One entire wall had collapsed on Biggers and Cosgrove and Fosburn. They weren't badly hurt, just scared to the point of peeing in their underwear.

The dust was so thick it was like a foggy night on the Barbary Coast. The dust was swirling around like whirlwinds. Smoke and Bad Dog each hurled another bundle of explosives, then got gone from the second floor of the general store, each carrying a bundle of dynamite to give to those hired guns out back.

But there was no need for that. Wolf and Barrie and Jenny had each tossed a charge and the back alley was a thick cloud of smoke and dust and hired guns lying unconscious on the ground.

The only building left intact in the center of the east side of the second block was Chung Lee's laundry. And Chung Lee was now, for the very first time, giving serious thought to returning to China. He was sure that feeling would pass . . . but not if this kept up.

Smoke and his party did not have to worry about blowing the pass. No one even heard them leave, much less pursued them as they rode and rattled down the back alleys and out of town. They came to the pass and Smoke signaled them on, staying behind for a moment or two. He sat his saddle and looked down at the town. The entire town was enveloped in a cloud of dust and smoke from a dozen small fires started by overturned lanterns and cookstoves.

Chuckling at the chaos that must now be reigning in the center of Red Light, he turned his horse and headed after the wagons.

Jack Biggers had been blown out of one boot. He was staggering and limping around, and looked down, certain he had been crippled forever by the loss of a foot.

Fosburn's pants had caught on fire and he just managed to put out the flames before they reached a critical part of his body. He was now standing outside the ruin of what had been his office, clad in very short pants and a shirt with no sleeves, wearing a very dazed look on his face.

Major Cosgrove crawled out of the rubble, his clothes sooty rags. He sat on the edge of what remained of the boardwalk in front of one of his several offices. He looked around him at all the carnage. He had never seen anything like it. There were men with broken arms and broken legs and busted heads and hands, and men lying dead in grotesquely twisted positions.

He felt like crying.

Then he saw Biggers limping around with a worried look on his face, and Fosburn standing in the middle of the street in short pants.

"Fosburn," he called. "Will you, for Christ's sake, put on some damn pants?"

Lonesome Ted Lightfoot staggered out of the dress shop, holding his aching head, the knot on his noggin compliments of Miss Alice and her flatiron. He pulled up short at the smoke and dust and fire and devastation before him. He thought for a moment he was dead and had gone to Hell.

Patmos sat down on the busted boardwalk beside Major. "Nineteen dead and twelve wounded," he told the man.

"How many of the wounded expected to live?" Cosgrove asked.

"Not very many."

"Make that twenty dead," Kit Silver said, walking up and sitting down. He took out the makings and started building a cigarette.

"What other wonderful news do you have to tell me?" Cosgrove asked bitterly.

"Five men pulled out during the lull in the fightin'. They were top guns, too."

"Why did they pull out?"

"A personal opinion?" Kit said, thumbing a match into flame and lighting up.

"Go ahead."

"I can send out the word and have you a hundred men in here in a week's time . . ."

"Do it!" Cosgrove said savagely.

". . . But no more than ten or twelve of them will be top-notch men," Kit went on as if the man had not spoken. "Fightin' Smoke Jensen has become known as a losin' proposition. And if you're half as smart as you think you are, you know why after this."

"He's just a man, goddamnit! He's just a flesh-and-blood man. That's all!"

"Sure," Kit said sarcastically. "Sure. Just a man who can

crawl up into a wolves' den and go to sleep cuddled up against a big ol' mama wolf. A man who had pumas for pets as a kid. A man who can call eagles to him. A man who when he lays down to rest has wild hawks guardin' him . . ."

"That's nonsense!" Cosgrove snapped.

"Some of it is, some of it isn't, believe me. I've been west of the Missouri all my life. I ain't never seen no human man like Smoke Jensen. And to tell the truth, neither has nobody else, either. I'll get your men in here for you, Cosgrove. But if you think this last bunch was scabby and no-'count, just wait until you see what'll come in now. Hiders and bounty hunters and wore-out buffalo hunters, all of them stinkin' and with fleas jumpin' on them."

"I don't care what they look like, just as long as they can do the job."

"Has anybody seen my pants?" Fosburn asked.

And in the valley, Smoke pushed open the door and smiled at Sally. "I told you I'd be back in time for supper."

19

"We have to move fast," Major Cosgrove said, one day after the fight on Main Street. "Several families have moved out of Red Light. They're sure to talk about this situation, and that will attract the attention of the territorial governor. He'll send people in here. We can't have that."

"We've already confirmed that Jensen is a real U.S. Marshal," Fosburn said. "He could legally arrest all of us for attempted murder, extortion, and God only knows what else. Why hasn't he done so?"

Biggers smiled grimly, a cruel twisting of the lips. "Jensen doesn't want to do this the legal way, that's why. Jensen doesn't pay much attention to written law. He wants us dead. All of us." He mumbled an obscenity.

"Kit says he can have gunhands in here," Cosgrove said. "I told him to go ahead. He left yesterday, right after the fight. By now he's sent the wires out and men are on the way. My God!" The man stood up from behind his new desk in his new office. "We're losing a fight against nine men, one woman, and two teenagers. To date our combined losses are about twenty-five dead and just about twenty wounded. Tough, top gunslingers are pulling out of this fight. Most didn't even wait around to get paid."

"I say we hit the ranch," Biggers said.

Club Bowers looked at the man, but offered no comment. Hitting the ranch would be suicide, in his opinion. One of his deputies had ridden out that way and reported back that the ranch looked more like a heavily fortified Army post than a working ranch complex. The land around the complex had been cleared and burned for hundreds of yards. Peter Hankins had finally checked back in after several days in the field and said there was no way he could get a shot at anyone on the ranch. Time was on the side of Smoke Jensen and family, and Club knew it.

Maybe it was time to pull out . . . he'd been giving that some serious thought.

"You have an opinion on any of this, Club?" Cosgrove asked.

"Yeah," the sheriff said. "Give it up and live and let live."

"Have you lost your mind?" Biggers almost shouted the words. "We *can't* give it up. We've got too much money invested in this fight. The gold in those mountains is worth a fortune!"

Club stood up and walked to the door. He put his hat on his head and turned to look at the men. "Is it worth your lives?" He stepped outside and walked to his office. There, he sat on the bench on the boardwalk and looked at the work crews clearing out the wreckage from the dynamite. Cosgrove had sent men from the mines to clear the mess and they were almost through. Now all that was left of very nearly a block was a great empty space in the center of town.

The man and woman who owned the general store had flatly told Cosgrove that either he paid for repairing the store and replacing the damaged goods or they would sue him and make certain every newspaper west of the Mississippi knew about it. At the prompt advice of Lawyer Dunham, Cosgrove told his men to go to work and told the store owner to order replacement goods and send the bill to him.

Club knew that Cosgrove had lost the upper hand in Red Light. The merchants had banded together and told Club they would no longer pay protection money to him. They all went armed now, and his deputies were very nervous. On this very morning, Club had told his men to enforce the law and that was it. They took orders from him, not from Major Cosgrove, Jack Biggers, or Fat Fosburn. The Big Three didn't much like that, but Club Bowers really didn't much care.

Deputy Modoc sat down behind him on the bench. "It's over, ain't it, Club?"

Club nodded his head. "Yeah, it is, Doc. The money men over yonder don't know it yet, but it's over. They'll be a lot more shootin', and a lot of killin', but it's over. It's like I told you boys this mornin'. From now on we enforce the law. We arrest whoever breaks it."

"Even them over yonder in the office?"

"Even them. I'm ridin' out to Miss Jenny's ranch and makin' peace with them folks and tellin' them how it's gonna be from now on. I'll see you later."

"Rider comin', Mister Smoke!" Jimmy yelled from his lookout position in the barn loft. "I think it's Club Bowers. He's alone."

Smoke stepped out of the house, buckling his gunbelt around him. He stood in the yard and waited. Club held up a hand. "I'm peaceful, Smoke. Can I step down?"

"Sure. Come on in the house and have some pie and coffee."

With coffee poured and thick wedges of pie cut, Club said, "From this day on, Smoke, me and my deputies enforce the law as it is written. You break the law, I'll arrest you, or go down tryin'. The same thing goes for Cosgrove, Biggers, Fosburn, or any of these no-'counts they're bringin' in. My office no longer takes protection money from any merchant. They say you can't teach an old dog new tricks. Well, I'm an old dog, and I think I can change. At least, I'm going to give it one hell of a try. Excuse my language, Miss Sally, Miss Jenny."

Smoke held out a hand and Club shook it. "Welcome to the right side of the fence, Sheriff."

Club smiled. "I think I like it over here, Smoke."

"How are things in town, Sheriff Bowers?" Jenny asked innocently.

Club chuckled. "Settlin' down, Miss Jenny. Been an awful lot of funerals, though. Boot Hill's rapidly fillin' up."

"How did Cosgrove take your decision?" Sally asked.

"I think he seen it comin', Miss Sally. Didn't none of them kick about it too much. I been uneasy about the situation in town ever since Miss Janey passed on."

"Did any of the Big Three have anything to do with my sister's death?" Smoke asked.

Club shook his head. "No. She died of the fever . . . or complications brought on by the fever. I know that. Van Horn held on to the ranch until Miss Jenny could get out here. That old man is randy to the core, let me tell you. You know there's gold up in the mountains?"

"I guessed as much," Smoke said.

"Worth a fortune, so Cosgrove says. I'll tell you what I think. I think Biggers wants Fosburn's spread, Fosburn wants Biggers' spread, and Cosgrove wants it all. These guns that's comin' in . . . well, I think they'll follow the orders of the man who offers them the most money, no matter which one of the Big Three they might be workin' for at the time. That's what I think."

"How about the townspeople?" Sally asked.

"They want things to settle down. They're tired of Cosgrove and all the trouble. And they've told him so. Still tellin' him so when I left. Chung Lee told him that if any more trouble happens, he was gonna starch his longhandles so stiff they'd look like a suit of armor standin' in the corner. Then he called him some things in Chinese that I'm pretty sure wasn't very complimentary."

"What's his next move, Club?"

"I wish I knew. All I know is that Kit Silver is wirin' for more gunhands to come in. And even Kit admits they'll be the scum of the earth. There is no law, yet, about two men settlin' their differences in the street. I can't interfere in that. But I am going to keep the peace in Red Light, Smoke. I mean that."

"Good. I won't push inside the town limits, Club. But I won't be pushed, either."

"That's fair enough. You know that damn back-shootin' Hankins has been snoopin' around here, don't you?"

"I suspected it. And some of the boys cut his sign yesterday."

Club ate the last of his pie, drained his coffee cup, and walked to the door. Just before he plopped his hat on his head and stepped outside, he smiled and said, "But on the other hand, it would be a real shame if somebody called that damn Hankins out into the street, now, wouldn't it?"

The fire in his belly had been so strong that Barrie had taken his blankets outside the bunkhouse and slept under the stars so the other men would not hear the occasional muffled moan of pain that passed his lips. He finished a bottle of laudanum and the pain eased, then went away. Breathing easier for the first time in hours, the town-tamer looked up and stared long at the stars in God's heavens and suddenly thought: this is my last time to see them. It has to be. I'm not goin' out layin' in some damn bed screamin' in pain, unable to control myself. That ain't no way for a man to go out. A man ought to have the right to pick and choose his time and place of dyin'. And I'm gonna do just that.

It had been a week since that fine time in town with Smoke and Bad Dog and Wolf and the girl. What a little gal Jenny was. Barrie smiled under the canopy of stars. He liked to think that his daughter would have been just like her. Couldn't ask for no finer.

And Barrie knew that Smoke had gotten word from Clemmie Feathers that the town was overflowing with two-bit gunhands on the payroll of the Big Three.

Barrie made up his mind. At four that morning, he was bathing in the creek and shaving as carefully as possible in what light there was. He'd had his black suit done up nice by Chung Lee and his handmade boots, which he seldom wore, polished to a high sheen. He put on a sparkling-clean white shirt and black string tie. He saddled up silently and strapped on his matched .45s, sticking two more .45s behind his gunbelt. He had made out his will during the first week he was at Jenny's spread and given it to Van Horn.

Van Horn, meanwhile, was sitting in his private quarters at the south end of the bunkhouse, drinking coffee and watching his old friend get ready to ride into Red Light and die. He longed to go with him, but knew that Barrie would resent it. Knew that the town-tamer wanted it this way. But there was something he could do. He smiled thinking about it.

Barrie had no sooner left the yard than Van Horn slipped out of the bunkhouse, saddled up, and took a shortcut to town. He could make damn sure that Club Bowers and his deputies didn't interfere.

Smoke lay beside Sally and heard both men leave. He knew what Barrie was going to do, and had a strong suspicion what Van Horn was going to do.

"Good-bye, Barrie," he whispered. "You're a good man."

"Did you say something, honey?" Sally whispered.

"No, dear. You must have been dreaming. Go back to sleep."

"Whahsiit?" the old man at the livery stable mumbled, still half asleep.

"I've rid hard to get here, old-timer," Van Horn said, gruffing up his voice. "Here's a dollar. Get over to the sheriff's office and tell him they's been a stage holdup at Red Creek Crossing. It's real bad. Dead folks all over the place. The outlaws took off up Devil's Pass. Move, man!"

Van Horn slipped back into the darkness, pretending to be seeing to his horse. The rummy-eyed old hostler beat it over to Club's place and within fifteen minutes, Club and his deputies were riding out for Red Creek. It would be a good five to six hours before they returned. By that time, Van Horn thought with a smile, it'll all be over.

All but the buryin'.

Van Horn walked over to Clemmie's and sat on the porch with Moses, who had just gotten up to stoke up the fire. The men sipped coffee as the sky grew silver in the east.

Barrie had a fine breakfast of biscuits and gravy and good strong hot black coffee. And then he bought a genuine five-cent cigar from the counterman. On the boards, he lit up and puffed contentedly. Man can't ask for much more, he thought. The fire in his belly was gone, and Barrie knew it would never return. He brushed his coat back, exposing the butts of his .45s, then went for a little walk. He stopped for a time to pet a stray dog. The dog licked his hand and Barrie was pleased. He'd always liked animals. He never trusted a man who disliked dogs . . . serious character flaw there.

Then he saw a knot of gunhands come walking out of the South End Hotel, on their way to breakfast. One of the men was Luther Cone, and with him was his sidekick, equally no-'count Jim Parish. Barrie had run both of them out of at least two towns that he could recall. After two suspicious killings.

"Might as well start here and now," he muttered. He stepped out into the street. "Cone!" he called. "Parish!"

The men stopped and turned to face Barrie. "Well, well," Cone said. "Would you look at this, Parish. It's old Barrie hisself. You ridin' the grub line, Barrie?"

"No," Barrie called. "I'm ridin' the killin' line."

"Huh? What you mean, the killin' line?"

"You workin' for Biggers, Fosburn, or Cosgrove?"

"All three, if it's any of your damn business."

"You come to make war against a fine little teenage girl, huh?"

"If you're talkin' about Janey's daughter, she's just like her momma, a slutty little two-bit whoor!"

"You'll not talk like that about her, Cone. Fill your hand, you scummy bastard!"

Cone and Parish drew—or tried to. Barrie's right hand flashed and his .45 roared. Cone and Parish went down in the dirt, both of them gut-shot. Barrie stepped two paces to one side and plugged a third man, a no-'count who fancied himself a gunhand and called himself the Arizona Kid. The Kid should have stayed on the farm, milking cows. Barrie shot him through the heart and then stepped back across the narrow street and into the alleyway as a hail of bullets came at him. One tugged at his sleeve, another clipped the brim of his hat, and another kicked dirt on his polished boots. Barrie knocked a leg out from under the man who dusted up his boots.

"Gettin' real interestin' up yonder," Van Horn said to Moses. "I think I'll just mosey up that way."

"I'll get my hat and join you," Moses said. "And my rifle."

Very few of the older, more experienced gunhands in the employ of the Big Three took any part in the shootout with

Barrie. Word had spread throughout the camps of the gun-hands, and when those with rooms in the town's several hotels heard about the town-tamer coming in all dressed to the nines and with polished boots and totin' at least four pistols, they figured what was coming.

The gunfighters put all that together and reached the conclusion that Barrie had come to town to die . . . but only after making sure a whole bunch of others got sent down that same dark road.

And a man like that would be hard to stop.

Barrie ran around the rear of a saddle and leather shop and slipped back up to the street, walking between it and a gaming house. He saw Dev White, a Utah gunslick, peeping around the corner of a hastily vacated cafe. Barrie sighted him in and the bullet knocked the man sprawling and hollering. A rifle roared and splinters tore into Barrie's right cheek. He ignored the bleeding and dropped to one knee, leveling his .45. A New Mexico punk was sent howling to the ground, his belly punctured by town-tamer lead.

Jody Thomas, a North Dakota kid who was wanted for murder, came running out of the Eagles Nest Hotel, his hands filled with .44s. Moses and Van Horn fired as one and Jody was knocked off his boots and went crashing through a window, back into the lobby.

"You're bleedin' all over the carpet!" the desk clerk hollered at the dying gunman.

Jody had no rebuttal to that. He simply closed his eyes and died.

"Stay out of this, you old goat!" Barrie hollered up the street at his longtime friend.

"We'll try to keep it fair," Van Horn yelled.

"Fair, hell!" Barrie said, reloading. "I got 'em outnumbered."

"Get that crazy fool!" Cosgrove yelled from the upstairs window of his new apartment over his mining office.

The street filled with guns-for-hire.

Barrie stepped to the other side of the alley, both hands filled with .45s, and yelled, "Here I am, boys. I'm half puma, half wolf, and Gloryland bound. So step up here and I'll punch your ticket to Hell!"

Then he opened fire.

20

Larry Brown, Johnny Newman, and two gunslicks from Texas stepped off the boards and onto the street and Barrie put them on the hellbound train, punching their tickets with .45 slugs.

A bullet clipped Barrie's ear and another one burned his shoulder. He didn't feel a thing. "Here's another for Miss Jenny and Smoke Jensen!" he yelled, jamming his empty guns into leather and jerking out two old long-barreled Peacemakers from behind his belt. He cocked and fired so fast, the sound was one continuous roll of deadly thunder.

When Barrie ducked back into the early morning shadows of the alley, the street in front of the hotel was littered with wounded and dead.

He ran around the gaming joint and a man opened the rear door and stuck out a sawed-off ten-gauge and a small sack of shells. "You don't remember me, Barrie. But I was bartender in a little mining town in Colorado you cleaned up. Give them no-goods hell, ol' hoss."

Before Barrie could thank the man, the door closed.

Barrie checked both barrels for blockage and loaded the Greener up. He began walking toward the corner of the building. Cosgrove was still shouting from the window, joined by Fosburn, standing in the door of his mayor's office.

The left side of Barrie's suit coat was drenched with blood from his mangled ear, and he had taken lead in his right leg. He limped on, ignoring the pain. He'd endured a hell of a lot worse from the pain in his belly.

Dave Stockton and John Robinson came racing around the corner of the keno joint. Barrie smiled at them and gave the pair both barrels from the sawed-off express gun. The worthless pair was flung back, nearly cut in two from the heavy charge.

Barrie stepped into the narrow passageway between buildings and saw Cosgrove, standing in his window, yelling and screaming and shouting orders. The range was far too great to do much damage with the shotgun, but Barrie gave the man both barrels to keep him honest. The shot had lost most of its punch when it reached Cosgrove, but it bloodied his neck and face and sent him hollering to the floor, certain he'd been mortally wounded.

At the ranch, Jenny sat down at the table with Smoke and Sally and the hands and asked, "Where are Mister Barrie and Mister Van Horn?"

"Barrie went into town to even the odds a little bit, Honey," Wolf told her. "I 'spect Van Horn went in to watch the show."

"You mean . . ."

"Barrie is dying, Jenny," Smoke told her. "This is the way he wanted to go out. After breakfast, Cooper, hitch up a team. Some of us will go in to bring the body back. Pasco, you and Ladd get shovels and ride up to the east slope, by that lightning-blazed tree above the spring. Dig a deep hole."

"Right, Boss," Pasco said.

"And be careful, that damn Hankins is probably prowling

around. He'll shoot anybody he sees on this range. If you see him, drop him."

"With pleasure," Ladd said, pouring syrup over his huge stack of flapjacks.

"I shore would like to be in town for this mornin's show," Wolf said. "When Barrie gets goin,' he's plumb hell with a short gun."

"I'll take that damned ol' has-been," a young man who called himself Rusty said, hitching at his fancy rig. He pulled both guns and stepped out of the saloon, where he'd spent the night, drinking and gambling and whoring. With both hands wrapped around the butts of .45s, Rusty marched right down the center of the narrow street.

"He'll last one minute," Kit Silver said, pouring a mug of coffee.

"Thirty seconds," Ned Harden shortened it.

"Hey, turd-face!" Van Horn called to Rusty.

"Ten seconds," Dan Segers said. "Van Horn just bought into it."

"Rusty's dead, then," Les Spivey said.

Rusty whirled around and took a shot at Van Horn, standing in the gloom under an awning. Rusty's shot went wide. Van Horn's aim was deadly. Rusty sat down hard in the street and commenced to bellering, his guns in the dirt and both hands holding his stomach.

"You should have stayed to home, boy, Van Horn said, punching out the empty and filling the slot.

Ray Houston stood up in the hotel lobby and started toward the stairs.

"Where you goin'?" Kit Silver asked.

"I'm through," Ray said. "This deal's done gone sour. They got a range war shapin' up down in New Mexico. I'm headin' for there."

"Hold up," Nevada Jones said. "I'll ride with you." Ron Patrick picked up his rifle and said, "That makes three of us. This war ain't for the likes of me."

Barrie's wounded leg was about to buckle on him and some lucky gunhand he'd not even seen had shot him in the side. "Time to end it," he muttered. He called out, "In the street, boys! Me agin you all. Holster your guns and meet me eyeball to eyeball. Who's got the sand to do it?"

Moses lifted his rifle and Van Horn put a gnarled hand on the barrel. "We're out of it unless they pull something sneaky, Moses. This is Barrie's show from now on."

Perry Sheridan, a tough from Oregon, stepped out onto the boards. "I'll meet you, Barrie."

"Well, come on, then," Barrie shouted, standing tall and bloody in the street. "I ain't got all the time in the world, you know."

Andre McMahon joined Perry, as did four others. The older, wiser gunnies stayed put.

"Fools," Kit said. "Can't they see that Barrie ain't got nothin' to lose?"

"Fifty dollars says they'll git him." A young squirt tossed the bet out.

"Oh, they'll get him," Kit said. "But they won't none of them be alive to brag about it. That's too high a price to pay for ten seconds of glory."

"If you want to call killin' a dyin' man something glorious," a lanky gunfighter said. "Hell with this. I'm haulin' my ashes out of here. Cosgrove and Biggers and Fosburn ain't fit to polish that Jenny girl's boots."

"That ain't what I'd like to polish about her," a brute of a man said with an evil grin on his dirty and unshaven face.

The lanky gunhawk lifted a .44 and shot him between the eyes, knocking him out of the chair. The gunhawk looked around the room. "Anybody else got anything nasty they want to say about that little girl?"

No one did.

"I don't like makin' war agin kids," Shady Bryant said, standing up. "I'll ride out with you, Slim."

Kit Silver poured a shot glass of whiskey into his hot coffee and stirred in a spoonful of sugar. "I tried to tell them money men this wouldn't work. It might take time, but the right cause near 'bouts always wins. And that kid's in the right. I'm out of this. I'm gonna stick around, but I ain't rightly sure what side I'm gonna be on."

"Then you better get clear of my sight," Curtis Brown said.

"You want to try an' make me?" Kit said softly.

"I think I'll stick around, too," Slim said. "I'm with you, Kit."

"And me," Shady said.

"I don't hear no shootin' out there." Brown changed the subject.

"Barrie's just standin' in the street, laughin' at them fools. He's sayin' something."

"Can you make it out?"

"Naw."

"What a pitiful-lookin' sight," Barrie said to the men facing him in the street.

"You're the pitiful one," Andre called. "Man, you're bleeding bad."

"I'll live long enough to kill you," Barrie told him.

Andre flushed, cussed, and grabbed iron. Barrie shot him in the chest and then dropped to one knee as he cleared leather with his lefthand .45. When the smoke cleared, Andre, Rusty, and their friends were down and hard hit. Barrie staggered to his boots, blood leaking from two more bullet holes. He almost fell while climbing up onto the boardwalk, but managed to stay on his feet and reload just as Eddie King stepped out from the doctor's office.

"My brother, Vern, just died, you son-of-a-bitch!" he shouted across the way.

Barrie turned. "Good," he said. "One less punk on the face of the earth." Then he lifted his Peacemaker and drilled Eddie right through the brisket.

A would-be tough and full-time bully leaned out of a second-story window and sighted Barrie in with a rifle.

"Not that way," Kit Silver said, standing on the boards. "He's too good a man to go that way." He palmed his gun and put a hole in the bully's head.

Leaning up against a post, Barrie looked at the man, questions in his eyes.

Kit shrugged. "It's a free country, town-tamer. I can change sides if I want to."

Barrie smiled as his mouth filled with blood. "That Jenny gal, she'll do, Kit."

"I'll see to it personal, ol' son. You save me a place where you're goin'. I figure this for my last fight."

Shady Bryant and Slim Waters stepped out to join Kit. "Count us in, too, Barrie," Slim said.

"Good men," Barrie said weakly. "All of you. You make me proud. I told all of you more than once, there was a streak of good in you. Even when I was runnin' you out of some damn two-bit town. You just proved me right. Now point me toward a nest of snakes whilst I still got the strength to do some stompin'."

"Second door to your left," Shady said. "But they're waitin' on you, Barrie."

Barrie smiled his bloody smile. "I wouldn't have it any other way." The town-tamer staggered to the door, kicked it in, and walked in shooting.

* * *

Smoke halted the wagon about a mile from town. Van Horn and three of Cosgrove's men were heading his way, leading Barrie's horse. Barrie, wrapped in a blanket, was tied across the saddle.

"These ol' boys here," Van Horn explained, "decided they didn't like the idea of makin' war against a young girl. Before he died, Barrie vouched for them. He said they might need a bath, but they was good boys."

"That's good enough for me," Smoke said, swinging down from the saddle. "Welcome to the spread, boys. I can guarantee you the finest food you ever ate."

"Miss Jenny and your Missus really make tubfuls of doughnuts?" Slim asked.

"Every day."

"Lord! I've found a home."

The men placed the bloodsoaked blanket containing Barrie into the hay-filled wagon bed. Cooper, holding the reins, looked back at the body. "I liked that man," he said.

"We all did, boy," Kit said. "Hadn't a been for him, I'd a been ridin' the outlaw trail. All three of us would. I ain't sayin' we're angels. But I ain't robbed nobody or done harm to a woman. And I ain't gonna start now."

"You should have seen him work, Smoke," Van Horn said. "He either outright killed or got mortal lead in twenty-six men this morning."

"Twenty-six!" Smoke said, clearly startled.

"That about passes your record, don't it, Smoke?" Slim asked.

"Certainly does."

"And them figures is right on the mark." Shady vouched for the number. "Barrie had nine slugs in him 'fore he finally give up the ghost. But he went out with a smile on his lips, knowin' he done a good thing. Cosgrove and Fosburn was in shock, I think. The undertaker was so happy, he was rubbin' his hands and smilin' to beat the band. Finally, ol' Fat Fosburn, he got to makin' threats about this and that and Shady, he went up to him and punched him in the mouth. Knocked him down in a big mud puddle. Cosgrove, he run off back to his office. There really ain't much to them men. Biggers neither, I'm thinkin'."

"Barrie went out gentle, talkin' about Jenny," Van Horn said. "I really think he started out likin' the girl and in a short time grew to love her like she was his own. Jenny's gonna take this hard."

"She knows why he left," Smoke said. "I told her, and Sally's with her now. They're all up on the east slope. Kit, would you boys mind staying at the ranch and looking after things while we have the funeral?"

"We'd be honored to, Smoke. And the ranch and everything on the place will be just like you left it. Or the three of us will be dead in the yard," he added grimly.

21

The burial procession left Slim, Kit, and Shady at the ranch, each man with a basket filled with doughnuts and a rifle by his side.

"I'd be plumb filled with ire if someone was to disturb me while I'm eatin' these," Slim said. "I might get so put out I'd have to kill somebody."

"If you do," Van Horn said, "I hope it's Hankins."

Slim shuddered. "I don't like that feller. He gives me the creeps. I can't abide a sneak, and that's what he is. I believe in meetin' a man eye-to-eye."

Wolf drove the wagon as far as it could go, and then Barrie was carried up the ridge overlooking the bubbling little spring. They'd dressed him up in clean clothes and wrapped his boots and spurs and guns in the blanket with him.

Pasco and Ladd had dug a deep hole and gathered rocks to shelter the mound once Barrie was covered.

Van Horn spoke a few words, Smoke read from the Bible, and then Jenny sang "O Valiant Hearts" and Sally sang

"What a Friend We Have in Jesus." There was a lot of nose-blowing and eye-wiping. Even ol' Wolf Parcell kept wiping his eyes and complaining about the "damn dust a-blowin' ever' which a-way."

If Hankins was around, he had missed the funeral procession from the ranch, and no long-range shots were fired. Which was wise on Hankins's part. Considering the mood of this gathering, had he tried a shot, the men would have tracked him into town and hanged him . . . along with Cosgrove, Fosburn, Biggers, and anybody else who might have gotten in their way.

The last words of the farewell prayer, offered by Sally, were just echoing away as the sun went down. Far in the distance, a big timber wolf howled.

"Look in on him from time to time, my brother Wolf," Bad Dog said, lifting his head, his eyes searching the horizon. "He would like that."

"Amen," Wolf Parcell said, and the service was over in the last fading light of the day.

Cosgrove, Biggers, and Fosburn were clearly in a state of shock over the killing or wounding of twenty-six newly hired gunhands and the defection of three top guns.

"One man," Biggers said, looking down into his coffee cup. "One sick and dying man breezes into town and we bury twenty-one men."

"And four out of the five who survived are not going to make it," Fosburn added.

Cosgrove was silent. He sat by the window of his office and stared out at the town that had once been his. Now he wielded no power. None. Once he could have snapped his fingers and the townspeople would have jumped. Now they just looked at him through eyes that held nothing but contempt. Mule Jackson had left Doc Blaine's small clinic and boarded the stage for God knows where. The man had picked up his wages and left. Still in pain and still badly shaken by the horrible beating laid on him by Smoke Jensen, Mule was only a shell of his former self.

Mule Jackson would drop out of sight, not to be heard from for a long, long time.

The town was still filled to overflowing with hired guns, but even they walked lightly around the citizens and caused no problems. Not after one had lipped off to a citizen and tried to bully a young boy. The boy's father, upon hearing the news, went home, got his shotgun, and shot the thug dead in the street. Club Bowers made no arrest. He had told Cosgrove, "Keep your pet hyenas on a short leash, Major. I can't be responsible for what these citizens might take it in their minds to do."

Cosgrove sat and listened with only half a mind to the talk around him. He knew what he ought to do: tend to his mining operations, fire all the gunhands, and live quietly and luxuriously with his considerable wealth.

He should do that, but he knew he wouldn't.

Major Cosgrove had never been beaten, in business or in a fistfight. Now, since Smoke Jensen had arrived, he'd been publicly humiliated, stomped on, and thwarted at every turn, and he'd had the entire town turn against him. Nearly all of his really good gunhands had left him. Hankins had not been able to get a clear shot at Smoke Jensen. Cosgrove could not understand that, could not understand that while Hankins hated Jensen, he was deathly afraid of the man. With Smoke Jensen, you only get one shot. Miss or wound the man, and Jensen would spend the rest of his life tracking you down and ultimately killing you.

One simply did not play deadly games with Smoke Jensen. Not ever.

Even Lawyer Dunham was keeping a very low profile, and gradually distancing himself from the Big Three.

"What are we goin' to do, Major?" Jack Biggers asked, breaking into Cosgrove's dark thoughts.

"Counting all hands, how many men can we muster?"

"Right at fifty," the rancher replied. "But if you're thinkin' 'bout attacking Jenny's ranch, forget it. That place is a fort. Since Smoke sold off most of the cattle, 'ceptin' for some of the finest bulls and heifers I ever seen, the hands ain't done nothin' 'cept work around the complex. Smoke sent a hand down south and brought a damn wagon train of supplies back. They got enough supplies out there to last a damn year. You can't get within a mile of the ranch—day or night—without being spotted. They started out by clearing two or three hundred yards. Now it's up to about three-quarters of a mile. Jenny's got ten first-rate men out there, not countin' Smoke and Sally. And you better not discount Sally Jensen."

"Tell me about it," Major muttered. The buckshot that Barrie had fired at the man had done little damage, but a few pellets—and rusty nails and so forth—had scarred his face, and Major Cosgrove was a vain man when it came to his personal appearance. All the more reason for hating the Jensens.

Cosgrove stood up from his windowseat and paced the office. He could no longer count on Sheriff Bowers or any of his men. Club was a changed man and the citizens were warming to him. He had pared down his deputies by firing Reed and Junior. If a general election were held this day, Bowers would be reelected by a landslide.

Everything, *everything* he had worked for was vanishing all around him. Most of his power was gone, and with it the prestige he had basked in.

Goddamn Smoke Jensen!

*   *   *

"Movement on the west side of the range," Slim said, handing Smoke the field glasses he'd been using up in the barn loft. "I think it's Hankins, and I think he's camped up there somewhere."

"Tonight I'll take the game to Hankins," Smoke said. "We've got to get rid of him. Once that's done, we can all breathe a little easier."

"You got a plan?"

"Yes," Smoke said, standing up. "Kill him."

Peter Hankins thought he had it all figured out. He had picked and then rejected two dozen different locations from which to shoot. Then he spotted one that was so obvious he had missed it from the outset. It was going to be a long shot, but he felt he could do it. He'd made shots from that distance before, but only during his many long hours of practice. He figured the distance at just under three-quarters of a mile. He could do it, he knew he could. And when he killed the legendary Smoke Jensen, from that moment on, Peter Hankins could name his own price, and men of a certain ilk would pay it.

Come night, he would work his way into position and wait.

Smoke dressed in dark clothing and slipped his feet into moccasins. He blackened his face with soot and tied a black bandanna around his forehead. He took a knife and his rifle only. He knew that this work would either be very close in, or long distance. There would be no in-between.

He did not underestimate the abilities of Peter Hankins. The man was a hunter and one of the best.

Smoke had napped through the hours of the afternoon, getting ready for the long night hours that lay ahead of him. Then he ate a good supper and slipped some jerky into his pocket. Jerky was swiftly going out of vogue in the early eighties but not with Smoke. He did not take a canteen. The area was dotted with springs, and he knew where they were.

He also thought he knew where Hankins had settled in for the night, patiently waiting for his morning shot.

Conversation at the supper table was sparse, with the men only picking at their food. None of them liked the idea of Smoke going out after Hankins alone.

"It oughta be me goin' out yonder after Hankins," Wolf Parcell grumbled. "I spent more years in the wilderness than you been alive, boy."

"You boys look after Jenny," Smoke had told them. He patted Sally's hand and slipped out into the darkness. He would rub his skin and his clothing with various types of grass and then dirt on top of that to mask the human smell.

Bad Dog chuckled as the door closed.

"What's so funny, *amigo?*" Pasco asked.

"Biggers, Cosgrove, and Fosburn have about fifty men on their combined payrolls at this time, right?"

" 'Bout that. Why?" Kit asked.

"They will have somewhat less than that by this time to-morrow, I am thinking. That was not Smoke's regular Bowie he was carrying for this night's work."

"What was it, then?" Slim asked.

Bad Dog met Sally's amused eyes. Mrs. Jensen said, "A Cheyenne scalping knife."

It took Smoke the better part of three hours to cover just over a mile. Twice coyotes trotted past him, unaware of his presence. Once a skunk came close to him and Smoke said a very sincere and silent prayer for the little animal to pad right on along and leave him alone.

Then the wind shifted and Smoke caught the unmistak-able smell of hair oil. Oh, vanity, he thought. It's going to get you killed, Hankins.

Ever so gently and soundlessly, Smoke eased around until he was pointing toward the smell of barbershop hair oil. With the wind blowing toward him, and the breeze freshening, there was no chance Hankins could smell him, and little chance of him hearing his approach.

Hankins stiffened at a slight unnatural noise and looked all around him, only the top of his head and his eyes poking out of the slight depression. He could see nothing out of the ordinary and he did not hear the noise again.

Hankins settled back into the natural hole, his rifle across his knees, and relaxed himself. It was silly of him to think that any cowboy was going to be able to slip unseen across a mile of burned-over ground without enough cover to hide a quail. He had seen those coyotes, hadn't he? And a man was a whole lot larger than a coyote.

Hankins longed for a hot cup of coffee and a warm bed. But he warmed himself internally by thinking of seeing Smoke Jensen falling dead with a bullet in his chest or back. Chest would be better, Hankins concluded. What a shot this would be. He would be talked about over campfires for the rest of his life.

If Hankins had any idea how short the rest of his life was, he would have been praying instead of mentally building monuments to himself.

Hankins almost peed in his underwear when someone tapped him on the shoulder. He tried to twist around, jerk up his rifle, and jump up at the same time. All he succeeded in doing was falling down in the hole and losing the grip on his rifle. He came up with a pistol in his hand and felt a powerful hand clamp around his wrist and jerk. Hankins went flying to land against the side of the earth depression, the wind being knocked out of him.

The last thing he remembered seeing through his panic-filled eyes was the dark, menacing shape of Smoke Jensen, a knife in his hand.

* * *

Sheriff Club Bowers thought he heard a horse walking slowly up the street of the town. With half-closed eyes, he could see the wall clock. Two o'clock in the morning. Must have been his imagination. He rolled over, pulled the blanket up to his shoulders, and went back to sleep.

He was awakened by a frantic banging on his door. "Sheriff!" a man hollered. "Come quick, Sheriff. Cosgrove and the mayor is about to have a conniption-fit. Get your britches on, man. Hurry, now."

Cussing, Club pulled on his pants and boots. It wasn't even daylight out yet. "This had better be good," he muttered. "I sure was sleepin' sound."

A crowd of men had gathered around a horse that was tied to the hitchrail in front of Major Cosgrove's offices. He recognized the animal as one that worthless back-shooting Peter Hankins had been riding.

Cosgrove and Fosburn were backed up against the outside wall of the building, both of them pale and looking like they wanted to puke.

Hankins' rifle was in the specially made saddle boot, and something was tied to it. Club pulled up short when he saw what it was.

A scalp.

Hankins' scalp. The man's blond hair was unmistakable.

"You reckon we're about to be attacked by wild Indians, Sheriff?" a man who was new to the West asked, nervousness in his voice.

"No. Hell, no, Adkins. Just calm down. The only Indians around here are tame ones, for the most part. Besides, Indians didn't do this."

"How do you know?" Adkins pressed.

"Indians keep the scalps, man. No Indian would have tied the top knot to this expensive rifle and turned this fine horse loose." This was the horse I heard walking up the street last night, Club thought. Oh, Jensen, you ballsy bastard. You got more guts than any ten men combined.

Cosgrove pointed a finger at the scalp flapping in the cool early morning breeze. "That's . . . something only a damn *heathen* would do!" His voice trembled as badly as his finger.

"Yep," Club said, rolling a cigarette. "For a white man to do this is almost as bad as a growed-up man who would try to steal a young girl's ranch and kill her in the process."

"I demand you go arrest Smoke Jensen!" Fosburn hollered. "I order you to arrest him!"

"You don't order me to do a damn thing, Fat." Club cupped his hand around the match flame and lit up. "And how do you know Smoke Jensen done this? Was you there? Did you see it?"

"Why . . . ah, no. Of course not."

"Well, shut your mouth then."

"You're all against me!" Cosgrove suddenly screamed out. "Every damn one of you. Well . . . well . . . by God, we'll see who wins this fight. I *own* this town. It was my money that helped *build* this town. No two-bit gunfighter is going to cheat me out of what is rightfully mine. I'll hire a hundred, a thousand gunfighters to kill that damn Smoke Jensen. You all hear me? And I'll have you all groveling at my feet, begging me to forgive you for turning against me. I . . ."

Lawyer Dunham had walked down from his quarters to see what the commotion was all about. "Mister Cosgrove, as the man handling your affairs, I would suggest, in the strongest possible terms, that you shut your damn mouth before you develop what is known as a buffalo mouth and a humming-bird ass."

"You're *fired!*" Cosgrove screamed.

"Suits me," Dunham said. He looked at the flapping scalp

and grimaced. "My word! I was going to the Grand Hotel for breakfast. I think I'll settle for coffee."

"I'll join you," Club said.

"What about that . . . scalp?" Fosburn hollered.

"He worked for you," Club told him. "You bury it."

22

Before the citizens of Red Light had settled down to breakfast that morning, twelve hired guns stuffed their saddle-bags, rolled up blankets in ground sheets, saddled up, and pulled out. Many of the residents of the boom town stood silently on the boardwalks and watched them leave.

Lawyer Dunham stood with Sheriff Bowers. "I have been such a fool," the attorney said. "The big money offered me by Cosgrove, Fosburn, and Biggers dazzled me. It blinded me to what is right and wrong and sent me down the wrong path."

"I been on the wrong path near 'bouts all my growed up life," Club said. "I do know what you're talkin' about. But ain't it a nice feelin' once you know you're back on track?"

"Yes. I started experiencing that sensation about a week ago. I feel as though a great weight has been lifted from me. Sheriff. I would like to handle Miss Jenny Jensen's affairs. And I won't even charge her for my services. Do you suppose I could safely ride out to her ranch without Smoke shooting me?"

Club chuckled. "Mister Dunham, you'll be surprised at how forgivin' Smoke is. I've spoke at length with half a dozen or more cowboys who right now still work for Biggers or Fosburn. They all, to a man, told me that Smoke could have easily killed them out on the range and had plenty of cause to do just that. Instead, he offered them a job on Miss Jenny's ranch once this fracas was over. Yeah. Really. I'd bet my last dollar—most of it, until lately, ill-gotten—" he admitted, "that you ride out there and they'll invite you in, give you coffee and pie, and everybody will shake hands and forget and forgive the past. Smoke has offered the same deal to the Big Three more than once, and they turned it down. He'll not offer it again. Come on. I'll ride out to the ranch with you."

As the sheriff and the lawyer were riding out one end of town, Jack Biggers and his entire crew, including the cook—an old outlaw wanted for murder in three states and two territories—were riding into town from the other end. Within five minutes, the hired-gun crew of Fat Fosburn came thundering in. Shopkeepers and store owners began closing and locking their doors. The Golden Cherry and the Golden Plum shut down. The town began bracing for a showdown the citizens knew was probably only hours away.

People called pet dogs and cats inside and tied them up or caged them. They began moving their horses out of the livery stables of Red Light and into corrals outside of town, out of bullet range. Thirty minutes after the heavily armed gunslicks rode into town, the long main street of Red Light was void of any decent person. Only the horses of the gunhands stood at the hitchrails. The hired guns sat in various saloons and waited for word to start the war.

"I will control this town," Cosgrove said, his eyes blazing with anger and approaching madness. "This is my town, and I give the orders."

Both Biggers and Fosburn felt it was their town, too; but they didn't bring that up at this time. Major Cosgrove had strapped on a gunbelt and had a rifle and a bandolier of ammunition on his desk.

The mine had shut down and the town was eerily silent. The miners were staying close to their tents and shacks on the slopes above Red Light. Whoever won, they would still have a job. They played cards, drank coffee, and waited.

On the Fosburn ranch, Luddy, Parker, and Dud packed up their few possessions and saddled their personal mounts. They stood for a moment, looking across the saddles at each other.

"Ain't nobody yet said where it is we're goin'," Parker broke the silence.

"I ain't no gunhand and never called myself one," Luddy said. "But I reckon it's time we seen if Miss Jenny Jensen might need some hands over to her place."

"I'll go along with that," Dud said.

The men swung into the saddle and put the Fosburn ranch behind them.

On the Triangle JB, Highpockets, Dick, Biff, and Howie saddled up and mounted up.

"I damn sure ain't leavin' no regrets behind," Biff said, picking up the reins.

"Me, neither," Highpockets said. "You reckon Smoke really scalped that back-shootin' Hankins like Biggers heard he done?"

"You want to ride into town and ask someone?" Howie looked at him.

"Hell, no! I don't want to get within ten miles of Red Light. That town's fixin' to explode."

"You know," Dick said, "Jack Biggers ain't got no family nowhere. They's gonna be a lot of work to be done around here once he's in the ground. And Smoke *did* say we could go to work for Miss Jenny."

"She's gonna own this place for sure," Biff said. "Let's ride over to her place and ask if we could please have a cup of coffee and a doughnut."

Lawyer Dunham sat in the lovely living room in Jenny Jensen's ranchhouse and drank excellent coffee and enjoyed some of the finest doughnuts he'd ever put in his mouth. He had gotten over his astonishment at the nice reception he'd received and was now talking legal business with Smoke, Sally, and Miss Jenny. Smoke had told him to put any past differences between them behind him. All that was in the past and best forgotten.

Lawyer Dunham was greatly relieved to do just that. Being hurled out of a second-story window was an experience he did not wish to relive.

"Rider comin'!" the lookout in the barn loft hollered. "It's young Billy Leonard from town."

The young man jumped from his horse and ran up to Sheriff Bowers, who had just stepped outside. "Deputy Brandt says to come quick, Sheriff. All the gunfighters has gathered in town. The men you fired, Reed and Junior, are workin' for Cosgrove. All the people in town are takin' sides, and they's gonna be a face-off before dark. It's bad, Sheriff. Real bad."

"More riders comin' in," the lookout called. "From north and south. I recognize Highpockets and Luddy."

"They've left the Big Three," Club said. "I spoke to them only a few days ago. They're good boys. I trust them to keep their word."

"So do I," Van Horn said.

Highpockets rode up to the front porch and tossed his hands into the air. The others did the same.

"What the hell . . . ?" Club said.

Smoke laughed at the men. "No need for that, boys. But I must say you have it down pat. You boys looking for work?"

"Punchin' cows and breakin' horses, yes, sir," Highpockets said. "We ain't hirin' out our guns. But we'll fight for the
brand if attacked."

"That's all anyone could ask. Put your stuff in the bunkhouse and the barn. When this mess is over, we'll rebuild the
bunkhouses on Fat's place and over on the Triangle JB."

"But the bunkhouse on the JB is in pretty good shape,"
Dick said.

Smoke smiled at him. "It probably won't be when all this
is over." He looked over at Van Horn. "Pick the men who
stay here, Van."

"Ladd. You, Ford, Cooper, and Jimmy stay here at the
ranch. Highpockets. You boys leavin' any saddle pals behind?"

"Not a one, Mister Van Horn. And I can speak for all of
us. They all drifted when the gunslicks started comin' in. If
you're worried about us tossin' lead at anyone who attacked
this ranch, you can put your mind to rest. Y'all didn't start
this war. Biggers and Fosburn and Cosgrove is in the wrong,
and so is any who ride for them."

"That's good enough for me. You men stay here and protect the ranch."

"You new men," Sally called from the kitchen window.
"Jenny and I just fixed a huge tub of doughnuts and the coffee is hot and fresh. Stow your gear and come on back here . . .
if you're hungry, that is."

The seven of them almost broke their necks getting to the
barn and the bunkhouse.

Smoke looked at the gathering of men. "Whoever is riding into town with me, get geared up for a fight. We'll pull
out in half an hour."

Smoke stepped back inside and looked at Sally. "Keep
some of those doughnuts handy, honey. The boys and me
will be hungry when we get back."

* * *

Eight men saddled up and rode out, heading for Red Light and a showdown with five or six times their number. Smoke headed the column. In addition to his matched .44s, he carried two more .44s tucked down behind his belt and his old Colt revolving shotgun slung by a strap over one shoulder, a bandolier of shells across his chest.

Beside him rode Van Horn, the legendary old gunfighter still ramrod straight and leather tough, his Remingtons loaded up full and ready to bang. Like Smoke, he had shoved two spare six-shooters behind his belt.

Behind Smoke and Van Horn rode Wolf Parcell and Bad Dog, both heavily armed, both carrying bows and a quiver of arrows.

Third in the column rode Pasco and Kit Silver. Behind them rode Slim Waters and Shady Bryant. Kit Silver felt in his guts that this would be his last fight. He had carried that feeling with him since the day he rode into Red Light. But if it was true, he would go out on the right side, and that gave him comfort.

The men pulled up at the pass and bunched. "You can bet they're waiting for us," Smoke said. "We'll go into town in pairs, two minutes apart. Just as soon as they open the dance . . ." He looked at Wolf, grinning at that remark. "Or, whoever opens the dance, we don't stop until it's over. I'll see the deputies first and give them Club's message. They'll clear out of town in jig time, you can bet on that. Club's giving us all a break by ordering his deputies out and by staying at the ranch until an hour before sundown. So it better be over by then. By now, with the fresh horse we gave him, Billy Leonard has delivered my message to the Big Three and found himself a safe hole. I want to thank you men . . ." Smoke paused, unable to find the right words.

Wolf said, "Just 'cause you was partly raised by that ol' windbag, Preacher, don't start actin' like him by makin' no long-winded speeches. You and that creaky, ancient ol' reprobate with you just ride on into town and get set. Me and the boys will be right behind you. I think it'd be best if we leave our horses at the crick, out of danger. Time the gun-smoke settles, this town will be tame and Miss Jenny won't be bothered no more. Now git!"

"Creaky ol' reprobate!" Van Horn hollered.

"Hee, hee, hee!" Wolf giggled, and the others smiled at the antics of the randy old mountain man, who was still tough enough to take on a grizzly bear . . . and would, if the opportunity presented itself.

"I'm gonna put a knot on your head when I get back," Van Horn warned Wolf.

Wolf laughed and slapped Van Horn's horse on the rump. "Go git 'em, Van!"

Van Horn and Smoke reined up at the creek, stripped the saddle and bridle off their horses, and hobbled them. They checked their guns and exchanged glances.

"See you at the other end of the street, young feller," Van Horn said, then hopped across the little creek and began working his way up behind the first line of houses and build-ings.

Smoke took the other side. But he stayed on the board-walks, at least for now.

There was not one living creature visible on the streets or boardwalks of the town. Not a dog, cat, chicken, horse, or man, woman, or child.

Smoke looked back. Wolf and Bad Dog were swinging down from the saddle at the creek. He walked on until he came to an empty building at the end of the first block of stores. All the stores that he could see were closed and locked.

Far up the street came the sound of a tinny piano and the high, shrill, false laughter of a hurdy-gurdy girl. Smoke looked across the street at the alleyway. Van Horn was standing there. He looked over at Smoke, shrugged his shoulders, and walked on.

Smoke paused, his eyes searching the second-story windows to his right. He was certain men with rifles had been posted along the way, but he could spot nothing that would give away their location. He resumed his slow walking.

The town was filled with gunfighters on the payrolls of Biggers, Fosburn, and Cosgrove; but where the hell were they? All scattered out in the town's many saloons? Some of them, yes. But he rather doubted that all of them were in the bars. Smoke stopped his walking. They had to be in the stores, all spread out along the narrow, twisting streets.

Smoke slipped off the boardwalk and stepped into the coolness of a shadowed alley. He slipped one of the spare .44s from behind his belt and jacked the hammer back as he walked toward the rear of the buildings. At the alley's opening, he looked back left, toward the Golden Cherry. Clemmie waved to him from a window on the second floor. Smoke returned the wave and walked on. By now, Wolf and Bad Dog would be a block behind him and Pasco and Kit would be hobbling their horses at the creek. The hired guns would know their quarry was in town. So why didn't they make a move?

That question was answered when a young man, who looked to be in his early twenties, suddenly stepped out from behind the rear of a building, both hands hovering over the butts of his guns. "Leather that six-shooter, Jensen, and face me like a man. I've come to kill you."

"Don't be a fool, man," Smoke told him, the cocked .44 in his right hand. "I've got no quarrel with you. Give this up and go on back home."

"Yellow, that's what you are!" the young man sneered.

"I'm offering you your life, partner," Smoke reminded the young man. "Take the offer. Don't die for nothing."

"You ain't gonna holster that gun and try your luck with me?"

"Not a chance, kid. This is not a game. Give it up, go home, and live."

The would-be gunslinger stood for a moment, cussing Smoke. Then, with a strange cry of desperation, his hands closed around the butts of his guns and Smoke fired, knocking a leg out from under the young man. The young tough hollered in pain, both hands grabbing at his shattered knee. Smoke walked up to him and took his guns from leather, noticing that one was a .44 and the other a .45. He kept the .44 and threw the .45 into the bushes.

He looked down at the young man, writhing in pain on the bottle- and can-littered ground. "Boy, if I ever see you again and you're carrying iron, I'll kill you on the spot. Do you understand all that?"

"Yes . . . sir," the young man groaned out the words. "I swear to God I'll never tote no gun again. But Jesus, I hurt something awful."

"Pain is good for a man. It's a reminder that you're still alive." Smoke walked on.

His shot had been the only one thus far. Smoke felt that was about to change. Now the hired guns knew where he was and they surely would be coming after him.

He heard a pistol bark and a man scream. That was followed by a crash of breaking glass and the thud of a body after it had fallen a distance. Van Horn had nailed one of those on a second floor . . . or a rooftop.

He heard running boots and stopped, filling his left hand with a .44. Two men sprang out of a narrow passageway between buildings and pulled up short, spotting Smoke. Smoke did not recall ever seeing the men before. But they cursed him, their guns lifting. Smoke had no choice but to open fire. He fired four times, the slugs taking the hired guns in belly and chest as the muzzles lifted. They spun around and jerked their way into the rapidly enveloping darkness of death.

Behind him and to his right he heard a curse, a shot, and a short cry of pain. He turned his head for a second, spotting ol' Wolf some distance behind him, both of his hands filled with guns.

Smoke walked on, now slipping into the dark and narrow passageway the hired guns had sprung out of. He stopped just short of the street, listening.

"I'll give a sack of gold for every dead Jensen supporter!" he heard Cosgrove scream. "A sack of gold, men, do you hear me? A sack of gold." The voice was slightly muffled, so Smoke figured Cosgrove was safely behind walls.

Boots sounded on the boardwalk and the entrance was suddenly filled with men from the Triangle JB.

"Is it a good day to die, boys?" Smoke threw out the question a second before he opened fire.

23

The booming of the .44s was enormous in the narrow space, and the alley became thick with gunsmoke. Smoke dropped to his belly and crawled under a building, leaving the Triangle JB men moaning and groaning on the ground. He inched his way toward the street, stopping just before he reached the high boardwalk in front of a saloon that he knew belonged to Fat Fosburn. Above him, the floor was heavy with pacing boots. He rolled over on his back and listened to the muffled talk.

"Goddamnit, there ain't but seven or eight of them. What the hell are we waitin' for?"

"I just caught me a glimpse of Kit," another said. "Damn turncoat! I can't figure what got into him."

The voice came from right above Smoke. He emptied one .44 into the floor above him, then swiftly rolled to his left, screams of anguish ripping from several men inside the saloon. Smoke was to the rear of the building and running up the littered way before the men in the saloon could gather their senses and start pouring lead into the floor.

He forced open the door to a barbershop, closing and locking it behind him, then ran to the front of the establishment. The door was bolted and the shades drawn halfway down. Kneeling down by the front and peeping out, Smoke quickly reloaded and caught his breath.

By now, all those backing him up would be in town and ready to force the hands of the Big Three. Smoke and Van Horn had cut the odds down some, but those supporting Jenny were still badly outnumbered . . . by how much was something none of them with Smoke knew.

Smoke had inflicted some damage by shooting through the floor back at the saloon. Maybe one or two men had caught lead. But so far, no class gunhand had showed himself, and there were about a dozen or so of them still on the payroll of Fosburn, Cosgrove, and Biggers.

Back of Wong's Chinese Cafe, Pasco came face to face with a slick who called himself the Lordsburg Kid. He'd killed a couple of Mexican sheepherders and raped one Mexican girl. The Kid thought he was hell on wheels with a gun.

"Damn greaser!" the Kid hissed at Pasco. "Anybody who'd work with sheep is scum."

"Oh?" Pasco said easily. "My cousin, Carbone, used to herd sheep as a boy. I do not think you would say that to him. If he's still alive, that is," he added.

"You ain't Carbone."

"This is true. I am better than my cousin, *amigo.* Faster, and a much more accurate shot."

"You're a damn greasy liar!"

Pasco drove the Kid's center shirt button all the way out his backbone with one slug. The Kid never even cleared leather. Pasco stood over the body and shook his head. "You should have learned some manners from your *madre* and *padre, amigo.* Now it is too late."

He walked on.

"Jenkins!" Van Horn called to a particularly vicious gun-hand who, he remembered, had said some terrible things about Miss Jenny.

Jenkins turned and grinned at Van Horn, his teeth yellow and rotted. "Why, you damned old wrinkled-up worthless coot! I doubt you even got the strength to pull them wore-out old Remingtons from leather. Will them things still fire?"

"Why don't you try me and see, Jenkins?"

Jenkins laughed at him and grabbed for iron. Van Horn shot him twice in the belly and left him dying in the alley. "Some folks nowadays just ain't got no respect for their elders and betters," Van Horn grumbled. "No tellin' what it'll be like a hundred years from now."

Wolf Parcell clamped a gnarled old hand on the neck of a Biggers rider and drove his head against the outside wall of a building. Several times. On the fourth try, the gunhand's head drove clear through the wood and Wolf left him dangling there by the neck, the toes of his boots dragging the ground.

"Either that was rotten wood or that boy's shore got a hard head," Wolf muttered.

Bad Dog just couldn't resist it. He had spotted a man on the roof of a hardware and guns store and quietly notched an arrow. The man finally presented him with the target he wanted, and Bad Dog let the arrow fly. It embedded about six inches into the left cheeks of the man's big ass. The gunslick dropped his rifle and went to bellerin' loud enough to wake the dead. A man ran out the back of Darlin' Lill's Saloon, both hands filled with guns, and Bad Dog gave him a Cheyenne present. The man dropped silently, an arrow through the heart.

The gunhand on the roof was trying to climb down, hollering and squalling each time he moved his left leg. Bad Dog put an arrow into his right leg and the man fell off the ladder to land hard in the alley. He did not move.

Slim Waters stepped into the rear of the Cards and Wheels Club, both hands filled with guns. He toed open the door leading from the main room to the storage area and stepped inside.

"This here's for Miss Jenny, boys," he announced, and started shooting.

Kit Silver stood facing five men, the class gunslick Val Davis among them.

"You're a fool, Kit," Val told him.

"Maybe," Kit replied. "But you're dead." Kit smiled and grabbed iron.

Shady Bryant faced three top guns, his hands by his side. "Well, boys, he told them, "I reckon this is my last hurrah. Let's make it a good one." Then he laughed, jerked his guns, and went to work, this time, on the right side.

Smoke heard the roaring reports of guns and knew it was root-hog-or-die time. He smashed out the window of the barbershop—remembering that he must be sure to use some Big Three money to replace it—and yelled, "Here I am, boys. You want that sack full of gold, come get me!"

Smoke ran out the back of the shop and around the corner just as men ran out of buildings and sought cover where they could find it and started pumping lead into the barbershop.

Standing by the corner of a building, Smoke dropped two before the men realized he wasn't in the barbershop and started throwing lead at him.

By that time, Smoke had crawled under a building and was working his way toward daylight on the other side of the establishment.

He paused to reload, shoved the Colts behind his belt, and pulled the sawed-off revolving shotgun from his shoulder. He checked the barrel for blockage. At short range, the ten-gauge was an awesome weapon. Smoke crawled out from under the building and looked at the backs of three men, Ned Harden and Haywood among the group—two of the more odious gunhandlers Smoke had ever had the misfortune to encounter. They would do anything, to anybody, at anytime. All that was about to stop—abruptly.

"You boys looking for me?" Smoke called, getting a good grip on the sawed-off, for its recoil could rip it from the grasp if a man wasn't ready for it.

The trio spun around, eyes wide and mouths open. "Jesus God!" Harden yelled, spotting the cutdown revolving shotgun.

There was about fifteen feet between them. Smoke started pulling and cocking and blasting. It was a good ten feet from the corner of the alleyway to the mud and dirt of the street, and that's where all three landed. Or what was left of them.

Smoke reloaded the hand cannon and listened for a few seconds. The shooting had stopped from inside the Cards and Wheels Club and from behind the apothecary shop. He had no way of knowing the outcome.

Kit Silver had taken five out with him. The gunfighter sat with his back to a building, four slugs in him; but he was not dead yet. He smiled at Val Davis, who lay mortally wounded, looking at him. The others with him were dead.

"Why'd . . . you do it, Kit?" Val asked.

"Felt like it. Felt good, too. Sorry you'll never get to know what it's like to do something right for a change."

"You've killed me!"

"Sure looks like it, don't it?"

Val put his head on the ground and died.

Kit shook his head. "I hope I live long enough to die among better company than this," he said.

The interior of the Cards and Wheels Club looked like a slaughterhouse when Pasco backtracked and entered the place. Slim was still alive, but just barely.

"I won't lie to you, Slim," Pasco said. "It's bad."

"Yeah, I know. In the side pocket of my jacket. A napkin. Get it for me, will you?"

"A napkin?"

Got . . . something wrapped up in it."

Pasco opened the napkin. One of Jenny's doughnuts. Slim held out his hand and grinned, the blood leaking from one corner of his mouth. He took a bite and chewed contentedly. "Mighty good, Pasco. Mighty good." He swallowed, closed his eyes, and his head lolled to one side.

"Damn!" Pasco said.

Shady Bryant lay with his hands still gripping the butts of his guns. Three dead gunhands lay in front of him. A young man who called himself the Red River Kid and fancied himself a fast gun stood looking at the scene. He shook his head and took off his gunbelt, slinging it over one shoulder. He started walking toward where their horses were picketed. The farm back in East Texas looked real good to him right now.

"Is that you, Red River?" a man called, sitting on the ground, his back to the outside wall of a privy. Bullets had broken both his legs.

"Never heard of him," the kid called over his shoulder, and kept right on walking. "My name's Frank Sparks."

"I'd a-shot him yesterday," the wounded gunfighter spoke to the slight breeze that wound around the buildings of Red Light. "But if I'd a-done what he's doin' twenty years ago, I damn sure wouldn't be in this fix now." The wounded gunslick watched the young man walk across the meadow. "Good luck, kid," he called weakly. "And to hell with this," he muttered. He pulled his guns from leather and tossed them into the tall grass.

Smoke walked into the Golden Plum, through the back door, and said, "Give me a beer, Jeff. I do believe I've worked up something of a thirst."

Jeff looked at him. "You're hit, Mister Jensen."

"Bullets burned my arm and scratched my side. Nothing serious."

Wolf and Bad Dog stomped in from the back, followed by Van Horn, who was supporting the badly wounded Kit Silver.

"Slim and Shady's dead," the old gunfighter announced. "It's down to us, now."

"No, it isn't," the voice came from the rear of the saloon, which was getting quite a bit of traffic. Moses stood there holding a rifle, a pistol belted around his waist. Clemmie and her girls stood behind him, all of them armed with various types of weapons.

"You put that ornery Silver on a pallet over here, Van Horn," Clemmie said, looking at Kit. "Me and that rounder go 'way back together. He's too damn mean to die."

Kit grinned at the madam as he was placed on a hurriedly made pallet of blankets.

Chung and Wong were next, both of them armed with long-barreled, ten-gauge goose guns. Wong said, "So sorry I could not bring some good Chinese food." He held up the shotgun. "Could not carry this and food at the same time."

Chung said, "Battle lines have been drawn, Mister Smoke Jensen. We are now all on this side of street, enemies on other side."

"Have drink of rye, Mister Jeff," Wong said. "Like cowboys do."

"You ain't never had a drink of rye in all the time I've known you. And you sure ain't gonna like it," Jeff warned.

Wong took the goose gun and loaded it up. "Warm belly, though. Might not get another chance for some time."

"He certainly has a point there," Smoke agreed.

Jeff smiled and set out shot glasses and bottles. "Serve yourselves, boys. I've got to get my guns!"

24

Above the town, on the slopes and ridges leading to the mine, the townspeople waited, watched, and listened. Most families had packed picnic lunches, and several of the saloon owners had transported barrels of beer and cases of whiskey and set up makeshift bars for the thirsty. No loving creature not directly involved in the fight had been left behind in the town. Pet cats were in boxes or crates, and dogs were on leashes. Chickens were in coops. Hens went right on laying eggs.

Across the narrow street, Cosgrove, Biggers, and Fosburn crouched behind the heavily barricaded front of the mayor's office and tried to make some sense out of what had happened and what was happening. All three had finally gotten it through their heads that this day was going to be the turning point in their lives—one way or the other.

Fosburn sat with his back to a wall. He had two guns strapped around his tubby waist and a rifle across his knees. His hair was disheveled and his face was dirty. His eyes seemed to have lost their sparkle. Of the three, Fosburn had turned realist.

"We were too greedy," the mayor spoke in quiet tones. "We had it all but wanted more. Now look where that's got us."

"Shut up," Jack Biggers snarled at him.

"Oh, he's right," Major Cosgrove said. "I don't have to like what he says, but I'm forced to agree with him. I do have to add this: none of us counted on Smoke Jensen."

"Make a deal with him," Fat said.

"I don't think that is possible at this stage," Major said. "The three of us have but two options left us—win or die."

"Jesus Christ!" Biggers almost shouted the words. "There can't be more than seven or eight of them over there. They're all in the saloon. We've still got about thirty-five hard cases and we have them surrounded. Why are we talking about dying and making deals?"

Fosburn stood up and walked to the shattered front window. "Smoke Jensen?" he called.

"I hear you," Smoke's voice rang out.

"I'll make a deal with you."

"What kind of deal?"

"You let me ride out with my money from the bank. I'll sell you my ranch at a fair price. You'll never hear from me again."

"You don't have a ranch." Smoke's words were loud and clear. "None of you do."

The Big Three exchanged glances. Fosburn shouted, "What the hell are you talking about, Jensen?"

"You men stole the land you're running cattle on. You killed the original land owners or ran them off. But you never properly filed on the land you stole. The quit claim and other deeds were forged. And bad ones at that. My wife has had two dozen lawyers and Pinkertons seeking out survivors and relatives. She bought the land from them. It's all legal. Your interests in the mine will go to the survivors and relatives of those you killed or ran out. Lawsuits are being filed now. U.S. Marshals are on the way here now with warrants and other legal papers. Neither you nor Biggers have a pot to piss in or a window to throw it out of. You're both dead broke. No deals."

Biggers and Fosburn were too astonished to speak. They stared at one another open mouthed.

"But I'm still rich, you bastard!" Major hollered. "You men working for me hear that? I've still got sacks and sacks of gold. And there's gold on Jenny Jensen's ranch. Up in the mountains. The richest vein in all of Montana. I'm giving it to you hired guns. You hear me? I'm writing out papers now. But you've got to kill the Jensens and all associated with them to get it. You'll all be worth millions if you do that. Think about it. You'll never have to work again. Never again have to sleep on the ground or worry about where your next meal or next dollar is coming from. You'll have fancy food and the best drinks and the fanciest women. For the rest of your lives!" he screamed.

"That's right, boys," the calm voice of Van Horn drifted out of the Golden Plum. "And all you got to do to earn it is kill me, Pasco, Bad Dog, Wolf Parcell, Kit Silver, and Smoke Jensen. Then you got to kill all the men out at Miss Jenny's ranch, and that includes Little Jimmy Hammon. Them's some bad ol' boys out yonder. And then you got to kill Miss Sally and Miss Jenny. And after that, you got to explain to the judges and the lawyers and the Pinkertons and the U.S. Marshals what happened to us all. Think about that."

"That's nothing!" Major yelled. "Without bodies, no one can prove a thing. Take the saloon, men. Take it, and be worth millions, or ride out with holes in your drawers and patches on your boots."

"They's still the townspeople," Patmos said to Whisperin' Langley.

"Kill 'em all and dump their bodies down a mineshaft and blow it closed," Whisperin' whispered.

"Hell," Bobby Jewel said. "They's five hundred or so people in this town."

"So what?" Jim Pell said. "We take the saloon, then the ranch, and have some fun with the women out there; then we kill Biggers, Fosburn, and Cosgrove, and we have it *all!*"

"Yeah," Sam Jackson said. "Let's do it."

"Pass the word," Whisperin' said. "We take the saloon. Now!"

"They're fools," Wolf said from his position in the saloon. "There ain't enough of them left to overpower us. We'll stack them up like cordwood out yonder in the street and back there in the alley."

"But they'll try," Smoke said. "They've got big money in their eyes now."

"Even if they should succeed," Kit said from the pallet, his voice weak—but his guns were loaded up and by his side—"they'll turn on Biggers and Fosburn and Cosgrove and kill them, too. All the real gunfighters has gone. Them with any honor at all has left or changed sides. That's pure scum out there now. Half of those bums out yonder have killed their own mothers and fathers and brothers and sisters for one reason or another. A horse turd has more value than all them out there put together."

Wong lifted his long-barreled goose gun, sighted in, and pulled the trigger. The charge blew the entire window out of its frame and tore the head off the rifleman who was getting set to snipe at the saloon. The headless body fell backward, bounced off a wall, and came catapulting out of the shattered frame, to crash through an awning and lie on the boardwalk.

Fosburn looked at the bloody, horrible sight about two feet from him and shuddered.

Wong picked himself up off the floor and reloaded the empty chamber.

Moses, Chung, Jeff, and the soiled doves from the Golden Cherry stationed themselves at the rear of the saloon, ready to repel any intruders. Clemmie stayed by the side of the wounded Kit Silver.

Stormclouds had been gathering all morning, and now a light rain began to fall. Lightning licked around the high peaks of the mountains that rimmed the mining town.

"That'll keep them from burning us out," Wolf remarked, chewing on a sandwich from the free lunch table.

Smoke nodded and lifted his rifle. A very small part of a leg was exposed across the street, the man behind a horse trough. Smoke sighted in and pulled the trigger and the man howled as the bullet shattered a shin. He staggered to his feet and turned to try to limp away, and Pasco nailed him from his position on the second floor of the saloon. The hired gun fell into the horse trough.

"Remind me to have that water changed," Smoke said. "I wouldn't want to poison a good horse."

There was a lull in the fighting while both sides tended to wounded, caught their breath, and had a drink, and while those aligned with the Big Three plotted unspeakable evil against fellow human beings.

Those in the Golden Plum waited as the rain picked up.

"I don't trust these men," Fat whispered. "I think they'd as soon kill us as anybody else."

"Where's your foreman, Waco?" Major asked Biggers.

"Gone," Biggers said sourly. "Pulled out last night. Said he didn't sign on to fight girls and women and to associate with the likes of them I got on the payroll. Man turned Christian on me or something. Wouldn't surprise me none to see him pop up over at Jenny's ranch."

Waco was at that moment riding toward Red Light, with a dozen of the area's small ranchers and farmers who had had quite enough of Cosgrove, Fosburn, and Biggers. Now that someone had finally gotten the ball rolling, they were in the game, root hog or die. From the edge of town, the men reined up, staring at the several hundred men, women, kids, and animals all gathered together at the mine complex.

"Must be hell in the streets of Red Light," Waco observed. "Let's go down and even up the odds a little bit for them on the side of Jensen."

Up on the mountain, the local Temperance League had gotten cranked up and there was preaching, singing, tooting, oom-pahing, and drumming.

Out at the Circle Cherry, Club and his deputies were playing poker with Sally and losing nearly every hand. "Ma'am," Deputy Brandt asked. 'Who taught you to play poker?"

"Louis Longmont," Sally said sweetly. "The bet is five dollars to you."

The sheriff and his deputies tossed their cards on the table. Louis Longmont was the most famous gambler in all of America, plus a noted gunfighter and a man worth millions and millions of dollars. "I believe we'll just get a breath of fresh air, ma'am," Club said.

Sally smiled and raked in her winnings. "Come here, Jenny," she said. "I'll teach you about cold-decking and palming."

Club and his deputies shook their heads and walked outside, Club saying, "That there, boys, is one hell of a woman. Can you believe that Smoke Jensen actually dries the dishes?"

Modoc looked at him. "Wouldn't you?"

"Riders coming into town, Smoke," Pasco called from the second floor. "It's Waco, and he's bringin' in a bunch of small ranchers and farmers."

"Waco's all right," Kit said. His voice seemed to be a little stronger. "I figured he'd get a gutful of Jack Biggers and leave." He started chuckling, and the others looked at him strangely. "It just dawned on me what Highpockets and Biff and them others was doin' that day at the ranch. Walkin' around, stoppin', then throwin' their hands up into the air. We all thought it was a new dance step. Then, when I seen Whisperin' and Val doin' it in the bunkhouse, I thought they had changed sides and was in love with one another!"

Clemmie started giggling at the very thought of Val Davis and Whisperin' dancing together, and it was highly infectious. Soon everybody in the saloon was roaring with laughter. Pasco had been sitting on the landing, looking out the window, and he almost fell down the steps, he was laughing so hard. Wolf Parcell was roaring with high mirth. The laughter reached those in the buildings directly across the street.

"What in billy-hell is so damn funny?" Jim Pell snarled the words.

"They must know something we don't," Al Jones said.

"Yeah," Dusty Higgens said, entering from the back door. "Believe me, they do. Like Waco and about twelve or fifteen men just rode into town and took up positions all around us. We got Smoke and them others surrounded in the saloon, and now we're surrounded in here!"

"Not with no twelve or fifteen men," Chambers said.

Dick Whitten stood up to look out the window and a rancher drilled him clean between the eyes with a .30-.30.

"You wanna bet?" Dusty asked.

25

"I've had it," a hired gun said to his buddy. They crouched behind the shattered windows on the second floor of a dry goods store. "I don't know what them others plan on doin', but I'm out of it."

"Me, too, Les," his friend replied. "I'm sorry I ever got into this awful situation."

Les took off his bandanna and tied it around the muzzle of his rifle, just behind the front sight. He stuck the barrel out of the window and waved it back and forth. Then he left the rifle balanced on the sill. The men took off their belts and laid them beside their rifles, in plain sight of anyone on the second floor across the street.

"Two of them giving it up," Pasco announced. "Second floor across the street and to our right."

In the rear of the saloon, four gunhands covering the back talked it over and decided they'd had enough of this town. They darted from cover to cover while those in the rear of the saloon held their fire and watched them leave. The gunhands made their horses and rode off. None of them looked back.

Moses slipped to the storage room door and called, "The back is clear, Smoke. The gunnies gave it up and rode off."

"The ones with any brains at all, and that ain't many of them, have sensed it's over," Kit said. "I figure you give some others the chance to ride clear and they'll go. That'll leave about twenty at most."

"Waco?" Smoke yelled.

"Right here, Mister Jensen!" the ex-Triangle JB foreman hollered.

"Hold your fire. Let's see if any want to ride out. If they do, let them have safe passage out of town."

"Will do."

"You men across the street!" Smoke yelled. "You heard it. Any who want to ride can do so in safety. Just clear out of this area and stay clear. It's up to you."

A moment passed before the call sprang from a building. "We're ridin' out, Jensen! They's eight of us. Hold your fire. You'll not see none of us again."

"Ride out, then!"

"Damn you all to hell!" Biggers shouted. "You're all dirty cowards!"

One of the retreating gunnies yelled out, telling Biggers where he could go and what he could do to himself while he was on the way. A couple more of those leaving yelled out some options for Biggers.

"That would certainly be an interesting sight to see," Clemmie muttered.

"Twenty-four or twenty-five left," Kit said, loud enough for Smoke to hear. "Maybe two or three less than that. But I could probably name those who stayed. They're the bad ones, Smoke. They'll not give up."

"Then they'll die," Wolf grumbled.

"They know that, too," Kit said. "They're worthless trash

and sorry human bein's, but they ain't cowards. They just ain't got good judgment."

Five hired guns rushed the front of the saloon. Rifles and pistols boomed and cracked from inside the Golden Plum. Five bodies lay still on the muddy street, the rain washing their blood into the wagon wheel ruts.

"How many?" Kit called.

"Five," Smoke told him, punching out the empties and reloading.

"Ruined," Fat Fosburn muttered from his position on the floor. "We had it all and now we have nothing. Jensen stripped us down to the bare bones. Even if we survive this, we're all looking at long prison terms or a hangman's noose. Too many people heard our offer to the gunfighters. I been to prison. I just ain't goin' back." He stuck the muzzle of his rifle into his mouth and pulled the trigger, blowing out the back of his head and splattering his brains on the wall.

Jack Biggers looked at the mess and swallowed hard. He cut his eyes to Major Cosgrove. "Now what?"

Cosgrove shook his head. "I don't know. There's only one way out of this damn town, and it's blocked by Waco and those men with him. All my gold is up at the mine. I've got to get it. It's all I have left. It's a fortune, Jack. Come on. We can't ride out, but we can walk out through the mountains. We can follow the ravines up to the rear of the mine office without being seen. All the townspeople have taken shelter from the rain in the sheds and the mouth of the pits. The gold is concealed under the office floor."

"We can't carry all that gold, man!"

"There are burros up there. They can go where a horse or mule can't go. They can tote the gold. We got no choice, Jack."

"If the gunhands see us leaving, they'll kill us."

"You have a better idea?"

Jack shook his head. "No," he said softly.

Jack Biggers and Major Cosgrove slipped out the rear of

the office and stood in the hard-pouring rain for a few seconds. The rain would help conceal their movements. The pair pushed off, running hard and staying low.

Since the abortive attempt to rush the saloon, no shots had been fired from either side. The bodies in the street gave mute testimony to the secure position of those inside the Golden Plum. It was a standoff, but a standoff that the gunhands knew they could not win.

"Whisperin'?" the hoarse call came from the outside, just loud enough to be heard by those in the front room.

Whisperin' moved to the busted window and looked out. Russ Bailey stood in the rain, pressed up close to the building. "Yeah?"

"Fat Fosburn is dead in the office. Looks like he blowed his own head off. It's a real mess, I tell you. Cosgrove and Biggers is gone."

Whisperin' mouthed an extremely ugly word several times. "We been sold out, boys," he told those in the room. "Cosgrove and Biggers has run. They got to be headin' for the mine. I suspect that's where he's hid all that gold he talked about."

"But there ain't no way out of that place!"

"Yeah, there is. Mule knew a way through and told some of the boys 'fore he left. There's a horse ranch just over the pass."

"Just over the pass means *walkin'* through them damn mountains, totin' the gold by hand."

"We can do it. At least, we can carry some of it. Come on, let's start slippin' out one at a time. Don't tell the others. Hell with them."

"Not me," Tom Wilson said. "I was caught in a thunderstorm in the mountains one time. If you ain't never seen it, you don't want to be in it. There's lightnin' dancin' and poppin' everywhere. They was three of us down in Colorado when we got caught. I was the only one who made it out. You ever seen a man hit by lightnin'?" He shuddered. "I have. Johnny's eyeballs popped out of his head. I'm stayin' right here."

"Somebody do something!" Russ said. "I'm freezin' to death out here in the damn rain!"

"Let's go."

Five men slipped out the rear of the building to join Russ in the rain. Lonesome was the last to leave. Tom Wilson stayed where he was, all right. Lonesome Ted Lightfoot had cut his throat to ensure the man's silence. They were all a real nice bunch of folks.

"Smoke!" Pasco called from the landing. "I thought at first I was seeing things. But now I'm sure. There's some men heading for the mine. I saw two about three or four minutes ago. Then about four or five more."

"That's it? No more?"

"Not yet. What do you think is up?"

"Rats desertin' the ship," Kit called.

"Probably," Smoke said. He checked his pistols and picked up a rifle, making certain it was loaded up full. "Hold it here, people. I'm heading for the mine."

"You want some company?" Van Horn called.

"No. You can be sure they're keeping a good eye behind them. One man alone will be much harder to spot. Besides, I think you're going to have your hands full with those still across the street. See you shortly."

Smoke was gone out the back door, running hard for the mine, keeping to the alley and out of sight of those across the street. At the mine road that angled off from the edge of town, Smoke darted across the crushed rock road and took the hard and long way up to the mine, clambering over huge rocks and jumping young rivers of water that would vanish when the rain stopped. Since this route was very nearly impossible for a man to climb, Smoke knew it would be the last place those above him would look.

Once, when he paused to catch his breath, he studied the

long stairs that led from ground level to the main offices. Since the mine was not working this day, the mule-drawn hoist was not being used and he could see two men just entering the offices, high above him. The big one was Cosgrove and the other one looked like Jack Biggers. It sure wasn't Fat Fosburn. The size was all wrong.

The angled steps had four landings, five if you counted the landing at the top. It was a good three hundred feet off the ground.

Then Smoke saw a knot of men running up the steps. Five, no, six of them. They paused for breath at the first landing. Unless you were accustomed to it, this high up was no place to be running, and it could sap your strength quickly.

Smoke climbed on while the storm raged, lightning dancing all around the high peaks above him. He had slung his rifle, muzzle down, and made sure his pistols were snug in their holsters and thonged down tight.

He was winded when he reached the top, but as far as he knew, no one had spotted him. The temperance band had stopped tooting and oom-pahing and drumming, and the singing had stopped. The townspeople had taken refuge wherever they could find it, and none were in sight.

Smoke studied the situation. There was no way he was going to risk climbing those steps; he'd be a very conspicuous target. Unless . . .

He studied the sheer wall of the cliff behind the steps, where the hoist was located. He could probably climb up a couple of hundred feet of dry cable, but damned if he was going to try it in a drenching rain.

Then he realized there was a road leading up to the mine proper. Naturally, dummy! he berated himself. How else could they build the damn complex way up there? The rain had obscured the narrow road, just wide enough for a wagon with a skilled driver at the reins and a stout rope or chain hooked to the rear of the wagon with the other end attached to a heavy-duty spoked gearbox of some type in case the wagon brakes failed.

Smoke left his dubious shelter and ran for the road. With his clothing soaked, he blended in against the gray water-soaked rock of the cliff the road had been carved out of.

Jack Biggers suddenly appeared on the top landing and started shooting at the men who were now at the second landing. The men returned the fire, driving the rancher back into the building.

Interesting, Smoke thought, as he squatted under a small overhang very near the mouth of the mine, which was on a level with the top landing. More steps led from the mine to the office. He unslung his rifle and wiped it as dry as he could, thinking: I'll just stay here out of the rain and if I'm lucky, maybe they'll kill each other.

No such luck. Patmos turned, spotted Smoke, and opened his mouth to shout out the warning. Before he could yell, Smoke drilled the gunfighter clean and Patmos went down on the slick landing. The shot was lost in the roar of rain, the howl of wind, and the crash of thunder.

For a few seconds—enough time for Smoke to leap out and run for a small foreman's hut—those on the landing with Patmos thought he had lost his footing and slipped. Whisperin' knelt down beside him and got the word from the badly wounded killer-for-hire. From his hiding place behind the hut, Smoke watched Whisperin' look wildly all around the spot where Patmos had pointed. Then the gunhand had to jump for safety as both Cosgrove and Biggers opened fire from above them, driving the gunfighters back. Whisperin' leaped away, leaving Patmos exposed on the landing. Patmos's body jerked in pain as half a dozen rounds were fired into him. He feebly lifted one hand, then the arm fell to the landing and he did not move again.

"That sure is a loyal bunch," Smoke muttered. "Certainly true to one another."

As he leaned against the hut, a thought came to him. Wherever miners are, there is bound to be dynamite. Smoke picked up a broken ax handle and used it to tear off a couple of boards from the rear of the hut. He smiled. The place was filled with cases of dynamite. Then he lost his smile as he realized what a lousy place he'd picked to hide behind. If a stray bullet hit the right spot, there wouldn't be enough left of him to pick up. Not even with a spoon and shovel.

He grabbed a dozen sticks and some caps and fuses and vacated the area immediately.

While those on the middle landing were being sniped at by Cosgrove and Biggers, unable either to return the fire or do much looking for Smoke, Smoke edged closer and capped and fused his dynamite. He lit a bundle and gave it a flip. The bundle of explosives bounced on the landing and went sailing off into space, exploding harmlessly in midair.

"What the hell?" Smoke heard Biggers holler from above him.

"You bastards!" Whisperin' yelled at the pair on the top landing.

"That wasn't us!" Cosgrove shouted.

There was only the howl of the wind, the rush of the rain, the snap and cracking of lightning, and the booming of thunder for a full half minute, as the men above and below each other gave that some thought.

"Oh, hell!" Lonesome Ted Lightfoot muttered. Then he raised his voice to a shout. "Cosgrove, Biggers! We better work together, boys. Smoke Jensen is up here with us."

"Hell with you!" Biggers shouted. "You look out for your own butt, gunfighter."

Smoke tossed another bundle of dynamite. It landed flat and stayed put on the slick boards. When it blew, it took about half the landing and forced the remaining gunfighters to press up against the face of the cliff. Patmos's body rolled off the shattered landing and fell to the rocky ground below.

Cosgrove and Biggers laughed at the men below them. Smoke stopped their laughter by tying a bundle of explosives to the broken ax or pick handle and hurling it up to the top landing.

"Jesus Christ!" Cosgrove yelled, as he and Biggers jumped for the dubious safety of the office building.

The charge blew off half the safety railing, tore a great hole in the floor of the landing, and shattered all the front windows in the office building. It also rattled the hell out of the office building constructed against the face of the cliff.

"That's it," Whisperin' said. "That's all for me. We can't get out, boys. We got the vigilantes below us, Cosgrove and Biggers above us, and Jensen over yonder someplace. I'm done."

"Might as well," Jim Pell said. The others nodded their agreement.

"Jensen!" Whisperin' shouted. "Can you hear me over all this damn stormin'?"

"I hear you," Smoke called.

"Can you see us?"

Smoke shifted positions behind crates and broken wagon wheels and other discarded debris. "I can see you."

"We're done, Smoke. You hear me? It's all over for us. We yield."

"Throw all your guns over the side. All of you. Unbuckle and toss everything over the side."

The men chucked it all over the side of the shattered landing. They even reached down into boots and behind their belts in the small of the backs and pulled out hideaway guns and knives. Everything went over the side.

"Now stay where you are. Press up against the face of the cliff. Cosgrove and Biggers can't see you or hit you with gunfire. Is there a back way out of that office building?"

"No," Dusty called. "They got to use this landing or the road you're on. They're trapped." Just like us, he thought.

Far below him, Smoke could see men gathering, taking up positions behind rocks and boulders and wagons and rail cars. Two dozen rifles or more were now trained on the office building. He could make out Waco and Wolf and Pasco and several others on his side. The storm had blocked the sounds of the final fight in Red Light. The outlaws were licked. Almost.

26

"It's all over, Cosgrove, Biggers," Smoke yelled from below the office building. "You have no more men. Give it up."

"Hell with you!" Major Cosgrove yelled. "Come and get us."

"Don't be fools! Look below you. There are two or three dozen rifles pointed at you right now. We can shoot that office building to bits. Give it up."

Cosgrove and Biggers chanced a look below them. Jensen sure wasn't lying.

"I hate Smoke Jensen," Major Cosgrove said. "I despise that man more than anything on the face of this earth. How the hell was I to know that Jenny was the blood kin of the last mountain man?" Then, out of sheer desperation, hate, fury, and frustration, he lifted his rifle and began firing at the men assembled far below the office building.

No one knows exactly what happened after that. And no one ever really will. The most popular theory is that Cosgrove had cases of dynamite stored in the building and the returning rifle fire touched it off. But still others say they saw a hideous flash of blue lightning strike the building.

Whatever the reason, one second the office building was there, and in the next instant it was gone, debris flying in all directions and raining down to the ground below.

But not one trace of Major Cosgrove or Jack Biggers was ever found. And neither was any of the gold. Some say there was a rear exit to the building, a natural cave that was sealed by the massive explosion. Some say they escaped.

All anybody knew for sure was that when Whisperin' Langely, Dusty Higgens, Jim Pell, Lonesome Ted Lightfoot, and Russ Bailey were finally rescued from the landing, they had to change underwear. The explosion must have given them quite a fright.

Sheriff Club Bowers and his deputies rode into town just in time to witness the explosion. U.S. Marshals had ridden into Red Light only seconds before the huge wall of flame blew out of the cliff.

Reverend Lester Laymon said it was the heavy hand of God that done it.

Violet said her husband was an idiot . . . as usual.

When all was said and done, all the legal papers served and filed and settled, the citizens of Red Light were the new owners of the mine and Jenny Jensen owned the entire valley of lush graze and flowing creeks and gushing springs . . . and the gold up in the towering mountains. That was never mined. All records of where the huge vein was located had gone up in the explosion and only Smoke Jensen knew the exact location, and he wasn't talking.

The gold is still there. Untouched.

Jenny's range stretched for miles, north to south. It's still in the family, and still producing some of the finest beef on the market.

Red Light was soon dropped and the town's name was changed. Kit Silver married Clementine Feathers and settled down. Club Bowers was honestly elected sheriff of the county and was sheriff until his death, well into the next century. Wolf Parcell vanished back into the mountains. But he kept a close eye on Jenny, until she got married a few years later. Van Horn remained foreman of the ranch until his death, years after the big fight in Red Light, Montana. Wolves still visit the grave of Barrie on the lonesome ridge above the little spring. All the hands stayed on and a hundred years later, the crosses in the cemetery on the ranch bear the names of Pasco, Clarence Bad Dog, Jim Hammon, Cooper, Ford, Ladd, and all the others who fought for and with Jenny Jensen and her Uncle Smoke.

Smoke and Sally stayed around long enough to see that Jenny would be all right, and then they mounted up for the long ride back to the Sugarloaf in Colorado.

Smoke would be back to check on Jenny from time to time. But that's another story . . . about the last mountain man.

THE LAST GUNFIGHTER SERIES BY
WILLIAM W. JOHNSTONE

MORE FICTION BY
WILLIAM W. JOHNSTONE